The Day Before
Forever

Also by Anna Caltabiano from Gollancz:

The Seventh Miss Hatfield
The Time of the Clockmaker

The Day Before Forever

ANNA CALTABIANO

GOLLANCZ

LONDON

First published in Great Britain in 2016 by Gollancz
an imprint of The Orion Publishing Group Ltd
Carmelite House, 50 Victoria Embankment
London EC4Y 0DZ

An Hachette UK Company

1 3 5 7 9 10 8 6 4 2

A CIP catalogue record for this book is
available from the British Library.

ISBN 978 1 473 20046 3

Printed in Great Britain by Clays Ltd, St Ives plc

www.annacaltabiano.com
www.orionbooks.co.uk
www.gollancz.co.uk

To the Henleys in our lives

'Death, only death, can break the lasting chain;
And here, ev'n then, shall my cold dust remain,
Here all its frailties, all its flames resign,
And wait till 'tis no sin to mix with thine.'
Alexander Pope, 'Eloisa to Abelard'

Prologue

I turned the doorknob and I was in. There was no lock, and why should there be? They rent rooms to harmless travellers. They had no thought that anything could go wrong.

The first room was painted in opposites – light and dark – but in the night it all looked grey. It was small, almost like a cupboard by modern standards, but I was used to such smaller dwelling places. I moved carefully to avoid bumping into the chairs lined up by the door. I didn't want to touch anything unnecessarily.

I had thought this through. I had thought *everything* through – especially during my many sleepless nights. I knew what every move should be, and I knew what every second held for me. Tonight's plan was completely premeditated. All that remained was to execute it.

I paused at the black table, as I had intended. There were many drawers but only the bottom one was locked. I opened the top drawer instead. There, nestled in the corner, was a set of keys. Predictable. People were all the same. Not even time can change them that much. I used the smallest key on the locked drawer and it opened for me without a sound.

Files. Paperwork. Names that meant nothing to me. And for the first time that night – the first time in a while – I felt apprehensive. How would I know which one was hers?

She could easily hide behind a false name. Then there it was, staring back at me. Her name. And another name, equally familiar. But it could not be *him* since he was not of this time . . . No matter. It was *she* who interested me. What arrogance and stupidity to use their own names. It led me straight to them and now I knew exactly where they were.

Two white doors met my gaze. Now, which one held what I was looking for? Or rather *who* I was looking for? I chose the left-hand door and was pleased when it opened to reveal a hallway. There were many doors on either side but none was the one I needed. I walked along the corridor, keeping close to the wall so the floorboards wouldn't creak under my weight.

Turning a corner, I saw it: a small, delicate blue flower amidst a background of white.

I took a hairpin out of my bag and set to work on the door, twisting it clockwise in the lock, waiting for it to catch on something.

Click.

I looked down at my hand. I expected it to be trembling, but it held the hairpin steady. Good. Now, a counter-clockwise twist with a little push. I wished I could have just broken a window to get in. That would have been so much easier, but far too haphazard. This was the best way. This was no time for sloppiness.

A creak sounded in the hallway behind me.

No.

I froze. If I could have willed my blood to stop flowing, I would have. I was so close. I had practised these very motions night after night. No one could stop me. Not now.

I stood there motionless, listening. No more sounds. They were not coming my way. *Thank you.*

My hand was still holding the hairpin in the lock. I turned it halfway clockwise then leaned gently against the door to open it.

Looking over my shoulder, I scanned the hallway behind me. Still empty. Everyone was asleep. It felt as if they had made it easy for me. But I wasn't doing this for the challenge, I reminded myself as I crept in. This was a culmination, of sorts – my last act.

Best to close the door behind me so no one would think anything was amiss. I did so, then slipped the hairpin into my bag alongside the knife and the small pocket watch I also carried.

There was no more time to waste. This had to be done now.

And then I stopped. For there she was, lying on the bed, fully clothed – not even underneath the covers – as if she had fallen asleep talking. This was too simple.

This was the first time I had seen her up close without the mask of darkness. When I tried to smother her before, it was too dark to see more than the outline of her face. But now I realised that she looked exactly like all the others I had ended.

This one's eyelashes fanned out against her pale skin. Deeply asleep, she was curled around a man lying next to her on the bed, as if her little body was trying to shield him from whatever might come through the door.

Me.

I almost laughed. She didn't have to worry about him. It was her I had come for, after all. But as I moved further into the room and stood over the bed, I saw his face and my breath stopped. *It couldn't be.*

Now I knew why she was curled around this man, trying to shield him. I remembered his face well. It was a face I

3

had seen before, centuries ago. He had been sick – dying, in fact. Mortal. But if he was here now, that could only mean he was immortal. She had turned him.

Pain shot through my jaw. I hadn't noticed I was clenching it that hard. If she had done this to him, she could be doing it to others.

I scanned the top of the bedside table. Just a string of plastic beads. Like a child's toy. How juvenile. Quietly, I opened the drawer. Stationery. Nothing important. I opened the closet door. Just a few articles of clothing. A black shift of some sort. A few men's shirts. Shoes on the floor. Nothing that would hold water. I made sure to put everything back in the right place. Next, I checked the adjoining bathroom very carefully. Still nothing. I had already searched the other woman's house in New York. Just like in this room, she had nothing that could have been what I was searching for – a filled glass or bottle of liquid.

But this woman . . . she would have needed the water to turn him. There was no other way to do it. She must have used the last she had on him – perhaps she would go back to acquire more? She had to. To turn more into her kind.

I had searched in Florida for the origin of the water but failed to find it. The others I had eliminated refused to tell me the location of their source before their deaths. Perhaps there was another spring to which she could lead me?

I peered at the bed again. I could do it in one motion. A twist of her neck. A swift gesture with a knife. Painless . . . almost. But what good would that do if I couldn't find her water source? I should keep her alive a while longer to help me find it.

I could keep him, too. She would confide in him. I could keep a close watch on them both. And he might also be useful in other ways. She appeared to care about her unnatural creation like she cared about no other thing or person. One might even call it *love*. Or weakness.

My eyes fell on the string of plastic beads on the bedside table. My hands moving instinctively, the motions familiar, I carefully wrapped the beads around his conveniently clasped hands. He did not stir.

It was too easy.

Chapter 1

'What's happening?' I heard Henley say.

Henley's – well, Richard's – eyes went wider than I had ever seen them. I knew a lot of strange things were happening, like the fact that Henley was now somehow inside Richard's body, which had been lying on a bed in fifteenth-century England just moments before, but nothing could have prepared me for Henley starting to shake uncontrollably.

Henley clutched first at his throat, then his chest. 'I-I can't breathe.' He took a few stumbling steps towards me. 'My chest—' In his panic, his other arm shot out to reach for me.

I grasped his hand. 'What's happening?'

He looked as if he was drowning in air. 'I—' He began, but it sounded as though his throat had closed up and his weight started to slump towards me.

'Henley!' I tried to keep him upright. His eyes were rolling back in his head. 'Look at me!'

His weight was too much for me to support so I tried to lower him gently. He hit the floor with a muffled thud. Henley's skin was flushed and sweat poured down from his hairline. There was a bit of blood at the corner of his lip, and I realised he must have bitten his tongue. I massaged his clenched jaw with my fingers to loosen the muscles as his body began to jerk on the floor. I felt under the side of his jaw like I had seen doctors on television do, but I couldn't tell if I was feeling his pulse or my own erratic heartbeat in my fingertips.

'Don't you dare do this to me,' I said. I tried to open his shirt to feel for his heartbeat, but my fingers were fumbling and his body continued to lurch beneath my touch.

There. I slipped my hand under his shirt and held him down, trying to quiet my breathing for a moment to listen for his heartbeat.

Henley's heart was still beating. Thank God.

Tears prickled in my eyes. I didn't know what was happening, but worse than that, I didn't know how to stop it.

'Henley?' I called, as if he was far away and not practically resting his head in my lap. 'Henley, dear. Stay with me.'

All I could do was beg and hope that this was just a fit that would soon pass.

I clasped his hand in mine. I couldn't lose Henley. I had fought for him. I thought I'd lost him once before. I couldn't lose him like this. It wasn't supposed to be like this.

I gripped his hand tighter, as if that was going to do any good.

We shouldn't have tried to travel in time so soon after Henley had somehow 'fallen into' Richard's body. I understood that Richard had been dying and Henley was just trying to help, but we – I – should have known it couldn't end well. Henley was half-immortal (whatever *that* meant or entailed) due to being the sixth Miss Hatfield's son, and getting sucked into Richard's body might have made Henley more mortal than immortal. There was really no way of knowing. But of course travelling through time this far into the future couldn't end well for him. I should have seen that. It rarely had for me.

7

Henley's fingers twitched in my hand. At first I thought it was the seizure, but I looked down to see Richard's – Henley's – eyes staring back at me.

I shuddered. I hadn't forgotten Henley was in there, but it was still so strange. I didn't know if I could ever get used to it.

'Henley?' I said his name clearly. 'Are you all right?'

He made to sit up but I put a hand on his shoulder. 'You shouldn't get up so quickly.'

He turned away from me and puked.

I rubbed his back.

'All right?' I asked.

'Yes.'

'You scared me.' I paused. If a full mortal travelled this far into the future, beyond his own lifespan, he would no longer exist, having killed himself by passing the point of his own death. Maybe Henley was still alive because he was half-immortal? 'Do you remember much?'

'I think I lost consciousness partway through talking to you,' Henley said. 'Then I was waking up on the floor and feeling nauseous . . . My head hurts, too.' He instinctively touched the side of his head, but as soon as he did so, his hand recoiled and he groaned. 'I'm not a fan of Richard's haircut, either.'

Henley looked serious, but I couldn't repress the small smile that had crept onto my lips. The quiet smile grew into a giggle I had to hold back as Henley turned his stranger's hands over, taking in the bizarre sight of being able to control someone else's hands. This was such a crazy situation.

A laugh escaped me despite my best efforts.

'What?' Henley pouted at me.

But sticking his bottom lip out just made me laugh harder.

'I go into some kind of seizure or shock and you just sit there laughing.' Henley shook his head, but he was smiling now, too.

I doubled over. The pinpricks of tears I had been holding back came pouring down my cheeks. Tears of relief. Laughing with relief. Relief all round.

'Thank God. Thank God you're all right.'

'I'm as all right as I ever could be, with you here by my side.' Henley poked me. It was all so strange – laughing and joking like this, as if he hadn't almost died a few moments ago. And not only that – Henley was finally here. In the flesh. Right in front of me. I had waited so long for this moment that I hadn't imagined it could ever happen. Maybe the laughter was some sort of nervous response?

My cheeks were aching from smiling when I felt the warmth of his hand against the side of my face. His touch was so careful, as if he was scared he would break me or otherwise shatter this perfect dream we were in.

I shook my head. It wasn't perfect. We didn't have time to be doing this.

Henley's laughter quietened as if he had just realised the same thing.

We had used the clock to travel in time, not only to save myself from the effects of staying in one period for too long, but also to run from a killer who appeared to have set his sights on me. *Miss Hatfield's killer*, I reminded myself.

Miss Hatfield – Henley's mother, as I had recently found out – had been my mentor, the only one I could really talk to about being immortal. Sure, she had caused my immortality by slipping water from the Fountain of Youth into my lemonade that fateful day, but she had helped me since then. Each Miss Hatfield created the next Miss Hatfield who would succeed her. Why? Was the impulse to do so

9

driven by the fear of spending an eternity alone? Was it out of a strange feeling of duty to immortality and to the Miss Hatfield name? I didn't know. But the first Miss Hatfield had turned the second, the second had turned the third, the third the fourth, and so on . . . Until I became the seventh Miss Hatfield. I was determined this curse would end with me. There would be no eighth Miss Hatfield.

There were so many rules to abide by as a Miss Hatfield that sometimes I was convinced the sixth Miss Hatfield had made up half of them. I was taught to be inconspicuous, not to make eye contact with people on the street and to look 'normal' at all costs. Miss Hatfield also taught me how to blend in with a given time period – to talk like they did, wear what they did, look like they did – and how to use the golden clock she kept on her kitchen wall to move in time.

The clock!

I frantically looked about. The clock lay glistening on the floor just a step behind me. Another wave of relief rushed through me.

After murdering Miss Hatfield – in front of me, no less – the killer had tried to come after me. I remembered the day when Miss Hatfield told me that immortality did not protect against bodily harm or accidents. An immortal can't die of illness or old age, but a murderer . . . that would do it. She said that the current Miss Hatfield always died in an accident – a ship fire, the Salem witch trials, while locked up in an asylum – shortly after she found and turned her successor. The idea of a murderer on the loose – that made me begin to question everything Miss Hatfield had told me.

When the murderer first attacked me, we got into a struggle during which the clock's hands were turned and sent us both to 1527 – the furthest the clock could move in time, and the exact year the clock had been made. After realising the clock had yet to be invented, it had been a real feat to get Henry VIII's court clockmaker to craft it for me.

I took a step and picked up the clock.

Of course, it wasn't me who convinced the clockmaker in the end. It was Richard.

Richard was a number of different things. He was charming, that was for sure, and funny, often muttering witty things to me under his breath during feasts at court. He had a way of making me feel like I was the only other person in the room. He looked at me and *really* saw me. I loved Richard.

Richard was also dead.

He was sick from the start. Consumption, they said. But Richard never told me till the end. He had a cough but I didn't think much of it. I was an idiot. Not that there was anything I could have done. I tried. In the end I asked Henley for help, and look where that had got us – Henley sucked into Richard's body when Richard died.

I really should be sadder about this – about Richard's death, I mean. I did love him. That hadn't changed. I still loved him. Yet I couldn't really mourn him when it felt like Richard was still here.

'Where are we?' Henley asked.

I stared into Richard's eyes.

We had been in Henry VIII's court about three minutes ago, and now we were . . . wherever this was.

I took in our surroundings for the first time. In my panic, I hadn't noticed much yet.

The floor was made of smooth stone cut into perfect squares. Pillars decorated with lavish gold and a greyish blue shot straight up, supporting a high ceiling decorated with a beautiful painted mural. Ornate crests and Greek-looking scrolls – definitely not Tudor-like – ran along the edge of the ceiling and the gold appeared to drip down the walls.

'All those angels looking down at us,' Henley muttered.

His voice carried and echoed in the large room. The ceiling was so high that I felt dizzy tilting my head up to take in the mural.

Something else echoed then and I swung to look at Henley.

'What's that?' I whispered, not wanting my voice to carry.

It sounded like a distant tapping echoing from the other side of the big room, yet the taps had no pattern.

'Footsteps,' Henley said.

And he was right.

Trying to think quickly, I put down the clock and arranged my long skirts to hide it.

The reason I couldn't make out the footsteps was that it sounded like more than one person. Many more.

I stood close to Henley, flattening my back against the wall, trying to disappear. He found my hand and squeezed it.

'. . . And please watch your step as we enter this next room.'

I held my breath but there was no way we wouldn't be found. Aside from the single door on the other side of the room – the side from which the voice was coming – there was no way out for us.

'Here we have the Painted Hall—'

A woman with an absurdly bright red scarf walked backwards into the room. At least fifteen other people followed her in, gripping little booklets and what appeared to be folded maps. With one glance, I could tell we were in the time of ripped jeans and baseball caps. Although the people following the woman in stared openly at us, she was too busy talking to notice.

'. . . This room was built by Mary II in 1692 as part of the Royal Hospital for Seamen at Greenwich. The hospital was closed in 1869.'

Two little girls appeared at the front of the crowd. They were playing tag and obviously not listening to the woman in the red scarf.

'You, there,' the woman barked, singling out one of the little girls. 'What did I say about running in these old buildings? You could break something, heaven forbid!'

The little girl was wearing a large pink fleece that almost went down to her knees. Her big eyes looked up at the woman before she suddenly ran back into the crowd, presumably to find her parents.

The woman with the red scarf continued lecturing almost forcibly to the crowd, harshly spitting out her words. 'From 1873 to 1998, this was the site of a training establishment for the Royal Navy.' Her face was almost as red as her scarf. I wondered if it was tied too tightly around her neck.

I turned my head to mention this to Henley, but he wasn't next to me any more. I hadn't even noticed him let go of my hand. I scanned the crowd for him. He couldn't have gone far. I was right – Henley was standing at the back of the crowd. What was he doing there? Squinting, I tried to make out if he was talking to someone. No, that wasn't it.

Henley was easy to spot as he was still wearing his Tudor-era nightshirt, since Richard had been on his deathbed only a few moments ago. I shook my head at how confusing that sounded. But even though he was standing just a few steps behind everyone, oddly no one appeared to be paying Henley any heed. They must have thought he had exited 'off stage' to give another performance in a different room.

The crowd continued to stare at me and their guide, waiting to see what I would do. I craned my neck to see what Henley was up to. I knew there had to be a reason why he'd moved there. Maybe he was scoping out the exit? As I stood on my toes for a better view, I saw Henley move close to a man standing at the edge of the crowd. The man didn't look particularly different from the rest of the party or important in any way; he just had a backpack slung over one shoulder. I had no clue what Henley was doing until I saw his hand flash forward.

I yelped and everyone, including the man standing right in front of Henley, looked up at me. I must have been quite a sight still in my Tudor gown, complete with a French hood headpiece, but I didn't think that Henley was going to do this. I wasn't prepared at all.

The tour guide shushed me. 'My God. Attention-seeking actors . . . The company should have warned me about their new promotions,' she mumbled, but she soon continued her lecture.

Henley had taken something from the man's backpack, something small, and I saw him hide it in his nightshirt. My shriek had distracted everyone – including Henley's target – and actually helped him pickpocket the man. I watched him move towards the other side of the room. I couldn't say anything to him with so many people around. Luckily, the woman with the red scarf was ushering everyone out and the group had started to head towards the exit.

I felt a tugging at my skirt and looked down to see the little girl with the oversized pink fleece. She wordlessly thrust something at me.

Confused, I took it, and before I could see what it was she ran off to rejoin the group. It felt small and cold in my hand.

'Please remember there's a step here!' the tour guide barked over her shoulder.

I looked down to see what the girl had given me. It was a coin. I wondered if her mother had told her to give it to the nice actor in Tudor dress standing mutely in the corner of the room. I turned the coin over in my hand. *One pound*, it said. Right, we were still in the UK, just in the future.

I waited for the last of the tour group to trickle out of the room and around the corner before I carefully stepped around the clock I was hiding and walked up to Henley.

'What the hell was that?' I said through gritted teeth.

'The little girl was just tipping you for your wonderful performance,' he said.

'You know that's not what I'm talking about.'

Henley dug into his shirt and withdrew a leather wallet. I wondered if his nightshirt had pockets, or if he had stuck it in the waistband of his pants. He tossed it to me and I barely caught it.

'Money,' he said.

'Money that's not ours.'

'I'm quite aware of that,' Henley said. I would have thought he'd feel guilty, or at least embarrassed, but he sounded strangely matter-of-fact. 'But it doesn't change the fact that we need some money to get away from here.'

I didn't want to admit it, but he was right. If there was one thing I had learned from living in New York, it was that you needed money to survive. New York was expensive and I guessed that London was, too. You need money to buy food, to find a place to stay, and even to get around. Money was tied to everything, really. So I opened the wallet.

'Reed Lory Glazen,' I read from the driver's licence. 'New Jersey driver's licence, so he's American.'

I pulled out his credit card and all the cash in his wallet: Visa card, £238 and $10.

Henley held out his hand, knowing I didn't have pockets. I handed him the credit card and the cash. I studied the driver's licence. The photo looked like a mugshot. It was issued in 2015 and expired in 2019.

My head spun.

I saw Henley gulp.

The sweatshirts and sneakers, among other things, had told me we were in the future. I was born in the forties – 1943, was it? – and Henley was born in the late 1800s. This definitely wasn't my time or his, or Tudor England, for that matter, but we were much further in the future than I had anticipated. Fortunately, this was a time period I knew a bit about. It was close to the year Miss Hatfield had been killed. Technically, the murder had only taken place a few years ago.

I tried to keep a level head. 'What about the wallet?' I asked.

'You should just drop it here,' Henley said. 'No sense in carrying it around, especially with someone else's ID inside.'

Since there was no table or window ledge on which to set it down, I put the leather wallet on the floor between us.

'We should go,' Henley said. But neither of us knew where.

'Wait,' I said. 'We can't walk around like this.' I motioned to what I was wearing.

I was worried that another tour group would walk in while we were changing, but we couldn't do much about it, except try to change quickly. I listened to make sure I couldn't hear footsteps before I took off the first layer of my clothing – the Tudor gown and the French hood headpiece, along with the pouch strung on a golden belt. As strange as the pieces of clothing looked, wearing them had become almost second nature to me in 1527.

Something rattled in the pouch as I took it off. I looked inside and found a small glass vial the size of my index finger. It had been a little present from Richard. I turned it over in my hands once before promptly putting it back into the drawstring pouch. I couldn't deal with it right now. We didn't have time. I couldn't think about Richard yet.

I had Henley loosen my corset and took a deep breath once it was off. Next came the stifling kirtle. I kept removing articles of clothing until I was left wearing only a white linen chemise with a pile of fabric at my feet. It wasn't much better, but at least I now had a minuscule chance of fitting in here – whatever the exact year was. Not to mention the fact that my entire body felt lighter and much less constrained.

'You're forgetting this.' Henley lifted the necklace I was wearing from around my neck and handed it to me. Even after hundreds of years, the garnets – or were they rubies? – glinted in the sunlight streaming through the room's tall windows. I paused before deciding to put the heavy necklace and matching earrings in the drawstring pouch along with the vial. I strapped the belt and pouch back on.

Wadding up the clothing on the floor, I looked around for a vase or something I could hide them in. Nothing. The Painted Hall was too bare. I decided I would just bring the garments with me for now. An abandoned pile of clothing would probably raise suspicion and likely attention we didn't want.

I cocked my head at Henley and he shrugged. There was nothing we could do about the way he was dressed as he was only wearing a linen shirt and old-fashioned hose. Maybe people would still think we were actors in costumes like the tour guide had, or perhaps adopting some brand-new fashion? We could only hope. Henley picked up the clock and put it under his arm. I followed him out of the room the way the tour group had left.

The doorway opened to the outside. The late spring, maybe early summer light was incredibly bright. I squinted forward and thought I could see the River Thames. Some things never changed. The gravel crunched beneath my flimsy leather shoes and Richard's bare feet as we stumbled towards the river.

'Wait a second,' I said.

I had spied a booth set up against the stone wall surrounding the building, just a little to our right. *Take photos with you as the King and Queen!* a sign declared. It was a tiny structure, barely accommodating the man behind the foot-long counter. I could see that he was all muscle even from where I stood, and it looked as if his body frame was the only thing keeping the booth upright. A family with a little boy were in the middle of taking photos a few steps away from the booth. They were dressed in period costume over their jeans and T-shirts.

I stole a glance at Henley. 'I have a brilliant idea . . .'

I took off towards the rickety booth and poor Henley had no choice but to follow me.

The man greeted us with a smile and began his sales patter. 'Hello there. Are you two looking to dress up as the Tudors did? The photos make a great Christmas card.'

'I'm sure it does,' I said, 'but we're not actually here to take photos—'

'Then move along,' he said.

His gruffness startled me, but I stood my ground directly in front of the counter.

'What are you trying to do?' he said. 'Scare away customers? I have a work permit—'

I didn't know why he was so defensive, but I wasn't about to ask. 'I'm sure you do. I don't really care about that. I'm just hoping to do some business with you,' I said.

'Some business? Who do you think you are?'

I ignored him. 'Look, we have a fine . . . *replica* woman's Tudor-era costume we think you'd be interested in and also find good use for.' I gestured to the family who were still absorbed in taking photos. 'How many of those costumes do you have?'

'Enough. Now get out of here.' He crossed his arms in front of his chest, causing the muscles in his arms to bulge. I could have sworn I heard Henley gulp.

'Well, how many of those do you go through in a year?' I asked. 'People aren't that gentle with them, are they? Buttons pop off, zips break. Worse still, the fabric itself rips sometimes.'

'Your point?' He still looked irritated that we were talking to him, but at least he sounded less suspicious.

'My point is that a certain amount of damage is fixable without the clothes looking horrible and putting a dent in your profits. But you'll have to replace the costumes eventually. You could put more costumes into circulation to lessen the amount of wear each one gets.'

The man still looked sceptical. 'And you have costumes to sell?'

'We do.'

Henley helped me set the pile of clothing on the narrow ledge of the booth counter.

'We have a complete woman's outfit. Gown, headwear, petticoat, kirtle – everything. *Exact* replicas of what they used to wear. Not a zip in sight,' I said.

The man started riffling through the clothing and holding items up to inspect the fabric and the seams. 'Not bad . . .' he finally said. 'Naturally, I've seen better . . . But not bad at all. How much are you asking for this set?'

I hadn't really thought about the market price of replica Tudor costumes. I looked at Henley, but he only met my gaze with a panicked look.

Ultimately, I turned to the man. 'What are you willing to pay for these?'

'Hmm . . .' He fingered the fabric of my skirt again. 'Two hundred pounds.'

I struggled to not widen my eyes. It was a lot more than I was expecting him to offer. I didn't know much about this time period, but when I lived with Miss Hatfield right before she was murdered, two hundred dollars was a lot. Two hundred pounds couldn't be that far off. 'Make it two hundred and fifty and you have yourself a deal.'

'Fine,' he said and dug into a pouch hanging from a belt around his waist.

I couldn't believe it. I thought I'd have to fight to get him to take our useless apparel off our hands. But I guessed he had seen the quality of the clothing; nothing's as good a replica as the real thing.

'Two hundred and fifty pounds.' The man counted out the money on the booth's tiny ledge and pushed it an inch towards us. Any further and it would have fallen off.

'Thank you,' I said, taking it and putting it in the pouch along with the jewellery and the vial.

'You, too. Now get out of here – you're taking up my counter space and I need it for customers.'

Henley and I were only too glad to leave.

'I managed to grab shoes,' Henley said.

I looked down, and sure enough, he was wearing period replica leather shoes. 'How—'

'I asked for them from the family.' He chuckled. 'They gave them to me, since they thought I worked here and they were done taking photos.'

We continued walking towards the river and away from the big stone building behind us.

'Look – there's a sign.' Henley pointed out a sign on a pole by the river. It read:

Built by Henry VII on the original site of the Palace of Placentia, Greenwich Palace was believed to have been his favourite residence. It later became the birthplace of Henry VIII, Mary I and Elizabeth I, before being demolished in 1695 and replaced by the Royal Hospital for Seamen, later the Royal Naval College, which was named a World Heritage Site by UNESCO.

I had been there. I saw Henry VIII address the court at the feasts he threw. I had been there and now it was all gone. The countess, Lord Empson, Lady Sutton – they were all gone. Dead. Richard was gone, too, of course. I was always alone in surviving everything, including time itself.

'Nothing stays the same,' Henley said, interrupting my thoughts.

I *had been* alone . . . but not any more. I looked up at him, so glad to have someone by my side at last.

'Things change you,' he continued. 'People change you. Not even you can stay exactly the same.'

I knew he meant well, but he was wrong. I *did* stay the same as everyone around me changed, and that was the flaw. It wasn't his fault that he couldn't understand.

'Come on,' I said. 'We shouldn't stick around. Let's go down to the river – it's probably our best bet for getting out of here.'

I started walking, not checking back to see if Henley was following. He would never understand. Not fully.

We took the stairs down to the water and headed for the end of the pier, where a large boat was docked.

'Should we take that boat?' I asked Henley.

It looked like a ferry touring London by river and people were embarking quickly, in a rush to see the next tourist stop. I recognised a few faces from the tour group that had come into the Painted Hall. Dozens of people were going up the ramp. I wondered if they would notice two extra passengers. I found Henley's hand and we followed the others aboard.

'Tickets, please.' A young man in a yellow vest stood by the entrance of the boat. 'Please have your tickets ready!'

It hadn't occurred to me that people would already have tickets and need to show them even to board.

'Your ticket, miss?' The man was looking at me.

'Would it be possible for us to buy them?'

'Certainly.' He reached into the pack belted around his waist and pulled out a stack of red tickets. 'Two?'

'Yes, two.'

'Twenty-four pounds, please.'

I pulled money would from the drawstring bag.

'Thank you. Have a good day.' The young man handed us the tickets as we moved past him. 'You'll see the best views from the top deck!' he called over his shoulder.

'Expensive . . .' Henley mumbled.

'You know the value of money is different in this time compared to yours? Inflation and all that?' This was still expensive, but not as much as Henley was probably thinking.

Henley chuckled. 'I would think I'd know at least a little more about money and finance than you, however much behind the times I might be.'

The seats by the boat's windows were all taken, and even more people were standing near them to see the views. We found a narrow spiral staircase at the far end of the boat and headed for the upper deck. I had to steady myself by gripping the railings as I climbed. The boat must have cast off since we boarded, since I could feel the sway as it moved through the water beneath us. A blast of cool air hit my face as we reached the top of the stairs. The boat's upper deck was open to the elements, and we passed rows of metal benches crammed with yet more people.

'I'm not sure we can find seats here,' Henley said.

I craned my neck to look for an empty section of bench, but Henley was right.

'Ouch.' I felt a sharp pain in my left foot. I looked down to see a sandal-clad foot on top of mine.

'Oh, I'm so sorry!' A platinum blonde was talking to me. She sounded American. 'There's just so many people on this boat. It's kinda hard to know where to step. You okay?' She looked down at my foot. 'Love, love, *love* your leather flats.' She squinted up at me as she was significantly shorter. 'Love your boho style in general.'

The woman's short, pale hair was in a pixie cut. She was wearing all black, which matched the harsh black eyeliner ringing her grey eyes. At least she sounded more cheerful than the way she dressed suggested.

'Boho?' I said before I could stop the word from coming out. Had I just embarrassed myself? Was that a term I should have known?

'Yeah, the white shift dress and all. *Very* boho chic,' the woman said. She glanced at Henley. 'Your boyfriend, too. Love the matching aesthetic.'

Out of the corner of my eye, I saw Henley grin at the word 'boyfriend'. It was a funny word when used to describe us.

We'd been through so much – life and death, quite literally – that it felt like too a trivial word to define our relationship. But if he wasn't my 'boyfriend', what else could he be?

'You guys looking for seats up here?' the woman asked.

'We were,' Henley said, 'but it's pretty full – everyone wants to sit up top.'

'It's like those double-decker buses London's famous for.' The woman laughed. 'I'm Alanna, by the way.' She stuck out her hand, first to me then to Henley.

'Rebecca,' I said, and Henley followed suit with his name.

'I'm sitting over there with Peter if you want to join us. We're taking up a lot more room than we really need – Peter likes to stretch his legs out and—'

'If you don't mind, that would be great,' Henley said, glancing at me for confirmation.

I didn't know why she was being so nice. Maybe we just looked lost?

We followed Alanna to the back of the boat, the second-to-last row, to be precise.

A man with braided blond hair lifted his head as we came closer. He took a long look at Henley, then at me, before he nodded hello in our direction.

'Making more friends already?' he said to Alanna. He also sounded American. I had registered quite a few American accents as we looked for seats. I was surprised how many Americans were aboard. I guessed boat tours of the Thames were a popular travel pastime for Americans.

'You know it.' She laughed.

'I'm Peter,' the man said. He was wearing a faded grey T-shirt with the logo of some band I couldn't place on it. His hair was tightly braided in neat rows down his scalp.

Alanna answered for us before we could open our mouths. 'This is Rebecca and Henley. They're from . . .

Where did you say you were from? The States? I'm just guessing by your accents, of course. So maybe I'm wrong . . . Did I guess right? Do sit down.' She pointed at the far seats closest to the side of the boat.

There was a newspaper spread out on the seats, presumably trying to save them for Peter to stretch out on, so I picked it up. I sat first, Henley next to me, and then Alanna next to Peter.

'You're completely right,' I said.

'So where in the States are you from?' Alanna asked.

'New York,' I said. 'How about you two?'

'We're from all over, but most recently we came in from Australia. We stayed right near Perth, if you know where that is.'

Henley nodded solemnly, and I wondered if that was because he knew where Perth was, or because he was trying to look attentive. Then he started asking her questions and they fell into a conversation about the native animals of Australia – wombats and all. I opened the newspaper.

17th June, 2016.

As soon as we arrived, I knew we had travelled into the future. But I had no idea that it was a whopping 489 years from where we had started.

I looked up to see Peter studying my face closely.

I couldn't let anything slip. I folded the newspaper and put it in my lap to take with me. It could give us valuable information.

'What's up?' he asked, leaning forward to talk to me, over Henley and Alanna.

I didn't know where to even begin answering that question. Everything was 'up', as he put it. Henley and I didn't know where we were heading, what we were going to do . . . Everything was a mess.

'This was a terribly last-minute trip,' I settled on in the end.

'You don't say?' Peter had a low, mellow way of talking. Not much emotion slipped out. 'A travelling-on-a-budget sorta thing?'

'Sure . . .' I said. A stolen credit card and limited cash counted as travelling on a budget, right?

'Did you guys at least figure out where you're staying tonight?'

I looked at Henley. He was still engrossed in his conversation with Alanna about the natural diet of dingos.

'Not yet,' I answered.

'If you're not set on something too central, Alanna and I are staying at a hostel. It's not the ritziest place, but it's not bad, either.'

'Yes!' Alanna chimed in. 'You *have to* stay with us! That is if you don't have a place to stay already?'

Peter shook his head.

'Then it's settled!' Alanna clapped her hands together like a child. 'It'll be like one big slumber party.'

Henley's brows were slightly raised. Getting too close to people made him wary. In that way, he was exactly like his mother, Miss Hatfield, but for very different reasons. My guess was that it made Henley uncomfortable because he didn't like to lie to others. Miss Hatfield only ever thought about herself and her own survival.

Chapter 2

As we wandered along the streets from the river to the hostel, I couldn't help but ask myself why they were being so nice to us. It was mostly Alanna, but Peter was friendly in his way, too. While Henley walked ahead chatting with Alanna about which sights they had already seen in England, Peter accompanied me.

'Sometimes it takes a bit to get used to her,' Peter said, nodding at Alanna. 'She doesn't know it, but she can be a bit . . . much.'

I smiled. So I wasn't the only one who was taken back by her openness that occasionally bordered on bluntness.

'She's just one of those naturally outgoing, naturally friendly people.' Peter shrugged. 'I was never like that, so we get along.'

'Counter-intuitive, don't you think?' I said.

'Opposites attract, right? Our personalities don't crash into each other.' Peter twisted the end of one of his braids as we rounded a corner. 'What about you and Henley? You're probably like that, too.'

'We do come from very different backgrounds,' I admitted. 'Worlds apart, really.'

'It's amazing how we can find common ground with those we love,' Peter said.

'The hostel's not far from here, I promise!' Alanna called over her shoulder.

I assured her Henley and I didn't mind the walk. 'We're getting to see more of London,' I said.

'When did you arrive, anyway?' Alanna slowed down to walk with Peter and me.

I glanced at Henley. I wasn't sure how much he had already told her.

'This morning,' I said, hoping Henley hadn't given her a different answer. He nodded – indicating he had more or less imparted the same thing – and I relaxed.

'Alanna mentioned that she and Peter have done a trip similar to this one before,' Henley said. 'Backpacking with barely anything more than the clothes they were wearing.' He looked at me intently as he spoke, and I could tell he was feeding me information.

'It was such fun!' Alanna ran her fingers through the short ends of her hair. 'Of course, it was Tibet for a summer and *soooo* much cheaper than London. It's a little harder to survive and travel with very little cash in an expensive city like London, but same idea. You two are just braver than we were. You'll survive.'

I wondered if she would count travelling in time as brave . . .

'It's so much more liberating than following a set plan,' Alanna went on. 'You can experience life more fully. There's something about trading what you have and living on necessities only . . . Speaking of which – keeping track of time is important, but what's the deal with that clock?' Alanna was gesturing towards the golden clock Henley was holding.

I saw Henley instinctively hunch over it.

'It's not that I have any problem with it,' Alanna said quickly, 'but it was one of the first things I noticed about you and—'

'Oh, we're just keeping it for a little while,' I said quickly.

Alanna raised her eyebrows. I held my breath.

'We found the clock in a store here,' Henley said. 'I collect vintage things, and Rebecca likes to decorate our new place with them. We want to ship it home but we've not had chance yet. Her mother wants her to go all modern with the new place, but, you know . . . there's charm in older things.'

Alanna cracked a smile, and I finally exhaled. This was Henley – always jumping in to save me. I shot him a grateful look, and got a shadow of a smile in return.

Alanna continued. 'Ah, I know how that feels,' she said to me. 'My mother and I always had different tastes—'

'When you see Alanna and her mother together, it's hard to imagine that one created the other,' Peter said.

'That's not nice, Peter!' Alanna said, but she giggled like a schoolgirl.

'Not nice doesn't mean it's not true,' Peter said.

Catching Henley's eye, I said, 'We probably should get a backpack or something to store the clock in, though, and we're going to need a change of clothes soon . . .' I hoped he was following my train of thought.

'There are little charity shops all around here,' Alanna said. 'Perfect.'

We could use the credit card – the *stolen* credit card, I reminded myself – to buy clothing and such. We had to do it sooner rather than later, before the theft was reported and the card cancelled – if it hadn't been already. Clothing didn't sound that important – in fact, it almost sounded silly and frivolous, but I knew that the first step to blending in was looking like we fitted the time period. And we had to blend in to avoid being found. We didn't need a lot. Just enough to start making our way.

'Let's stop at the next shop, then,' Henley said.

'If it's the next one you're after, it doesn't get any closer than that.' Alanna pointed across the street.

Sure enough, there was a small shop with a mannequin in the window and a sign promising to donate a percentage of all profits to a children's charity. At least the money was going to a good cause, even if it wasn't our money to begin with.

A bell rang as we opened the door and entered the little store. Inside we found rows of racks and boxes with mismatched clothing thrown over them. Velvet was tossed in with chiffon. Skirts were hung with braces.

Behind the back counter was an old woman whose stature looked proportional to the size of the store. She was reading and didn't make a move to stand. She only glanced up briefly to smile at us before going back to her book.

'What do you need?' Alanna asked me.

'For starters, a bag would be nice. Something big enough to carry everything.'

I watched Alanna walk the perimeter of the store, slowly taking everything in, surveying the wares. She headed for a green plastic bin in one corner, reached in and grabbed a neon backpack in each hand.

'What about matching backpacks?' she said.

I tried to laugh off her absurdly bright choices. Blending in would be impossible with such eyesores.

'You know, when Peter and I went to Greece a while ago, we got matching backpacks,' Alanna said. 'We even had our names embroidered on them – isn't that right, Peter?'

'Yeah, sure,' was all that came out of Peter.

He didn't look too thrilled about the concept of matching backpacks, either. It must have been another thing Alanna had talked him into.

'Let's just pick up one backpack.' The neon monstrosities were the only ones in sight, so I settled for a bright green one. If it would hold the clock and a few other things, it would have to do. 'And some clothes . . .'

Alanna perked up at the mention of clothes. 'Oh, wonderful! What type of clothing?'

'Um . . .' I was tempted to just say 'anything' but wasn't sure if that would be appropriate in this time period. I didn't know how I was supposed to act or what was acceptable.

'Let's try to find something very *you*,' Alanna said. I had no idea what that meant, but I was thankful she was leading the way. 'Something casual,' she said, rummaging through the racks. 'Something fun . . .'

'Uh, whatever you think will work,' I said.

Peter chuckled. 'Probably not the best idea to say that.'

Henley was standing with Peter, leaning against the wall. He already had clothing under his arm. I was amazed he had been able to pick something out so quickly.

Alanna shushed Peter. 'This is the fun part.'

I left her to sort through the boxes of clothing while I took in the other items the store sold. I wondered where all this stuff came from. Wandering travellers who had to sell their things to move on to a new place? People who were done with a certain stage in their lives and didn't just want to throw away their possessions? Maybe even people who wanted to get rid of old memories?

'Oh, Rebecca – look!' Alanna was already on to the next thing. 'Maxi skirts!'

'Maxi skirts?' I examined the bunches of fabric Alanna had grabbed.

'Long, billowy maxi skirts.' Alanna paused. 'Don't these kinda look like the dress you're wearing now? Of course, yours is better and much more stylish . . .'

I guessed they were a current fashion. But Alanna had already moved on again.

'What do you think of this?' She held up a short black dress that looked more like a lacy slip.

I glanced at Henley, wondering if he'd be comfortable with me wearing something like that. I had grown used to seeing those styles when I was in the twenty-first century with Miss Hatfield, but Henley was from a much more conservative time period. In 1904, not even underwear had been this revealing! But this *was* a different time with different rules, and how I dressed myself *was* my choice. Miss Hatfield would have sniffed at the so-called 'dress' with disdain, but I nodded.

Alanna looked pleased with herself. 'And this?' She held up a tiny shirt that looked like it would fit a child better than it would fit me. 'The crop top comes with a matching skirt – I think it would be so cute!' The skirt she held up was, unsurprisingly, equally short.

'Why not?' I said. 'But maybe I should get a pair of these, too.' I pulled a pair of jeans from a bin that looked like they would fit me.

'Do you want to try these on?' Alanna lifted the bundle of clothing she now held.

I glanced around the shop but it didn't look as if there were any changing rooms.

'I'm fine,' I said. 'Let's just get these.'

I took the now-rumpled clothing from her and walked to the desk at the back of the store. I made sure to add the neon-green backpack to the pile.

'Finally done?' Henley joined me at the desk, leaving Peter and Alanna talking softly out of earshot. He added the clothing he was holding to the pile on the desk.

The older woman put down her book. 'Will this be all?'

I tried to catch a glimpse of what she was reading. It looked like a mystery of some sort.

'Yes, thank you,' Henley responded.

The woman moved away from the counter to get a bag ready for our purchases.

'No matter the time period, you always take a long time to shop,' Henley murmured while her back was turned.

I shoved him playfully.

With Henley there were no secrets – nothing I had to hide from him. He knew my entire history and I liked that I could be open with him.

I almost forgot to remind Henley about the credit card. I turned to him with a more serious expression. 'We should probably use the credit card, before—'

'I know,' he said.

He understood. He always did.

Henley withdrew the credit card from the inside of his shirt.

I had explained the concept of credit cards to Henley, and he appeared to understand it best when I told him it was like putting something on his father's tab in his day – a way of promising to pay the amount later.

When the woman had placed all the clothing in the bag, she took the card from Henley. We watched her insert the card into the machine. I clasped and reclasped my hands together, but I knew this would work. I was just overthinking it.

'Could you enter your PIN number, please?'

I froze. PIN number? What on earth was a PIN number? We didn't have a PIN number. I was seriously considering making a run for it when the woman looked more closely at the machine.

'Oh, I'm sorry – this is an American credit card, isn't it? American credit cards have chips but don't need PIN numbers. A signature will be fine.'

Henley didn't blink an eye when he wrote 'Reed L. Glazen'.

I still half-expected it not to work. Or maybe for police to come running into the shop. But neither of those things happened.

'Thank you,' he said, taking the bag, the credit card and the receipt.

'Have a nice day, Mr Glazen!' The woman waved as we rejoined Alanna and Peter near the door. I hoped they hadn't heard that. The bell chimed again on our way out.

Realising I was still clutching the newspaper I had found on the boat, I stuffed it into the bag Henley was carrying, which also had the clock in it now. As I did so, Henley slowed down to let Alanna and Peter walk ahead of us.

'That wasn't too bad, was it?' he said, turning towards me to smile at me.

'I never thought I'd do something like that.'

'Well, there's certainly a first time for everything.' With that, he increased his pace to catch up with Alanna and Peter and I followed suit.

'It isn't long to the hostel. Promise,' Alanna said.

'I'm pretty sure you said that ten minutes before the shop,' Henley teased.

She laughed. 'No. It's close now. Honest.'

'If you say so,' I said.

'Bet you're looking forward to putting everything down and grabbing a bite to eat, eh?' Peter said.

'Well, Henley's the one carrying everything, but that's the idea.'

Henley lifted the bag. 'I am ever the pack mule.'

Alanna shrugged, not missing a beat. 'That's why we keep you guys around.'

'Let's see,' Peter said, interrupting the conversation. 'It's on this street here.'

'The hostel?' I asked.

'Yeah. It's hard to find – we kept walking past it on our first day here. There's only one sign—'

'There it is.' Alanna cut Peter off, pointing to a tall, narrow sign reading 'The Brock Terrace Hostel'.

A narrow monochrome door matched the plain sign. Peter was right: it would be easy to miss if you didn't know what you were looking for.

'Watch your feet,' Alanna said, hopping over the single step leading up to the door.

I wasn't sure how run-down or just plain *off* this place would look inside, but when she pushed open the door, I was pleasantly surprised firstly by how clean it looked.

The door led into a parlour of some sort which was so small that the four of us took up most of the available space. Like the sign and the door outside, the tiny front room was decorated in black and white. A narrow white table faced the door, offering barely enough space for a black computer monitor and a small silver bell. Behind it were two white doors I supposed led to the rest of the hostel. Two identical black chairs were placed on either side of the doorway to the street. They were wooden and not upholstered, so they didn't look particularly inviting.

Alanna went up to the desk and hit the bell.

A few moments later we heard the shuffle of feet from the next room. One of the white doors opened and a burly man with a shaved head and a full beard the same size as his face squeezed through it.

'Alanna! Peter!' The man clapped Peter's back. 'And you brought friends. Wonderful!' He sat on a stool on the other side of the desk. 'What can I do for you?'

Nothing about this man matched the decor of the place. He wore a green flannel shirt tucked into faded jeans held up by a wide belt around his middle. The silver buckle gleamed like his shaven head. He squinted at us, and I was sure he was smiling, but his heavy beard hid everything from view.

'Do you have room for our friends, Henley and Rebecca?' Alanna said.

'I'm afraid it's a bit last minute—' Henley started.

'Nonsense!' the man said. 'The best travelling is done last minute. You can't plan out adventure.' He began digging through the drawers on his side of the desk. 'Henley, you said?'

'Henley Beauford.'

'And Rebecca Hatfield,' I volunteered.

'I'm Aaron. I'm guessing you'd like a private room rather than a bed in one of the dorms?'

'That would be preferable,' Henley said.

The man pulled out a few forms and started jotting down information. 'And how would you like to pay for the room? Credit card? Traveller's cheques? We can also do cash if that's more your thing.'

Henley didn't even hesitate. 'Cash, if that's all right.'

'Certainly.' Aaron turned the form he was filling out towards us. 'Just sign here. It's thirty pounds a night. How many nights will you be staying with us?'

'We're still not sure . . .' I said. 'Maybe a week?'

Staying a week would be hard on us financially, but I hoped that would buy us time to find additional funds. Money was crucial for everything, and there was no telling when we might suddenly need more of it than we currently had. If either of us got in trouble with the police and couldn't produce ID for this time period, or if we needed to make a quick getaway – all that would require money.

Then there was the fact that I couldn't even stay in this time period for long. That was one of the side effects of immortality: keep time travelling or slowly lose my grip on reality and ultimately be driven insane.

'Of course. That's fine. Let's put you down for a week and you can always extend your stay if you need to.' Aaron made a note of that on the form. 'Would you like to pay for that week up front, or just give me the hundred-pound deposit now?'

'We'd best do the deposit first,' I said, before quickly clarifying. 'We need to stop by an ATM soon.'

Henley shot me a curious, if not slightly confused, glance. I needed to remember to explain what an ATM was to him at some point.

'You can always pay by card,' Aaron said. 'Save you a trip.'

I saw my mistake. 'W-we'd rather go with cash, if you don't mind.'

Aaron gave us a quizzical look but didn't say anything more.

Henley counted out a hundred pounds and handed it across the desk.

Aaron put the money away and locked the drawer. 'Here are your room keys.'

He passed us each a metal key with a wooden tag attached. The tags were decorated with a painting of a flower and the words 'Blue Flax'.

'These are beautiful,' I said.

'Thank you. I did the paintings myself. We named the private rooms after flowers. Shall I show you to your room?'

At this point we parted ways with Alanna and Peter.

'Why don't you come down when you're ready for dinner?' Alanna said. 'We can meet here in about an hour? Is that enough time for you to get settled?'

We assured her that was fine and followed Aaron through the white door closest to us. He led us down a cramped corridor so narrow that his shoulders took up most of the room, and I couldn't see ahead of him to where we were going. We stopped in front of a white door with small painted blue flowers spanning the wood.

'Why don't you try your key?'

I had almost forgotten I was holding it.

The room was simple enough – a bed, a blue bedside table with an alarm clock, a free-standing wardrobe in one corner and a rickety door I assumed led to the bathroom. The walls were the same stark white as the mini-lobby. The hardwood floors creaked ever so slightly as Henley headed for the bed to unload the bag of clothes he was holding. As he did so, the newspaper I had stuck into the bag fell out.

'This is perfect,' I told Aaron.

'We have an optional cleaning service – just a daily tidying up and a weekly change of sheets, if you end up staying with us that long. It's an extra charge, of course – would you be interested?'

I opened my mouth to answer but Henley responded before I could. 'No, we're fine. Thank you.'

'Very well,' Aaron said, backing out through the door. 'If you need anything, just stop by the front desk and let me know.'

There was a click as the door shut behind him, and finally Henley and I were alone.

I yawned inadvertently.

'That's exactly how I feel about today,' Henley said. He sat on the edge of the bed and kicked off his shoes.

'The day's not over yet.' I reminded him we had promised to meet up with Alanna and Peter shortly.

'They're almost . . . *too* helpful,' Henley said.

I studied his features carefully. His eyes were a little narrower than usual. I didn't like him being *this* on edge, *this* suspicious. But recent events just kept giving him more reason to be this way.

I walked over to the bed and sat next to him on the bright red quilt pulled taut over white sheets. The bed was so small that I was squished into his side.

'I think they mean well, though,' I said. 'It would have taken us twice as long to find a place to stay tonight by ourselves.'

'I know . . . I just can't help being cautious.'

Henley said 'cautious' but I knew it was more a sort of paranoia. I knew that because I had the same feeling in the pit of my stomach. It was a feeling that made it hard to trust anyone. First there was the whole immortality thing, and then this murderer getting ever closer to me – that would be enough to set anyone on edge, but I didn't want it to become a reason to not trust anyone ever again.

'Some people are just good people,' I said.

Henley leaned back on his forearms. The bed shifted with his body weight and I was comforted by feeling him – all of him – right next to me.

'We need to get home,' I finally said.

'Home? You mean to Miss Hatfield's house?' Henley said.

He forgot it was my house, too. And in some ways, it was his only home now. We didn't have anything else.

'The same house the killer trashed? He knows where you *live*. He knows *exactly* where to find you, Rebecca.'

'Do you have any better ideas?' I asked.

'We have to get away,' he said. 'From the murderer. From this place. From all of this.'

'Of course, but that doesn't really answer the question of where we're going, does it?'

'We can't just stay here.'

He was right, of course.

Henley continued, 'It's a foreign country. We don't know anyone here. We may not be close in time to the killer but we're close geographically.'

The last we saw of the murderer had been in the Tudor court in England. This wasn't 1527, but it was still the same country and we weren't far from that location.

'I guess we need to make our way back to the States,' I said. 'But to do anything, we need money.'

'We currently have three hundred and sixty-four pounds,' Henley said.

'And ten dollars,' I reminded him.

There was a pause.

'That deposit took a lot of our money,' I said.

'There wasn't much to begin with.'

And it wasn't even our money, of course, I added mentally.

I got up from the bed and reached for the bag on the other side of Henley. Wordlessly, I started going through the clothing we had bought and saw the tags still attached. Did the hostel rooms have scissors? I opened the single drawer in the bedside table. Postcards. Pens. More stationery. No scissors. I began ripping the tags off instead.

'What did you get for yourself?' I asked, even though I was already pulling out the clothing Henley had bought.

'Just a shirt and some jeans,' Henley said. He crossed his arms behind his head to prop himself up. 'Jeans seem very popular here. Have you seen how many people are wearing them? It's as if it's mandated somewhere that every second person must be wearing jeans when in a group in public.'

'I guess it's just like how everyone wore gloves in your time,' I said, still tearing off tags.

Henley scrunched up his face. 'No . . . No, it's different.'

I tried not to laugh. He sounded so certain. I picked up the now slightly crumpled newspaper that lay limp on the other side of the bed and tossed it to Henley.

'You might as well read up on current news and learn something useful instead of just lying there.' I was teasing, but Henley actually picked up the paper and started reading it intently.

I took the bright green backpack we had bought and contemplated its many zippers. It might have been conspicuous, but at least it had a lot of pockets. The biggest compartment looked spacious enough to hold the clock. After losing it in Tudor England, there was no way I was going to leave it in the hostel room when we went out. I picked up the clock and tried it for size. It fitted well.

Deciding it would probably be best to change into something more contemporary, I took off the belt and the purse around my waist, along with the flimsy linen shift I was wearing. Oddly, I didn't feel at all concerned about changing in front of Henley. Though things were a little different now because he had a body, I figured he had seen everything before.

Looking at my choices, I settled for what Alanna had called a 'crop top' and the jeans.

Try as I might – and I did try very hard to tug the shirt down – the top only half-covered me. I heard Henley laugh behind me and I turned.

'What?' I asked, as the left corner of my mouth twitched up into a half-smile.

'I think that's how it's supposed to be worn,' he said, eyeing me. 'I'm not the biggest fan of jeans but I like them on you.'

41

'I thought I'd change for dinner so we don't stick out as much.'

'I always miss the best things,' Henley grumbled. 'Like you changing . . .'

Apparently he'd been too engrossed in the paper to notice what I was doing. I shook my head at him but a giggle slipped out.

'Regardless of which century I'm from, I *am* a man.' Henley folded the newspaper.

'I'm quite sure you saw your fair share when you were bodyless like a ghost.'

'You forget that I'm also a gentleman!'

He feigned feeling hurt and I threw the nearest piece of clothing I could find – his jeans – at him. They landed harmlessly in his lap.

I changed the subject. 'Did you learn anything useful from the paper?'

'Everyone's worried about the government and the economy. It's the same in every time.' Henley stood up.

'So nothing interesting?'

'I didn't say that,' Henley said. He started taking off his shirt. 'I figured out how we're going to get more money.'

'What are you doing?'

Henley froze. 'The same as you. Changing.'

'I . . . Can't you wait until I turn around?' I quickly turned my back towards him, but not before he saw how red my cheeks were growing.

'I figured we're close enough by now for me to change in front of you.' He laughed. 'It's not as if we haven't been through centuries of life-or-death situations together.'

'Well . . .' True. But somehow it felt different. *This* was different. While Henley might have watched me change a multitude of times when he was without a body, this was one of the first times I had seen so much of him.

'Well, what? Being hunted by a murderer doesn't faze you as much as a man changing near you?' Henley laughed his full, all-encompassing laugh. It was the kind of laugh that made other people pause to appreciate it. 'I hope I never stop being able to make you blush so furiously.'

I still had my back towards him but my shoulders were shaking now from laughing with him.

'Don't you want to ask me how we're going to get more money?' he asked. 'Or did whatever caused your blush make you forget all about that, too?'

I *had* completely forgotten but I wasn't going to give Henley the satisfaction of knowing. 'So how are we going to get money? Not by pickpocketing again, I hope?'

'God, no. I hated doing that the first time round. I was amazed it worked, though. I only did it a few times as a child.' Noting my raised eyebrow, he added, 'Best not to get into that now. What I was about to say was that we could sell your jewellery.' He pointed to the pouch tied to the belt I had just taken off. 'There's no harm in pawning that stuff. It's not as if we'll have any use for it here.'

'But who'll take it?' I paused. 'And even if we do find someone who'll buy it, they'll only give us the price of costume jewellery. No one would know the pieces are worth far more than that.'

'They would if they were experts.' Henley grinned, opening the newspaper and tapping an advert on one of the pages for *Carter House Auction Specialists*. 'They even have a jewellery expert,' he said. 'It's perfect.'

'It is pretty perfect,' I had to admit. 'They could just write us a cheque and then we'd just have to figure out a way to cash it . . . But before you go on feeling pleased with yourself, did you come up with an explanation for why we have this old jewellery in the first place? It doesn't even look *vintage*. It's jewellery straight from Henry VIII's court, without centuries of ageing.'

'Not exactly a normal find on the street, no, but we'll think of something.' Henley sounded so sure of himself. 'And we don't even have to sort it all out now. We can go to dinner, maybe sleep on it. We have some time.'

'Our money will run out quickly, though,' I reminded him.

'We have a fair bit left. You could even say we're comfortable. Three hundred and sixty-four pounds isn't too bad. It's enough for a few dinners, at least.'

I shrugged. I didn't have any idea how much dinner would cost. We would definitely be able to afford it tonight . . . But a week's worth of food in addition to the rest of the money for the room? I wasn't sure we had enough.

'Just order small amounts of food,' Henley said.

Henley was worse off than me, I reminded myself. Although he had been a successful businessman in his time, I remembered he had never carried cash. People knew his father and he just put everything he bought on Mr Beauford's tab. Despite what he might believe, Henley had no concept of money, period.

Chapter 3

'Here they are,' Alanna chirped as she saw us come out to the mini-lobby. The early evening sun shone lazily through the window onto the floor in front of her.

'We were beginning to take bets on whether Alanna had scared you off permanently,' Peter said.

'Sorry we took so long,' I said as Henley lifted the back-pack from my shoulder.

'No problem. Settling in takes time,' Alanna said. 'And I see you've changed! That outfit fits you perfectly.'

'She has a tendency to look lovely in whatever she wears,' Henley said behind me.

Being the topic of conversation made my cheeks burn.

'Shouldn't we get going to dinner?' I said.

'Do you have any food preferences?' Alanna asked. 'Paleo, pescatarian, vegan?'

I shook my head. I didn't know what any of those things were.

'That makes things easier for us. Why don't we go to this pub we found a few nights ago, then? It serves food, too.'

'That sounds great,' Henley said, wrapping an arm around me.

Henley had his white button-down shirt tucked into his jeans. It was very much like him to look so neat and well groomed even when we had barely unpacked and were staying in a hostel.

'You couldn't have just bought a T-shirt?' I whispered to him as we set off walking.

'They all had "I heart London" on them. Couldn't have that sort of atrocity on my person, could I?'

'I'm wearing a shirt that doesn't come down to my belly button.' I tried to say it sternly and keep a straight face, but Henley's smirk got me laughing.

'Oh, stop being such a cute couple,' Alanna said. 'We're at the pub already.' She turned to Peter. 'Do you think we look like that to other people?'

Peter twisted a braid. 'Are you asking me if we stare sappily into each other's eyes and sigh all the time? Probably.'

Alanna shoved him, but Peter only looked amused.

'Is this it?' Henley was looking up at a double door painted black. A sign hung above: Goldmann's Pub.

'It is.' Alanna ushered us in. 'You *have* to try the fish and chips. Very touristy, but so good here.'

My eyes took a minute to adjust to the dim lighting. Everything was hardwood here – the floor, the ceiling, the bar were all panelled in dark wood. A handful of old blown-glass lighting fixtures completed the murky look. I'd expected there would be tables, but as there were none in sight, I followed Alanna and Peter to the bar and took a seat between Peter and Henley. Alanna sat on the other side of Peter.

'Good evening.' A man with slicked-back hair walked up behind the bar. 'Thanks for joining us at Goldmann's. You'll find the stack of menus right next to you, but before we can serve you, could I see IDs?'

He looked like he should be working at a five-star restaurant rather than a pub. He also sounded like he took his job rather seriously.

46

'IDs?' I didn't know who said it first, Henley or me, but we looked at each other with wide eyes.

Alanna and Peter calmly took out their drivers' licences and showed them to the man at the bar.

'Good, good.' He nodded. Turning his attention to us, he added, 'It's policy to ask to see the ID of anyone who looks younger than thirty. Is that a problem?'

'We—' I started.

'We don't have our IDs with us,' Henley said. 'We must have left them back in our room.'

'I'm sorry,' the barman said. 'You can't sit in the pub without showing ID.'

Henley nodded and stood up.

'Do you want to eat somewhere else?' Alanna asked. 'Or we could buy food and take it outside. The weather's so nice, anyway.'

'That actually sounds like a great idea,' Henley said and started digging through his pocket for cash.

'No, no,' Alanna said.

'But—'

'Absolutely not.'

'Thank you,' I said.

Henley looked a bit defeated as he pulled me outside.

Once we were outside, I squinted at Henley past the lowering sun. 'Why couldn't you just say we don't have IDs instead of telling him we left them in our room? What if Alanna wants us to get our IDs for something else later?' I hissed.

'You can't travel without some form of identification,' Henley said. 'That's true in any time.'

I sighed, looking down at my shoes. He was right and there was no way around it.

I heard a cough and looked up, about to ask Henley what he wanted now. But it wasn't Henley.

A man in an oversized sweatshirt was approaching us from around the corner of the pub. His greying facial hair looked like it hadn't been shaved for a week. His brown hair was plastered to his forehead and the sides of his face with what looked like sweat.

He had a gruff voice. 'Saw you guys get kicked out.'

'And what of it?' Henley drew himself up.

'You need ID to sit in there.'

'So we heard,' I said.

The man grinned, revealing a mouthful of yellowed teeth. 'I know someone who could hook you up.'

'Hook us up?'

'My guy specialises in IDs – driving licences, passports . . . He does other things, too.'

Henley's hands were clenched. 'We don't—'

'How much?' I asked.

Out of the corner of my eye, I saw Henley's face blanch, but I kept my eyes trained on this strange man.

'Rebecca, you don't mean—'

I ignored him. 'How much?' I asked again.

'Nothing we can't negotiate,' he said.

'Would we have to pay up front?' I asked.

His eyes darted the length of the street. 'I'd prefer not to discuss this here . . . Where are you staying?'

'Rebecca—'

'The Brock Terrace Hostel.'

'Nice and close.' The man leered at me. 'I'm looking forward to doing business with *you*.'

Just at that moment, Alanna and Peter came tumbling out through the dark doors of the pub.

'Don't drop it, Peter!'

The man looked alarmed for a second. 'I'll find you,' he quickly said before heading back the way he'd come.

48

'Well, that man was sure creepy.' Alanna stood with her hands on her hips. 'Wherever you go, all across the world, every country definitely has its own creeps.'

I didn't think they'd caught much of what the man said, so I simply smiled.

Peter walked towards us with paper plates of fried fish and a mountain of French fries, and we sat on the curb.

'Fish and chips!' Alanna squealed. 'I didn't know if you liked salt, vinegar, tartar sauce or ketchup, so I just put them all on the side.'

My stomach gurgled its thanks. I couldn't remember the last time I had eaten.

'Let us pay you back—' Henley started, but Alanna stopped him, touching his shoulder.

'This one's on us. You can get the next meal. Besides, someone sounds hungry.' She laughed, looking at me.

'You heard that?' I was already grabbing a handful of fries.

'I've never understood why fries are chips here and chips are crisps.' Henley was loading his fish with a massive amount of tartar sauce. 'It's so complicated.'

'Got enough sauce there?' I teased.

'It looks like he has more sauce than fish.' Alanna wrinkled her nose. 'Look, Peter does the same thing, except with vinegar.'

Sure enough, Peter was busy drowning his fish in the little cup of vinegar.

'I like it with a tang,' he said.

'That's so gross.' Alanna was eating her fish plain.

'Eh.' Peter just shrugged.

A phone buzzed, and Alanna and Peter simultaneously held their forkfuls of fish with one hand and patted their pockets for their phones with the other hand.

'Oh, it's mine,' Alanna said, looking at her white iPhone. She turned to me. 'My friend had the cutest baby! And they finally posted pics.'

'Janice?' Peter said.

'Yeah, Janice. And the baby looks just like her. Give me a second and let me pull up the photo on Facebook.'

Alanna handed me her phone. 'Isn't she just the cutest?'

The baby was peering at the camera, open-mouthed. If Alanna hadn't told me, the only clue to the baby's gender was the giant bow that looked as if it was taped onto her bald head.

When I grabbed the phone from Alanna's hands, I accidentally tapped a banner at the bottom of the screen and a new page popped up. An advertisement of some sort? No – a news article: *Regency Keepsake Box Excavated in London Parking Lot*.

But it was the photographs underneath the title that really caught my eye. One showed a letter next to a wooden jewellery box. The letter looked ancient and the ink was faded in places, but the text was magnified in a separate photo. It began: *Querida Emilia* . . . I scanned the letter. The entire thing was in Spanish, but two words made me stop.

Juana Ruíz.

That was the signature on the letter.

I wondered if I had read that right. I skimmed the article. It mentioned that the letter was written in the 1500s while the box was a Regency piece. The article also mentioned that Juana might have been the first European woman to set foot in the Americas.

So was it her? The woman who drank from the Fountain of Youth with Ponce de León, the discoverer of both Florida and the source of immortality?

The article said that the artefacts were found during a construction project for what would become a parking lot somewhere in London. I took note of the address. The article didn't say much else after that.

'Still looking at the baby?' Alanna said.

I quickly clicked out of the page and handed Alanna her phone.

'She's adorable,' I said.

The conversation continued around me but I was barely listening. Juana. Why hadn't it occurred to me before? If all the Miss Hatfields were dead and killed by someone immortal who had gone back in time to murder them one by one . . . Maybe Juana was the killer. She had drunk from the Fountain of Youth with Ponce de León. What if she never died? She was the only plausible suspect I could think of. I had to talk this through with Henley, but I felt the letter could be a starting clue.

And then there was that man who had just come up to us . . . I knew he was more than a little 'off' and might potentially be dangerous, but he was really our only option. We couldn't just sit here for ever. I glanced at Henley. Although he was sticking a huge piece of fish into his mouth, he had a worried crease between his brows.

'What do you think, Rebecca?'

I looked up into Alanna's expectant face. She must have said something but I'd completely missed it.

'Uh, sorry?' I said.

'Much too into your fish and chips, I see. I was just saying that Peter and I are going to do some touristy stuff tomorrow – Buckingham Palace, the London Eye – you and Henley should join us,' she said.

'Oh, we'd love to, but . . . Henley and I have a few things we need to take care of,' I said.

'What kind of things?'

'We just received news that a family member of mine passed away,' Henley said suddenly.

'A family member?' This time it was me with my mouth open in surprise. 'Um, yeah. A family member.' I tried to recover.

'My grandmother, actually,' Henley went on. 'We just have a few matters to clear up.'

'Of course,' Alanna said. 'I'm so sorry to hear that.' Luckily, she seemed oblivious to Henley having to step in to save me.

'She's resting much more comfortably now,' Henley said.

When we were done with our food and had thrown our plates away, I took Henley's hand and began to excuse us.

'But the night's still young,' Peter said.

'We've had a rough day of travelling,' I said. 'We both need some downtime and we should also get some rest.' I looked at Henley and he rubbed his eyes on cue.

'They're right,' Alanna said to Peter. 'It's been a long day for them.' To us, she said, 'Let us at least walk you back.'

Though it further postponed me talking with Henley alone, we agreed. There was only so much we could protest. We started back to the hostel, Peter walking ahead with Henley, Alanna by my side.

'Such a shame about Henley and his grandmother,' she said.

'Yes.' I tried to keep from biting my lip. I didn't want to lie to Alanna, but things like this occasionally had to be done. And when they were done, they had to be seamless.

'Were they close?'

'As close as any grandchild is to his grandmother, I suppose.'

'Was it sudden?' She had tears in her eyes and I was taken aback.

'Oh, no.' I tried to reassure her. 'She'd been sick for a while. We saw it coming and had time to prepare.'

'Prepare and try to come to terms with it, I guess, right?'

'Yes.'

'Well, I don't think anyone can really come to terms with family dying. It's not something I've ever managed, at least,' she said.

We walked in silence for a few strides before she spoke again.

'Sorry,' Alanna said. 'My own granny died six months ago. It's still a difficult subject for me.'

I felt a sudden wave of guilt for the lie Henley and I had told. Although he had come up with it, I had helped him by elaborating on it.

'I'm sure she was a wonderful woman.'

'Yeah, she was . . . Nothing like my mother,' she said. 'Anyway . . . I'm sorry I brought that up. I just wanted to tell you that Henley's lucky to have you by his side at a tough time like this. I don't know what I would have done without Peter.'

'It's the least I can do. Henley's been with me through a lot. I can't begin to even the score.'

'How long have you two been together?'

Her question gave me pause. How could I answer it? Barely a year? Five centuries and counting?

'A while,' I said. 'It feels like for ever, but also like we only met yesterday.'

Alanna smiled. 'That's when you know it's serious.'

I laughed. 'I suppose you could say that. I can't imagine being with anyone else.'

'He understands you, doesn't he?'

'More than anyone,' I said.

'So you think he'll put a ring on you soon?'

I stumbled. 'Come again?'

'A ring,' she said. 'He's so in love with you. Head over heels, in fact. It's obvious.'

I looked ahead to see Henley glancing over his shoulder at me. Henley had in fact given me a ring long before, in 1904. And although Henley knew me well even then – better than anyone – he had no idea I was immortal. No idea that I couldn't stay with him. And he'd asked for precisely that: Henley had got down on one knee and asked me to marry him. I had refused. Instead of telling him I was immortal, I croaked out that I didn't love him. That couldn't have been further from the truth. He made me take the ring anyway, insisting, 'It's not an engagement ring any more.' I still remembered it like it was yesterday.

I realised I was still staring at Henley, and he was still looking my way.

'You all right?' he called back.

'I'm fine,' I mumbled, though I knew he was probably too far ahead to hear me. 'Just tripped.'

Henley and Peter waited in front of the hostel door for us to catch up.

'I don't know him that well, but even I can tell he doesn't look at everybody like that,' Alanna said as we came up to the black door. 'It's only a matter of time.' She squeezed my shoulder. 'Get lots of rest and we'll hopefully see you tomorrow.'

Alanna took Peter's hand, and for the first time, as she waved goodbye, I noticed an oval diamond glittering on her ring finger.

'Ready to go in?' Henley said.

'Not quite. We should probably stock up on some food for the week ahead, don't you think?'

'Oh, we could have asked Alanna and Peter where the closest shop is—'

I stopped him. 'I didn't want them to come with us. You know them – they would have offered to walk us there, and it might look a little suspicious to buy more than a small amount of food with cash only.'

'So then why don't we use the credit card?'

I shook my head. 'It's probably been too long since it was stolen. He must have reported it missing by now. Better to just use cash.'

'Let me pop in and ask Aaron where the nearest grocer is, then.'

I waited outside for him. He wasn't gone long.

'It's only three blocks that way. He said it's pretty small – a local little thing – but it sounds like it'll have every-thing we need.'

'We don't need much,' I said, starting to walk in the direction he had indicated. 'Just enough to sustain ourselves.'

'Naturally.'

We walked quickly through the streets. It was getting late and the early summer sun was starting to set, the shadows growing ever longer as we hurried along.

'Let's make this visit as quick as possible,' I said when we saw the grocery store in front of us. 'It'll be night soon, and I don't want us to have to walk in the dark on our way back.'

Henley nodded. 'Even from the outside it looks bigger than any grocer's shop I've ever seen.'

'And have you seen many?' I teased.

'Well . . . our cook did do most of the food shopping, but I passed the food districts occasionally,' he said.

I rolled my eyes. 'Let me guess – from inside your carriage?'

'That was just how it was done,' he said. There was a defensive tone in his voice.

I shook my head, getting back to the task at hand.

As we approached the doors, they parted for us.

'Like magic,' Henley whispered.

I didn't know if he was talking about the doors or the astonishing sights inside. Cold air blew across our faces as we entered.

'My God . . .'

I glanced up at Henley. His lips were parted like he was going to say something more, but nothing was coming out.

'. . . This is wonderful,' he finally managed to utter.

Rows of shelved food greeted us. There was a row of nothing but bread and another filled with cereal. A round table just for bananas. Another set up with a mountain of pastries.

I grabbed a shopping cart.

'They have *everything*,' Henley said.

I realised Henley hadn't seen a real grocery store . . . or at least not a modern one like this.

Henley took off running down the first aisle with the cart. 'What should we get?' He grabbed a box of children's cereal. 'I-it's so colourful,' he said as he stuck it in the cart. Then he picked up a loaf of French bread, a box of frozen dumplings and a miniature chocolate cake in the dessert section.

I'd expected him to be hesitant to try food he hadn't seen in his time, but I think he was so excited by the prospect of eating again in human form that he wanted to try everything immediately.

'Henley! We can't buy the whole store.'

'What?' Henley froze in the middle of the produce aisle with two apples in his hand.

'Put those down.'

Obediently, he put the apples down . . . in the salad section.

'No, take them back where you found them,' I said.

He slowly took the apples and returned them to the right place.

'Henley, I know this all looks good, but we can't buy everything. We have a limited amount we can spend on food and no fridge to keep it cool.'

'Surely those few things can't cost *that* much,' he said.

'You'd be surprised.' I knew the high cost of food from living in New York. 'Now let's go and put most of this back.'

I walked with Henley from section to section until he had replaced everything where he'd found it. He was most reluctant to give up his chocolate cake, claiming that, 'We could use the sugar after all that we've been through,' but eventually he complied.

'Now, let's start from the beginning and choose carefully – we want foods that are as cheap and as filling as possible.'

Who knew grocery shopping on a budget would be this hard?

We picked up a loaf of wholewheat bread, the cheapest brand we could find, then a hunk of cheese and some canned kidney beans. We also found an oat cereal discounted if we bought two boxes, so we took that, too.

'Look for sales,' I said.

We added a jar of peanut butter, some celery, a bag of granola and a bag of cinnamon rolls.

'That should last us a while, right?' I asked once we were in the checkout line.

Just to be safe, Henley ran and grabbed another loaf of bread.

'Cash, debit or credit?' the cashier asked.

'Um . . . cash,' I said. The stolen credit card had probably been reported by now.

I counted out the appropriate number of notes.

'Thank you,' the cashier said, handing us the receipt and our bags.

'Wait a second,' Henley said as soon as we left the store and ran back inside.

'What was that about?' I asked when he returned.

'I just threw away the credit card,' he said. 'You said we couldn't use it any more—'

'That's right. We don't want someone tracking us down with it, and I'm sure Mr Glazen probably already had it reported as stolen.'

We walked quickly, lugging the flimsy bags. I hoped the kidney beans didn't break through the bottom of the bag. There were a handful of people in the street, all wearing orange shirts with something written on them and passing out trinkets.

'What do you think that's about?' Henley asked.

One of the orange-shirted people came up to us. 'Free beads?' she asked, holding out two strings of orange plastic beads with a tag that said 'Friday Free Beer Nights at Cassoni's'.

'Sure, why not?' Henley grinned.

The girl placed them over our heads. 'Remember to come on Fridays for free beer from four-thirty to six-thirty!'

'Interesting . . .' I said as soon as we were out of earshot.

'I wish they did that back home,' Henley said.

I knew he was talking about the early 1900s.

We resumed our walk to the hostel. It was the golden hour and everything was cast in a soft glow.

'It's my favourite time of day,' Henley said. His face looked golden, too, emphasising his – or rather Richard's – honey-coloured eyes. 'Everything looks ten times more lovely in this light.'

'And magical,' I said.

'And magical.'

There were instances like this when I would remember that those were Richard's eyes and Richard's hands. These moments came suddenly and unexpectedly, and I would catch myself feeling guilty that I didn't mourn Richard more. I did miss him, but . . . never like I had missed Henley. The awareness of Richard's absence in my life was incomparable to the deep-rooted ache I suffered without Henley. I felt terrible about it, but I couldn't help it.

The hostel's mini-lobby was empty when we arrived, and we didn't run into Aaron as we made our way to our room at the back of the building. I'd been planning to tell Henley about the sixteenth-century letter found in the parking lot and my idea that Juana was the killer as soon as we got back, but something stopped me. Maybe I didn't want to spoil this perfect moment.

'What a couple,' Henley said, sprawling out on the bed.

'You mean Alanna and Peter?'

Henley nodded.

I found it interesting that Henley was thinking about them all of a sudden. 'What brought this up?'

'Nothing really,' he started. 'I was just thinking about us. And them. And how we were different. And all the ways we were similar.'

I looked at Henley's face closely. Sometimes I felt that if I stared hard enough, I'd finally be able to read his thoughts.

'Do you ever feel that some things were meant to happen?' Henley went on to say. 'Like you and me?'

I smiled back at him. 'Now you're just being mushy.'

'It may be a little overly sentimental, but it's true.'

We both took off our beads and put them on the bedside table. Not having anywhere else to put the shopping bags,

I set them down next to the bedside table. I wished we had a mini-fridge, but even I knew that was too much to ask for in a hostel. I put the backpack containing all our valuables, including our cash, the clock and Richard's vial, under the bed.

'That's beginning to look like your go-to position,' I said.

'What? Lying on the bed? There aren't many seating options here, in case you haven't noticed.'

I walked over to the window and perched on the narrow sill. We didn't have much of a view, just the whitewashed brick wall of the next building (apartments, I was guessing), but there was a narrow side street between our window and the wall and I watched the occasional person stroll past.

'I hope you know what you've got us into,' Henley said behind me.

Hearing the suddenly serious tone of his voice, I knew he was talking about the man from earlier.

'What else could we have done?'

I was suddenly conscious that we were talking in 'we's' instead 'I's', and the corners of my mouth twitched up into a smile as I thought of how close Henley and I had become.

'Something less dubious might have come—' Henley began, but I interrupted him.

'We can't wait. We don't have time.'

Henley was silent. He knew as well as I did that time was always the one thing we never had enough of. Which was ironic, considering I had an infinite amount of it.

'Let's not think about that now,' I said, turning from the windowsill. 'We have to figure out how to get him the money.'

Henley shook his head. 'One step ahead of you there. Remember my "grandmother"?'

'Your grandmother? You mean the one you created out of the blue and killed off just to give us an excuse to have time to ourselves? That was awful, even for this messed-up situation. Especially as Alanna told me she'd recently lost her own grandmother—'

'We could tell the auction house that my grandmother – God rest her soul – has bequeathed me things in her will, including her treasured Tudor jewellery passed down for generations. How simple is that?'

I chewed my lip. It would have normally mildly irritated me that Henley cut me off when talking about something serious like this, but his plan sounded like it could work.

Henley went on. 'No need for problematic paperwork detailing how the necklace was bought or acquired if it's been passed down through a family for long enough.'

'Nice and simple . . .'

'No holes,' he said. 'We get the man his money, which gets us IDs—'

'And passports,' I said.

'And passports,' Henley repeated. 'And we're out. And then what?'

'New York.'

Chapter 4

The woman stood in front of me in a haze of white. I couldn't see where she was – I could only focus on her. She was dressed in white, with only the faintest rose colour in her cheeks. She was *pure*. She was *good*. She looked like some sort of immovable Roman statue. Her eyes were marble and her lips frozen, and her auburn hair fell gently down her back. I reached out – I didn't know if it was to comfort her or to unfreeze her somehow – but try as I might, I could never reach her.

The woman smiled, suddenly animated, and both our gazes travelled down to watch a red flower bloom from her body. As its bright petals unfurled, the red began to engulf her.

I glanced back at her face and all at once she looked terrified. How could I have mistaken that grimace for a smile? She was horrified by what was happening to her. She was in pain. She started to scream.

I tried to reach her but I couldn't move. I tried to cry out, but there was only silence. All I could do was watch her die.

I woke up, blinking into the dark. My breath was coming in ragged bursts from crying in my sleep. *Everything's okay. Just breathe.*

I sat up slowly. The room was ink-black, and although I strained my eyes against the darkness, I couldn't see a thing. I felt Henley next to me, the side of his body pressed against mine, and he was warm.

As I moved to swing my feet to the floor, my hand brushed over something cold and smooth lying against Henley's skin. I recoiled. *What was that?* I frowned and fumbled for the light switch, which I thought was above the bedside table. When the lights flickered on, I choked.

Henley was lying flat on his back. His hands were clasped together, and wrapped around them . . . the plastic beads we had been given on the street yesterday.

He looked like a corpse.

Roused by the light, Henley's eyes flickered open. 'Rebecca . . . What time is it?' He looked from me to his hands and the colour drained from his face. 'You didn't do this, did you?' His voice wavered.

I shook my head, unable to speak.

He sat up with the beads still wrapped around his hands. 'If you didn't do this . . .'

'Someone else was here.'

I immediately dived for the backpack under the bed. Panic churning in my stomach, I pulled it out and unzipped it, emptying its contents next to Henley. The clock was still there, thank goodness, along with Richard's vial. And the cash, too. Nothing important was missing.

'It's all here,' I said.

I glanced at the bedside table. The other set of beads we had been given remained untouched.

Henley was already walking around the room, examining everything else. 'It doesn't look like anything's been touched . . . Maybe I grabbed the beads in my sleep,' he said, but we both knew that wasn't true.

My hands were still shaking, but I managed to return everything to the backpack and slip it under the bed again.

'So what does this mean?' Henley said.

I bit my lip. I didn't know. 'Whoever did this, they tied your hands together with the beads – is that supposed to invoke chains?' *Was it supposed to mean something to me?*

'The man on the street yesterday—' Henley started.

'No. He has no reason to do this.'

'Then he found us,' Henley said. 'The killer. He's tracked us down.'

I sank back onto the bed in disbelief. He couldn't have. Of all the time periods he could be in, he had managed to find ours. This was a person on a mission. He wanted me – and maybe Henley, too – dead. That was his goal, I was sure of it – but now I started to wonder if that really was his goal . . .

Henley startled me by rushing over and grabbing the backpack from under the bed. I watched nonplussed as he began throwing our clothes into it.

'What are you doing?' I asked slowly.

'What do you think I'm doing?' he snapped. 'Someone's toying with us. I'm packing so we can get out of here.'

'And go where?'

'Anywhere. Does it matter as long as it's not here?'

'Henley,' I said, not moving from my spot on the bed. 'We have no place to go.'

He ignored me and continued packing.

'Henley, are you listening?' I asked, but he still didn't stop. 'We have no place to go and not much cash. We can get money, but that'll take time.'

Henley dropped the backpack in front of me. 'My God, Rebecca, he'll kill you. He'll kill you, you know that?'

I shook my head. 'We were asleep last night and he didn't kill either of us then. He had the opportunity, but he didn't take it.'

Henley roughly pushed back his hair. 'And what makes you so sure that he won't take the next opportunity he gets?'

'I can never be sure,' I said, 'but I can guess. And my gut feeling—'

'This isn't the damn time for gut feelings.' Henley's cheeks were red. 'This is someone who tried to smother you in your sleep. He killed my mother!'

'He's changed since then. I can't explain it, but he's different somehow. He doesn't just want me dead. He wants me to . . . understand.'

'Understand what? There isn't time for *understanding*.'

'It's hard to explain,' I repeated. 'I just *know*. He could have killed us last night but he didn't. There's something more he wants.'

'So you expect me to just let you stay here?'

'I want you to trust me,' I said.

'What? Trust that you're right, and when you're not, simply watch you die?' Henley was breathing heavily, trying to keep his voice down. 'You can't ask that of me,' he said. He didn't say it, but he must have been worried for himself, too.

'That's the only thing I ask,' I said. 'There's no other way. We can't go far without passports. Say we switch from here to a different hostel or hotel, or travel to a different time – what then? If he could track us down to this specific place and time, what would stop him from doing it again?'

'At least travelling to a different time could buy us some breathing space.' Henley was pleading now.

'Not enough. It would take more time to set ourselves up in the new period – we'd need money, a place to stay, a background story . . . And the toll on your body – your new body . . .' I said. 'You almost died this last time.'

That finally got Henley to at least sit down. 'So you need to time travel without me.'

'You can't be serious,' I sputtered.

'I know you don't want me to bring it up, but we both know you'll need to time travel soon,' Henley said. 'It's been on my mind . . . I mean, how could it not be? Every moment you're here puts a greater strain on you. You need to time travel—'

'So I don't go insane,' I finished for him.

'So you don't suffer the side effects of immortality.' He put it more tactfully.

'You know I can't leave you.'

'You can—' Henley started to say.

'I can't. I don't *want* to. After all that's happened . . . You think I could leave you again, just like that?'

'You need to. There's a killer here and you're not safe.'

I was about to argue with him when I remembered the sixteenth-century letter found at the parking lot construction site.

'Okay . . .' I said slowly. 'I will.'

'You'll get out of this time period?' Henley said.

'I will.'

He looked surprised that I was agreeing with him suddenly, so I started telling Henley about the article I had read on Alanna's phone.

'So Juana signed the letter?' Henley said.

'That's exactly what it looked like. It could give us some clue.'

'Some clue that would confirm that Juana is the killer?' Henley looked at me intently.

'I think that's a safe bet. Our only bet, in fact.'

'And you want to travel back in time just to see what this letter says?'

'Well, it would help me not go insane from staying in one time period for too long,' I said.

66

'You don't even know what time period to travel to,' Henley said. 'Did the article mention any specific dates?'

I shrugged. 'I could guess.'

Henley looked incredulous.

'It's a sixteenth-century letter in a Regency-era wooden box. It obviously has to be Regency-era onward. The Regency period wasn't that long. If we picked a year in the latter part of the Regency period, it'll be more likely that the box will exist and that it'll be there in that exact place.'

'And what if Juana happens to be there? Or what if she finds you.'

'Juana could be anywhere,' I said. 'If she is the killer. He – *she* was obviously here last night.'

'I don't like this,' Henley said.

I didn't tell him that I thought the killer would follow me, and therefore I could protect Henley by keeping away from him for a little bit.

'We're doing the best we can,' I said.

'What if that's not good enough?'

I couldn't answer that.

I moved closer to Henley and placed my hand on his shoulder. 'There's nothing more we can do until the sun comes up. Let's try and get some more sleep and then track down the parking lot. Somehow everything will work itself out.'

'I hope so.'

'It won't take long.'

Chapter 5

After a few more hours of fitful sleep, we grabbed the backpack and went straight to Aaron to ask for the quickest way to get to the address mentioned in the article.

'Oh, are you going to the shopping centre there?' he said. 'It's quite nice.'

Neither Henley nor I corrected him as Aaron pointed out the location on a map.

The walk wasn't as far as it looked on the map, although I had enough time to wonder what the scene would be like once we arrived. It was an excavation of some sort, so it could just be a hole in the ground. There might be a crowd of onlookers since the archaeological find had been in the news. Would barriers and lots of yellow tape make it difficult to get in there?

But once we arrived, I was surprised to see very few people around. Occasionally someone stopped on their way past to peer into the gaping hole in the ground, but that was pretty much it. The construction site was bigger than I had imagined and the hole in the ground where I guessed the artefacts had been found looked to be about the size of the foundations for a house. The only caution tape was around the hole itself and I spied a ladder descending into it on one side. This wasn't going to be too difficult.

Henley had already removed the clock from the bag. I kissed him on the cheek and took it from him before ducking under the caution tape and making my way towards the ladder.

'I'm sorry. This is a restricted area—' I heard as I descended into the pit. 'Miss!' The voice was coming closer.

As soon as my feet hit the bare dirt at the bottom of the hole, I started turning the clock's hands.

Regency period. It ended in 1820. So that year would do, right?

I'd never get used to time travelling. The act itself was simple enough: a turn of the clock's hands was all it took. But the world around me dissolving and a new one taking its place – that would never become commonplace.

I watched the hues of the objects around me fade, the sky becoming a blue sheet that ran into the white clouds like watercolour. The ground appeared to melt, softening as it turned into carpet beneath my feet. A different world came into view as new objects hardened in place.

Then something sharp hit my chest and I put my hands out to steady myself. A crash broke me out of the strange feeling of peace.

No sound came out of my mouth, as I looked about at the many shards of what looked like porcelain that encircled my bare feet.

'What in tarnation—'

At the sound of the unknown male voice, I looked down at my nakedness. *Quick. Do something.* My eyes darted to a standing screen in the corner of the room. Four leaping steps across the carpet and I was behind it, clutching the clock to my chest.

'What's going on?'

I peeked around the side of the screen. I only meant to steal a glance, to see what I was up against, but instead my gaze locked with two grey eyes staring back at me from across the room.

'Rebecca?'

At first I thought I had heard wrong. There was no way this stranger could know my name. He didn't know where I'd come from. He didn't know me.

'Rebecca Hatfield? Is that you?'

I took in the sight of the man in front of me, standing tall in his dark jacket. He couldn't have been that much older than me. Freshly shaven, curly hair combed back, neatly trimmed sideburns and what looked like some type of necktie secured beneath his chin. I didn't have to be near him to know that he smelled like a bouquet of meticulously picked flowers.

'Rebecca, come out here this instant,' he said.

I looked down at my nude body. 'Umm . . .' Something in the authoritative tone of his voice made me want to obey – it actually felt safe to obey – but my present situation gave me pause.

The man also heard my hesitation and remembered why I had run behind the screen in the first place.

'Uh, yes . . . I'll, uh, send for Mrs Becker. She'll know what to do.' He actually had the decency to look embarrassed. Or at least that's how I figured he was feeling as he took a sudden interest in his shoes. Then he left abruptly without giving any indication of when or even if he would be back.

Who was he? And how did he know my name?

I didn't have much time to dwell on these questions before there was quick knock on the door.

'Um . . . yes? Come in?' I said, placing the clock by my feet.

A woman in a brown pinstriped dress swept in with a tower of boxes clutched to her chest. She sidestepped broken shards of what I assumed had been a vase without even glancing down.

Bobbing a quick curtsy, she set the boxes on a table. 'Ethel will see to your dressing today. I am afraid Lucy is not with us any more.'

'Dead?' I asked automatically as a young woman with wheat-blonde hair scuttled in. I had no idea what made me say it.

The older woman in the brown dress tried to look away as the corner of her mouth lifted with amusement. 'No. She simply sought employment elsewhere. I'm afraid much has changed since your last visit, Miss Hatfield.'

My skin rose in little bumps at being addressed that way. I must have travelled to a time and place where a former Miss Hatfield once lived . . . But which Miss Hatfield? I'd assumed all of them had been in the US.

'Ethel, why don't we dress Miss Hatfield in the deep-blue gown that was always her favourite?' Mrs Becker took the lid off of the topmost box. Turning towards me, she said, 'I'm afraid the dress will be a bit wrinkled. It's the best we could do without notice. We didn't know you would be arriving so . . . soon.'

She stared at me and I realised she was waiting for a response.

'Of course,' I said. 'The blue dress will do.'

Ethel and Mrs Becker continued to unpack white under-garments and yards of blue fabric and ribbon that made up the dress. I tried to glance around the room for the keepsake box but there was only so much I could see from my position behind the screen.

71

Ethel joined me and started dressing me as Mrs Becker edged towards the door, where she paused. 'Will that be all?'

'Uh, yes.'

'Very well. I shall leave you to your room.'

My room?

I was so preoccupied with what she might have meant that I only just heard her say, 'I believe Mr Percy will be in his study when you are ready.' With that, she slipped out, barely glancing at the broken vase on the floor as she left.

Blending into a time period was a lot like a child's game of dress-up. Occasionally it felt juvenile, but I guess it was a testament to how little things changed. Sure, the fashions altered with the years and people might speak a bit differently, but that was it, really. People's relationships with each other stayed the same. Their desires stayed the same. And for the most part, even their values stayed the same.

When I was finally wearing enough layers of undergarments to satisfy Ethel, she asked me in a quiet voice if I would like her to do my hair. I gave her a nod and she led me to a vanity on the other side of the screen. She began poking and prodding at my hair as soon as I took a seat.

'Something simple will be fine,' I said, biting my lip. This wasn't what I was here to do.

'Of course, Miss Hatfield.'

Ten minutes later, with my hair off the nape of my neck, Ethel led me back behind the screen to finish dressing me. She lifted the top layer of the dress over me and the blue fabric fell around me. Ethel's deft fingers made short work of the buttons and then flew down to rearrange my skirts. I was pleasantly surprised to find the dress had pockets, but I suspected they were more decorative than for practical use. With the blue dress piled around me, I looked like I was drowning at sea.

'Thank you, Ethel,' I said, giving her a nod to dismiss her.

Ethel crept out, barely turning her back to me.

When she closed the doors behind her, I was finally left alone to take in the room. It was a surprisingly big space. Not too many books, trinkets or furniture, but that was to be expected of this time period. A bed in the middle of the room was covered with a blue fabric that matched my dress. There were two wooden bedside tables, a dressing table with a mirror and a chest with drawers against the far wall. I noticed there were no windows, but the high ceiling kept it from feeling stuffy.

Now, where would that wooden jewellery box be? I had no idea what size it was, but it didn't look too big in the photo. I scanned the tops of the bedside tables. Nothing.

I pulled out the drawer of the left-hand bedside table. Empty.

Going over to the other side, I held my breath, expecting this drawer to be empty, too. I pulled the handle and the first thing my eyes saw was a Bible. I picked it up, thinking I'd flip through it, but as soon as I lifted it, I noticed something underneath. The wooden box.

It was wedged into the drawer so there was no space to see any of the sides of the box save for its top, but it was unmistakable. The same colour wood. The same engravings on its lid. I prised it out using my fingernails. The box opened so easily.

There was a rosary in the box but I pushed it aside. It was of no interest to me. I'd come here for the letter. I grasped the paper at the bottom of the box.

Querida Emilia . . .

This was it.

I pocketed the letter, gripping it tight.

73

This was all I had come here to do . . . and yet there were still so many unanswered questions. Which Miss Hatfield's life was this? Why was Juana's letter here?

I walked out of the room, deciding one more conversation with Mr Percy wouldn't hurt. If anyone could answer these questions, it would probably be him.

Mrs Becker had said that he'd be in his study, but where would that be? I didn't even know if I was currently upstairs or downstairs. Wait . . . were there even multiple floors? No matter. I decided I would check the rooms nearby first.

The door next to mine was locked, so I moved on to the next door in the hallway. The doorknob turned easily, but upon poking my head in, I saw loveseats and a card table. A sitting room of some sort? I moved along the hall door by door. Some were locked. Others looked like dusty closet spaces or other bedrooms. I was beginning to think I wouldn't find the study on this floor when I neared a room with an open door.

'Yes. Yes. Certainly.'

I could hear voices – or rather, one voice – from the open door as I approached it.

'Of course I know she's a threat to herself . . . Yes, I know it's important to get her back,' Mr Percy said.

I refrained from walking into the room because I wanted to hear more of the conversation. Who was he talking with? What was this about?

His voice got low. 'I-I just don't want it to be like last time. I know we had to force her to go, but watching it . . . it all but broke me.' There was a long pause. I couldn't hear the other person but I supposed there was a response. 'Of course I know that. But she was going to be Mrs Benjamin Percy. I was in love with her. I still am . . . I can't help it. You forget that I almost married Rebecca.'

I faltered hearing my name . . . or rather that of one of the previous Miss Hatfields. But what I heard next almost made me sick.

'She sounds as if she's in one of her more reasonable moods today, so come tomorrow. Yes, she only broke one thing today. No tantrums so far. Come tomorrow, then you can take her back to the asylum.'

He said it so casually that I almost missed it. The asylum. As in a mental institution. But in this time, I knew it would be more of a prison than a hospital.

But he said he loved her – *me*. So why was he doing such a thing?

And then it hit me. I knew which Rebecca Hatfield this was. The fiancé, the asylum . . . it all made sense. I remembered what my Miss Hatfield – the sixth Miss Hatfield – had told me. The fourth Miss Hatfield was committed to an asylum because she told her fiancé everything and asked him to accept her for what she'd become, if he could still find it within himself to love her. Needless to say, he thought she carried bad blood and helped them lock her away. It wasn't clear exactly how she died, but my Miss Hatfield told me the fourth had died in the asylum. She said it was probably the torture they put her through which ultimately did her in.

I shivered.

That's why there was no former Miss Hatfield here. When a Miss Hatfield dies, she gets erased from time completely. This Miss Hatfield was locked away and tortured to death. Or maybe the killer had something to do with this, too?

I had the letter now. I needed to go back.

Taking care not to make any noise, I walked quickly along the hall into the room I had come from.

The clock was still where I had placed it on the floor behind the screen. Checking once more that the letter was in my pocket, I turned the hands of the clock.

When I looked up, all I saw was sky. There was no ceiling. To either side of me was dirt and mud. I spotted the ladder to my left and started climbing before anyone official could stop me.

'Rebecca!' Henley ran over and helped me under the yellow tape. 'Is everything all right? Are *you* all right?'

'Yes. I'm fine.' I quickly patted my pocket to make sure the letter was still there. 'I got it.' I felt ridiculous wearing an ancient dress while Henley was in a shirt. 'How long has it been?'

'Let's start walking back.' Henley looked around as his arm encircled me. 'For me? Less than ten minutes. What happened?'

I was intending to tell him about Mr Percy and how I had slipped into a former Miss Hatfield's life, but that wasn't what I said.

'What would make you stop loving me?'

'Where did that come from?' Henley looked at me closely. 'Did something happen?'

I shook my head. 'Answer the question.'

'I don't know . . .' he said slowly. 'I don't think anything you could do would make me unlove you. I don't know if you can really even "unlove" someone . . . You sure something didn't happen?'

His arm felt warm around my shoulders like a cloak. I didn't want to worry him. I decided to drop the subject and there was silence between us all the way back to the hostel.

'I don't like this,' Henley said, pacing the room.

It was the day after I had last seen him in his time.

'I think that's all you ever say nowadays,' I said.

Henley continued to walk back and forth. 'Well, I don't like feeling helpless.'

'And pacing is all you ever do.'

Henley stopped and faced me. 'What else is there to do other than sit and worry that we'll be killed today?'

'We can do some research on that auction house you found.'

'Research? How?'

'The Internet, silly. It's an amazing contraption. Besides, we need to translate the letter I brought back. The Internet can also translate.' During my time with Miss Hatfield in the twenty-first century, I had grown quite fond of computers and the wealth of information available on the Internet. 'We just need to find a computer. We can ask Aaron at the front desk,' I suggested.

Henley nodded slowly, sitting down. He looked resigned.

'Now, let's get out of yesterday's clothes,' I said. It was like leading a child by the hand.

Henley remained seated. 'You should change, but these were the only clothes I bought.'

'Okay.' I pulled out the now rumpled black dress from the backpack.

As I began to change, I made a mental note to also ask Aaron to see the lost-and-found box, if they had one. People were bound to leave articles of clothing behind at a hostel like this, and maybe something would be Henley's size.

'Ready,' I said.

Henley glanced at me. The way he sat hunched over, the grey cast to his face, the troubled look in his eyes – he must be exhausted.

I held out my hand but he stood without taking it. He grabbed the backpack and I made sure I had the key to the room tucked away in the one flimsy pocket of my dress. When I opened the door, I found two scones on a paper plate set right outside for us.

Picking up the plate, I handed a scone to Henley. 'At least breakfast is free,' I said, taking a bite out of mine.

'Blueberry,' Henley said with his mouth full. 'My favourite.'

'I never knew that.'

'There are still things for you to learn about me,' he said with a wink as we rounded the corner. At the end of the hallway he opened the white door for me.

'Good morning,' Aaron called from behind his desk as we walked into the tiny lobby. 'I trust you slept well?'

'We did,' I was quick to say. I glanced at Henley's haggard face and wondered if I looked the same. I'd not had time to take a peek at myself in the bathroom mirror before we left. 'Some jet lag, though.'

'I can imagine. Where are you both from?'

'New York,' I said.

'The city?'

'Right in the middle of things.'

'I've always wanted to visit, but my partner's actually more one for the countryside. Me, I've always been a city person.'

I tried to look interested.

'Anyway, can I help you with something? Oh, let me give you two a map! We try to give all our guests these complimentary maps so you don't pay more than you have to in a tourist trap.' Aaron dug behind his desk.

A man in green horn-rimmed glasses entered the lobby through the white door and passed us on his way towards the main exit.

Aaron glanced up from behind the desk just enough to see who it was and call out, 'Have a nice day, Eddie!'

Eddie waved as he exited the hostel.

I thought back to the scene I had woken up to with the beads ominously wrapped around Henley's hands. 'Do you get many guests this time of year?' I asked.

'The weather's finally nice, so yes, but it's not quite full-swing tourist season. The tourist rush has barely started. And even when we're busy, though, this hostel's small enough that I still remember everyone's names. That and I'm good at remembering names and faces.'

Henley perked up. 'So you remember everyone who comes in here?'

'Proud to say I don't forget a single one.'

I tried to think of a casual, nonchalant way of asking if anyone had come in last night, but Henley beat me to it.

'Did someone you didn't recognise come in last night?' he asked.

Well, that was blunt. Even for him.

'Last night, eh? Only Alanna and Peter, a bit after you two. I was surprised no one was out drinking last night. When I went to the pub, it was pretty empty . . . Why? Were you expecting anyone?'

'We just found these delicious scones outside our door and were wondering who put them there,' I said. 'I noticed none of the other rooms had scones waiting for them.'

That was reasonably smooth. I hoped.

Aaron smiled. 'That's because Alanna and Peter took them to you. And I'm glad you enjoyed them – I bake them fresh every day and put them at the front desk for people to take on their way out. They assumed the scones would all be gone by the time you two got to the lobby, so they decided to leave them there for you. Wasn't that nice of them?'

Henley and I agreed it was.

79

'Oh, almost forgot,' Aaron said, passing us a folded sheet of paper. 'Here's the map. The hostel is clearly marked on it.'

'That will be most helpful,' Henley said. He took it and put it in the backpack without even looking at it.

'Is there a computer here for guests to use?' I asked.

'I'm afraid not, but the local library has some.'

I shot a look at Henley.

'That would be perfect,' he said.

'The library's marked on the map – it's only a short walk from here. Anything else I can help you with?' Aaron asked.

'Just one thing – do you have a lost-and-found box or something like that?' I asked, remembering Henley's lack of clothes.

'Lost something already?' Aaron chortled. 'Lucky for you, we do. It's right down the hall from your room – just keep going past your door and you'll see it. Everyone seems to leave something behind. It's positively overflowing!'

I thanked him, then grabbed Henley by the arm and walked him back to the room.

'You wait here,' I said. 'I won't be a minute.'

He didn't even look surprised as he unlocked the door and let himself in.

Hearing the door shut behind me, I kept walking down the hall as Aaron had instructed. I passed the Daffodil room, the Poppy room, the Foxglove room and a few others with flowers I could not place. Towards the end of the corridor I found a bright blue wooden crate with random items spilling out of it. At first glance, I saw everything from a baseball mitt to a few paperback books.

The first article of clothing I pulled out was a toddler's dress with a pink stain running down the front of it. Strawberry jam? Next was a woman's blouse that was much too big for me. I continued rummaging until I found a black men's T-shirt. Sure, it was wrinkled from being stored under the mountain of objects, but it was reasonably clean and looked to be about Henley's size. I found another shirt that said 'Jefferson Airplane' on it, which I guessed was a movie title or a band. It would have to do. For me, I found a turquoise polka-dotted shirt that didn't look like it was from this era.

With the three shirts slung over my arm, I headed back to the room and fumbled with my key. I had barely got the key in the lock before Henley opened the door.

'Shirts?' I grinned up at him.

'From the lost-and-found box? Won't someone come looking for them?'

I slipped past him. 'I don't think so – these look like they've been there a while.' I tossed him the two shirts I had picked out for him.

'They look clean enough,' he said, his tone a bit dubious, 'although I'm not keen on the concept of wearing things other people have worn—'

'Oh, like we have a choice,' I said. It was so like Henley to comment on something as trivial as this when there was so much more to think about. 'You can wash them in the bathroom sink if you want.'

'I think I'll do that,' he said. He grabbed my shirt, too, before taking them to the bathroom. He left the door open so he could still hear me. I sat on the bed, and from there I could see Henley's reflection in the mirror hanging on the inside of the bathroom door.

'Jefferson Airplane?' Henley asked as he started scrubbing with the tiny bar of complimentary soap.

'Your guess is as good as mine,' I said.

'Sometimes I feel as though I've missed out on quite a lot between the early twentieth century and whatever year we're now in.'

'2016,' I reminded him. 'And you have.'

'Thanks for being mindful of my feelings.'

'Careful, your sarcasm is dripping everywhere.'

Henley laughed. 'So that's how you treat a man who's currently washing one of *your* shirts? You know, where I come from, this is a woman's job.'

'Welcome to the twenty-first century. And thank God we're not "where you come from",' I said.

I expected a laugh from Henley but his voice grew serious instead.

'It wasn't that bad, was it? My time, I mean; 1904 wasn't that bad.'

I watched him put down the shirt he was washing and the soap. He stared at himself in the mirror above the sink, but I couldn't tell what he saw.

'It was hard,' I admitted. 'There was a lot of fitting in to do. Mannerisms, dress, speech – all the things you took for granted. But that's always the same in any time.'

'I suppose you're constantly adapting.'

'We have to.'

In that moment, I didn't know whether that 'we' encompassed Miss Hatfield and me, Henley and me, or all three of us.

He wordlessly resumed washing and only came out once he had draped the shirts over the shower curtain rail to dry.

'Ready to go to the library?' I asked, heading for the door. I already had the backpack slung over my shoulder, the weight of the clock and the jewellery resting against the small of my back.

'Just let me get my key from the bedside table . . .'

We were careful to lock our door, although I didn't know why we were bothering. A murderer had already walked in, after all. We waved goodbye to Aaron at the front desk and made it a block before having to pull out the map.

'We're going in completely the wrong direction,' Henley said. He sounded convinced, but he kept turning the map this way and that.

'Do you even know how to read that thing?'

'Of course I do.' He jabbed a finger at the paper. 'We're here . . . And it says the library is . . . Here.'

Because Henley held the map at his height, I had to stand on my toes to peek over the map. 'That's not the library.'

'No, but—'

'See, look – it says museum.'

'Fine. Then why don't you—'

'The library's here.' I pointed across the page. 'It's clearly labelled and we're walking in the right direction.' I took the map from Henley and folded it up before returning it to the front pocket of the backpack.

Henley huffed, but I knew he was just being playful.

'Oh, what would you do without me?' I poked his side.

We walked for about ten minutes just like that – quipping at each other instead of talking about the more difficult things. Clearly we both wanted to forget about what was at stake, even though it was constantly stuck in the back of our minds.

A flight of white steps led up to the entrance of the library. It didn't look like a big building, but it felt larger on the inside than it appeared on the outside. Whitewashed walls gave way to stacks and shelves of books and the circulation desk was right in front of us as we walked in. A curly-haired woman behind the desk eyed us sharply as I approached her.

'Excuse me. Would it be possible for us to use the computers here?'

She looked at us quizzically.

'Yeah . . .' was all she said.

I didn't get it. Was I not supposed to ask? Did I ask a question with a very obvious answer?

I saw the computers to our left. Perfect.

'Come on,' I said to Henley.

I took a seat at the first computer, with Henley next to me. There was a sign stuck to the monitor and we read it carefully.

'I don't understand.' Henley was the first to speak. 'We're supposed to pay for the use of this computer by the minute? Isn't this a library? Aren't things supposed to be free in a library?' He squinted at the sign again. 'It says a penny a minute.'

I moved the mouse to wake the computer. A text box came up on the screen, prompting us for a credit card number.

'Let me go and talk to the woman at the desk.' Henley made to stand but I stopped him.

'What are you going to say?'

'Just that we only brought cash with us.'

I let him go. Henley unzipped the backpack and found a pound coin we'd been given as change by the grocery store. I watched him walk to the desk and begin talking to the curly-haired woman. She didn't look happy. Her lips were downturned, and I didn't think they were naturally that way. Her chin bobbed as she said something to Henley. I watched him pause and tilt his head before replying. He was probably choosing his words carefully. The woman shook her head, but took his pound and counted out some change.

I looked away as they came walking towards me and pretended I was picking at a loose thread at the hem of my dress. I watched out of the corner of my eye as she executed a few speedy keystrokes and typed some sort of code into another text box that had popped up. She clicked on something else and soon all of the boxes disappeared, leaving us with an unlocked computer.

'Thank you,' I mumbled as she stalked back to the desk.

'I bought us thirty minutes,' Henley said. 'Is that enough?'

'More than enough,' I said.

I realised this was the first time Henley had used a computer – well, *physically* used one, anyway. I say that because on one occasion he manipulated my laptop when he was still without a body to send me a message. That was the first time I learned he was still out there.

I clicked the first icon and the web browser opened a search engine.

'This is the Internet?' Henley's eyes were fixed intently on the screen.

I would have laughed at the look of reverence on his face then, but knew I had worn the same expression when I was first introduced to computers. It didn't take Miss Hatfield long to teach me the basics of Internet searches and some beginner computer terminology. I was an eager learner. After that, picking up more computer terms and uses were just a function of using the computer often and trying different things.

'Let's start with a search for an online translator,' I said, clicking through various options. I pulled out the letter. 'The first words are *Querida Emilia.*' I typed them in and *Dear Emily* popped up on the screen.

'So you just type it in and the computer spits it out in English?' Henley said.

'Basically.' I continued typing in the rest of the letter. 'There.'

We both craned our necks towards the computer screen to read the translation.

'That's it?' Henley asked.

The translation hadn't revealed much. It looked like Juana was just writing to a friend. She asked how her other friends and extended family were doing and mentioned that she missed playing her harpsichord and recorder. The only thing that felt significant was a couple of sentences at the end: *I feel as if I should be happier, and yet I'm not. Forgive me for not being able to bear to show my face to you. I fear I have become something I am not proud of.*

'That's it,' I said. 'That's what we've been looking for.'

'"I feel as if I should be happier . . . Forgive me." That doesn't say much at all,' Henley said.

'She says she can't bear to show her face to her friend – it's because she's turned immortal and she knows it. What else could it be? And she even says that she fears she has become something she's not proud of!'

'That means nothing.' Henley sighed. 'She could be talking about anything. That she's stolen something and become a common thief. That she's committed adultery with a married man. That she thinks she's a bad daughter to her parents—'

'No,' I said insistently, cutting him off. 'It *has* to be immortality. It fits so well and there isn't anyone else who could potentially be immortal. And if she hates it as much as it seems in this letter, it's no wonder she's killed all the Miss Hatfields.'

'All the Miss Hatfields save one,' Henley corrected.

I shrugged off my mistake. 'Now let's find out about the auction house,' I said, quickly pulling up another window on the screen. Glancing over at Henley, who was still slack-jawed at how the computer worked, I asked him if he wanted to type.

'Can I?' His grin stretched across his entire face.

'Of course.' I turned the keyboard towards him. 'Do you remember the name of the place that said they specialise in jewellery among other things?'

'Carter House.'

'Why don't you type "Carter House Auctioneer", just to be safe?'

Watching him was agony. Henley painstakingly scanned the entire keyboard before finding the letter he needed. Then he slowly pressed that one key, as if worried he would break the keyboard. The result so far was 'CaaarteerHoo'.

'Do you mind if I finish?' I would have left him to it had we not been in such a hurry. In his time I had been the clueless one fumbling through social etiquette and tripping over my own curtsies. Now it was Henley's turn to be a fast learner.

Henley pushed the keyboard over to me. He looked relieved.

'Here's the space bar.' I showed him while finishing the word. Then I pressed 'enter' and we watched the page of results scroll up.

'Try the first one.' Henley prodded the screen with his finger.

'Henley,' I said, 'one of the first rules of using computers is that you never touch the screen. Especially not that hard.' Unless it was a touchscreen, but I didn't mention that. It would only have confused him.

I looked over my shoulder at the circulation desks and sure enough, the curly-haired woman was watching us with her birdlike eyes.

I clicked on the first link, which took us to what looked like Carter House's official website. *Purveyors of fine art and museum-quality antiques. Own a piece of history today!*

flashed across the screen. There was a special tab for jewellery, so I clicked it. *We accept verified vintage jewellery from all eras. Call for more information.*

'I wonder what "verified" entails?' Henley said.

'They'll probably have a specialist look at it or something,' I said. 'Would you mind asking the woman at the desk for a piece of paper and a pen so we can take down the number?'

Henley did as I asked and returned with only a pen. 'She wouldn't give me paper. Said she didn't have any,' he muttered as he jotted the number and address down on the back of his hand.

'Just remember not to wash your hands before we call.'

'What do you take me for?' Henley teased.

I didn't answer that, instead glancing up at the clock on the other side of the room. 'We still have a few minutes left on the computer.' I pulled up the search engine and tried to think of something useful to look for. I typed 'Rebecca Hatfield'. Holding my breath, I hit enter.

The search results popped up. Pages of them. There were pages of links to people with the entire name 'Rebecca Hatfield.' After that, there were links to online directories of people with the first name 'Rebecca' or the last name 'Hatfield.' I didn't realise there would be so many. As I scanned the later pages, the results became ever more random and less relevant.

'I don't know if you're trying to look up yourself or my mother,' Henley said.

I didn't know, either. I only wanted to find some record of me – of her. Some record to show that we existed then and that I still existed now.

'Why don't you try me?' Henley said.

I typed out his name and as the page started filling up with a list of results, I drew a long breath.

'Henley – these are all you,' I said.

Henley A. Beauford.

The last time I had read those words was on his grave.

'Look, there's even a photo of you!' I clicked it and Henley's face filled the screen.

He looked young, almost as young as I remembered him from 1904 . . . Maybe a few added wrinkles and worry lines . . . Not that you could tell much from the black and white photo. He was wearing a tuxedo with a white bow tie. I remembered the white bow tie from when he first wore it to dinner in 1904. Tuxes were just coming into fashion then and Mr Beauford, Henley's father, had hated the way it looked. He thought it was much too casual. Mr Beauford would have been shocked if he could see what his son was wearing today, and the notion made me laugh.

'What?' Henley said. 'You're not laughing at how I look, are you? You need to remember that the flashes they used then were incredibly bright and *that* is the only reason I'm squinting—'

'You look fine,' I said. Of course, he bore no resemblance to his past self now, in Richard's body.

Henley clicked to see the next photo. In this one, Henley was on the left and an equally familiar face peered at me from the right-hand side of the frame. Eliza.

Eliza had visited Henley and his family along with her snobby sister when I was also at their country home – well, it was more of an estate than a little home. Eliza was sweet and gentle, unlike her older sister Christine who, though a beauty, believed everything revolved around her. There was also the fact that Christine had designs to marry Henley for his father's money and influence – that hadn't made her too popular with me.

89

Eliza had been left blind and frail by a fever when she was younger, but the fact that she had survived at all was probably a big reason for her piety and faith in God. She had maintained all the faith and conviction I didn't have. Henley had gone on to marry Eliza, and although Eliza had only survived a few years after she and Henley wed, I was happy that two of the people I loved the most had been able to enjoy a life together, however brief.

I wondered about many things Henley had done after I left his time. It was easy to forget that he had lived a full life before returning to me; he had married, buried a wife, built a business . . . But most striking of all, he had grown old and died. Then again, it wasn't a permanent death since Henley was Miss Hatfield's son and therefore half-immortal. His corporeal death was only the end of his life in his own time period and the beginning of his existence as a roaming ghost without a body.

'You're quiet. What are you thinking about?' Henley's warm eyes sought mine.

'All the lives you've led,' I said.

His face was thoughtful and mirrored my own. He didn't ask me anything further.

As I continued to click through the images, we saw photos of Mr Beauford's car (he was so proud of owning one of the first 'automobiles' in the city), a few objects that used to belong in the city house and the blueprint of the country estate. They all felt so familiar to me yet so far away, and I knew Henley was probably feeling this even more than I was.

I instinctively gripped his hand and he gave me a little squeeze back. I had missed that feeling of reassurance when Henley was without a body.

'I wonder where they're getting all these photographs from?' Henley said.

'The better question is who are "they"? Who would have access to them?

A few clicks took me to the website's homepage: *Beauford Family Estate*, it said.

'You have a family estate?'

'Of course I do,' was Henley's response. 'It's probably run by some descendant of mine.'

My eyes went wide. 'B-but you didn't have any children . . . And you don't have any siblings . . . Is there anything you haven't told me or forgot to mention?'

'Not that I know of. I meant distant relations – like the great-grandchildren of my cousins or something along those lines,' he said.

'Thank God.' I let out the breath I didn't know I'd been holding.

Henley raised his eyebrows. 'Were you thinking I was going to admit to fathering four children you didn't know about?'

It sounded absurd, but I guess I hadn't known what to expect. 'It's just that—'

'You know I've told you everything.'

Except about your life after I left, I thought to myself.

'I haven't kept anything from you,' he went on. 'Why should I?'

I bit my tongue. We only had a minute left on the computer and I wanted to find out more about who was running this site. I scrolled down to the bottom of the page to a small 'About' section.

Muffy Beauford. Great-granddaughter of Philip Beauford—

That was all I could read before the computer cut off. We were out of time.

'Damn it,' I said.

Henley looked appalled. 'I haven't heard you swear like that before. A woman like you—'

'I'm just disappointed,' I said. 'Don't you want to find out more about this Muffy Beauford? We could pay for some extra time.'

'It's not worth it.'

I was surprised Henley thought that. 'What do you mean? You're related to her in some way – aren't you curious? All I saw was that she's the great-granddaughter of a Philip Beauford.'

'Philip was my father's younger brother. They didn't get along, so I don't remember him. Supposedly I met him once but I must have been young – I don't recall. Reading about this Muffy won't let me know her. And if you're going to ask me if I ever want to meet Muffy or anyone else, the answer is no. I don't know them. They're not family.'

I had to let it go. It wasn't as if it would be easy to contact them, either. They'd probably laugh if we said Henley was their long-lost great-uncle. Or worse – call the police.

'However,' he added, 'just knowing that a Beauford Family Estate exists is helpful in itself. It's a perfect back-story – we can tell the auction house that the jewellery was passed down from them.'

'Now that *is* a good idea – let's get back to the hostel so we can call the auction house before it closes today.' I still couldn't understand why he wasn't more interested in his family, but it was time to move on.

We hardly had time or breath for conversation – not that we had much to say to each other – on the brisk walk to get back to call Carter House before it closed, so I was surprised when Henley suddenly stopped short across the street from the hostel.

'What are you doing?' I asked. 'It's right there. We need to call before—'

'That man's out front.'

For a moment, I had no idea what he was talking about until I saw him myself. The man from the pub was pacing in front of the hostel. I recognised him by his oversized sweat-shirt and his sweaty hair – he obviously hadn't changed since last night. I walked towards him before Henley could stop me.

'There you are,' the man said when he saw me. 'Took you long enough.'

Standing in front of him now, I noticed a brown stain near the front neckline of his sweatshirt. He'd probably missed his mouth when eating something and hadn't both-ered to clean up.

'Why were you waiting for us?' I braced myself as he approached me. I didn't want to know what his breath smelled like.

'We have business to take care of, don't we?' The man ignored Henley, who had come to stand protectively behind me.

'We want—'

'Not here.' The man turned and walked around the corner of the hostel.

It took me a second to work out I was meant to follow. Trailing him, I realised this was the small street I could see from the window in our room, between the hostel and the apartment building next door. Now I was in it, however, it looked more like an alleyway than a street.

It was the perfect location: devoid of people and no security cameras as far as I could see. The man had flattened himself against the wall of the hostel and was standing precisely where he could not be seen from the hostel or the apartments. He'd clearly done this sort of thing before.

'Next time you wait ten more seconds before following me, yeah?'

I nodded quickly.

'So what do you want?'

I had to think on my feet. We ultimately needed passports to leave the country, but we surely didn't have the funds to pay for them right then and we'd probably have to hand over some kind of deposit in advance. For the time being, we needed something to show the auction house. Henley's cover story for how we came to own the Tudor jewellery meant that the auction house would probably ask him for ID rather than me, but I needed one, too, for showing to bar staff in pubs and so on.

'We need two IDs. One for me and one for him.' I pointed at a fidgeting Henley. A deep furrow lined his forehead.

The man rubbed his short beard but made no reply.

'Perhaps a British driving licence?' I offered.

'Of course not. That won't do. Your accents tell me that you're obviously not from around here, so a British licence would raise questions. Do you take me for an idiot?'

'Um . . . no?'

The man crossed his arms. 'So where are you from?'

'The States,' Henley said.

'I know *that*,' the man snapped. 'I meant what state.'

'New York,' I said.

'Him, too?' He jabbed his thumb in Henley's general direction.

'Yes.'

'Then you want New York driver's licences,' the man said.

'And you can do New York driver's licences?' I asked.

'Of course we can. Don't insult me. You have the address and names you want on them?' The man pulled a scrap of paper and a pen out of the pocket of his sweatshirt.

I took them and tried to write Henley's name, but the capless ballpoint pen didn't work.

'Do you have another pen?' I asked.

'Do I look like I have another pen?'

I took that to mean 'no' and kept scribbling on the corner of the paper. At last some ink came out and I carefully wrote down Henley's full name, my name and Miss Hatfield's address. The man took the pen and paper back from me when I was done.

'Two names. Two cards. Same address,' I said.

'How much will that cost?' Henley asked.

'I can do them for eighty pounds.'

'Eighty pounds?' I said, raising my eyebrows.

'Well, sweetie, you're not exactly ordering in bulk.'

'We're ordering more than one,' I said, giving him a withering look.

'Fine. Sixty.'

'That better get us quick delivery too,' I fired back.

'Who's calling the shots?' he grumbled. 'Tomorrow quick enough for you?'

'As long as it's morning.'

'I'll get it to you early,' he said.

'And how do we know they'll be good enough to pass muster?' Henley said.

'Oh, they'll be good. But if you're so worried, why don't you pay half now and the other half when you see them?' The man seemed so self-assured.

Henley looked at me. That sounded reasonable.

'Give him the money,' I said.

Henley dug into the backpack and pulled out the money. Each bill was neatly folded down the middle.

The man was quick to pocket the cash and produced his phone. Even a shady man like him had a glossy iPhone.

'I need to take pictures of both of you.' The man pointed to the white-painted brick wall behind us. 'Stand there.'

The photo was taken as soon as Henley got in front of the wall.

Henley opened his mouth. 'But I—'

'Wasn't ready?' The man sniggered. 'That's the first thing about fakes. The photos aren't supposed to be good. If you look too good, it's a tell-tale sign the ID's a fake.' He jabbed a finger at me. 'You next.' I complied and he quickly took my photo.

'When will they be ready?' Henley asked.

'Calm down, boy. It'll take as long as it takes. I promise quality, not speed.'

Henley's face flushed. 'We need them fast. We're paying—'

The man looked at me with his hard eyes. 'I don't like this boy. You should lose him as soon as you can.'

I ignored that and tried to ask the question in a way the man would understand. 'We want to use the IDs as soon as possible.'

The man mopped his sweaty forehead with the sleeve of his sweatshirt. 'You have something in mind?'

'We'll be putting them to the test as soon as we get them,' I said.

'Oh, they'll pass. You'll see.'

'I sure hope they do.' I surprised myself with how cold I sounded.

The man grinned. 'I like you better than your boy there. Tell you what – I'll rush my guy for expedited service and

I'll only charge fifty per cent more. Because I'm that kinda businessman.'

I nodded to Henley and he gave the man another fifteen pounds.

'The IDs will pass whatever test you throw at them,' the man said as he walked away from us.

For a second, neither Henley nor I moved. When the man was long out of sight, Henley finally turned towards me.

'So that was that?' Henley said. 'The man will just find us when he's done making the fake licences?'

'He'll probably be pacing in front of the hostel again,' I said.

We went inside and Henley made to go back to our room, but I stopped him.

'Aren't you forgetting something?' I pointed to the phone number scrawled on the back of his left hand. 'Weren't we going to call the auction house?'

'Oh, right. Yes.' It was obvious he was a little out of sorts after the encounter we'd just had.

'Given we don't know when exactly we'll have the IDs, hopefully we won't need them for our first meeting . . .' I felt as if I was talking to myself more than Henley.

I rang the bell at the front desk and waited a few minutes. I didn't want to come across as too impatient, but when no one arrived, I rang it again.

I heard a distant, 'Yes!' through the walls. A moment later, footsteps.

'So sorry,' Aaron said as he bustled through the door. He tried to wipe what looked like flour from his shirt but only managed to smear the white powder even more. 'I was just baking. Can't leave the oven unattended for long! What can I do for you?'

'Sorry for taking you from your baking,' I said.

'Oh no, I'm here to answer your questions.'

'In that case, is there a phone we could use?'

Aaron reached behind the desk and pulled out a phone. It was a landline and connected to the wall, so he made sure to move the cord around the computer monitor. 'There you go.'

Thanking him, I reached for the phone and stopped.

'Why don't you make the call?' I said to Henley.

Aaron was still standing awkwardly behind the desk, watching us. He didn't look like he was going to move any time soon. It was as if he had forgotten that he had something in the oven.

Henley picked up the receiver and began dialling, glancing at the back of his hand every few seconds as he read the number. He put the phone to his ear and I heard it ring.

'Carter House Auction Specialists.' It was a young female voice at the other end of the line. 'Hilary speaking.'

'Um, yes, Hilary. I'm Henley Beauford and I was hoping to come in to talk to you about a piece of jewellery I would like to sell.'

'Jewellery. I can certainly put you in touch with one of our specialists for a consultation and evaluation.' Hilary spoke crisply, enunciating all her letters so that even I could hear every consonant she uttered. 'Might I ask the decade this piece is from?'

'Uh, well it's actually a set – a woman's necklace and earrings – and it's very old. Um, early sixteenth century?'

Hilary didn't miss a beat. 'Could you briefly describe it for us? I'd like to take a few notes to give to our specialist before the meeting.'

'Sure . . . it's gold. With rubies.'

'Or garnets,' I whispered.

'Or garnets,' Henley repeated. 'Red stones, anyway. Um, and the earrings match.'

'They're in very good condition,' I prompted Henley.

'They're in very good condition. *Very* well preserved,' Henley said.

I glanced at Aaron and wondered how much he could hear of the woman on the other end. He was listening in, for sure – this probably wasn't the type of phone conversation he was used to at the hostel.

'Yes.' Hilary sounded like she was taking notes furiously while she was talking. 'And finally, when would be most convenient for you to come into our offices so we can assess the jewellery and discuss our sales process with you?'

'We . . . my . . . girlfriend and I are travelling from the States and will be staying briefly in the UK, so as soon as possible would be ideal.'

'We can see you first thing tomorrow morning at ten, if that would be convenient for you?'

'Yes, that would be fine. Thank you.'

'We look forward to meeting you, Mr Beauford.'

Henley and I waited for the click of the phone on the other end. When we heard it, it was accompanied by a sigh of relief, but I didn't know if the sigh had come from me or Henley. Henley put down the receiver and we both thanked Aaron once again.

'We're trying to take care of a few things while we're in town,' I tried to explain.

Aaron asked no questions. He only nodded and disappeared.

I asked for some paper and a pen and wrote down the number from Henley's hand before we headed back to our room.

'So – "girlfriend", huh?' I said.

Henley chuckled. 'What else was I supposed to call you? I heard Peter use the term when he described you. That was appropriate, right?'

'Yes,' I said. It wasn't perfect, but there wasn't really a word for what I was to Henley and what he was to me. I guessed it was close enough.

Chapter 6

I knew it was morning before I opened my eyes. Light streamed into our room and I felt its warmth through my eyelids.

I kept them closed and turned over onto my side. I could feel Henley next to me – his palpable warmth, the cadence of his breath and the way his body fitted around mine. In that moment, everything else was secondary. Henley was here next to me and that was all that mattered. I was the happiest I had been in a long time.

I sighed and turned onto my back again. It was so comfortable in bed, but I knew I should start to get up. I unglued my eyelids and stared straight up at the ceiling, which was plain and set lower than I had noticed before. My eyes followed every bump and bubble of the paint. Uninterested, I turned to Henley again. This time, with my eyes open, it was a different experience.

With my eyes closed, Henley was Henley alone; he was the Henley I loved and the Henley who existed in my memories. With my eyes open, Henley was Henley *and* Richard. Henley had come back to me and I still loved him, yet he was so different – *this* was so different. Every morning when I woke up, would it be like this? Feeling Henley, hearing Henley and expecting to see Henley, only to find Richard by my side?

Frowning, I turned away.

'Good morning.' I heard Henley groan as he stretched beside me. 'Sleep well?'

I rolled towards him, almost anticipating Henley's clear blue eyes, but of course I was met with Richard's caramel.

'Yes, I did,' I said.

'I had a dream I was back home,' he said.

Home. It was amazing he still considered his former residence that way. Eventually, Henley would probably stop thinking of the house in his original time period as his 'home', but not yet, apparently.

'What happened?'

'Not much.' He tucked his hands behind his head. 'I was walking the grounds of the country house. Everything was there – the tree we sat by, the stables you loved, the original main house before it burned down . . .'

We lay in silence for a while.

'We have a long morning ahead of us, don't we?' Henley finally said.

'Yes . . .' I glanced at the clock on the bedside table. 'We have enough time, but we should get dressed and eat a quick breakfast before we leave.'

Henley sat up without warning. 'What do we wear?'

I had slept in one of the shirts I had got Henley from the lost-and-found and Henley had slept in his pants. We couldn't really go as we were.

I shrugged. 'The nicest we can manage. That button-down shirt of yours will look good with the jeans, and I'll wear a dress.'

'And shoes?' Henley ran his fingers through his hair. 'What about shoes?'

I shrugged again. It was just like Henley to panic about shoes.

We both got up and changed into our respective outfits. I was spreading peanut butter on a slice of bread when Henley came back into the room. I was hungry and so absorbed in preparing breakfast that I hadn't noticed him leaving in the first place. I turned to him with the bread in my hands, about to ask him where he had been until I saw that he was clutching a pair of shoes in each hand and had a shirt draped over his arm.

'The lost-and-found crate out there is a gold mine.' Henley grinned. 'It's as if we have our own personal shop right outside.' He tossed the shirt onto the bed. 'Even got something to wrap the jewellery in.'

I laughed and offered him the bread I was holding. 'I'll trade you a scrumptious breakfast of peanut butter and bread for those shoes.' I pointed at the women's leather shoes in Henley's right hand.

'You drive a hard bargain,' Henley said, pretending to think about it. 'But for *that* piece of bread . . . I think I'll have to accept.'

He set the shoes in front of me and I stepped into them. Henley took the bread from me and bit into it while looking me up and down.

'A little big . . . but surprisingly not bad,' he said through his full mouth. 'Try walking around in them. Hopefully you won't step completely out of them.'

I walked to the other side of the room and back. He was right – not bad at all, especially for something exca-vated from the lost-and-found. I picked up another piece of bread for myself and spread peanut butter on it.

'That crate has everything,' he said. 'I swear there are more things in the lost-and-found than there was food in that grocery store. The world could end tomorrow and we'd find survival supplies in that crate.'

I thought it funny that the grocery store had made a big impression on Henley.

'Try yours on.' I took a bite out of my bread.

'Already did,' he said, but he put on the shoes anyway. 'Aren't they nice?'

Henley's shoes actually looked like they were his.

'Fortunately my jeans are long enough that you can't see the big scuff mark on the instep.'

'They look perfect for the meeting.'

'Speaking of which . . .' Henley glanced at the clock on the bedside table. 'We should get going.'

I devoured the rest of my bread while Henley wrapped the jewellery in one of the shirts we had taken from the lost-and-found bin and put it in the backpack along with the clock.

'Anything else we need?' Henley asked.

'IDs,' I said, 'but it looks like we won't have them.' I wished we could have ordered them from the man sooner.

'They probably won't need something like that at a first meeting,' Henley said. But we both knew that was a complete guess. Neither of us had a clue about the auction house's policies.

We walked down the hall to the mini-lobby.

I spotted a map behind the counter and pulled it towards me. I scanned the page for the street Carter House was on.

'Here we go.'

I saw Henley take one of the hostel's business card from in front of the computer. That was a smart idea, in case we ever got lost or had to call the hostel.

'We need to take a left up there,' I said as we stepped out of the building.

Before Henley could answer, we both caught sight of the ID man. He was leaning on the wall of a building across the street, watching us.

Catching our eyes, he simply nodded, before slinking around the corner as he had last night. We remembered to wait longer than before and then followed him down the alley.

'Finally!' he said. 'You two take so long. Did you sleep in or what?'

I noticed the man was wearing different clothing at last before Henley instinctively stepped in front of me.

'Well, you don't need no more beauty rest—' The man glanced at Henley. 'Maybe *you* do, though – you look more horrible than your picture.'

'So you have them, then?' I asked. 'The fake IDs?'

He grinned and his yellowed teeth shone. 'Here you go, princess.' The man held up the licences, and from where I stood, they looked a lot like the IDs Miss Hatfield had made for both of us in New York.

Henley tried to reach for them, but the man snatched them away.

'Uh-uh. You see the cards. I see the money.'

Henley dug into the backpack and came up with the extra forty-five pounds. We watched the man count it out before stashing it in his pocket, after which he wordlessly handed us the IDs.

Henley leaned over me as we both peered at his card. He was pale and dissatisfied in the photo, but it looked as if it had been taken in bad lighting in the Department of Motor Vehicles. Henley's name was spelled correctly. The address was also correct. There was even a fake signature and an estimated height. The card read 'New York State Driver License' and looked official enough, as did mine.

'So?' The man stared expectantly at us. 'Tell me that's not the best damn job you've ever seen. It's perfect.'

I was about to tell him that I wouldn't know since I had nothing to compare it to, but decided against and just nodded.

'Thank you,' I said.

'For a sweetie like you? Any day,' he said. 'The name's Carl, by the way.' He squinted hard at Henley. 'You're lucky you have this one,' he told him.

'I'm quite aware of that,' Henley said.

'Well, Carl, we'd best get going,' I said. We weren't late for our meeting yet, but I didn't want to be. I suddenly thought about the passports we'd require soon. 'How can we contact you if we want something else?'

'You, sweetie, can have my number.'

Carl pulled a pen out from his trouser pocket and walked towards me. It took everything in my power not to step back. He grabbed my hand and wrote his phone number on the inside of my wrist. The tip of the pen scratched as it dug into my skin.

'Th-thanks,' I managed to get out.

'Call any time you need anything. That's what prepaid phones are for . . . That and making sure you don't leave a trail, of course.' Carl flashed us a lazy grin. 'If that's it for now, I'd best be off, too. You know how it is – places to go, people to see.'

We left the alley first, while Carl waited an extra minute so he wouldn't be seen leaving at the same time as us.

'That was . . . strange,' Henley said once we were safely a block away.

'Would you expect anything else when you're buying an illegal fake ID?'

'You do have a point . . .'

Henley consulted the map to get his bearings before we started power-walking to the auction house address.

Henley pulled open the heavy glass door and, seeing my hesitation, walked in first. I followed the muffled sound his loafers made on the floor, clutching the backpack in my arms.

The lobby was empty and vast. The smooth black stone walls were in complete contrast to the green tiles beneath our feet, which sparkled where we stepped. The only furniture was a black desk at least three times the size of the cramped one back at the hostel. A woman with a perfectly coifed bun eyed us from her seat behind it as we walked in. I suspected we probably looked different – a little younger, less conservatively dressed – from the people she usually saw walking into the building, but hopefully not *that* different.

Henley looked confident – at least from behind – as he strutted up to the woman.

'We're visiting Carter House,' he said.

She gestured to the far side of the lobby. 'The elevator would be that way.'

Henley walked past me and I followed closely at his heels.

The elevator looked imposing, its tall doors highly buffed to a gleam where the sun hit it.

'What company, sir?'

The voice surprised me – I hadn't noticed the man in uniform standing next to the elevator. He had already pushed the button to summon it.

'Carter House, please,' Henley said.

Unlike the phone call he had made yesterday, there were no 'ums' and 'uhs'. This was a different Henley. A confident Henley. He must have been used to this type of lavish business environment. I wondered if this was the Henley everyone saw when he did business in his own time.

The elevator dinged and we walked inside. The elevator man wedged himself between me and the buttons. He pressed for the fourth floor and we went up.

I watched my reflection in the heavily burnished silver doors. The woman I saw didn't look as nervous as I felt, but she looked so out of place. Her dress was riding up and her shoes were large enough that there was a gap between her heel and the back of the shoe. She held her backpack so tightly that her hands were turning white. She wasn't of this world.

The elevator dinged again and I felt it come to a stop.

The uniformed man held the door for us as we stepped out. 'Have a good day. Sir. Madam.'

I tried to smile at him but Henley didn't even acknowledge his existence.

The fourth-floor lobby matched the one downstairs, with the same colour scheme of emerald and black, but it was smaller with a smaller desk. A seating area with a large emerald couch and black velvet armchairs also took up space.

'Hello. How may I help you?' The woman at this front desk had a nicer smile than the last. Behind her, a large sign proudly announced *Carter House Auction Specialists*. At least we were in the right place.

'We have an appointment for ten this morning,' Henley said.

The woman glanced down, presumably at a computer hidden from sight. 'Why, yes. Mr Beauford?' She tucked a flyaway blonde strand behind her ear.

'Yes.'

The woman smiled at me. 'Please have a seat, Mr and Mrs Beauford, and we'll be right with you.'

Henley didn't bother to correct her and went straight to one of the single-seater black velvet armchairs. I sat on the green couch. The backs of my thighs stuck to the leather upholstery. There was a single door between the seating area and the desk. I guessed it led to the rest of the office and that someone would appear through it to call our names.

'Coffee or tea while you wait?' the woman asked from the desk.

Henley waved her away.

'No, thank you,' I said.

I stared hard at the door, willing someone to materialise, but when no one did, I looked at Henley instead.

He was leaning nonchalantly against one arm of his chair, his legs crossed, as if he often visited offices like this. For once, he looked cold and distant. He made no move to talk to me. He wasn't even looking in my direction. Instead, he was staring aimlessly towards one corner of the room. It felt as if he was purposefully distancing himself from me. I didn't know if it was all an act or not.

I noticed a black smudge on the back of his hand where he had written down the number for the auction house. The skin around it was pink, as if Henley had tried to scrub it off. I looked at my own hand with Carl's phone number scrawled along the inside of my wrist in black ink. I should remember to keep my wrist down so as to not draw unnecessary attention to it. I also needed to make sure I didn't accidentally smear it.

Finally, the door I had been watching opened. Another polished woman crisply dressed in a black skirt suit walked out and headed towards us.

Sticking a hand out first to Henley, then to me, the woman introduced herself. 'Tabitha Webley.' Her hand was as cool as her voice. She didn't smile, but I could see as she pronounced her name that her teeth looked sharp. She didn't look like a woman I would want to trust.

'Henley Beauford.'

'Of course,' she said. The woman's polite formality matched the room in appearance and in attitude.

'This is Rebecca Hatfield,' he said. I couldn't help but notice he didn't use any labels for me. No 'friend'. No 'girlfriend'.

'It's a pleasure,' she said. 'Now, if you'll please follow me into one of our conference rooms, our sixteenth-century jewellery specialist will be joining us in just a moment.'

When Tabitha held open the door for us, I saw that the rest of the office was mostly conference rooms, identically furnished with dark wooden tables. As she sashayed through the halls, I peeked into glass-walled rooms that looked like human-sized fishbowls. Each one we passed was empty and dark.

'This way.' Tabitha finally opened the door to one of the rooms.

It looked like an arbitrary choice – there was nothing special about this one compared to the others, but it was set up and ready for us. The lights were already on. There were orchids in the middle of the table and a pitcher of water accompanied by glasses with intricate, lace-like designs cut into them.

'Coffee or tea?' she asked. Her voice didn't have much inflection. It was smooth like ice.

We shook our heads.

Tabitha took the far chair, while Henley sat across from her. I pulled out a chair next to Henley, right by the door. Just as we sat, the door behind me opened and I felt a soft gust of air.

'So sorry to keep you waiting.' A short man in a black suit walked in, smoothing his burgundy tie. 'Ronald Burgess,' he said as he shook our hands. He sat next to Tabitha.

The people of this company appeared to like their black suits.

'So, shall we begin?' Tabitha said. It was clear she was running the meeting and Ronald was just there for the ride.

'My grandmother recently passed away and I inherited a few things from her,' Henley said.

'We're very sorry for your loss,' Tabitha said. She said it so quickly, it was obviously a practised answer.

'Thank you. We received the news while we were travelling and had this jewellery sent to us, along with some art and a few small antiques. We'd like to sell it quickly and move on with our lives.'

'Would you be interested in selling the other objects with us, Mr Beauford?' Tabitha asked smoothly. 'We have many different experts who specialise in different things. Selling inherited jewellery, art and, of course, most antiques, especially period furniture, is what we do best—'

'This jewellery is the only thing we're considering selling for now,' Henley said firmly.

'Very well,' Tabitha said. She looked obviously miffed, but her voice was still smooth. 'Are you familiar with Carter House's auction process, Mr Beauford?'

'I imagine it is aligned with that of other highly esteemed auction houses around the world,' Henley said.

'Indeed. We're an international auction house and we adhere to standard international protocols. We also take special pride in the quality of the items we put up for auction. Consequently, we meticulously vet the items we choose to take on. The process includes a background check that no similar pieces have been reported missing from museums and public and registered private collections – only a formality, of course . . . I'm sure you understand that we have an obligation to both our sellers and our buyers.'

'Certainly.' Henley draped his arms over the armrests of his chair.

'So you will agree to have Ronald appraise the jewellery?'

Henley looked at me for the first time since we set foot in the building. I unzipped the neon-green backpack and took out the jewellery that was floating loose in the bottom of the bag.

Tabitha and Ronald wore identical looks of surprise. I didn't know whether it was because we had brought priceless jewellery in a touristy backpack that had a colour scheme only a seven-year-old would approve of, or whether it was because the necklace and earrings tumbled out of an old T-shirt instead of being ensconced in a protective case of some kind.

'May I?' Ronald said, after recovering from his shock. He held out his hands and I gently placed first the necklace and then the pair of earrings into his palms.

I felt an immediate physical and emotional lightness as soon as I handed over the jewellery. Releasing the physical weight felt like letting go of all the memories I had of that life in Tudor England. Most of all, it felt like letting go of Richard.

Ronald produced a single-lens magnifying tool to take a closer look at each of the gemstones. He studied the necklace first.

'Remarkable,' he breathed.

Even Tabitha looked a bit excited.

'Absolutely stunning.'

Henley was expressionless, watching him.

Ronald turned the necklace in his hands to examine the gold plating. 'This isn't without its flaws,' he said. 'There are obvious scratches from workshop tools and a little wear from the necklace being worn . . . But aside from that, this is amazing.'

'And?' Henley said.

Ronald put his magnifying tool down, his cheeks rosy from his barely contained excitement. 'You might not believe this,' he started softly, 'but I think this might be original jewellery from the Tudor period.'

'Wonderful,' was all Henley said.

Not getting the thrilled response he had been hoping for, Ronald looked to me.

'What fantastic luck!' I offered, trying to sound as delighted as Ronald.

'Very lucky indeed. I've never seen anything like it . . . It's exceptionally well preserved – as if someone just plucked it off the neck of a lady at court yesterday.'

Ronald was closer to the truth than he realised.

'How did you come to acquire these pieces again?' he asked Henley.

Henley took it smoothly. 'My late grandmother.'

'Yes, oh yes. And she was an avid collector? Did she specialise in specific pieces? Only jewellery? Or items from a specific time period? A Tudor fan, perhaps?'

'She was a woman of many curiosities,' Henley said.

'She had a great eye,' Ronald said. 'This must have cost a fortune and a considerable amount of time to acquire.'

'Do you think I'll get much of that investment back?'

'Of course.' Ronald's eyes were glued to the earrings now. He took his magnifying tool and held one of the earrings to the light. 'Items like these only appreciate in value, especially when they're in such great condition. I don't know if you realise how rare a thing you have here, Mr Beauford.'

'What would Carter House pay for it?'

'Directly?' Ronald finally put his lens down. 'We don't often buy directly from any of our clients . . .' He glanced at Tabitha.

Tabitha stepped in. 'It's not Carter House's common practice to buy directly from our sellers. We normally put the object up for auction and charge a commission on the final sale value.'

'And how long will that take?' Henley sighed heavily. 'Weeks, at least? Perhaps even months to advertise the auction appropriately? I would like to bury my grand-mother's memory and be done with it. I'm not interested in dragging it out like some show.'

Ronald continued giving Tabitha a strange look, as if trying to communicate something to her. She caught his look and pretended not to notice. Finally she spoke.

'As I said, while it's not our common practice to buy directly from our clients, it has been done before in cases where a client wanted to *alleviate* himself of the burden of a specific sale.'

I wasn't sure what she was trying to get at.

'Selling directly to us will not give you the highest price you can receive on this object, Mr Beauford,' Tabitha said. 'It'll certainly be a faster transaction since you won't have to wait for the auction to take place, as you said. But it also means that the sale price would be whatever we deem fit.'

'I understand,' Henley said. He hadn't moved from his position with his arms on both armrests.

'At auction, there could be a bidding war, or a buyer might fall in love with a specific piece and pay more than market value. That will not happen if you sell directly to us.'

'Of course.'

Tabitha's eyebrows rose at how calm Henley looked.

'I've already made my decision,' Henley said. 'I won't make my sale at Carter House unless I can sell to you directly. If not, I will take my business to another auction house – perhaps one back home in the States might be more . . . accommodating?'

That made Tabitha pause. She glanced at Ronald, but it was evident that he desperately wanted her to make the purchase if it meant more time with the jewellery.

There was a knot in my stomach. Surely Henley was bluffing. If we couldn't persuade them to buy the jewellery from us we wouldn't have the money to get home, and we'd most likely starve waiting for an auction to take place.

'We can make you an offer,' Tabitha said at last.

Thank God.

'Of course, we'll have to send the jewellery out for further appraisal by our experts.' She looked at me, as if I might object to this. 'We like to be certain we're getting exactly what we pay for. You'll be able to make a final decision to sell or not once the appraisal is complete.'

'Naturally,' Henley said. 'How long will the appraisal take?'

'Typically, anything from one to two weeks.'

'Two weeks?' Henley raised his brows. 'We're travelling. We can't stay in one place for long. I still have to make arrangements for my grandmother—'

'Of course,' Tabitha said. 'I'll expedite the process and have the appraisal done in about a week.'

'That would be marvellous,' Henley said, but the way he said it, it sounded as if that was the bare minimum they could do.

'Then it's settled,' Tabitha said. 'Could I please have your ID to make a copy of it for our records? Any form of identification is fine – a passport, a driving licence . . .'

Henley handed her his fake licence. Thank goodness Carl had delivered them before the meeting.

Tabitha scanned the ID in her hand and it appeared to pass her scrutiny. 'Please excuse me while I get the appropriate forms and make a copy of this.' She left the room.

'Pleasure meeting you both,' Ronald said, shaking our hands a second time. 'Thank you for giving me the opportunity to look at these incredible pieces. I'm sure the other jewellery specialists will be equally thrilled to study them.' And with that, Ronald followed Tabitha out.

Henley and I were alone in the room at last. I breathed a sigh of relief but Henley didn't move. His back remained rigid and his hands were still.

'Looks like we did it,' I said.

'It's too soon to tell,' he said. 'But hopefully they'll pay enough for the jewellery after they authenticate it.'

I tried to think through the logistics of what would happen next. 'Whatever they pay, they might do a bank transfer – which is fine because Miss Hatfield has an American bank account and she made me memorise the number – but then I don't think we can withdraw the money immediately.'

'That's the only problem? Why can't we ask for some of the money in cash?' Henley said.

'Because . . .' I started. 'Actually, that's not a bad idea . . .'

'Maybe the hardest part is over,' Henley said.

Maybe he was right. Carter House was definitely interested, that much was clear.

Tabitha returned with a small stack of pink forms. She took her seat and passed the papers to Henley along with a pen.

'This looks daunting, but you don't need to fill out all of them at this point,' she said. 'just those confirming your understanding that this is only an agreement for an appraisal. Neither party is required to go through with the transaction.' Tabitha pointed a perfectly manicured finger at various sections of the forms. 'Just put your full legal name here. Address of main residence here and temporary address here. A phone number we can contact you at here – hotel numbers are fine. And then sign here and here.'

Henley nodded. He took out the hostel's business card and carefully copied the details onto the forms. I was glad all over again that he had thought to pick one up earlier. I looked over his shoulder as he signed the various pages and printed his full name: *Henley Ainsley Beauford*. I'd always known his middle name started with an 'A' but not what it was.

'Which address should we put down as our main residence?' Henley turned towards me. 'The town house or the country house?' As his lips said one thing, his eyes were telling me something else: Miss Hatfield's home was the only permanent residence we could call our own and he didn't know the address.

I took the pen and paper from him and pretended to think about it. 'Why don't we use the city house? Most of our mail is sent there anyway.'

'What a good idea,' Henley said, as if he hadn't known I would give him that answer.

I quickly scrawled down Miss Hatfield's address in the city, which was one of the first things she made me commit to memory. She had been worried that I wouldn't be able to find her again in 1904, but thankfully street addresses don't change much and it was the same in 2016. I passed the page back to Henley, who gave it and the other forms a once-over before handing them back to Tabitha.

'Thank you,' she said, beginning to stand.

'One more thing,' Henley said. 'Since we're still travelling and potentially won't be home for a few months, would it be possible to receive part of the amount in cash?'

'Cash?' Tabitha's eyebrows were raised so high, I thought they'd meet her hairline. 'We usually do a bank transfer. Cash is—'

'Yes, cash,' I chimed in. 'Say . . . ten thousand pounds?'

'That's *highly* irregular. I'm not sure—'

'Once the jewellery is dated, appraised and authenticated by Carter House,' Henley said, 'we will proceed immediately with the transaction. Unless, of course, Carter House would be unable to pay part of the sale price in cash. In that case, we'd have no other choice but to take our business elsewhere, would we, Rebecca?'

I nodded as I watched Tabitha grow more flustered.

'I-I'm not sure what Carter House's policies are in that regard . . . I'd have to check with someone from the management team. May I request your bank information at this time so that we can prepare the relevant documents for your next visit?'

'Of course,' I said.

'Please excuse me.' Tabitha left the room again. Thankfully, she was less pale by now, having recovered somewhat from the shock we'd given her by asking for cash. She was almost back to her usual colour.

She returned a few minutes later and sat down with a laptop in front of her. 'Could I first have the name the sale would be under?'

'Let's put it under my name, dear,' I said, making a show of patting Henley's hand. 'It'll work better for our taxes.'

'Good idea,' Henley said.

I turned to Tabitha. 'Rebecca Hatfield.'

Tabitha clicked furiously. 'Let's see . . . I'm just verifying your online presence – another mere formality, I'm afraid.'

My mouth went dry. That was something I hadn't planned for. I glanced at Henley and saw that worried crease in his forehead.

'I'm sorry, sometimes this takes longer than it should,' Tabitha said. After a minute, she clicked her tongue. 'Mmhm. Everything is in order. And where do you bank?'

I allowed myself to breathe. 'Chase,' I said, as Miss Hatfield had taught me.

'And your bank account number.'

I prattled off the number that was ingrained in my mind.

'And you'll want ten thousand pounds in cash? I'll make a note of that in here and get all this to our finance department.' Tabitha shut her laptop.

'Wonderful,' Henley said.

As Tabitha stood, she reached to shake our hands in turn. 'It's a pleasure working with you. I'm sure we'll find your grandmother's jewellery a fine home.'

Henley was as slick as Tabitha when he spoke. 'The pleasure is ours, working with an institution as professional as Carter House.'

'Please, let me walk you both out.' Tabitha held open the conference room door for us and we followed her down the hall. I didn't know how much time we had spent in that room, but the other conference rooms were still empty and dark. I wondered how many clients they saw per day.

'Thank you again,' she said as she opened the door that led out to the lobby. 'We'll see you again in a week.' She turned on her heel and left, the door swinging shut behind her.

As Henley summoned the elevator, the woman at the Carter House lobby desk called out, 'Hope you had a good visit!'

I thought we had, but I wasn't sure if Henley agreed.

'Kidney beans?' I asked, handing Henley the can.

It was a good thing we'd had the foresight to ask Aaron for a can opener on our way back to the room.

'Fine,' he grumbled, sitting on the edge of the bed.

'You don't *have* to eat them,' I said.

'No, I do, since I'm hungry and that's practically the only food we have.'

'We *could* buy—'

Henley cut me off. 'Things are still uncertain. Something unexpected might cost us a lot of money down the line so we need to be prepared. Knocking back kidney beans is fine.'

Since we didn't have any utensils, he started slurping up the kidney beans.

'That's so—'

Henley put down the can and wiped his mouth with the back of his hand. 'Disgusting?'

'Yes, precisely. Disgusting. You're going to wash that, right?' I looked pointedly at his hand.

Henley got up in a huff and handed me the beans on his way to the bathroom. When hungry, he became irritable like a child would have. His child-likeness often had the potential to be cute or annoying. Here it was definitely annoying. I heard him turn the taps on as I stared down into the can. Henley had left a few bites – or rather sips – of beans for me. How thoughtful of him. I started to drink. After two sips, I screwed up my face at the taste. It just wasn't worth it.

When Henley came out of the bathroom, I handed the can back to him. As I handed it to him, I noticed the writing on my wrist. Carl's number. Of course. I watched

Henley down the rest of the beans, throw away the empty can and go to lie on the bed.

I quickly wrote down Carl's phone number from my wrist. I couldn't relax while worrying I might accidentally rub it off.

'So I guess all we can do now is wait,' Henley said. He still sounded a little testy, but it was so much better now that he had food in him.

'Yeah . . . Do you want some celery?' I was already getting out the head we had bought. We needed to finish eating it before it went bad. At least it'd taste better than a canned bean smoothie. I also took out the peanut butter and climbed on the bed.

'You're the only woman I know who comes to bed with celery,' Henley said.

I pretended to whack him with it. This was so much better than hungry, cranky Henley.

'Everything's set in motion,' I said, 'so hopefully every-thing will go according to plan.'

'Everything *will* go according to plan. And then we can get out of here.'

'You're so focused on leaving everything here and getting back to New York,' I said.

'And you're not?'

I sat cross-legged and opened the jar of peanut butter. 'No, I am . . . just not as intensely as you—'

Henley sat up. 'You're the one who can't physically stay in a particular time period for too long without going insane.'

'I know that.' I took a piece of the celery and dipped it in the peanut butter. 'It's just that you remind me of your mother sometimes.'

'Miss Hatfield,' Henley said, as if he was correcting me.

'Yeah . . . I guess it's strange that I got to know your mother better than you did,' I said, taking a bite of the celery.

'You guess?'

'Did you *want* to know her?'

Henley didn't answer that question immediately. He took a piece of celery from me and dipped it into the peanut butter. He bit off a piece, chewed and swallowed before replying.

'I don't know,' he said.

I waited for him to say more.

He took another bite. 'Sometimes I wonder if she would have liked me.'

'Of course she would have liked you – you're her son!'

'Besides that, I mean. As a person.' Henley bit his lip. 'Moreover, I'm not sure "son" had much meaning for her. She left me with Mr Beauford, after all.'

'You know she couldn't have raised you,' I said. 'People would have noticed that she wasn't ageing and worked out that something about her was different. And it wasn't as if she could take you with her – you're only half-immortal.'

'I know . . .' Henley said. 'It's just—'

'You think about the way things could have been.'

'I suppose you do that, too? Wonder what might have been if Miss Hatfield hadn't turned you immortal?'

'Sometimes I'm amazed by how well I took it,' I said.

Henley wrinkled his forehead, trying to understand.

'When Miss Hatfield first aged me and then turned me immortal, sure, there were tears and hysterical sobs, but there wasn't any screaming or locking myself in my room.'

Henley shook his head. 'You were in shock,' he said, as if he had been there.

'Of course – but more than that, I knew it wouldn't do me any good. Once it happened, there was no going back.'

Henley turned his face away from me.

'I know you can't think of your mother as all good, but—'

'Rebecca, she took you away from your family and did . . . *this* to you.' He spoke through clenched teeth.

'And then she became my only family. She had her reasons,' I said. 'Neither of us might agree with them, but she wasn't cruel.'

'You were too kind to someone like *that*.'

'I didn't fight her that first day because I was resigned to my fate. I knew she was right – I couldn't go back to my family after she'd aged me and taken away death. It wasn't kindness. It was resignation.'

Henley finally turned towards me. 'But what about now? The woman is dead and you speak of her almost fondly,' he said.

'I speak of her as a mentor and the only family I had for a long time. Look, you didn't know her—'

'You're right, I didn't.'

I wished I hadn't said that. 'But don't you want to?' My voice was soft.

'Want to know your kidnapper? Of course not.' Henley sat up.

'Your *mother*,' I corrected. 'Just because we don't agree with what she did and just because I have no intention of continuing Miss Hatfield's legacy doesn't mean Miss Hatfield didn't do what *she* thought was right in any given moment.'

Henley looked at his hands. 'You can't separate out the different parts of people to suit yourself.'

'You can and you have to,' I said. 'Every person wears different faces and plays different roles. It's not just your mother – everybody shows different versions of themselves, and one version is no truer than another. It's something we all do.'

Henley was silent, but I knew he was listening.

'She would have wanted to know you,' I said.

Still no response, so I continued to tell him about his own mother.

'Her hair was a little lighter than yours, with more of a red undertone. She liked to wear it up, but at night she took it down and it fell in waves down her back.'

I watched Henley's chest rise and fall with his breathing.

'She spoke sharply and believed in always enunciating the ends of her sentences. Her statements never died off in a mutter. She wasn't like that.'

I studied Henley for a sign that he was taking in my words, but he was very still.

'You have her nose . . . *Had* her nose,' I corrected myself. Henley wasn't in his own body any more, of course. 'And the way your eyebrows furrowed and made creases in the middle of your forehead when you worried – those mannerisms were hers, too. You carried a lot of her. You can't run from that.'

Henley blinked at his lap.

'And for the record, she cared about you. That day you took me out to get ice cream, she was there. You caught sight of her, remember? You thought she was a friend of mine from home. I suspect she was there hoping to catch a glimpse of you. And you know what? She asked about you. She asked after Mr Beauford's son specifically. So think what you want about your own mother, but I won't let you believe that she didn't care.'

Henley's hands were trembling. They started to shake, with bigger tremors moving up his arms and through the rest of his body until he was shuddering.

Sitting there with a jar of peanut butter in my lap, I touched the back of his neck, and he took a deep breath.

His body released the first sob. A second slipped out. A third, a fourth . . . until his whole body was racked with them. I kept my hand against his warm neck but his body didn't want to be soothed. His body only wanted to get out all the pain.

When he was done, he stood up and walked in silence to the bathroom. He didn't look at me. The bathroom door closed and I heard the shower turn on.

We didn't talk about it afterwards. We just changed clothes – me into one of his large shirts and him in his jeans – and got into bed. With the sheets tucked up to my chin, Henley stroked my hair gently as I drifted to sleep. It was as if I had been the one crying.

Chapter 7

Something shoved me in the shoulder.

'Rebecca.'

Henley was being awfully loud for morning. I turned and buried my face in the pillow.

'Rebecca, get up.' He began tugging the sheets down.

My arm flailed, trying to grab hold of the sheets so he couldn't take them.

Henley chuckled. 'Rebecca, you're behaving like a child. It's almost ten . . . Don't you think it's time to get up now?'

We were sleeping well for people whose room had been sneaked into, but it never felt like enough. This was only the fourth day in London, but all the worrying, all the preparations left us exhausted at the end of each day.

'Shh,' I mumbled into my pillow.

I felt the weight distribution change on the bed. Then two hands grasped my legs. Henley was now trying to pull me out of bed by my ankles.

'Rebecca!'

'No. No you don't,' I said, though by this point I was wide awake. I noticed that he was already dressed. Typical Henley.

'Oh yes, I do . . .' Henley pulled again. He dragged me out of the sheets and half onto the floor with him. We were both laughing as we slid the rest of the way down to land in a heap.

'What was that for?' I said, swiping my hair out of my eyes. 'Look what you've done. Now the duvet and the sheets are on the floor.'

'You were asleep till ten!'

'And . . .?'

'And today I thought we could do something special.' He chuckled again when he saw me visibly perk up at the word 'special'.

'So what are we doing?' I asked.

Henley took my hands and helped me stand. 'We are going on a date. Our *real* first date.'

I thought back to all the time I had spent with Henley. I guess none of our experiences in Tudor England counted since he technically didn't have a body or the choice of being there or not. The latter part of the time we spent in 1904 was difficult thanks to his father's death and the growing unease I was experiencing from staying in one time period for too long. And the beginning of our time in 1904 . . . Well, I suppose that had been a little closer to what a real date would be like. I remembered Henley taking me shopping and for ice cream – that was what people did on dates in the movies. Of course, the shopping was for clothing to fit into the time period so I could pose as Henley's cousin and fool his father . . . And the ice cream was cut short when I saw Miss Hatfield there, which reminded me I was on a mission. There was also the fact that I hadn't been able to tell Henley anything about myself. I had to either lie to him or keep everything vague. So I guess that wasn't really a date, either.

'Rebecca?' Henley's brows were furrowed.

'Yes?'

'Is that all right with you?'

'Is what all right?' I said.

'If we were to go out on a real date.'

I laughed. 'Of course. Why would it not be?'

'Well, you didn't answer, and . . .'

I thought it funny that Henley could think I would say no to my first official date with him when I had been with him for centuries, and often as my only confidant.

'So what are we going to do?' I asked.

'I don't know yet,' Henley said. 'There must be lots to do in London. But first, get changed.' Henley walked across the room and tossed me my black dress.

'Hmm . . .' I fingered the fabric.

'What now?'

'My dress feels a bit damp.'

'I washed our clothing while you were still asleep,' Henley said. 'I hope you don't mind, but I much prefer my women in clean clothing.'

I rolled my eyes at him and began to change.

Ever the gentleman, Henley turned to face the wall to give me privacy. I wondered if that would ever change.

'You can turn around now,' I said when I was finished.

'You look stunning, as always,' he said, grabbing the backpack with all our things in it.

'You sound sarcastic, as always.'

'I'm just trying to give you a compliment, but if you can't take it, that's on you.'

Henley held the door for me as we left.

In the lobby, we ran into Aaron.

'Beautiful day out for a walk,' he said.

'That's exactly what we intend to do,' Henley said.

'Oh, where to?'

Henley glanced at me. 'We're not quite sure yet. Maybe we'll do some of the most touristy things.'

'The London Eye, perhaps?'

I wasn't sure whether Henley knew what that was. It certainly didn't exist in the early 1900s.

'Whatever my lady wants,' Henley said, looking at me so sincerely I couldn't help but feel a bit shy in front of Aaron. 'I'm spending a day with her, after all.'

'Right you are.' Aaron looked like he was about to swoon. 'I wish my partner was that romantic.' He winked at me. 'Oh, before I forget, Alanna and Peter were asking after you. They're going to a comedy show and wanted to know if you'd like to join them.'

Henley looked at me again. It was almost the same gentle look he always gave me, but there was some underlying intensity in his eyes. I thought I would be scared by it, but this was Henley and he always made me feel safe. This new intensity seemed to kindle some similar emotion in me.

'Tonight might be a bit difficult,' I said. 'But we're hoping to catch up with them later.'

'No worries,' Aaron said. 'I'll let them know when I see them.'

Henley put his arm around me.

'Have a lovely day,' Aaron said. His head was tilted, as if we were the sweetest things he had ever seen.

As we walked down the road, I kept waiting for Henley to pull out his map.

'You're not going to look up directions?' I finally asked.

'Directions? To what?'

'Well, I don't know. Something you want to see?'

'Wandering is best when you don't know what you want to see. Let something find you for once,' Henley said. 'This road will turn onto a main street soon, and there's bound to be something to see if we keep walking along it.'

Henley was right. As we neared the main street, we heard the bustle of people and traffic – that much was normal – but then we started to hear music.

'What do you think it is?' I asked as we turned the corner.

For the most part, traffic was at a standstill. People clogged the sidewalks, jockeying to buy food and snacks from little carts. A stilt-wearing, eight-foot-tall man slowly walked past us, and a clown was making balloon animals for a mass of children on the other side of the street.

'Some kind of festival, I guess,' Henley said. He grabbed my hand. 'Here, let's walk down that way a bit. The people with popcorn and balloon animals seem to be coming from that direction, so it must be closer to the action.'

Henley pushed into the throng of people on the pavement. I was glad I had hold of his hand as I would surely have lost him otherwise.

'This is what I was talking about.' Henley's eyes twinkled with excitement over whatever he'd glimpsed through the people ahead.

When we reached a gap in the crowd, I saw that the road was closed off and lined with stalls selling all manner of goods and kiosks offering fairground games.

'Isn't this better than the London Eye, whatever that is?' Henley said.

I laughed. I could barely hear him over the crowd. He had to step closer to me and bring his mouth next to my ear.

'Now, what should we do first? Games?' Henley was raring to go.

'Don't these games and things cost money?' I said, but Henley couldn't hear me.

'Hmm . . . Let's try that milk bottle game first. I think you'll be good at it!'

'I don't know about that . . .' I said, but he didn't hear that, either. I had to tug on his shirtsleeve like a child to get his attention. 'Don't these games and the stuff in the other kiosks cost money?' I said. 'We have to be careful with the money we have left – I don't want to spend it on frivolous things.'

'I'm not sure how much they cost . . .' It was obvious the thought that these games weren't free hadn't even crossed his mind.

Of course, we might be murdered in our sleep tonight and all this saving money would have been in vain. Maybe we should have some fun while we were still alive.

We watched the little boy in front of us. I didn't see him hand the man any money in return for his plastic rings for the ring-toss, but I could easily have missed it.

Soon the boy was done and it was our turn.

Henley pushed me forward. 'Ten rings for this lady here.'

The man in the kiosk simply handed me the rings. I guessed it was free, after all.

'You want to toss them around the necks of the bottles,' the man said.

I nodded gravely and threw my first ring. It missed the bottles completely.

'Try throwing it like a Frisbee, perhaps?' he said.

I had no clue what a 'Frisbee' was. I glanced at Henley, but he looked like he had no idea, either.

In the end, the man had to walk over and show me how to throw the ring.

'Firmly plant your feet – yes, like that – and then it's a little snap of the wrist,' he said.

'Okay . . .' I tried again. This time the ring hit one of the bottle-necks.

'Very close!' Henley cheered from the sidelines.

'I just can't get it over,' I said, offering him the rest of the rings.

'No, no,' he said. 'At least give it another try.'

I did, and the ring hit a bottle's lip this time.

'I'd like to see you have a go,' I said. 'Bet you can't do any better.'

Henley wrinkled his nose and I laughed at the goofy expression he made.

'Is that a challenge?' He took the rings from me and made a show of firmly planting his feet.

'Go on,' I said, but I was giggling.

Henley whipped his wrist back and sent the ring flying. It hit the first bottle and fell perfectly around its neck.

I gaped. Henley flashed me a cocky grin.

'Not fair!' I said. 'You saw the man teach me how to hold and throw the rings before you went.'

'That's called strategy,' Henley said. 'You go first so I can learn from your mistakes.'

I made a show of pouting.

'You look too adorable when you do that.' Henley threw his second ring and it slid into place on top of the first. 'Third time's the charm,' he said, and his third ring slipped around another bottle-neck. 'I think I just found my new favourite game.'

'Now you're just showing off.'

'Finally – something I'm naturally better at than you,' he called as he neatly dropped the last of his rings around the bottles.

'Hey, you had horse riding, too.'

The man gathered his rings, and Henley thanked him.

'Your prize,' the man said, handing Henley a plastic bag emblazoned with a large company logo.

I noticed a fuzzy mascot walking past us with the same company logo on its shirt. I think the mascot was supposed to be a cow. This whole carnival event must be sponsored by the company.

Henley pulled a disposable camera from the bag and slowly turned it over, inspecting it, marvelling at the click of the dial as he wound it. 'I saw these so often when I was . . .' He trailed off but I knew what he meant. When he was without a body.

Before I could say anything, he took a photo of me. '*Naturally* better,' he said, returning to our previous conversation as we began walking again.

'What's that supposed to mean?'

'I was only better at horse riding than you because I grew up around horses at the country house. You'd probably never ridden one before, yet in a month you already had the skill it took me years to build up.' Henley wound the camera's dial again.

'I still wasn't as good as you.'

He smiled at that. I thought he was going to jokingly pat my hand, but he took another photo instead. 'We can't always have everything we want, my dear.'

I almost stuck my tongue out at him. 'Someday,' I said, 'if we ever go horse riding together again, I'll practise till I'm as good as you.'

'I'm looking forward to that.'

'Excuse me, sir?' Henley tapped a random man on the shoulder.

The man was wearing a baseball cap backwards and looked as confused as I was.

'What are you doing?' I whispered.

Henley handed the man the camera. 'Would you mind taking a photo of us?'

133

'Not at all,' he said, peering through the viewfinder. 'Should I take a few?'

'That would be great.'

Henley stood next to me, our shoulders touching.

'Smile,' Henley whispered. 'We don't have any photographs of us together.'

'One. Two. And three . . .'

I smiled.

'One more . . .'

'Rebecca?'

I squinted up at him.

'Thank you for humouring me,' he said.

After the man had taken several photos, Henley thanked him and put the camera in the backpack.

'Do you want to get something to eat soon?' he asked as we ducked into the shade of one of the nearby tents. It offered face-painting and was filled with kids asking for princesses, mermaids and Batman logos on their cheeks.

We had been playing carnival games like the ring-toss for much of the last hour. Henley won most of them, but I beat him in the sack race, so all was forgiven. He also continued taking photos until the camera ran out of film.

'Sure. I was just getting hungry.' It was more that I had only realised how hungry I was when he mentioned it.

We scanned the food carts near us.

'Any idea what you want to eat?' he asked.

We checked out stalls selling giant pretzels, candy floss trollies and popcorn pushcarts. My mouth was watering thinking of all the different combinations of sweet and salty flavours.

'I think I'll go with a hot dog,' I said, spying a cart selling gourmet hot dogs with every possible topping a person could think of.

Henley paid the woman selling the hot dogs. Wrapped in tinfoil, it was warm in my hands. It smelled absolutely delicious, but I wanted to wait for Henley to get something before trying it. Henley had already ordered something from another cart and was waiting for his food.

'I got a meat pie,' he said. 'It's the perfect savoury, filling treat.'

'We should probably find shade while we eat,' I said.

The sun was hotter than usual today, or maybe we just felt it more because we hadn't spent much time outdoors for a while. The back of my head was blazing hot to the touch. We walked until we came to a row of square granite stones jutting from the pavement in the shade of some tall buildings. Their tops were flattened and polished, and other people were already sitting on some of them. One stone looked like it would comfortably fit two people.

'Here?' I suggested.

Henley sat to my left.

'This pie is *divine*.' He stretched out the word.

'You're eating already?'

'Wasn't that the plan?'

'I mean you're not waiting for me.'

'Everything's better when it's still hot.'

I followed suit and unwrapped my hot dog. I took a bite and relished the warmth of the sausage. It was a little salty but tasted just right with the sweetness of the ketchup and the little kick of the onions and peppers.

'Exactly what I needed,' I mumbled.

'I never thought of warm food as a privilege before.' Henley took another bite.

'It's always the little things . . .'

And it was always the little things that made the biggest difference when you travelled from one time to the next.

You missed them the most and – thinking of Henley in the grocery store – it was the little things that astounded you. It was also these same little things that reminded me that Henley was from such a different time from my own. And he had already lived a full life. He had seen and done things that I might never have the opportunity to do.

'What was it like being married?' My question came out more abruptly than I had hoped.

Henley looked a bit taken aback and paused mid-bite. He put his food down. 'It wasn't so different from not being married, truthfully. Part of the reason it felt like that was probably because Eliza was already a friend and I didn't see her any differently after we were married.'

'I suppose it wasn't a conventional marriage?' I only asked this because it lasted so briefly.

'No, not really,' he said. 'But it was a good one. It worked.'

I knew it had been dear, sweet Eliza, but the thought of Henley married to another woman was . . . strange, to say the least. I couldn't get it out of my head. 'You two slept in the same bed.' It came out more as a statement than a question.

Henley scratched his neck. 'Well, yes, for a bit when we were first married . . . Don't give me that look – all we did was sleep! Eliza's health was much too fragile for *that*.'

I wasn't aware I had been giving him a look.

'And besides, as I said, I didn't see her that way. She was like a younger sister. I married her to give her a home. To protect her . . . And also to save me from marrying her sister, of course.'

Henley tried to make a joke out of that point, but I didn't feel remotely like laughing.

'And what happened after that?'

'Eliza's health declined.'

'And?'

'And she died,' he said bluntly.

'And then?'

'And then? Then I lived alone.'

'At the rebuilt country house?' I asked.

'No. In the city house.'

I was confused. I remembered Henley telling me the house in the country was his favourite and that he had never cared much for the house in the bustling city.

'The country home had . . . too many memories. Memories of you. Even when I had it rebuilt, your ghost was still there.'

After he said that, I couldn't ask any more questions. I knew leaving him was the only thing I could have done, but that didn't mean I didn't feel guilty. We sat in a comfortable silence until Henley felt ready to talk again.

'What do you miss the most?' Henley said.

There was a beat before I said, 'Pardon?'

'I'm sorry . . . It's just that I've never really asked how it was where you came from. We always talk about my time but I've never asked much about yours.'

'Does it really matter?' My words came out sounding more downhearted than I intended.

'Yes. Yes, it does,' Henley said intensely. 'I want to know. I want to know about you, where you came from . . . all of it. I want to understand the context you grew up in.'

'I've changed since then.'

'I still want to know.'

'Okay then . . .' I didn't know where to start. 'The last time I remember being in *my* time was 1954 . . . I was eleven and still playing with dolls. That was the type of girl I was – I knew I was much too old for them but I couldn't let go. And . . . what else do you want to know?'

I took a bite of my hot dog. After starting this conversation, the food tasted less good to me, somehow.

Henley was thoughtful. 'Did you have any siblings?'

'No,' I said. Then, more carefully, 'Not that I remember.' I remembered playing with dolls and even little details about my parents, so surely I would remember whether or not I had a sibling. But I wasn't sure any more. I couldn't trust my memory.

Henley chewed his bite of pie. 'What were your parents like? Was your father anything like mine?'

'My father . . .' I began. In truth, when I said those words, a specific scene came to mind.

It was dinner time and my father had just arrived home – it must have been from work, though I couldn't remember what his job had been. My father would come in through the front door and follow the same routine: take his hat off, hook it up, take his trench coat off, hook it up – in the winter it was a dark wool coat, black, maybe? – and come into the kitchen to kiss my mother.

That was what I remembered when I spoke the words, 'my father'. Not a face. This man I remembered didn't even *feel* like my father.

'He loved my mother,' I said. I felt as if I was trying to deduce a stranger's character by their actions. Only this wasn't a stranger. It was my father.

Henley let it go, choosing instead to finish the rest of his meat pie in one bite. 'And your mother?'

'She was beautiful,' I said. Not because I remembered her face, but because I remembered other women – many of them my mother's friends from some club or other – telling me so.

'So that's something you remember from back then,' Henley said. 'They must have been wonderful parents.'

'I-I don't recall.' It was strange. I didn't feel any sort of love towards these shadow people in my – or, more accurately, Cynthia's – memories. I didn't actually feel *any* sort of emotion towards them. I felt ambivalent, at most.

'It must be difficult,' Henley said. 'Forgetting, I mean.'

'It's not really forgetting.' It was hard to explain. '"Forgetting" implies you knew something before. Me . . . Well, I feel like a completely different person. Cynthia isn't me, so in a way, I feel completely fine not knowing her memories.'

'Cynthia,' Henley breathed.

It hit me that this was the first time Henley had heard my original name.

'Yes, Cynthia.' It was silly, but I felt nervous. For some reason, even though it wasn't mine any more, I wanted him to like the name.

'Cynthia . . . Do you remember your last name?'

I shook my head.

'No matter,' Henley said. 'Cynthia.' He was still trying it out on his tongue.

I liked the way he said it. It sounded sweeter in his voice. Less uncertain than in mine.

'I'm not sure it suits you, but I like the name,' he said.

'A lot of things changed when Miss H – when your mother came.'

'And yet you don't speak of her with disgust.'

I turned so I could better see Henley's face and read his expression. 'What do you mean?'

'She pulled you out of your life and changed you for ever so you couldn't return to it. Most people would despise someone who did that to them.'

'You don't understand,' I said. 'She was my stability, the only person I had—'

'Only because she made it that way. I can't comprehend why you don't find that disgusting. She took everything you had—'

'It's not that simple,' I said quietly. 'She had her reasons, too, you know. Everyone does.'

'It must have been hellish getting used to that new life.'

'Miss Hatfield was one of the few comforts I had. She taught me everything I know now.' Even if I had no intention of passing on that knowledge, I thought. Still, I wished I could consult her about our current situation. I could only hope that Miss Hatfield truly *had* taught me everything I needed to know. 'She was strict on some of her rules, but I think she meant well. Some of her rules were also harder than others.'

'Such as?'

The remainder of my hot dog had gone cold . . . not that I had any appetite left. I poked it once before rewrapping it in the tinfoil to save for later.

'Such as taking care not to form attachments,' I said. I sounded like Miss Hatfield.

'"Attachments"? Like me?'

'You and me in this way – it wasn't supposed to happen. Or at least, not like this.'

'I'm glad it did, though.' Henley's hand found its way towards mine and lingered atop my fingers. 'You'll never be alone any more once I become an immortal. I'll always be by your side like I am now.'

There was a crash as one of the food carts nearby fell over. The poor old man running it was yelling at someone in the crowd while he picked up packets of crisps.

I pulled my fingers away from Henley's. 'I-I don't think I can stand by and watch that happen.'

'What do you mean, Rebecca?'

'I wouldn't wish immortality on anyone. Least of all you,' I said. 'Don't you see? You of all people should know what it does. You can never *stay* anywhere. You can never build a life. You're left without a time to belong to.'

'And what of that? We can wander together.'

The thought of having Henley for ever . . . I shook my head. I couldn't be blinded by that fantasy. He wasn't getting it.

'Your life loses meaning without death,' I said. 'I don't want that for you.'

'And you're not understanding what I'm saying. I'm not going to lose you again. I'm not going to let you walk away from me again.'

'Henley, I don't want this for you.'

'I'm not asking for permission any more. You need someone. You can't go on like this – even you know that. And besides, I need you, too.'

There was a break in our conversation as I didn't know what to say next.

'What were you thinking of doing?' Henley asked, his voice soft. 'You know you have to leave this time period soon. Your body just can't take it. Were you planning to leave me behind, too?'

'I-I don't know. I wasn't thinking that far ahead.' And it was true. I'd been so focused on the fact that I had finally got Henley back – and with a body, too – that the thought of me having to leave this time period hadn't crossed my mind. 'Maybe I could leave and come back—'

'And what then? You'd keep doing that until this body's life is over?' Henley crumpled the food wrapping in his lap. 'People would notice you not ageing.'

'I don't care—'

'*I* care.' Henley's gaze held mine. 'You'll be alone again after I'm gone – *truly* alone. No one deserves that.'

The irony was that we were back where we had started. In 1904, I had been forced to leave because I was immortal and Henley wasn't. This was no different.

'No one should have to give up their life, either,' I said.

'This? You call this a life? I don't *exist* to anyone in this time period except you. I'm the man everyone glimpses in passing on the street but never talks to. I might as well not be here.'

'Turning you immortal won't fix that . . . If anything, it'll only intensify it. You won't be able to connect with anyone—'

'As if I connect with people now . . .'

'You seem to be doing fine with Alanna and Peter.'

'That's a bit superficial, though, isn't it? I mean *really* connect.' Henley scoffed. 'But at least we'll have each other.'

'You just . . . You don't understand.' I stood up and Henley stood up with me.

'You're right. I don't,' he said. His face was flushed and he spoke slowly. I couldn't tell if he was more hurt than angry or the other way round.

I struggled to explain what I was thinking in a way that would make sense to him. 'Being immortal is like . . . It's like reliving the same year of your life for ever. You're never going to change. Things change around you, but you can't even stay to watch that happen. You're always leaving people behind.'

I tucked the remainder of my hot dog into the backpack. It wouldn't taste as good later, but it was a waste to throw it out when we were so strapped for cash.

Henley was stubborn. I knew that well. But he wanted something he didn't fully comprehend – and how could anyone fully understand a concept so vague and weighty as immortality without experiencing it first? He had *some* understanding, but it was very limited. I was only trying to protect him. He had to see that.

I felt a hand on my shoulder.

'Rebecca—'

'No, stop.'

And just like that, our first date was over. Henley started the walk back to the hostel beside me, but little by little, he fell behind. I didn't know if it was because I was walking faster or if he had slowed down, but all I wanted was to be alone. Going back to the room wouldn't give me that, but my feet were still moving fast, trying to get me there as soon as possible.

We turned the last corner and I could see the hostel ahead. The door was swinging shut, as if someone had just walked in or out. I jogged the last few steps between me and the building and hopped onto the single step leading up to the door. Let Henley follow if he wanted to. I entered to find the small lobby packed with people.

'Rebecca!'

I looked up to see Aaron, but it wasn't him who had called my name.

'I'm so glad we ran into you!' Alanna rushed up to give me a hug.

I wasn't prepared and my arms were awkwardly trapped by my sides as she pinned me to her.

'We thought you two might have left. We haven't seen you for a while.' Peter was there, too. Today his braids were held back by an orange headband. Luckily he made no move to ensnare me in a hug.

'Speaking of which, where's that Henley of yours?'

That 'Henley of mine' was being a bit of a stubborn jerk. I smiled. 'He's probably right behind me.'

'That's perfect,' Alanna said. 'Peter and I were about to go out for some late afternoon ice cream. You should come with us!'

'Uh, I don't know about that—' I began.

Alanna looked panic-stricken. 'Why not? Are you lactose intolerant? Because we could—'

'Oh, no. Nothing like that. It's just—'

Henley walked into the mini-lobby behind Alanna and Peter.

'Hey there.' Peter took Henley's hand and initiated what I could only describe as a one-armed hug.

'We were just talking about you!' Alanna said.

'Oh, were you?' Henley raised an eyebrow at me.

No, I didn't tell them anything about us, I wanted to reassure him, but Alanna spoke before I could open my mouth.

'We were just saying what a great idea it would be if we all went out for ice cream.'

'You were, were you?' Henley said, looking directly at me.

Not me, I wanted to say.

'It's the perfect treat for a nice hot day like today and Peter and I were already going out to get some.' Alanna was talking fast. When Henley and I didn't say anything, she prompted us with, 'Now, doesn't that sound great?'

Henley's eyes never left mine. We were both hung up on our conversation from before – a conversation that Alanna couldn't know we'd had.

Unfortunately, she took our silence for agreement. 'Then it's settled!' she said and pulled me outside by my hand, then took off down the street with me in tow. I guessed Henley and Peter were following, but Alanna didn't give me a moment to turn and check.

'Aaron recommended this speciality gelato store,' Alanna said. 'He said it has the best gelato around. Just like Italy.'

I wondered if she realised I was only half-listening because she abruptly changed the subject.

'So what have you and Henley been up to?'

The first thing I thought of was our meeting with the auction house. 'We've been taking care of a few things . . . after Henley's grandmother passed.' I bit my lip, remembering Alanna's original reaction to Henley's lie about his 'grandmother' dying. I shouldn't have mentioned it again. It was such a raw topic for her. I held my breath, waiting for her response.

'Anything Peter or I could help with?' she said.

I breathed out. 'No – but thank you for offering, though. It's just a few minor details here and there.'

'I imagine Henley wants to move on,' she said.

And although it had nothing to do with the current conversation, Alanna's comment made me think of Henley wanting to be immortal. He believed it was easy to simply 'move on' and reinvent an identity and a new life every time a new period required it. It wasn't. Beyond the complex logistics, it was emotionally difficult. Becoming an immortal meant losing a lot more than the promise of death. He simply didn't understand.

'It can be very hard to come to terms with the passing of a loved one,' Alanna said.

I froze, realising I must have said at least some of my thoughts aloud.

'We still have a little way to go,' Alanna said, still ushering me along.

I thought I heard footsteps behind me and turned to take a peek. It couldn't have been Henley or Peter as they were much further away. Henley wasn't looking my way for once. His gaze was on the ground in front of him as he talked and laughed with Peter. I wondered what they were discussing . . . Certainly not what was on my mind.

Remembering the footsteps I had heard, I quickened my pace.

'What else did you two do these past couple of days?'

'Um . . . Well, we went to a street fair today,' I volunteered.

'There was a street fair?'

'A carnival of sorts, back that way.' I pointed behind us.

'And we missed it?' Alanna looked heartbroken.

I chuckled. 'I'm sure there'll be others.'

'Peter wants to head to Scotland soon, so we'll see.'

'How long have you been travelling?'

'A few years. Maybe three?'

My eyes widened. I was expecting her to say a few months at the most.

Alanna saw my look of astonishment and laughed. 'That tends to be the response we get from people. I'm used to it by now.'

'But . . . why?'

'Why do we travel, you mean?'

'If you don't mind me asking.'

It was a blunt question but there was no other way of putting it.

Luckily, Alanna smiled. 'Life at home doesn't really suit me,' she said, 'and Peter's nice enough to let me drag him around the world.'

I had so many questions, like how they were able to afford all the travelling without holding down a job, but I made sure not to overwhelm her with them.

'You're probably going to ask, "But what about your families?"' she said.

That thought hadn't crossed my mind, but I nodded.

'Peter makes sure to visit his every once in a while – he'll head to Ohio for about a week.'

I was taken back. 'That's where he's from?' Peter looked too 'alternative' to be from somewhere as 'normal' as Ohio.

'It's the braids, isn't it?' Alanna laughed, mindlessly patting her own platinum-blonde hair into place. 'He's worn those cornrows since before I met him. Hard to imagine Peter as a middle-America boy eating processed foods.' She wrinkled her little nose at the word 'processed'.

'I guess people change,' I said and glanced back over my shoulder at Peter. He was wearing a tie-die shirt with cut-out armholes today. Definitely not what I imagined when I thought about 'Ohio'.

'What about you?' I asked. 'Are you from Ohio?'

'Me? God, no. The one thing my parents did right was not birthing me in Ohio.'

What that a joke? I didn't know whether I was supposed to laugh or not, but since Alanna remained serious, so did I.

'I'm from LA,' she said, 'but I like to tell people, "I'm *from* the world." Only born in LA.'

'What was it like there?' I thought back to all the depictions of LA I remembered from the movies and television shows I had watched with Miss Hatfield. 'Sunny?'

'Yup.' Alanna popped the 'p'. 'Full of people who think they know it all – who they are, how they're supposed to live their lives – but actually don't know a thing. People like my mother, basically.'

'And your father?' I said carefully. I probably shouldn't have asked about him. I didn't want to cross any lines I couldn't see, but Alanna appeared to take everything in her stride.

'He's the quintessential Los Angeles plastic surgeon. Went to med school to help children born with cleft lips. Came out and was quickly indoctrinated by society singing, "Get rich. It's the only way you'll look like a person of value."' Alanna tugged at the hem of her shirt. 'But at least he started out well. His biggest mistake was marrying my mother.'

147

For someone who hated her mother so much, Alanna kept bringing her up. I was afraid to ask, but fortunately I didn't have to.

'My mother's a shark. She survives on pushing people.'

'I'm not sure I understand,' I said.

'She riles people up just so she can push them to their maximum. Their max operating potential. Their max abilities. Their max everything.'

I frowned. 'Isn't that a good thing?'

'It breaks people,' Alanna said. 'She's the type of person who knows *exactly* what your weakness is – the worst thought you've ever had about yourself, the biggest insecurity you hide from the world. If she doesn't know it, she makes it her job to find out. And all so that she can use you to her advantage.'

Alanna looked different as she spoke about this side of her mother. Sure, she was talking mostly in generalities, but something had changed in her face. Were her eyes a bit narrower? Was there a tiny crease on her forehead not there before? Were her eyes a little glossier? I couldn't put my finger on it, but I knew from her face that she was speaking from experience.

'She's ultimately the reason I travel.'

So that was it. I finally understood her. 'People travel for two reasons: to seek something out that they need to find, or to run from something in their past.'

'Don't judge me,' she said, 'but I'm definitely the latter.'

I was the last person who could judge her. 'Don't worry, I won't.' Because I was the latter, too. I was running from the past itself.

'This looks like it!' Alanna pointed out a small shop with a pink door and a sign illustrating three scoops of gelato on a cone. 'See how cute it is.'

An old-fashioned bell rang as we opened the door. My first thought was that Henley would like it. Although physically different from the ice cream parlour he'd taken me to in 1904, it somehow *felt* the same. The room was much smaller than the parlour in 1904 and could only fit two tables by the front window. The walls were painted the same cheery pink as the door. It wasn't a sickly bubble gum pink and managed to look sleek paired with the white chairs and the stainless-steel counter. I heard the bell ring for a second time when Henley and Peter came in. Henley didn't say anything, but he walked up to stand next to me.

'Welcome!' A man with a rounded stomach waved us in. 'What can I do for you?'

'We'll order some gelato in a second,' Peter said, 'but for now, we're still browsing.'

'Let me know if I can get you samples.'

I peeked through the glass into the display. The traditional flavours were on the left – chocolate, vanilla, strawberry – and the right side had the newer, more unconventional flavours: Nutella and strawberries, caramel macchiato, roasted banana.

I already knew what Henley would choose. Though he liked blueberry scones, when it came to ice cream he always got strawberry. It was his favourite.

I watched Alanna make her decision. I expected her to go for one of the unconventional flavours. She would be the type of person to wonder if the caramel macchiato used actual coffee beans, and if so, whether the coffee beans were fair trade and sustainably produced. She'd probably end up picking the Nutella and strawberries or the roasted banana.

Next, I eyed Peter. Underneath his rebellious outside, he was still an Ohio boy. Not only that, but he still cared about it enough to visit. I had a feeling he'd stick with one of the safer, traditional flavours. Maybe even something as safe and classic as vanilla.

'I think I'm ready to order.' Alanna stepped up to the counter first. 'Could I get a cone of the roasted banana?'

I smiled. I had been right.

The man came over with a small tasting spoon. 'Do you want to try it first? It has a bit of an unusual smoky banana flavour, so it's a tad hit or miss with people. Some folks think it tastes a bit burned.'

'Oh, no need for that – being surprised by something new is part of the fun, whether you love it or not.'

'Okay . . .' The man put the spoon away. 'Cones come with two scoops. Would you like another flavour, or just two scoops of the roasted banana?'

'Just the one flavour's fine.'

The man heaped two scoops of the pale yellow ice cream onto a cone. Alanna gleefully took it from him and tasted it straight away.

'Mm . . . So. Good,' she said, between licks.

'Guess I'm next.' Peter approached the counter after glancing at both Henley and me. 'Vanilla, please.'

Two out of two. I was feeling smug.

'On a cone?' the man asked.

'Sure.'

'Two scoops of that?'

'Yeah.'

Peter soon had his vanilla gelato. He grabbed a napkin but didn't start eating immediately, presumably waiting for Henley and I to order before he started on it.

Henley looked at me. 'You want to go before me?' It was the first time he had spoken to me since our earlier argument.

'No, it's fine. Why don't you choose?' In truth, I was waiting for my last prediction to be proved correct. Henley I knew better than anyone.

He looked like he didn't want to argue over something so little. 'Strawberry for me, please.'

Right again.

'And then Nutella and strawberries for the second scoop.'

I tilted my head. I couldn't decide whether the second scoop was characteristic of Henley or not.

'Miss, are you ready to order?'

The man was looking at me. Henley already had his cone of gelato.

'Two scoops of the Nutella and strawberries for me as well.'

When we all had our gelato, Alanna started to walk up to the counter by Henley to pay.

'Oh no you don't.' Henley playfully shooed her away. 'You got dinner last time. This is our chance to make up for it and save face.'

We both knew we still had to save money, but this was Henley trying to look inconspicuous and fit in with Alanna and Peter.

'You sure?' she said.

'Of course!'

'Well, only so you can look good in front of Rebecca.' She winked at him, then made her way to sit at the tables near the window.

Peter and I followed. He sat down next to Alanna, putting his feet up on a spare chair and draping his arm around her. She looked so small sitting there with her shoulder enveloped by his arm.

Henley joined us as soon as he had finished paying. I watched to see which chair he would take – the one next to me or the one across from me. He took the one across from me.

'Thanks for the treat, Henley,' Alanna said.

'How's your roasted banana?' he asked her.

'It's really good. You want a bit?'

Henley shook his head. 'I'm sticking to my strawberry combination.'

'Is the strawberry good?' I asked.

Henley hesitated, and I knew it was because I was speaking to him. 'Yes, it is. Would you like to try it?'

I declined.

'It tastes like real, freshly picked strawberries,' he said.

'That does sound good,' Alanna said.

'Henley's always had this thing for strawberry ice cream,' I told her.

'Just like how Peter here loves his vanilla.' Alanna poked Peter. 'I always tell him that's boring and he needs to branch out, but—'

'But I like it.' Peter finished off for her.

'You need to be more adventurous!'

'I'm adventurous with other things, but some I stick to because I like them: vanilla ice cream and you.'

Peter leaned in for a kiss, but Alanna jokingly slapped him away. It was clear she loved the attention, though.

Did Henley and I look like that sometimes? Did we have moments when we were wonderfully absorbed in each other and nothing else existed . . . or rather, didn't matter? Yes. Yes, we did.

'How did you two meet?' Henley asked. He was grinning at Alanna and Peter. 'That's surely an entertaining story neither of you has told us yet.'

Alanna giggled. 'This one here' – she pointed at Peter – 'this one was actually interning in my father's office one summer.'

'What does your father do?' Henley asked before I could fill him in.

'Plastic surgeon with a God complex,' Alanna answered without batting an eyelid.

It was clear Henley didn't know how to respond to that. 'Ah . . .'

'Anyway, for some reason, this doofus thought he might want to work for a plastic surgeon.'

Peter spoke up. 'In my defence, this was *many* years ago and I was an impressionable young man.'

Alanna waved him quiet. 'As I was saying . . . Oh yeah, so I was on vacation from university that summer. My father had forgotten something at home and texted me to ask me to drop it off – Peter, what was it?'

'His lunch, I think.'

'That's right! Mother had just started him on the Paleo diet, so he couldn't eat with everyone else at the nearby café. And Peter just happened to be working the front desk, isn't that right?'

Peter nodded. 'This beauty walked into the waiting room among all those women with bandages across their noses and all those men waiting for a pec implant consultation—'

'And you know what he said to me?' Alanna cut in. 'His first words were—'

'Dear God, I hope you're not getting a nose job. That little nose is perfect on its own. Don't you dare touch it,' Peter finished off for her.

Henley's lips twitched up in a smile as he watched them laugh in unison.

'And then I told him that he was bad for business since he should be encouraging people to get procedures done, not discouraging them.'

'I had no idea Alanna was the boss's daughter. They look absolutely nothing alike,' Peter said.

'I'll take that as a compliment. That's saying I look nothing like a balding post-middle-aged man.' Alanna looked pleased.

'That's why I love you.'

The rest of our time in the gelato shop went similarly – Alanna and Peter did most of the talking while Henley and I sat silently. They were so effortless together. Their banter reminded me of the way Henley and I sometimes were, but we didn't have their easiness. Henley and I needed so many heavy conversations just to stay in sync with each other. Discussions about living eternally together versus having a meaningful life alone would put a spanner in most relationships, including Alanna and Peter's, I suspected. It certainly had in ours.

Chapter 8

Later, back at the hostel, I reflected that it had been a relatively quiet week compared to normal. My last long conversation with Henley – the argument, if you could call it that – was still hanging between us. I was uncertain whether we had really made up. It wasn't as if he was giving me the childish silent treatment. Henley was talking to me – he had even talked to me in the gelato shop before we left – but things weren't normal yet.

I looked at him across the room from my spot by the window. He had parked himself on the furthest corner of the bed from me and was just lying there staring at the ceiling. I knew we couldn't go on like this.

'Henley.'

He didn't move or respond.

'So what are we going to do?' I said.

He knew I was talking about us. I didn't have to say it.

'Do you want me with you?' Henley spoke to the ceiling.

'You know I do—'

'Then I don't understand why there's a decision to be made.'

I hesitated, then said, 'Because I feel selfish making that choice merely to keep you with me for ever.'

With those words, Henley turned to look at me. 'I *want* to be with you. How does that make *you* selfish?'

'Because you don't know what that entails. You're giving up a lot more than you realise.'

I waited for Henley to argue with me. But he simply said, 'I know.'

'You do?'

'Of course I do, Rebecca.' Henley got off the bed and walked to my side. 'I haven't experienced it myself, but that doesn't mean I haven't watched how you've dealt with it. You're strong. Sometimes I wonder if I can be as strong as you. But whatever happens, I know I can't stand losing you again.'

I braced myself against the window. 'We need to make a decision soon, don't we?' I already knew the answer to that question.

Henley nodded. 'We also need to figure out what our next steps will be.'

'And you're truly willing to make your life meaningless and to give up one of the things that makes you human?'

'To keep you? In a heartbeat. Besides, how human can I be if I'm half-immortal already?'

I tried to even out my breathing. It was as if I kept forgetting to inhale.

'Rebecca, I love you, but you know this isn't your choice to make.'

'I know,' I said.

Henley's eyes bored into mine, trying to read me.

I nodded slowly. 'If you're set on this, then we'll turn you immortal.'

Henley cupped my face in his hand. 'Are you sure you're okay with this?'

'Yes.'

He stroked my cheek with his thumb. 'We can be happy.'

'We can have *a shot* at happiness,' I corrected. Our future happiness wasn't totally up to us. 'We still have this murderer to deal with. We're not in control.'

Henley stepped away from me, his face turning dark. 'So what are we going to do about it?'

'What do you mean?'

'We can't just sit and wait for him to find you.'

I was tired of the waiting game, too. 'But what else can we do?'

'We have to end this,' he said.

'It's only going to end when one of us is dead.'

Henley looked at me. His eyes were wild. 'Then we have to make sure it isn't you.'

'Kill this person, you mean?'

'They're after you. We have to stop them.'

I massaged my temples. 'I know we need to do something, but how do we kill someone we know nothing about? We don't even know for certain that it's a *he* and not a *she*.'

'We have to find them,' Henley said.

He couldn't be serious. 'That's much easier said than done. How in the world are we supposed to do that?'

'Simple. They're looking for you. You're our bait,' Henley said.

I sat down on the bed. 'So we wait till they come to kill me?' Of all possible ideas, this one had to be the worst by far.

'No. Prepare ourselves so we're ready to strike first when they make their move.'

'That sounds impossible.'

'Well, it's the best option we have.'

There was a knock on the door and I jumped.

I frowned at Henley, but he was already going over to the door to open it. I hoped whoever was out there hadn't overheard our conversation. There was no peephole to look through to see who it was.

Henley opened the door. It was Aaron.

'Oh, good! You two are in,' he said. 'There was a phone call for you and I wasn't sure whether to wait until you passed through the lobby again or if I should just come up—'

'A phone call, you said?' I joined Henley at the door.

'Yes. Let's see . . .' Aaron paused as he tried to remember. 'It was from a place called Carter House.' Aaron leaned against the doorway. He looked at us expectantly for a sign of recognition.

'And?' Henley prompted him.

'And they asked you to call back.'

I didn't know if this was good news or not.

'How long ago did they call?'

'Oh, about twenty minutes ago, I'd say.'

'Thank you,' Henley said. 'We'll be right down to use the phone.'

'Of course.'

Henley started closing the door before Aaron turned away, and he had to take a step back so as not to get caught between door and doorway.

'What do you think they want?' Henley whispered. Perhaps he was worried that Aaron might be eavesdropping on the other side of the door.

'It has to be good news, right?' I whispered back.

'It's not as if we're trying to sell them knock-offs,' Henley said. 'I can't imagine anything going wrong . . .'

We both knew that wasn't true. Carter House could refuse to buy directly from us because it wasn't 'standard protocol'. Henley was probably thinking the same thing but we didn't dare voice it. We didn't want to jinx it.

'Well, the only way to find out is for me to call them back,' Henley said. He grabbed the piece of paper with the phone number off the bedside table.

I followed Henley to the lobby. Surprisingly, Aaron wasn't there, though he *must* have been curious about our business with Carter House. Henley smoothed out the piece of paper and punched in the phone number. I could hear it ringing at the other end as Henley held it up to his ear.

'Carter House Auction Specialists, Hilary speaking.'

'Hilary, this is Henley Beauford.'

'Why, hello, Mr Beauford. Calling about the Tudor jewellery set?' Hilary was as chirpy as before.

'Yes, I am.'

'Let me put you through to Tabitha. Please hold.'

Classical music started pouring out of the phone before Henley could respond. He ran his fingers through his hair and sighed. At least they had chosen good music – it sounded like Beethoven.

'Tabitha speaking.'

'Tabitha? This is Henley Beauford.'

'Mr Beauford, a pleasure to hear from you so quickly.' Her voice sounded colder over the phone than it did in person.

Henley started pacing the floor in front of me, but I put a hand on him and stopped him. I wanted to be able to hear both ends of the conversation.

'We wanted to let you know our experts have authenticated the jewellery set as Tudor era – early sixteenth century. This would have normally taken at least a week even with an expedited process, but Ronald was so excited for this find that he did the research immediately. He stressed that this was a remarkable find. In addition, the Carter House Management Group also approved a direct-sale transaction with a portion in cash up front.'

'Brilliant. Have you settled on a price?'

'We're very close to making an offer, just going over some last-minute details. We will be happy to discuss the exact amount in person at your convenience. We would also like to complete some additional paperwork to finalise the sale.'

'Tomorrow, then?' Henley said.

'If that works for you?'

'Yes, that would be fine.'

'Wonderful. I will have Hilary schedule that. Until then, is there anything else I can help you with?'

'No, that will be all.'

'Then thank you. We look forward to your visit tomorrow.'

There was a click on the line and Henley put down the phone.

'Did it go well?' I asked, although I'd heard the conversation. The conversation sounded good to me, but I wanted the reassurance.

'Well enough, I believe . . . So far so good.'

We went back to the room. Things were so much better between us now that we'd cleared the air and set up what would hopefully be the last meeting with the auction house.

Henley took over the bed as usual, so I sat on the floor at the foot of it. I reached underneath for the backpack. I didn't really need anything from it, but sometimes I just liked to hold the clock in my arms. I knew how strange that would probably look to anyone else, but the clock had been through everything with me. It was linked to Miss Hatfield. It was linked to me. But when I reached into the backpack, my hands closed around a smooth glass surface instead of the clock. I took out the vial – Richard's vial.

Rolling it around in my hand, I saw there was still liquid in it. I brought it to eye level and sighed. It was silly but I couldn't bring myself to throw the vial away. I knew the liquid didn't do anything. Richard and the court's royal alchemist had created it to make people immortal, but it was plain water as far as its abilities went . . . Although had it worked, it would have made turning Henley a lot easier. I couldn't part with it because it was the last thing of Richard's I possessed. Henley inhabited his body, but that wasn't Richard any more. The vial in my hand was a part of Richard that Henley couldn't touch.

'You're holding that again?' Henley didn't sound bitter. He hopped off the bed and came to sit by me on the floor.

'Just a little memento of my past,' I said.

'That's from Richard, isn't it?' He said it without judgement, but I could tell he was treading carefully.

'Yeah, it is.'

'I'm sorry about what happened to him,' he said.

'Me, too.' I gripped the vial tighter in my fist.

'W-when you kissed him . . .' Henley began. It was the first time he had brought this up since he'd exploded right after it happened. In truth, Richard had kissed me, but I knew it wouldn't help to correct Henley. Richard had thought we were alone, but Henley was there, watching as he leaned in and kissed me. I hadn't *not* liked it. I hadn't pushed him away.

I was confused, but I knew I liked Richard – I'd loved him, in fact. But what I felt for him was different from what I felt for Henley.

'It's over,' I said.

'Because he's dead or because you didn't love him?' Henley's voice wasn't harsh at all. He sounded sad, desperately trying to understand what had happened that day and what had happened between us to ever cause someone like Richard to almost replace him.

'I loved him. I still do. I don't think that'll ever change.'

Henley recoiled initially but recovered quickly, moving to sit closer to me.

'I'm sorry,' I said. 'I'm just trying to explain how I feel about all this.' Henley already knew the facts of what had happened. The last thing I wanted to do was hurt him.

'I appreciate you being honest with me.'

'I loved him, but I'm not *in* love with him. I never was.' I tried to better collect my thoughts. I wanted Henley to understand this side of me, however confusing it might be. 'He was kind, wonderful, brilliant even. He had this strong, almost . . . addictive passion for everything. I loved that. He exerted this draw on me—'

'And you loved him for that, too.'

'Yes, I did.'

'He burned bright, but he burned quickly,' Henley said.

'So you understand?' I said.

'In a way, I do. Eliza was my Richard.'

'Now that's someone who *really* burned bright.'

Henley clasped my hand. 'And she burned so quickly.'

I had an image of Eliza fixed in my mind as the brightest star in the night sky, and the first star to burn through its fuel and die out.

'I don't believe we're meant to love just once,' Henley said. 'I don't think we're built like that – to scour the Earth for the one person we're destined to be with. Every love we feel is different. One isn't better or more important than another. We need them all to function and live full lives. But ours is the type of love that lasts.'

'It won't just blow away?' I asked.

'No, it won't.' Henley sounded sure in his answer. 'It's not that I can't live without you – I can and I have. It's more that I've seen a world without you and I don't want to live in such a world. So I'm choosing to be with you.'

I squeezed his knee. 'Sometimes I wonder what I did to deserve you.'

'You deserve far more,' he said. He sounded sure of that, too.

Chapter 9

We woke up late the next morning. I swear I had celery-and-kidney-bean breath as that was what I'd had for 'dinner' last night, if you could call it that. We'd bought enough of each food so we weren't technically hungry, but it had been a while since either of us had felt contentedly full. Henley ate cereal along with his beans. Not the best combination.

I poked him.

He opened one eye, still half-asleep. 'What was that for?'

'Should we go and buy food?' I said. '*Real* food?'

Henley smirked. 'Hungry?'

'Not technically, but not satisfied, either.'

'I know we're very close to having the cash from Carter House, but we don't have it yet and all kinds of things could go wrong.'

I turned over with a sigh. 'You're right, of course, but we do need to eat . . .' I got up and went to fetch the food. I took one bite of the bread. It was horrible, but I had to satisfy my stomach.

I looked back at the bed, expecting to see Henley fast asleep again, but he was up. Although he was just standing there doing absolutely nothing.

'Are you all right?' I said, going closer to him. 'Henley?'

He didn't seem to hear me.

'Sorry. Pardon?'

'Are you all right?' I repeated.

'Yes. Um . . . fine.'

But he shuffled his feet and shifted his weight from one leg to the other. Then he crossed and uncrossed his arms.

'What is it?' I asked.

'Nothing.'

I wanted to believe him, but next he paced a few steps to the left, then turned to his right and walked the other way. He kept stretching his hands out and then balling up them into fists.

'It's obviously not nothing,' I finally said.

He turned to me and his eyes searched my face. 'You're not going to like this . . .'

'Just spit it out, Henley.' His reticence was driving me nuts.

'I need meat,' he said slowly. 'I need *hot* food.'

I froze, looking up at him, and burst out laughing. Soon I was howling and couldn't stand up straight any more, so I bent over, clutching at my sides.

'It's not *that* funny,' Henley said, watching me with his hands planted on his hips. 'I'm serious.'

That only made me cackle even more. He waited in that pose until my laughter died down enough for me to speak.

'You . . . You looked *so* serious,' I said. 'I was worried you were going to tell me something absolutely horrible.'

'Your face is red.'

I stuck my tongue out at him. 'I know you want hot food, but like you said, we have to save money. We have leftover bread and kidney beans.'

'I don't *want* hot food. I *need* hot food.' Henley's face was grave. 'I can't eat another meal of cold canned kidney beans. This is a matter of survival. Doesn't meat sound good? Besides, we can call it a slightly early celebratory lunch – we're getting the money today.'

I had to agree with him – meat did sound good. As soon as he mentioned it, all I could think of was a plate of chicken. And as he said, we were getting some money soon anyway.

'What's one little meal?' Henley said. 'We'll go to the cheapest place in the area. We could ask Aaron.'

'You want this really badly, don't you?'

Henley nodded like a bobblehead.

My stomach gurgled. I couldn't argue.

We washed up and got dressed. Grabbing the backpack, we made our way directly to the lobby, where Henley was quick to ring the desk bell.

'Oh, it's you two.' Aaron smiled as he came in. 'What can I do for you?'

'We're looking for meat,' Henley said.

I giggled. 'A place that serves meat, he means. A *cheap* place.'

'If you really want cheap, there's McDonald's, but I understand if that doesn't appeal. We also have—'

'That's the cheapest?' I asked.

'Well, yeah . . .' Aaron looked confused. 'You could get chicken nuggets for about three pounds.'

I didn't know much about McDonald's, except for the advertisements I'd seen on bus stops in New York. Miss Hatfield never ordered from there and we never went. But I was sold as soon as Aaron mentioned 'chicken'.

'McDonald's would be perfect.'

'It's only three blocks down the street that way.' Aaron waved his arm to the left.

We barely heard the end of his sentence as we dashed towards the door.

166

I hadn't realised how much I'd missed hot food in general and meat in particular. I tried to remember the last time I'd eaten either – was it at the court feast in 1527? No, I did have that hot dog with Henley, but that was so little food.

Henley pointed out the lighted 'M' sign and began to jog towards it. I caught up with him in front of the restaurant counter.

'What are you going to get?' he asked me.

'Chicken.'

'Chicken nuggets? What are nuggets? Just little pieces of chicken?'

I was so looking forward to warm food that I couldn't even enjoy Henley figuring out chicken nuggets.

'I guess that makes sense,' Henley was saying. 'Chicken nuggets are little nuggets of chicken. How clever. I'll get that, too. They look good in that photo.'

'How may I help you today?' A girl with braces on her teeth and a red visor tilted her head at us as we approached the counter.

'Chicken nuggets, please,' I said.

'The Chicken McNuggets? How many pieces?'

'How much is a good amount for two people?' I asked.

The girl looked bored with my question. 'You could get the Chicken McNuggets share box with your choice of Pure Honey, Tangy Barbeque, Sweet 'n' Sour, Hot or Honey Mustard, Sweet Chilli, Ranch, Spicy Buffalo, or Tomato Ketchup.'

'How much is that?'

'Three pounds and ninety-nine pence,' she said, reciting from memory.

'We'll get two of those,' Henley said. 'And . . . with ketchup.'

'To go or for here?'

'For here,' I said. Why not? The place was mostly empty anyway.

'That'll be seven pounds and ninety-eight pence.'

Henley handed over the money and took his receipt, then we stood aside to wait for our order. The smell of food was thick in the air and I could almost feel the texture of chicken in my mouth. I grabbed ketchup to distract myself, which came in little pouches like the soy sauce Miss Hatfield used to get with our Chinese take-away.

'I'm excited,' Henley whispered. His face was flushed and his eyes were glued to the people making French fries in the kitchen.

'I can see that.'

'Classic burger. No pickle.' A loud voice boomed over the intercom, making me jump.

A woman standing next to us walked up to the counter and grabbed her paper bag of food. Even though it hadn't been sitting there long, grease had already started to soak through the bottom and sides.

'I think we're next,' Henley said.

Sure enough, a few minutes later, the voice came back on the intercom. 'Chicken McNuggets share box.'

Henley was already by the counter and took the tray of food directly from the man who dropped it off from the kitchen.

We sat down at the first table we saw, though all the tables were empty. Perhaps we had just missed the lunch rush and were eating late. I sat by the window and Henley sat across from me. He was already opening the first box of food. He popped a chicken nugget into his mouth before I could even get a ketchup packet open.

'Don't eat all of them yet!' I said.

'Heavenly,' Henley said, taking a second nugget. 'Your loss if you're slow.'

I carefully dipped my chicken nugget into the pool of ketchup I had made in the corner of the paper carton. The piece of chicken was hot to the touch.

'This is how you do it,' I said as I took my first bite.

Henley was right, it was heavenly.

'I haven't eaten chicken – or any meat, actually – since . . . since I had my old body!' Henley said between mouthfuls.

I was glad no one was within earshot. They would have thought he was a lunatic.

'You had that meat pie,' I said.

'That's a bit of ground beef. That doesn't count.'

I had absolutely no idea what that meant, but I didn't question his logic.

When was the last time I'd eaten McNuggets? Maybe by myself in New York, since Miss Hatfield never ordered from McDonald's? Had I eaten them back in 1954 when I was called Cynthia and I was still mortal . . .? Before Miss Hatfield moved into the neighbourhood and changed everything? Did my mother – Cynthia's mother – take me to get chicken nuggets after school? Did we have chicken nuggets then? Were they invented? I didn't remember.

What did Cynthia's mother look like? I scanned my memories and recalled the beautiful pastel dresses she used to wear, but try as I might, her face was always blank or greyed-out, somehow. It was frustrating, so I stopped trying. I wasn't Cynthia any more.

'Doesn't it feel good? This warmth with each bite?' Henley went on. 'That's what you miss with a diet of bread and kidney beans.'

'You're forgetting the cheese and celery. Not to mention the peanut butter and cereal,' I teased through a mouthful of chicken.

Henley waved a nugget in my face. 'Doesn't this beat cheese?'

When we had scarfed down the first box, Henley went to get us water. I watched him ask an employee how to use the soda machine. I'd never used one myself, but apparently there was a button for water. Henley was beaming when he brought the cups over to the table.

'You look so smug,' I said.

'I'm proud of myself. Those contraptions are no match for me.'

I rolled my eyes. 'Whatever you say . . .'

I don't think Henley heard me as he was busy opening the second box of chicken nuggets.

We spent a good hour at McDonald's. Henley was in better cheer after warm food and I felt happier after satisfying my strange craving for chicken. Soon enough, it was time to head over to the auction house for our meeting.

When Henley and I walked into the tall, imposing building the second time, it wasn't quite as tall and imposing as I remembered. Yes, our shoes still made the same clicking sound on the green-tile floor as we walked across it, but at least this time we also knew to go directly to the elevator where the operator was waiting.

'Fourth floor, Carter House,' Henley said.

The elevator doors parted and we walked into the second lobby.

'Hello, Hilary.' Henley greeted her first.

Hilary's face perked up. I wondered if it was unusual for a client to remember her name.

'Let me buzz Tabitha to let them know you're here,' she said. 'Please take a seat. Coffee or tea?'

Henley sat down on the green leather couch and sprawled his arms out, hooking his elbows around the couch back. 'Coffee, please.'

I sat beside him. Maybe this time I would peruse the magazines on the table in front of us while I waited.

'And for you, Mrs Beauford?' Hilary asked me.

A smirk materialised on Henley's face, though neither of us corrected her.

'Coffee for me as well, please,' I managed to get out.

'I quite like the sound of that,' Henley said when Hilary had left the lobby.

I blushed so hard, my cheeks burned.

'I'm going to take that as a sign that you like it, too.'

I was too embarrassed to answer him, so instead I changed the subject. 'You're so comfortable in these grand rooms and situations – was your business like this?'

'You mean was it conducted like this? Well, yes – it was a lot of sitting around doing nothing and waiting for people to show up.' His eyes had a mischievous gleam. 'The world of business doesn't change much. It'll always be about people – you work with people, you work to understand people. That's all it really is.'

'So you were "working with people" and "working to understand people" in luxurious settings like this?' I threw my hands up, gesturing to the room we were sitting in. 'I don't even want to think about how much the couch we're sitting on cost.'

Henley laughed. 'It's all about appearances. But yes, my business often took me to people's houses and their private studies were my meeting rooms.'

'Private studies that looked like this, I'm guessing?' Henley would never – and *could* never – guess at the difference in economic backgrounds between his upbringing and Cynthia's. I didn't remember much about Cynthia's house, but I knew it wasn't anything like this or Henley's country estate.

Henley said something I didn't quite catch.

'What?'

'Penny for your thoughts?' he said with a chuckle. 'You're tilting your head like you're in the middle of a difficult debate with yourself.'

'I'm just thinking about the differences between Cynthia's upbringing and yours.'

'Is there that much of a difference?' He stretched his shoulders.

'More than you know.'

We heard the door open and Hilary came in carrying a wooden tray with two porcelain cups filled with coffee. She set it down carefully on the clear acrylic table in front of us.

'Enjoy,' she said, then returned to her station at the desk.

There were brown sugar cubes in a matching porcelain sugar bowl. Each piece of porcelain had a different geometric design etched in gold. As I looked closer, I realised the tray wasn't made of real wood. It was aluminium or some other metal painted to look like wood.

Henley noticed the fake wood tray, too. 'A metaphor for this time, don't you think?' he whispered to me.

I watched Henley completely disregard the sugar and drink his coffee black.

'Don't you want some sugar in that?' I said. 'Look, there's even some cream.'

'Sugar's for the weak,' he said.

I made a point of putting two cubes in my coffee. And also a bit of cream.

'Why, hello there.'

Tabitha walked into the lobby as if she hadn't known we would be there. Perhaps she'd kept us waiting on purpose, even if she didn't have anything else to do that day. She had a leather portfolio with her.

'Why don't you bring your drinks and follow me, please?' As we stood and picked up our cups and saucers, Tabitha opened the door for us. 'I trust you've been having a fine day so far?' Her smile was so practised, it almost looked genuine.

'Indeed we have – and yourself?' Henley ushered me in front of him, so I was trapped between him and Tabitha as they spoke over me.

'The typical work day,' she said. 'Enhanced by caffeine, of course.'

I caught sight of one room with the lights on. Was it the same room we had been in before? I looked through the glass walls and thought I recognised the arrangement of orchids in the middle of the table.

Tabitha opened the door for us. 'Please, take a seat.'

Henley chose the same seat as last time, as did I. I set the backpack on the floor between us. Tabitha sat across from us behind a stack of forms already on the table.

'Nothing to be afraid of,' she said. She looked so calm and collected. 'Just some formalities that require your attention. Let me begin by relaying what our jewellery experts said.' Her smile was more like a baring of teeth. 'They were quite pleased by how wonderfully the pieces have been preserved – the garnet is practically without scratches. Your late grandmother – and those who owned it before her – must have been especially diligent about that, Mr Beauford. Our experts haven't seen anything like it, and therefore we are willing to make you a significant offer.'

I thought back to when we sold my dress as a Tudor 'costume'. Even that had gone for a great deal more than I'd expected. I couldn't imagine what the jewellery would bring in – would it be an amount we could even manage? My mind started to race. Tabitha had mentioned a bank transfer and I hoped that wouldn't cause any problems since we didn't have a bank account in the UK and this money would be coming from overseas. A truly vast sum might raise red flags with the authorities.

'How much would you offer for the earrings alone?' I asked.

Tabitha's eyes darted to me in surprise. I wasn't sure if it was the question itself or me asking it that startled her out of her usual composure.

'The earrings alone? Six hundred thousand.'

'Six hundred thousand?' Henley and I said, almost simultaneously.

'That's our highest offer,' Tabitha said. 'You won't match that anywhere else selling directly.'

Their highest offer was definitely a potential problem.

'In that case, we'd like to only sell the earrings,' I said.

Calm and collected Tabitha wasn't so calm and collected any more. 'Pardon?'

I looked at Henley as I spoke. 'At this moment, we'd like to only sell the earrings directly to Carter House.'

Tabitha's face was beginning to blanch. 'B-but, Mr Beauford, our prior agreement—'

'You said it wasn't a final deal until today,' Henley jumped in. 'At our previous meeting, I believe you said we were only making an agreement for an appraisal. And I recall something about neither party being required to go through with the transaction.'

Thank God Henley was backing me up on this change of plan even though he probably had no idea what my reasons were for suggesting it.

'We're not even cancelling the transaction,' I said. 'We're only modifying it.'

'You won't find a higher price elsewhere by selling the necklace directly,' Tabitha said.

'You're probably right,' I said.

Henley took my hand in his and gave it a squeeze where Tabitha could see the gesture. 'Rebecca's just looking out for me. She knows this jewellery set has sentimental value for me; they're the objects that remind me most of my grandmother. I didn't see it before, but selling the entire set now would not be the right thing to do. Surely you understand, Tabitha?'

Tabitha's gaping mouth scrambled to figure out what to say, but Henley didn't give her a moment to speak.

Instead, he continued, 'Were this a run-of-the-mill auction house, I wouldn't even sell you the earrings, but Carter House is a superior institution and its clients are some of the most refined connoisseurs of art and jewellery in the world. I'm sure you'll be able to find a buyer who cares about these earrings almost as much as I do.'

There was a pause.

'Well, what do you say, Tabitha?' Henley prompted.

'Let me print out new paperwork,' she said, still so flustered that she forgot to excuse herself when she left the room.

'That was wonderful,' I whispered to Henley.

'I hope that was worth it – and you'd better explain everything later,' he said. No one else would have trusted me so fully.

'It is and I will, I promise.' I didn't want to go into it there for fear that someone might walk in and overhear our conversation.

Ten minutes later, Tabitha returned with a new stack of papers and a suede pouch. The papers were so fresh from the printer that they were warm when she passed them to us.

'The necklace,' she said as she slid the suede pouch to our side of the table.

I took a look and, sure enough, my necklace was inside the pouch. It looked positively regal – and so much more expensive – wrapped in suede. They also appeared to have cleaned it, as both stones and metal sparkled more than they had before.

I turned my attention to the forms Henley was already going through. 'Tudor-era garnet earrings' were the only item listed for sale and the price was six hundred thousand pounds, as promised.

Tabitha had regained some of her composure by this time and was talking Henley through the forms. 'Could you please verify that the information is correct from our last meeting and then sign the highlighted sections?'

Henley scanned the addresses and personal information. 'It looks all right to me.' He signed his name on the various pages.

'Should we send the remittance advice to the New York address?'

I answered that one. 'Yes.'

Tabitha was taking notes on a sheet of paper in front of her. 'The bank transfer will be made as soon as possible on our end, but please remember it might take a while for it to clear overseas.'

'And the cash?' Henley asked.

'Is right here.' Tabitha took out an envelope from her leather portfolio and passed it towards us. 'Ten thousand pounds, as agreed. Please feel free to check it.'

I peeked inside and saw stacks of notes secured with rubber bands around them.

'No need to double-check such a prestigious company.' Henley put the envelope in the backpack.

'Now, if that will be all for today . . .' Tabitha stood and we followed suit. 'Please let me escort you both to the lobby.' She opened the door and led us to the waiting area. 'If there's anything else that we can do, please don't hesitate to give us a ring.' Tabitha smiled. 'Carter House would love to be of service.'

She shook Henley's hand, then mine. Her fingers were so cold compared to mine that I expected them to sizzle upon contact with my hand.

Tabitha left us in the lobby and I called the elevator. Henley gave Hilary a quick wave before we stepped in.

'Lobby, please,' Henley said. The elevator operator pressed the lowest button.

A few moments later, the doors opened and we glided through the main lobby and onto the street. We were barely outside before Henley demanded an explanation.

'So what was that about selling only the earrings?'

I walked us further away from the buildings before answering him.

'Firstly,' I explained, 'we definitely don't need more than six hundred thousand in British pounds – that's a lot more than I thought we'd get for just the earrings.'

'Secondly?' he prompted.

'Secondly, transferring such vast sums of money overseas may raise a lot of flags and we don't want that kind of attention from the authorities.'

Henley was now cradling the backpack in front of him like an infant.

'That looks even more suspicious,' I said, pointing to the way he was carrying it.

'I don't care.' Henley dropped his voice. 'Did you see how many bills were inside that envelope?' Even so, he changed the position of his arms so he looked less like he was carrying something valuable.

'So that's what ten thousand pounds looks like,' I said.

'I know . . . but my God!'

I knew what he meant. It was one thing to imagine ten thousand pounds; it was another thing entirely to actually see that much money in front of you.

'We should go back to the room now,' I said, already starting to drag Henley in the direction of the hostel. 'I'm very uncomfortable walking around with that kind of money – I feel like you might get mugged at gunpoint any moment.'

Henley quickened his steps. 'That would indeed be a problem.'

We rushed the rest of the way to the hostel. Most of the walk – almost a jog, really – was a blur, but I paused at one point when someone thrust a flyer into my hand. We were hurrying back, so I grabbed the flyer without much thought to look at it.

Once back in our room, we counted the money in the envelope and returned it to the backpack, which I put under the bed. Although it would be a risk for us to leave it behind, it was definitely a relief to stop fretting about being mugged on the street.

'There has to be a better hiding spot,' Henley said. 'There's much too high a likelihood of that being found. If I were to rob a room, that's the first place I'd look.'

I was distracted and reading the flyer that had been handed to me on the street. It was advertising for a free film. A *Fine Experiment*, it read. The title wasn't that interesting, but beneath it was a picture of an old woman holding a young man's hand. It struck a chord, for some reason, and stuck in my mind. They listed a few showings. It was playing today too, actually. Maybe we should see it later on? Frugality was less of a concern now, but free opportunities still sounded better than something that required money. I made a mental note of the address.

'Do you see another place we could put it?' I said, finally answering Henley.

Aside from the bed, the only other furniture was the bedside table, but the drawer was too small for the back-pack and the table itself too small for us to hide the backpack behind.

'Good point,' Henley conceded.

'Limited places to hide.' As soon as I said that, I real-ised those words could be applied to describe Henley and my current situation. Limited places to hide. And a high likelihood of being found.

Chapter 10

'Now that we have the money, we should call Carl again for the passports.'

It had only been a few hours since we had got the money from Carter House, but I was anxious to start the passport process.

'That dreadful man?' Henley didn't bother to hide his distaste.

'I know you don't like him—'

'I don't feel comfortable with him.'

'We're not paying him to make us feel comfortable. We're paying him to make us passports.'

That was a little blunt, but it appeared to work as Henley followed me down to the hostel lobby without further complaint.

'Why don't you make the call?' Henley looked at the ground between his feet. 'I'd do it, but, um . . . he likes you better than he does me.'

I would have laughed were I not so nervous about calling Carl myself. Sure, he had been nice enough to me, but he was still a criminal. Nevertheless, I had no choice but to pick up the phone and dial.

It rang.

'Anything?' Henley asked.

'Not yet.'

The phone rang again.

'Still nothing?' Henley was putting me on edge.

'You'll hear it if he answers,' I said.

I was about to give up when I heard a click on the other end.

'Hi . . . uh, Carl?'

'Yes?' He sounded even more intimidating on the phone than he did in real life.

'This is Rebecca and Henley,' I said.

There was no response. I would have thought the call had been dropped if not for the breathing I could hear.

I chose my words carefully. 'We met in front of the pub?' I couldn't exactly say, 'You helped us get hold of fake IDs, remember?' while we were in public.

'Where are you calling from?'

'Um, the hostel lobby?'

'The hostel you and your boy are staying at?'

'Yes?'

'God, woman. You should never use a phone connected to where you're staying.'

'Sorry . . .?'

'Are you at least using a payphone?'

'No . . .' I wondered if he would hang up on me.

'Seriously, are you trying to get yourself arrested?'

If only he knew. I had bigger problems. Like an unknown killer after me.

An uncomfortable pause followed. Henley was looking pale.

'We need—'

He shut me down immediately. 'Not on here. We'll talk later, yeah?'

My mind scrambled for the best way to express how urgent this was without causing him to hang up. I went with: 'We'll be leaving London in a day or two.'

Another pause, shorter this time.

'Just so happens that I'm in the neighbourhood. I can be there in ten – you'd better make it worth my while.'

Before I could respond, the line went dead. I steadied my shaking hand as I put the handset down.

Henley was already pacing in front of me. Clearly, he'd heard everything.

'Let's go outside,' I said, hoping it would stop Henley's pacing. Unfortunately, he continued when we got there. We had decided to leave the backpack behind in the room, which was unusual for us, but we decided that it was less of a risk than taking all our valuables to meet a criminal.

'You really think he can do this?' Henley asked.

'He's the best shot we have,' I said. 'And they did a great job on our IDs.'

'This had better work . . . It'll probably cost a fortune.'

I thought so, too, but didn't see any point in sharing my concern that we might not have enough cash to cover it.

Ten minutes later, practically on the dot, Carl arrived. Today he was wearing a navy sweatshirt – also with a stain down the front like the last one. Perhaps his entire wardrobe consisted of dirty sweatshirts he never washed.

'My favourite twosome,' he said.

I was getting used to him leering at us.

He tilted his head towards the alleyway, his preferred venue for our conversations, and sauntered off in that direction. We gave it a full minute before we followed.

'Not bad,' he said when he saw us. 'You're naturals at this. Pretty soon, you'll be just like me.'

That was exactly what I didn't want to hear.

'So, let's talk business, eh?' Carl only had eyes for me. 'What do you want this time?'

'Passports,' Henley said.

'First, let me clarify . . . We're talking American passports, right? And you want the real deal? I mean, they'll
still be fakes, but damn good ones – with the electronics
inside and get you through airport security.'

'Yes. That's exactly what we were thinking,' I said.

Carl shook his head. 'Sorry, sweetheart – that's going
to drive the cost up for you.'

'Just because they're American?' Henley looked bemused.

'We live in a post Nine-Eleven world, kid,' Carl said,
not that it meant anything to Henley.

'It's okay,' I said quietly to Henley. 'So how much are
we talking?'

'In dollars? Seven thousand five hundred and up for two.'

My jaw dropped.

Seeing my reaction, Carl said, 'We're talking complicated
stuff – working MRZs, authentic microchipping, passport
numbers that work online. Basically, we get stolen passports, strip them and rebuild them—'

We already owed around £50 for the hostel room after
the deposit. And then there were plane tickets . . . What
would they cost? £850? More? 'We can't afford that,' I said.

'Not my problem.'

Which meant we were going to be stuck on this continent with no way out. If I travelled back to a time period
where I could take a boat across the Atlantic with limited
documentation, I'd potentially be stuck on a boat for weeks
on end with a killer after me. If he could find our hostel
and our room in a specific time period, he could certainly
find me trapped aboard a boat. Not to mention, how would
I deal with the effects of being in one time period for so
long while making the crossing? And what of Henley? I'd
have to leave him here.

Tears pricked at my eyes.

'Woah – don't you go crying on me.'

I sniffed. 'I can't help it.'

'Yeah, you can!' Carl said. 'Tears don't do anything for me.'

By now they were streaming down my face. Henley put an arm around me.

'Stop it,' Carl hissed. 'God damn, woman, stop it.'

But by this point I was blubbering. 'I just want to go home—'

'Then find some other way,' Carl snapped.

That only made me cry harder. 'There is no other way. We tried.'

'Get someone to send you money, then. You got relatives, right?'

'I don't have anyone,' I sobbed. '*We* don't have anyone but each other.'

'An orphan already? Hate it when relatives bugger off without leaving money,' Carl said. 'For God's sake, stop the crying now.'

'I'm trying!'

'I'll . . . I'll cut the cost if you stop your crying.'

I sniffed. 'To how much?'

'How much can you afford?'

'We only have a little over four thousand pounds,' Henley said quietly. We had more, of course, but he had clearly done some calculations, too, taking the hostel room into account and leaving us with enough for plane tickets and whatnot.

'Woah – that's a massive cut. You're practically asking me to get my guy to do this for free. Are you insane? Absolutely not.'

By 'free' he meant he was still getting three-quarters of his regular cost. My tears started again.

Finally, Carl spoke directly to Henley. 'Can't you get your woman to stop crying?'

'I'm sorry,' I said. 'I honestly can't help it. I just want to go home to the States.'

Carl sighed. 'All right.'

'W-what?' I wasn't sure if I'd heard correctly.

'I said, all right, woman! Don't make me repeat myself...'

Henley hesitated, then asked, 'So you'll do it for four thousand pounds?'

Carl crossed his arms. 'I can, but you're paying in full now – none of that half-up-front-and-half-later stuff . . . I'll basically have to give up my cut for him to keep his.'

'A-and you'd do that? For us?' My eyes were so wide, the tears made a film over them.

'Don't get all glossy-eyed on me, woman. That's almost as bad as crying. Call it my yearly pro-bono work. Can't be doing this all the time, but gotta get the big guy in the sky to let me into heaven somehow, right?'

I had no clue whether someone who brokered forged passports and IDs would be getting into heaven – if there even was such a place – but who was I to judge? I could have hugged Carl in that moment, stained sweatshirt and all.

Carl pulled out his phone and took photos for our passports.

'How quickly can we get them?' I asked.

'Making more demands already?' Carl said. 'Even if we do a rush job, it'll still take two weeks or so.'

Two weeks. That was a long time to stay in one place with the killer still on the loose. And there was the whole fact of slowly going insane as I stayed in one time period for too long. It wouldn't be long until the first symptoms started showing themselves. Staying was dangerous. But what else could we do?

'Thank you,' I said. 'Thank you so much.'

Carl blushed and rubbed his cheeks as if trying to erase the embarrassment. 'Don't go telling your friends that

Carl here went soft for a crying woman. Can't stand the waterworks . . .'

I smiled. Tough guy Carl had a heart after all.

'We *really* need these passports as soon as possible,' I said.

Carl sighed. 'What room are you staying in?' He tilted his head in the direction of the hostel.

'The Blue Flax room,' I said.

I saw Henley stiffen. I knew he wouldn't like Carl knowing that, but if it helped somehow, I was willing to take the risk. I wondered if Carl was planning to deliver the passports directly to us, even though he was usually cautious about conducting his business in public.

'If it's just drop-off, I can do that at the room,' he said, answering my question. 'I know the housekeeper. It'll be fine.' He gave me a nod. 'Now bugger off and get my money so I can do my work and tell my guy he'll be working overtime this week.'

Henley went back to the room to fetch the cash. He wasn't at all happy about leaving me alone with Carl, but he insisted that one of us stay with him until he had his money. When Henley returned, Carl quickly counted the cash and gave us a nod before sauntering off down the alley. We gave him a couple minutes before following.

We'd planned to go straight back to the hostel, but Henley got sidetracked when he saw a chemist across the street advertising that they developed photos. He dragged me into the store without even asking me if we had time to go in.

'These stores have *everything*,' he said, half to himself.

'We don't have room in our budget for getting photos developed. Not today, anyway.'

'Just this once,' he said, already walking up to the photo counter. 'It can't be that much. Besides, we don't have any photographs of us together.'

But it won't be of us together, I wanted to say. *It will be of me with Richard.* Like Henley, I wanted a tangible memento, but I had no desire to see Richard in that photo instead of Henley.

It was too late to explain that, however, as Henley had already paid and handed the attendant the camera. A few minutes later, we heard the faint thrum of the machines in the back processing the film. Twenty minutes after that, we were handed an envelope of photographs.

Henley couldn't wait and dumped the contents on the counter.

There were many of me looking off into the distance – Henley must have taken them without me realising. There were also the ones of us standing hip to hip, grinning into the camera, that someone else had kindly taken for us at the street fair. I watched him finger each photo. I couldn't tell if he was looking at my face in the photos or his – or rather, Richard's.

'Rebecca . . .'

There was one photo – it was probably my favourite – in which I was staring up at Henley while he smiled at the camera. I looked so at peace, gazing into his face. It illustrated how I felt when I was with Henley.

'Rebecca, look.' Henley was pointing to the photo I was looking at.

'I really like that one, too—'

'No – not us, *this*.' He tapped a black blur on the left-hand side of the photo with a fingertip.

I squinted at it. 'That's just some stranger's shoulder,' I said. 'It looks like they were trying to get out of the way.'

Henley pointed to the left side of another photo. It was the same left shoulder.

'I don't—'

Henley spread all the photos out along the counter. The same black-clad shoulder was in every single shot.

'It doesn't make sense,' I said. 'We took these photos in different places.'

'Exactly . . . So were we being followed?'

My stomach lurched.

There wasn't much to go on. The shoulder was blurry in many of the photos, and even where it was clearer, it was impossible to tell if it belonged to a man or a woman. All we knew was that the person always wore black and stood to our left – which was the side I favoured in these photos. But that had to be a coincidence . . . right?

'It looks as if whoever this is ducked out of the frame at the last second,' Henley said.

I glanced behind us now and thought I saw something dark slip into one of the other aisles. I felt paranoid, but still walked along one end of the aisles to check. Peering down each of them, I couldn't see a single person.

'Let's go,' Henley said.

As we walked outside, Henley threw the photos in a bin. I thought he might keep them as evidence of some sort, but perhaps he didn't want to hang on to something so ominous. Any sentimental feelings he had towards our first photos together were probably gone thanks to this mysterious stranger.

'Yeah, let's get out of here.'

Chapter 11

'Grab your things,' I said, a bit later that day.

Henley looked surprised that I sounded so urgent. 'So now you're ordering me around?' He smirked.

'I don't know what you're talking about . . . I've always ordered you around.'

'Now, that's true.' Nevertheless, Henley grabbed the backpack and stood. He was smiling.

'Come on,' I said as I led him out of the room and through the lobby.

'Where are we going?' he asked outside the hostel.

'Anywhere normal.' I continued walking.

He looked confused but increased his pace to catch up.

'I figured we needed a do-over date,' I said. 'I mean . . . our last one ended on a sour note.'

'With you so mad that you were turning red?'

'Excuse me, but I think you're confusing me with yourself.' I stuck my tongue out at him.

'So, a do-over date?' Henley looked at me intently. 'What does one do on a do-over date?'

'What any normal person does on a normal date.'

'And what's that?'

'I'm . . . not quite sure yet as I've never been on a *normal* date.' Where nothing went wrong . . .

Henley grinned and held out his hand. I took it and it was nice to feel his warmth.

'We need a normal date,' I said. 'And by normal I mean that we're not allowed to talk about any of that immortal or time-travelling stuff.'

'Not *allowed*? Like a strict rule?'

'A strict ban on anything not normal,' I said.

'So what do normal people do?'

'Well, I was thinking . . . Normal people take people they like to the cinema.'

Henley looked taken back. 'A film? You're taking me to see a film?'

It had never occurred to me that he might not like them. 'D-do you not like films?'

'No, it's not that. It's just . . . Doesn't it cost money?'

I grinned. 'I thought that would come up. It's a free screening, some sort of independent production. I was handed a poster for it earlier today.'

'So you've been planning this?'

'I don't know if this actually counts as *planning*,' I said. 'Now take that map out of the backpack and let's try to find it.'

Henley did as I asked and held it so we could orientate ourselves.

'There's the venue.' I pointed out an intersection on the map. 'And we're walking in the right direction since it's north of here . . .'

'Looks easy enough to get to,' Henley said.

The late afternoon sun warmed our backs as we continued walking north.

Once we were in the right neighbourhood, we started to ask passers-by for directions, since without street signs on the smaller roads, our map was useless.

'I can't believe they're not all labelled,' I said. 'Even New York streets are neatly organised and labelled.'

'Oh, stop your muttering. We're close—' Henley ran off across the street in the middle of his sentence. 'Excuse me, could you please tell me . . .' I heard him saying to a girl wearing a long dress and combat boots, who pointed behind her. 'Thank you!' he called back as he crossed the street towards me. 'We're so close – it's only one block that way. She said we'll probably start to see some people heading to the same place.'

The girl was right. As we got closer, we saw people of a very specific type milling around. They were a younger crowd in their twenties, maybe early thirties at the oldest. The men wore plain white or discoloured shirts with slogans on them under their army-inspired jackets, and most had jet-black hair spiked up in the front. The women were dressed similarly, in black jeans so ripped that the top half above the knee looked completely separated from the bottom half, which were either artfully rolled to show their ankles or tucked into heavy work boots. The majority were stubbing out cigarettes to go inside before the movie started.

'Shame we didn't get the dress-code memo,' Henley said.

I giggled. I couldn't imagine him wearing distressed black denim.

The people were all entering through the same metal green door.

'I guess that's where we're headed,' I said.

I thought we would get looks as we entered the building since with our neon-green backpack we looked nothing like the others, but surprisingly, no one appeared to care.

Upon entering the building, my senses were assaulted by an overpowering smell in the air. I couldn't identify it – it smelled like skunk. Inside, the building was so dark that

I couldn't see Henley standing shoulder to shoulder right next to me. I grabbed hold of him as we moved further in while my eyes adjusted.

'What is this place?' Henley muttered by my ear.

I could tell his eyes had adjusted to the dark because he was already looking around.

We were in what appeared to be a large multi-purpose room of some sort with a low ceiling that Henley could almost touch if he put his arm up. I didn't know what the room was used for normally but there was a permanent-looking wooden bar on the left. That was a popular spot right now as people jockeyed for the single bartender's attention. I presumed they were buying drinks before settling down to watch the movie.

Aside from the bar, there wasn't any other permanent furniture and with the exception of the area by the bar, people were either standing in the back or sprawled out on blankets, large pillows and beanbags strewn on the floor. The whole room was probably a fire code violation.

'Where should we sit?' Henley said. The only reason I could hear him above the roar of everyone else's conversations was because he had leaned over to speak into my ear.

We scanned the room for an empty patch of floor. Finally, I pointed to an unclaimed blanket by one wall. It was so dark that I couldn't even tell what colour it was. We had to step over people already seated to claim our spot before someone else took it. I sat down quickly and was amazed by the plushness of the blanket. I could still feel the wooden floor beneath me, but the blanket was of short faux fur that provided a warm barrier between our bodies and the cold ground.

'Wait right here,' Henley said, before disappearing into the crowd of people standing behind us.

Someone tapped me and I looked up. Henley was holding a large pillow out to me and clutching another by his side.

'Where'd you find these?' I asked as I took the pillow.

Henley put his down on the blanket. 'I just asked people where they found theirs.'

I wedged my pillow between his knee and my back.

'Making a backrest?' Henley said with a laugh.

'Exactly.' I lay down to see if it was any good. The pillow was softer than it looked and it was in the perfect spot for me to lean against.

'So when's this supposed to start?' Henley had to lean down to talk to me as my head was practically in his lap.

'It was supposed to start maybe ten minutes ago—'

'Then hopefully I still have time to get one more thing.' Henley wiggled his knee until I moved and then stood up again.

That man never sat still.

Alone again, I focused on the people around me. Some were with groups of friends but it looked like the majority were couples. I leaned my head against the wall next to me. In front of me was a girl with a long fringe falling over her eyes through which she was peering at a man in a leather jacket sitting next to her. The way she kept glancing at him made me think they'd only just started going out. She looked so happy. She probably *felt* happy, as if the universe was going her way all of a sudden. The couple behind me were already making out. Thankfully the sounds of people talking and the low background music managed to block out whatever noises they were making.

'Here we go . . .' Henley was back. He gingerly stepped around me, taking care not to stand on anyone's legs or fingers, and squatted down next to me. 'I bought you a drink.'

He passed me a glass bottle. I squinted at the label but the writing was too small to read in the low light.

'Thanks.' I took a sip and grimaced as I struggled to force it down. 'What did you buy me?'

'Beer.'

'Beer?'

'Yeah, I didn't know what was good here, so they recommended the most popular dark beer.'

'Did they ask to see your ID?'

Henley looked like he was laughing but I couldn't hear him in the loud room. 'My dear, do you *think* we're in a place where they would ask to see identification?'

He had a point.

I took another sip of my beer to see if it would taste any better the second time around. Surprisingly, it did. Henley sat down, balancing a glass in his right hand.

'What did you get?' I asked. The liquid looked clear, but that could also have been due to the lack of lighting.

'Gin and tonic,' he said. 'I was actually surprised they had gin, but I suppose I shouldn't have been.' He gestured around us. 'All these fine film devotees probably know their drinks.'

I couldn't figure out if Henley was being sarcastic or not by calling them 'film devotees', but they certainly knew their drinks if 'knowing their drinks' meant they had a lot of practice chugging them down.

'I think a lot of these "film devotees" of yours might be more interested in each other than the actual movie,' I said.

'You don't know that,' Henley said. 'The film hasn't even started.'

'Hey, mate!' The man next to us leaned over his companion to tap Henley on the shoulder. He said something when we turned but it was lost in the music, and Henley cupped his hand around his ear to increase his chances of hearing.

'You need any spliff, mate?' the man yelled.

'Spliff?' Henley said.

I heard his confusion but didn't think the man could.

'No thanks,' I called over. 'We already did the "spliff" back home before we came.'

What's spliff? I thought. *And what on Earth is one supposed to do with it?*

'Nice . . .' the man drawled.

I guessed I'd given an appropriate answer.

'If you change your mind later, my man Ricardo in the back got you covered.'

Henley nodded his thanks.

The man appeared to be looking out for us. His date must be proud. I smiled at her and she winked back.

The sound system screeched and the music stopped.

'Okay . . .' A male voice came through the speakers but I could barely hear him over the people talking. 'Okay, settle down. I'll wait.' As soon as he said that, the voices started to hush. 'Glad to hear that line still works. Now, contrary to some of our beliefs, we're not here just for the cheap drinks. That's a valid reason to come, but we're mainly here to watch my boy Danny's new film!'

At that there was some whooping and hollering.

'So where's my boy Danny?' the announcer said.

I turned to scan the crowd behind us and a man with a neatly trimmed goatee standing by the corner of the bar raised his hand slowly.

'Give it up for Danny!'

People yelled and stomped their feet. Henley and I simply clapped.

'Start the damn movie!' Danny yelled.

There was laughter and someone finally turned on the projector, illuminating the far wall in front of us. The title –

A *Fine Experiment* – flashed up, accompanied by flute music.

I didn't have a clue what the film was about and wondered if I had made the wrong choice in bringing Henley here. I tried to glance at him without him noticing. His jaw was slightly slack and I could see the title reflected in his eyes. He was already engrossed and it hadn't even started properly yet. Suddenly, Henley looked up and stared at the ceiling. Then he looked back at the makeshift screen. Then at the ceiling again. Finally, he twisted his entire body and peered towards the back of the room.

A slow smile crept onto my face. Of course – Henley was trying to figure out where the projector was and how it worked. That would probably keep him engaged more than the actual movie itself.

The screen flickered. Old movie effects, maybe? The camera followed an old woman being led around a garden by a young man. So far, the only soundtrack was music. I didn't know this was supposed to be a silent film.

'We're having the stereotypical date,' I whispered to Henley. 'We're out watching a film.'

'Dinner and a movie minus the dinner?'

'We're becoming normal.'

When Henley returned his attention to the screen, I took in the people around us. A man up front was already completely absorbed and scribbling notes furiously into a notebook on his lap. Film student, perhaps? Or someone who *wanted* to be one? Next, I noticed the man's polar opposite: a girl more interested in examining her hair for split ends than watching the film.

For the most part, the entire middle section of the room looked like they wanted to be there. Nachos, pretzels and sweets were being passed around, but everyone's eyes were glued to the screen.

The back of the room was different and looked more dense. The people looked more squished against one another and I could hear the low murmur of their conversations from where we were sitting.

Henley leaned towards me, his eyes not leaving the screen. 'You don't look like you're paying attention to the film,' he whispered.

'I am. Honestly, I am.'

For once, there was no cheeky reply. Henley was too busy watching the film.

Maybe it was because I missed the first few minutes thanks to my people-watching, but the rest of it made no sense to me. There was neither narrator nor apparent plot, and the characters appeared to be doing random things. Bits of dialogue between the old woman and the young man were interspersed with the music, but the lines sounded random and nonsensical. I decided to keep drinking my beer and try to follow along as best as I could. In the end, a character who looked like the personification of Death came and took the old woman away, forcing the young man to continue his life without her. I still couldn't make head or tail of it.

When the credits started rolling, people were already clapping. Some in the centre and towards the front were even standing up – they appeared to have loved it.

'Bravo!' someone shouted. A few people even whistled.

I heard the word 'wondrous' more than once, and someone nearby said, 'Meaningful poetry.' The folks at the back of the room, however, didn't appear to have even noticed that the screening had finished and were still busy drinking and talking.

'That was superb,' Henley said. He sounded breathless.

'Really?' I asked.

'All the colours . . . And the sound was so good.'

'Amazed by the changes in technology since your time?'

'Well . . . yes.'

I had to laugh. He was almost as impressed as when I showed him how the computer worked.

There was a crackle as the speaker system turned on again.

'My God, was that some deep mind-boggling stuff, am I right?' It was the announcer from before. 'Let's hear it again for my man Danny!'

The applause was loud and more people whistled than before.

'Danny, do you want to say something?'

'Free beers on me!' he yelled.

There was a mad stampede towards the bar.

'My Lord . . . I can't believe it,' Henley said. There was nothing but disdain in his voice.

'The rush of people towards the bar?'

'The fact that they're still acting like children even though they all appear to be adults,' he said.

'I'm not so sure about that. Those *children* seemed to understand the movie much better than I did,' I said. 'Maybe I didn't understand it because I don't understand death.'

'You know that's not true. You're probably just over-thinking it.' Henley paused. 'I know the film is over, but I'd like to say a while, if you don't mind.'

'I don't mind at all.'

I glanced around at the other people in the room to see what they were up to. Still chatting, still drinking.

Henley stretched out on the vacated pillows around us. 'Do you sometimes feel that the only place you can be alone is in a crowd?'

It was hard to put into words, but I knew that feeling. 'We're doing it right now, aren't we? Having this private

conversation in a room full of people. Everyone's so preoccupied with their own lives that we're alone.'

Henley raised himself up on his forearms. 'Do you want
another beer?'

I glanced over at the beer bottle a foot away from my
arm – it was still half-full. 'Not beer.'

'Something else, then?'

'Sure,' I said. I had very little knowledge of alcohol.

Henley left to get our drinks. The crowd by the bar
had dissipated after everyone had claimed their free beer.
Whoever was tending the bar was probably having a good
night full of happy customers.

Henley returned carrying two plastic cups.

'Plastic?'

'They ran out of glasses,' he said.

Henley's looked like another gin and tonic. The drink
he held out to me was tinted green.

'What did you get me?'

'A green apple martini,' he said.

Hesitantly, I took it. I was worried it would taste like the
beer. People had always told me that alcohol was an acquired
taste. It certainly wasn't a taste I had the opportunity to
acquire before I had been turned immortal. I took a sip.
It was good. In fact, the drink was *really* good. It smelled
faintly of an apple orchard and it tasted like it smelled. I
liked it better than the wine I had at court in 1527. I took
another sip. And another.

'I'm glad you like it, but you might want to slow down,'
Henley said.

'It's okay,' I said. I was already more than halfway through
my cup – which hadn't been full to begin with – and I felt
fine. Completely unchanged, in fact. Then my cheeks started
to grow warm as they did when I blushed, but instead of

embarrassment, I was filled with pure, radiating warmth. It felt good.

'Can I have another?' I asked Henley.

'You can if you promise to drink it much more slowly.' He waited for me to nod, then got up to go to the bar.

I tried to remember if anyone I knew drank much. Miss Hatfield never did, of that I was certain . . . At least, not in front of me. I couldn't remember whether Cynthia's parents had . . . maybe a glass of wine, only during holidays? Or maybe they drank all the time and I just couldn't remember it.

Henley was soon back with another cup. I reached out to take it from him but he held it out of reach.

'Slowly,' he said, before handing it to me.

'I know. I know.'

I relished the way the sweet drink warmed my throat on the way down. The slow burn might have come with a syrupy texture, but it was smooth and almost too easy to drink. I tilted my head back and smiled. If I'd not had anything else to worry about, this moment would have been perfect.

'Are you all right, Rebecca?'

I wanted to tell Henley that of course I wasn't 'all right' – I had a murderer after me and I was stuck on the wrong continent – but I remembered the promise we had made not to talk about any of that while we were on our do-over date.

So I said, 'I'm fine.'

'You're looking a tad rosy there,' he said.

I rolled my head to the side to look at him. 'Am I?'

'You're getting a bit tipsy, aren't you?'

'Am I?' I asked again. I looked down at my cup. It was empty. I could've sworn I hadn't drunk it all.

'Wait . . . This is your first time drinking, isn't it?'

'I've had wine before,' I said, but the word 'wine' stretched out unnaturally in my mouth.

I couldn't tell if he looked concerned or if he was smirking. It's very hard to figure out someone's expression when you're staring at them sideways with your head tilted.

'Do you feel like you're in control of yourself?' Henley asked.

I began to shake my head but the room moved. I didn't like that. I steadied myself on Henley's shoulders.

'It's nice to feel less in control than I normally do,' I said.

'It's nice to not feel in control?'

'That's what I said . . . Would you buy me another drink?'

Henley took my hands off his shoulders. 'I don't think that's what you need right now. What you need right now is some water . . . I can't believe you drank those martinis so quickly. You know there's vodka in them?'

I gave him a blank stare.

'Wait right here. Don't move.'

I tried to focus as I watched him walk away from me.

'Hey, can I buy you a drink?' Someone was tapping me on the shoulder.

'Oh, that's nice of you. An apple martini, please,' I said. It was dark, but I think the man was blond.

'Sounds good. The bartender's a friend of mine, so skipping the line will be easy.'

He flashed me a grin. His teeth were so white, they glowed in the dark.

As he made his way to the bar, I wondered if he whitened his teeth with one of those handheld devices they sold on television. What were they called? I couldn't remember. But regardless, it was so nice of him to go round buying drinks for random strangers. I wondered if the host was paying him to do it, to make sure people had a good time.

He was back almost immediately with my drink.

'Thank you!' I said, taking a sip.

'So you're a martini girl?'

'I guess you could say that.' It was also the only cocktail drink I could name, but he didn't need to know that.

I saw Henley coming towards me. I waved to show him where I was – I hadn't moved an inch since he told me not to.

'Who are you waving at?' the man asked.

'Henley,' I said.

The man looked surprised and left. I had no idea why he didn't want to stay to say hello to Henley. Henley could've used a drink, too.

'Sorry that took a while – the line was long. And all that for them only to tell me they're out of water. What kind of bar is ever out of water and ice?' Henley said. 'And who was that man?'

'I'm not sure,' I said. 'But he bought me a drink.'

'He did what?'

'An apple martini.'

I lifted my new cup and he took it from me.

'Hey – go and get your own,' I said. 'Besides, I've already drunk most of it anyway.'

'You're not supposed to take drinks from strangers,' he said. He actually looked mad.

'Like Miss Hatfield. Oops.' I covered my mouth, but it was too late.

'It's dangerous.' Henley didn't appear to have noticed my slip-up. 'And what did I say about slowing down on the alcohol? We should probably start walking back and get you some water on the way.'

'Hydrating is good,' I said, taking his arm. 'You're not upset to miss the rest of this party?'

'No. I don't need that,' he said.

When we stepped outside, the cooler air hit us in the face. It was dark out already. The sound of music and voices escaped through the door with us and leaked out onto the street until we closed the door. It had to be soundproofed – or maybe it just seemed that way because our ears were ringing.

'I didn't realise it was *that* loud in there,' Henley said, confirming my last thought. 'I'm yelling just to hear myself now.'

'Shh, we don't want to disturb other people on the street.'

Henley said something.

I shook my head. I couldn't hear it.

'How are you feeling?' he said, much louder. 'I don't care that I'm yelling in the streets – you're the one who's drunk so early in the evening.' He teased.

He linked arms with me and I leaned my head towards him as we walked. It felt good. Everything felt good.

'You know something?' I tilted my head up to look at Henley.

He was patient with me. 'What?'

'We're going to be okay.'

'I hope so.'

Henley wheeled me through the hostel lobby past a baffled Aaron. 'She's drunk already? It's still early evening,' I think I heard him say. He was laughing.

Henley leaned me against the wall outside our door.

'Did you forget the key?' I asked.

'No, but I thought we'd end this stereotypical date in a stereotypical way.'

I was confused.

But then his lips were on mine. It was the first time he had kissed me since 1904. It was worth a century's wait. Even through the alcoholic haze, he tasted sweeter than any drink. He made my cheeks warmer – all the way down to the base of my neck. And there was something else, something I felt with my whole body.

He pulled away. 'Had to end our first proper date with a proper kiss on the doorstep.' Henley unlocked the door and held it open. 'Ladies first.'

I ducked under his arm and made a beeline for the bed. I didn't know what to think about the kiss and about Henley. It was obvious how much he meant to me from the start. But that kiss. That was something else that made the pit of my stomach drop out from under me and made my head feel warm. It felt good, but I definitely needed to sleep off my martinis.

Chapter 12

The bed moved beside me and I opened my eyes.

'Had a nice nap?' Henley asked.

I realised I had fallen asleep on my stomach. As I slowly turned over, I became aware of how sore my body felt. Finally on my back, I rolled my shoulders against the mattress.

'You slept pretty soundly,' Henley said. 'You didn't move at all. At one point, I thought I should make sure you were still breathing.'

I'd probably also slept strangely on my arm, which explained why I was so stiff.

'You even snored.'

That got my attention. 'I did?'

'Yes, you did. A lot.'

Now *that* was embarrassing. Especially in front of Henley.

'It was probably from the alcohol. At least you know what it does to you now.'

'Makes me feel warm and good?' I said.

'And able to sleep through the end of the world.' Henley propped himself up with his pillow.

'How long was I asleep?'

'Just a few hours,' Henley said.

'Why didn't you wake me?'

'You looked like you needed it,' he said. 'Besides, it's not as if there's anything we need to do right now. I did take the opportunity to talk to Alanna and Peter, though.'

'You talked to them? Without me?'

He playfully poked me. 'Don't look so shocked. I like having friends and socialising, too. Anyway, they invited us out for drinks.'

I turned over and groaned into my pillow. 'Ugh, drinks.' I'd enjoyed the green apple martinis but felt so tired after drinking them. I just wanted to stay lying down.

'That's exactly the reaction I thought you'd have,' Henley said, 'which is why I suggested breakfast tomorrow instead.'

'Thank you, thank you.'

I didn't even have to look at Henley to know that he was smirking.

The next morning started off rushed.

'We were supposed to be in the lobby ten minutes ago to meet Alanna and Peter!'

'I know, I know.' I was struggling to get my shoes on.

Henley grabbed the backpack and pushed me out through the door, locking it behind us.

I ran down the hallway, not caring who I woke. It was time they were up, anyway.

'There you guys are!' Alanna rose from one of the chairs flanking the lobby door to give me a big hug.

A week or so ago, that would have scared me, but by now I was sufficiently used to it to remember to hug her back.

Henley caught up with us. 'Peter.' Henley gave him a nod.

'Why is it that men don't hug as much as women?' Alanna wondered. 'It's not unmanly to hug it out, you know.'

'Oh, we know, honey,' Peter said. 'Just let us do our own thing.'

Alanna rolled her eyes, muttering, 'Stubborn men,' under her breath.

'So I heard you and Henley had some fun yesterday?' Alanna linked arms with me and pulled me out into the street.

'Yes, we did . . .' I was hesitant, not knowing how much Henley had told her. Had he mentioned me being tipsy for the first time?

'I also heard that you found a new drink that you liked.' She nudged me conspiratorially.

'Yes. A green apple martini,' I said.

'Very good. I like mine extra dry. I like that it's sweet, but not so sweet that you can't have it with appetisers.'

'I don't drink very often,' I said.

'I can imagine—'

I gave her a look. 'And what's that supposed to mean?'

'Henley mentioned you got a little drunk yesterday and it wasn't quite even dinner time.' Alanna giggled.

'I'm not going to live that down for a while, am I?'

Alanna pretended to think for a moment. 'Um . . . Nope.'

I changed the subject. 'So where are we going?'

Her pace was quickening. 'We found this *marvellous* crêpe place. It's just *divine*.'

'That good?' I said.

Alanna paused at a crossing. She looked both ways and even over her shoulder once before stepping into the road. '"Good" doesn't even begin to describe it,' Alanna said, walking even faster.

'She's not kidding when she says it's out of this world,' Peter said, rushing to keep up with her. 'Not that Alanna would actually know since she never gets the crêpes . . .' he muttered.

'See! If Peter says it's good, you know it has to be,' Alanna said, ignoring his last comment.

'You two are walking so fast, it's like you think this place will run out of food!' Henley said.

Alanna looked at him with a serious expression. 'It's so fantastic, I wouldn't be surprised if it did.'

I grinned. 'I guess we'll have to put it to the test, then – right, Henley? You do know that New York has some of the best breakfast places.'

'Oh, I agree with Rebecca,' Henley said. 'We need to see if your crêpe place is all it's cracked up to be.'

'I'm sure you'll love it as much as we do,' Alanna said. 'You just *have* to.'

We ended up walking into a restaurant that looked like a kitchen from a home-improvement magazine. The floor was tiled with black and white symmetrical patterns. The lights hung from upside-down brass cups that swung ever so slightly with the air conditioning. The room was full of light reflecting off the cutlery and white dishes.

'Four for brunch,' Alanna told the hostess.

She led us to a table with a view of the street. I squeezed myself beside the window and Peter since Henley and Alanna had taken the other side.

'Here are your menus,' our waitress said. 'Could I start you off with something to drink? Coffee or tea, perhaps?'

'Water for all of us, please,' Henley said.

Alanna raised a hand. I noticed that it looked freshly manicured. 'A mimosa for me, please . . . Because I'm not Rebecca.' She smiled at me, causing the confused waitress to glance my way.

'A coffee for me, please,' I said.

Henley and Peter stuck with their waters.

Our waitress was soon back with our drinks. I plopped two sugars into my coffee, trying not to splash it everywhere.

'Looks like someone has a sweet tooth,' Peter said. 'Don't worry. I won't tell Alanna . . . or else she'd make you eat kale or something dreadful like that.'

'Kale?'

'Yeah, she's a health freak. Or haven't you noticed?'

I glanced at Alanna, who was busy scanning her menu.

'She told you the crêpes are amazing here, right?' Peter said.

'Yeah . . .'

'Well, she only knows that because I order them,' Peter said. 'She'll order the healthiest thing she can find on there, like plain steamed broccoli or a boring salad sans dressing.'

'And you? You're not into healthy eating?'

'Am I a health freak? Oh no, thank God. I wouldn't be able to live with myself.'

The waitress returned. 'Are you all ready to order?'

I had forgotten to look at the menu. I started scanning it furiously, hoping to find something before the waitress got to me.

'I'll have the salmon crêpe,' Henley said.

There was a pause as our waitress wrote that down. 'And you, miss?'

I glanced up. Thankfully, she was talking to Alanna.

'Oh, could I have the house salad?' she said. 'But without the dressing?'

'Told you . . .' Peter whispered.

'And you, sir?'

'The chocolate, banana and strawberry crêpe, please.' To me, he said, 'I have a sweet tooth, too.'

I saw Alanna momentarily wrinkle her nose at Peter's order.

'And you, miss?'

'The mushroom and poached egg crêpe, please.'

When the waitress left, Alanna looked carefully at Peter.

'Here comes the lecture,' he murmured.

'Eighty-twenty,' she said. 'You're supposed to eat healthily eighty per cent of the time and eat what you want twenty per cent of the time. We both had fish and chips a few days ago. *And* gelato. You need to eat healthier, Peter,' Alanna said.

'Yes, ma'am.'

Alanna huffed, but luckily Henley distracted her with a question.

'She means well,' Peter said. 'She does it because she loves me. And by "it", I mean drive me raving mad. That's why I chose to spend the rest of my life with her and not someone else.'

I smiled at that.

'You saw the ring, right?' Peter tilted his head at Alanna. 'It's pretty good, isn't it?' He looked proud.

'Yes, I've noticed it before.' I turned to look more closely at it now. An oval diamond glittered on her finger, comple-mented by a rose-gold band. Simple yet unique.

'It's beautiful,' I said.

'It should be – it took me for ever to save up for it. So many odd jobs to scrape the money together . . . I was even a substitute teacher once. Me. A teacher. Can you believe that? They wanted me to cut my braids but I put my foot down. Totally worth it. Alanna likes it, and she's worth everything. I can't wait to make it all official.'

'Official?'

'You know . . . marriage. The real deal,' he said.

That brought a smile to my face. Even a modern, some-what unconventional couple like Alanna and Peter were traditional enough to want to get married and have the bond between them validated by society. Yes, even a man who refused to cut his dreads.

He leaned in. 'Can I tell you a secret?'

'Sure.'

'Alanna wants me to cut my dreadlocks for the wedding, but I probably won't.' He smirked. 'If she loves me, she'll take me as I am, dreads and all.'

I could imagine Alanna throwing a fit. 'Not sure how happy she'll be with that,' I said, 'but hopefully she'll warm to the idea.'

'Oh, I'm not planning to tell her. I'm thinking of just showing up on the day of the ceremony with my dreads.'

It was lucky for Peter that the restaurant was too loud for Alanna to hear him right now. I couldn't imagine that going over well at all.

When the food arrived, Alanna's face lit up.

'I can't wait to dig in,' Henley said.

I raised my fork.

'Stop!'

We both looked up at Alanna, since she had been the one to bark at us.

'You can't eat yet,' she said. 'I need to take a few photos. Put that fork down!'

Somewhat bemused, I obeyed as Alanna pulled out a phone and stood over the table to begin taking photos.

Henley's eyes met mine. There was something urgent in them, something he wanted to tell me, but not in front of them. 'Later,' he mouthed.

'Alanna always photographs her food before she eats it,' Peter said. 'And if you're eating with her, she'll snap yours, too. That's like a Cardinal Rule of Alanna.'

'So . . . what does she do with all these photos of her food?' I asked.

'She posts them online. Sometimes to her blog, but definitely to Instagram,' Peter said.

I had never heard of Instagram.

Alanna sat down again once she was done. 'You guys can go ahead and eat now.'

'Blog?' I asked Peter as I picked up my fork again. Talking kept my mind off worrying about what Henley wanted to tell me.

'Yeah, Alanna blogs. She didn't tell you that?' Peter looked surprised and then glanced at Alanna. 'You didn't tell them that you blog?'

'I must have mentioned it sometime,' she said. She gestured at the restaurant around us. 'You know my parents' money doesn't pay for *all* of this.' Alanna laughed.

'Give them one of your business cards,' Peter said.

'Let's see if I have one . . .' Alanna dug into the black cross-body bag she was carrying. 'Here you go.' She slid it across the table to me and I picked it up.

Alanna Santelli – Blogger of Colourful Plate and Dress.

'So what do you write about?'

'The three "f's" – food, fashion, fun. And basically anything else that comes to mind,' she said.

'And, most recently, travel,' Peter added. 'Don't forget that.'

'Right. My blog's been getting loads more hits from the outfit posts I've been doing at each place we travel to. And more hits means more sponsors.'

'And what do the sponsors do?' Henley asked.

'Sponsors do everything from donating stuff for free giveaways to providing me with clothing to wear in my posts. Sometimes restaurants in the cities we visit sponsor me and we'll have a free meal provided I blog about it.'

'Interesting . . .' Henley said. I could almost hear the gears churning in his mind. 'Sounds actually profitable, if you do it the right way.'

He was ever the businessman.

'Peter looks after the finances for me,' Alanna said. 'He also takes the photos for the outfit posts.' She leaned across the table to touch Peter's arm. 'He's incredibly helpful.'

Peter looked at me. 'It's how I earn my keep.' He chuckled. 'Practically the only way I could persuade her to say yes when I got down on one knee.'

Alanna slapped his hand playfully. 'That's not true.'

'So when are you two getting married?' Henley asked.

'We're still figuring everything out,' Peter said, then tilted his head at Alanna. 'That's because this one here can't make up her mind between a summer or a winter wedding.'

'And that changes *everything*,' Alanna said. 'On one hand, an outdoor summer wedding with wisteria in the garden would be so beautiful. On the other, can you imagine the lights and the snow outside during a December wedding?'

'So we need to decide that before we can plan anything else. That'll dictate inside or outside, the location, everything.'

Alanna smiled. 'There's only one man crazy enough to marry someone as indecisive as me.'

'She means stupid enough,' Peter said, earning himself another smack.

They looked perfect together.

'But we're definitely thinking of doing it this year or next, depending on venue availability,' Alanna said. 'You know, you both should come. In fact, you *have* to come.'

'To your wedding?' Henley looked a little startled.

'Of course! It'll be wonderful to have you there. Wouldn't it be wonderful, Peter?'

'Yeah, definitely.' Peter smiled.

I knew what Henley was thinking: there was no way we could be there for the wedding. We'd either be in another time period . . . or dead.

Seeing that Henley wasn't going to address that issue any time soon, I stepped in with, 'We'd love to try,' I said, 'but I'm afraid things are up in the air for us as well.'

'Well, promise me you'll try hard,' Alanna said.

'I promise.'

The rest of brunch was small talk. Alanna and Peter sounded so excited for the future. They were going to buy an apartment some day, finally settle down. An apartment with a yellow door, since that signified happiness to Alanna, for some reason. They wanted a dog. The big, scruffy kind. Peter wanted to learn to cook. And Alanna wanted a closet bigger than the kitchen.

I was happy for them but couldn't help feeling a bit envious. They had everything planned out. They could afford to dream about the future because it was going to happen for them. Every time I thought about actually having a future with Henley, I felt like I was going to jinx it. We had to live day by day. Yes, that meant we were thankful for every moment we had with each other, but it just wasn't fair. I wanted to think about kitchen counters and argue over the colour of bedding, too. I wanted that with Henley.

When we were back in the room, I thought Henley was going to say something about Alanna and Peter getting married. In 1904, Henley had proposed to me in one final attempt to persuade me to stay. He now understood why I had to say no, but it must have been on his mind ever since.

But instead, Henley's face turned cold. 'Alanna and Peter's room was broken into.'

My breath caught in my throat. I struggled to swallow so I could speak. 'Was anything taken?'

'Not that they could tell,' Henley said, 'but they asked Aaron for a room change anyway.'

'D-do you think . . .?'

'The killer?' Henley said slowly. 'Maybe.'

'Tell me exactly what they said.'

'Peter thinks they probably just forgot to lock the door behind them when they went out, but Alanna swears she remembers locking it.'

I bit my lip. That wasn't much to go on. 'Anything else?'

Henley nodded. 'Alanna said some of the stuff in their room had been moved ever so slightly—'

'As if someone was looking for something,' I finished for him. 'Money, perhaps.'

'Yes, if they were a common thief. But what common thief would walk into a hostel and take the time to go to a specific door all the way down the hall?'

He had a point. But if their door was unlocked it would have been an easier target for a thief.

Henley continued, 'If I were a common thief, I'd break into the first door I saw. Better yet, I'd go straight for the front desk. Odds are Aaron keeps some cash there. That would be quicker and less risky.'

'So if it's *not* a common thief . . .'

'We don't know for certain, but we can guess,' Henley said.

Henley paced the room in front of me. It made me impatient and anxious just watching him, so I looked away.

'Guesses are all we have right now,' I said. 'The only thing we know for certain is that this killer will keep coming after us.'

'So we've got to move as quickly as we can.'

'Yes. And although I don't like it, we need to turn you immortal. And then we confront him.'

But before we went to bed, Henley wedged a chair under the doorknob.

'Just in case,' he said.

I took the scissors from the desk and put them under my pillow.

We both knew that such makeshift measures wouldn't be much of a deterrent, but at least we'd hear someone trying to break in and be prepared. Hopefully.

Chapter 13

'Well, we can't just sit here and wait for everything to fall into place,' Henley said the following morning. 'If we're going to make me immortal and find this killer, we need to *do* something.'

I was as antsy as he was, but I didn't show it.

'We should do some research,' I said. 'We need to work out what our next steps will be to locate the Fountain of Youth.'

'Good. Good. And how do you propose we do that?'

I looked up at him. 'The Internet, of course.'

We walked over to the library again. This time we knew to bring change, but we still didn't have a credit card. I hoped someone different would be working the circulation desk today. Thankfully, it wasn't the bitter curly-haired woman from last time. This woman was older and had her greying hair tucked into a bun at the nape of her neck. She actually looked nice, unlike the first librarian we had met.

'Hi – we'd like to use one of the computers here, but unfortunately we've only brought cash.'

'Oh, no problem at all,' the woman said, putting on her reading glasses.

I handed her a pound coin. 'Could we pay for an hour of computer use?'

'Certainly.' She rummaged behind the desk before coming round and leading us to the first free computer she saw. 'Would this one be all right?'

'Um . . . Could we use that one over there instead?' Henley pointed to a computer at the back of the room.

'Certainly.'

After she'd logged us in and returned to her desk, we sat down and I opened up the Internet browser.

'Where do we start?' Henley said.

'Let's start with the Fountain of Youth.' I typed quickly and pulled up a map of Florida. 'Where's Islamorada?' I whispered, trying to find it.

Henley pointed at the bottom of the map. 'Is that it?'

I nodded, zooming into the map so I could see all of the Florida Keys. 'That's the island.' I pointed.

'So we'll want to stay near there,' Henley said. 'Will that be possible?'

'It's the Florida Keys,' I said, but of course Henley didn't know what I meant. 'It's a place where people like to go on vacation – there'll be lots of places to stay.' A few clicks later, a list of hotels and resorts flooded the screen. 'See?'

'So many palm trees,' Henley muttered, looking at the photos.

'Let's go for the cheapest one we can find.' I reordered the list from least to most expensive. 'Here we go. There's our place.' I pointed to the first link. 'Creekside Pointe Resort.'

'Sounds like a trite name,' Henley said. 'Let's see the photos.'

I clicked the photo link and scrolled through several images, and there were indeed palm trees everywhere. The lobby had mini potted palm trees. The views from the rooms included palm trees. Even the photo of a suite's bathroom had a palm tree leaf jutting in through the window.

'Not bad,' Henley said. 'We should write this down.' He went to the circulation desk and returned with a pen and a notepad.

'You couldn't just take one sheet of paper?'

Henley shrugged. 'She gave me the whole thing.' He made a note of the name of the resort, along with a phone number. 'How much is it for one night, so we can budget?'

'That's a great idea.' I began clicking around until I found a list of room rates. I stopped short.

'Well, how much is it?'

'It's *from* $250 a night,' I said.

Thank God we had some cash. But there were always more things we would need.

'We really should get a credit card so we can avoid looking suspicious,' I said.

'And where would we obtain one of those?'

'New York.'

Henley paused and opened his mouth. Seeming to think better of it, he closed it again, and shook his head. 'New York it is.'

'We can buy the plane tickets online ahead of time with the Visa gift cards,' I told Henley as we walked towards the shopping centre Aaron had suggested. 'I made sure of it. And we can book the tickets from here to New York first. Once we're there, we can get a credit card so we'll have steady money. We'll have more than enough credit to buy tickets from New York to Florida, and we can also book the hotel room then.'

'I still don't understand why we're going to the mall right now,' Henley said.

'Because we'll look suspicious if we arrive at a resort without anything remotely resort-wear-ish. Aaron also said they have a tech store where we can get one of those phones that Carl uses – the prepaid ones.'

'Do we really need to ensure that people can't trace our phone calls? It's not like we're doing anything illegal.'

'Well, we have no idea how much the killer knows about us. What if he can track a regular mobile phone? We need a phone – I just don't want to sign up for a plan,' I said.

'A plan? What sort of plan?' Henley asked.

'There's more to modern life than you can imagine, Henley.'

We entered the shopping centre, which appeared to be divided into a large department store on the left and smaller stores and boutiques on the right.

'Let's get this phone first and I'll explain the rest later,' I said, spying the electronics store on the right – *Tech House*, the neon sign read.

An older man walked out from behind the desk to greet us as we entered.

'We're just browsing,' I said automatically. I scanned the shelves full of colourful boxes but couldn't see any phones. Henley was looking on the other side of the small store. Maybe they didn't carry any prepaid phones.

'You sure I can't help you with anything?'

The way the old man trailed around after us made me think his store didn't get too many customers.

'We're looking for a prepaid phone we can use here and in the States. Do you sell those?'

'Indeed we do.' The man straightened his short-sleeved checked shirt. 'They're right here in the back.' He walked us over to a row of different phones. 'These are the pay-as-you-go phones we stock. I'm afraid they don't have all the bells and whistles of the new smartphones, but they get the job done, and they all should work in America. Would you like two of them?'

I picked up one of the boxes. It didn't matter which brand we got as long as it did the basics. We didn't need anything fancy, either. I read the price sticker on the back of the box. Twenty-five pounds. Not bad.

'No, just one is fine,' I said.

'But you'll need something to call your sweetheart,' the man insisted, looking at Henley.

Henley had a smug look on his face. So he thought this was amusing?

'I'll give you a discount on two – eight pounds off.'

'No, really. It's fine—'

'Ten pounds, then,' he said.

'We only need one.' I walked to the desk, making the older man follow me.

'What about Visa gift cards?' the man said. 'We sell those, too! You can use them to top up the phone when you run out of credit.'

That stopped me in my tracks.

The word 'Visa' went with 'credit cards' in my mind, but I had never heard of Visa gift cards before.

'What exactly is a Visa gift card?'

'Think of it as a prepaid debit card,' the man said. 'You can buy a hundred-pound Visa gift card with cash and then use it wherever you like . . . Of course, there's a small administrative fee of five pounds.'

'We can use it wherever? Including the States?'

'Anywhere you desire.'

This could work.

'And you can buy anything with them? Say . . . plane tickets, for example?' I asked.

'Of course. Any place that takes credit cards will take Visa gift cards.'

Using a Visa gift card might be the way to go, I thought. It would definitely look less suspicious than cash and let us book things online.

'What's the biggest amount we can put on each card?' Henley asked.

'Five hundred pounds.'

I looked at Henley. His eyes were rolled up at the ceiling as he did the maths.

'We need a fair few,' he said, grabbing a rackful of the cards and dumping them on the table. 'We'll take these, too.'

'Good.' The man looked pleased as he rang up our purchases.

When Henley handed the man cash, he looked even happier. He set up the phone for us before putting it back in its box and handing it over. I stuck the box and the gift cards inside the backpack.

'Have a nice day!' the man said as we walked off.

'I'm guessing the department store is next?' Henley said, already heading in that direction.

When we walked in, everything was glittering. The floors, the glass cases, the mirrors – all were polished to a high shine.

I was expecting Henley to gawk, but instead he simply said, 'Some things never change.'

'You used to shop in department stores?' *No way.*

'Of course we did – how old do you think I am?' Henley chuckled. 'Lord and Taylor, Macy's—'

My jaw went slack. 'Macy's? You had a Macy's in the 1900s?'

'Don't be silly – of course we did,' he said. 'Now, which department should we look at first?'

Since we were already in the men's clothing section, we decided to start there.

'I don't need much,' Henley said.

'I know – I want to save money, too, but we have to make you look like you're actually going to a resort in the Florida Keys.' I grabbed a pair of green shorts.

Henley shook his head. 'There's no way I'm wearing those.'

'What's wrong with them?'

'Too bright.'

I put them back, opting for a brown pair instead.

Henley raised his eyebrows wordlessly.

'Out with it,' I said. 'What's wrong with these?'

'Do you see how short they are? No self-respecting gentleman would wear such a thing.'

'You're not a "self-respecting gentleman" in this time period,' I said, though I put back the shorts. 'You're supposed to be a normal twenty-first-century guy, so act like it.'

Henley reached for a pair of navy shorts. 'If I have to show leg, these would be appropriate.'

I held on to those while we continued looking through the racks.

'Let's see . . . We have shorts now, and you can wear the shirts you already have. What are we missing? Swimming trunks.' I found the swimwear section and held up a pair of board shorts. 'You do swim, right?'

'Of course I do,' Henley snapped. 'You make me sound ancient.'

He actually looked a bit insulted, but I had to laugh. 'I'm sorry, but sometimes I'm not sure what you do or don't know. How about these, then?'

He took the board shorts from me. 'They're fine.' He sounded like a sulky child, but like a sulky child, I knew he couldn't hold a grudge and he'd get over me hurting his feelings quickly.

I started walking towards the checkout desk.

'Where are you going?' Henley asked.

'To pay for these.'

'Don't you want to look at the women's section?'

'I'll be fine wearing the clothes I already have – they're certainly skimpy enough,' I said. 'Miss Hatfield will also probably have left some clothing I can use back in the house.'

'She had resort wear?'

'She had everything,' I said, thinking of the many chests of clothing I had glimpsed, each containing dresses and undergarments from different centuries. 'Are you ready to pay, then?'

'One second,' Henley said and steered me away from the checkout desk and towards the jewellery section, which was even more well lit than the menswear department. Light from the fixtures above us bounced off sharply cut jewels.

'What are we doing here?' I asked.

'You'll see.'

Henley walked up to a case filled with rings. Immediately, a shop attendant swooped in.

'May I help you with anything, sir?' The man wore a fitted waistcoat and talked with his hands.

'Yes, actually, you can.' Henley pointed out a ring in the case. 'Could I take a look at that one at the back?'

'Why, yes – of course you can.' The man took out his keys and unlocked the case, then withdrew a delicate-looking ring. He glanced at me. 'Is it for this lovely lady here?'

'It is,' Henley said, before I could stop him.

The man waved me closer and motioned for me to hold out my left hand.

'Slender fingers,' he observed.

Embarrassed, I started to pull my hand away, but he grasped it gently but firmly in his own.

'I think this will be a perfect fit, though.' He looked at Henley. 'Would you like to do the honours?' Henley nodded and the man handed him the ring.

Henley took my hand and slipped it onto my ring finger.

'You're right – it's a perfect fit.' But Henley was looking at me.

'What are you doing?' I whispered.

Henley didn't answer. I wasn't sure why not, but perhaps it was because of the shop assistant.

'Might I offer my congratulations?' the man said.

'Congratulations for what?' I said, without thinking.

The man waved his hands. 'On your engagement, of course!'

'Of course . . .' I muttered.

'How do you like the style of the ring?' the man asked.

The ring was just as simple as the first one Henley had given me. But instead of two small diamonds flanking a stone the colour of Henley's eyes, this one had a solitaire diamond enclosed in engraved vines.

Taking my silence to indicate dislike, the man busied himself looking through the rows of other rings. 'Don't you move an inch. I'll find you some other options.'

'Do you like it?' Henley asked me when the man disappeared.

'Yes, I do, but—'

'Then it's yours,' Henley said.

'But it's just not practical. The money—'

'Surely we can spare some for this. I don't *really* need those shorts, and I'm sure there are other things we don't *really* need.'

'It's not only the money,' I said. 'It's just not that practical. I lost the first ring you gave me when I travelled back in time to 1527 because the ring hadn't been created

225

yet. I'm eventually going to have to travel in time again, and then I'll only lose this ring, too. I can't limit myself to time periods where this ring exists. It's beautiful and I appreciate the thought, but it's simply not practical.' I slid the ring off my finger and placed it gently on the glass counter in front of us.

Henley picked it up. The ring was dwarfed by his fingers. 'You do understand, right?'

Henley didn't answer my question. 'Some day I want to buy you a ring. Call it a replacement for the one you lost.'

'Henley, I don't need a ring—'

'I *want* to give you a ring,' he said firmly. 'You might not understand why, but it's important to me. I'm a little old-fashioned like that.'

'But it's not—'

'Practical?' He set the ring back on the counter and faced me. 'What is *ever* practical? Sometimes we do things because we *want* to do them, not because they're practical at that moment.'

The man who was helping us came back before I could reply.

'I found all these lovely possibilities,' he said, setting a collection of gold and silver rings before us.

'I'm sorry. We're done here,' Henley said.

The man's mouth opened as if he was going to object.

'I'm sorry,' I repeated.

I pulled Henley away from the jewellery section. 'Let's just pay for your clothes and go.'

That night, I woke up parched. It was pitch-dark – maybe it was early morning already? I gently moved Henley's arm, which he had wrapped around me. It was so dark I couldn't see his face, but I hoped he was sleeping peacefully.

I got up slowly, trying not to shake the bed. There was a foul smell in the room. Maybe we had forgotten to close one of the windows?

I crept towards the bathroom with my arms outstretched to find the doorknob.

Then my foot sank into something wet.

I froze.

Wet. Squishy. Vaguely sticky.

'Um . . . Henley?'

Of course there was no answer – he was fast asleep.

I took another step. *Squish*.

I leapt towards the wall with the light switch. Feeling around blindly, I finally hit it and the light flickered on.

Blood.

I inhaled to scream, but my throat felt blocked.

'Rebecca?' Henley's eyes fluttered open and he sat up. 'My God – are you hurt?'

He jumped out of bed and took a couple of bounding steps towards me, but he slipped on the blood and instead came crashing down next to the body of the dead snake that had been dragged across our floor.

After I helped him up, Henley looked more closely at the snake.

'I woke up to get a glass of water and stepped on this,' I said.

Henley was silent for a few seconds. 'You know who did this, don't you?'

'The killer?'

'Who else could it be? It's a warning,' Henley said. 'And see how the snake's arranged.'

I looked down and realised that the snake's tail was in its mouth. It was an unnatural position, almost as if the snake was trying to ingest its own body.

'It's an ouroboros,' Henley said. 'The sign of eternal return. And look at what the killer's done to it.'

I wasn't sure what he meant, but I followed Henley's gaze to the snake's head. It was cut clean from its body.

'The eternal circle is broken,' Henley said.

He took the sheet off the bed and wrapped the snake's body in it. Then he did his best to mop the blood off the hardwood floors.

'Rebecca, open the window.'

I was still in shock and trembling, but I did as I was told.

Henley threw the bed sheet and the snake's body out through the window into the alley between our building and the next.

'There. It's all done. Now wash and get back to bed. Don't worry about finishing cleaning off the floor. That's something I can do.' Henley moved to comfort me, but stopped short when he realised that his hands were slick with blood, as if he had killed the snake himself.

Chapter 14

Our passports arrived on the one rainy day we had. It was ten days from when we had seen Carl. Those days were spent mostly in the hostel room, as Henley deemed it safer than walking the streets.

We heard the rain tap against our window as we got washed and dressed.

'It's summer – it's not supposed to rain this hard,' Henley said.

I was washing my face, having just got out of bed. Hearing a shuffling noise by the door, I walked out of the bathroom with my face still dripping wet.

'Henley?'

An envelope had been pushed under the door. I wiped my hands dry on my shirt before picking it up. It was a hefty envelope – thick and bulky. The flap wasn't sealed, only tucked in. I opened it above the bed and two navy-blue American passports came tumbling out.

'They're here,' Henley said. He sounded incredulous.

Thank goodness. We had already bought our plane tickets online using some of the Visa gift cards and were set to leave in three days. If the passports hadn't come in time, we would have had to pay an additional fee to change our plane tickets.

We each picked up a passport. I opened mine and my face stared back at me. I knew it was the picture Carl had taken in the cramped side street, but here it looked official with a white background somehow Photoshopped in.

'The man Carl uses is good,' Henley said. 'Really good.'

'I just hope they're as convincing as the real thing.' I tilted my passport and an official-looking stamp appeared. 'I wish there was a way of testing these – we won't know if they work until we try them at the airport.'

'On the bright side, if we get caught with fake passports, at least you could use the clock to time travel out of prison,' Henley said.

'They would probably take the clock off me, before putting me in a cell,' I pointed out.

And even if I did somehow have the clock, I'd have to leave Henley behind since his body wouldn't be able to take it, I mentally added. I shuddered to think what would happen if these passports didn't work. I took Henley's and put them both into the backpack with our other valuables.

'We should see if we can pay Aaron the remainder of the room cost ahead of time,' I said. 'We have a morning flight and need to get to the airport early. It'll be one less thing to worry about.'

Henley concurred, so we went down to the front desk. I rang the bell.

'Haven't seen you two in a while,' Aaron said. 'How have you been?'

'Well, thanks,' I said.

'So what can I help you with?'

'We'll be checking out early on Thursday morning. Any chance we can pay the balance we owe for the room now, leave one less thing for us to do that morning?'

'How early's early?'

'The flight leaves at eight-fifteen,' Henley said.

'Yikes. Now that's *is* early, given you need to get there at least three hours before. Security can be a mess – that alone could take an hour. I understand – you can pay the balance right now, if you like.'

'How much is it?' Henley asked, already taking out a couple of the Visa gift cards.

'The total comes out to five hundred and forty pounds, so subtracting the deposit, that'll be four hundred and forty pounds.' Aaron took the gift card Henley offered him and ran it through his machine. 'I see you're not using cash any more.'

'We figured it was safer,' I said when Henley couldn't come up with a response.

'Sign here, please.' Aaron passed us the electronic screen. Henley baulked.

'Just sign with your finger,' Aaron said, matter-of-factly.

Henley did as he was told and gave him his autograph. I saw a smile forming on his lips, as he watched the touch-screen work under his finger.

'Great, thanks,' Aaron said.

'We're all square, then?' Henley asked.

'Indeed we are.'

We turned away from the desk and found ourselves face to face with Alanna and Peter. I hadn't even heard them come in.

'You two must have really quiet footsteps,' Henley said. 'How long have you been standing behind us?'

'Long enough to see that you're checking out.' Alanna pouted. 'When are you leaving?'

'Thursday,' Henley said.

'Well, at least it's not today,' she said. She glanced at Peter. 'I'm glad you told us. We really must take you out to dinner before you leave.'

'Oh, you don't have to do that,' I said. 'You've done so much already.'

'Nonsense!'

'We insist,' Peter said. 'Really, you'll be saving me from listening to Alanna going on and on for ever about wanting to have dinner with you guys before you leave.'

Alanna stuck out her bottom lip. 'Yes, I will. So when are you free. Tonight? The night before you go?'

'Why don't we do dinner tonight?' *The sooner, the better*, I thought. I looked at Henley for confirmation. He nodded.

'Should we meet you here in the lobby?' Henley asked.

'Why don't you meet us at the restaurant? At six, maybe?' Alanna said. 'It's called Bezels. Funny name, isn't it? It's right on the corner next to the grocery store if you know where that is.'

'Sure. We'll see you there,' Henley said.

We spent a bit of our morning folding what little clothing we had, and preparing to bundle everything into the backpack at a moment's notice. We double-checked our inventory and made sure we had cut the tags from Henley's new shorts and swimming trunks. Still finding we had a lot of time left before dinner, we decided to spend the day touring the city, as we didn't have much time left in London.

We saw a little bit: Trafalgar Square, St Paul's Cathedral, the London Eye. The touristy parts, of course. But both Henley and I were too antsy to enjoy it. We'd been all set to leave for a while now, especially after that horrifying incident with the dead snake. Everything was happening too slowly.

That evening, Henley and I entered Bezels to see Alanna and Peter sitting at the back of an empty restaurant. Alanna waved us over.

'I would have thought it'd be packed by six,' I said as we took our seats across from them. 'Isn't it prime dinner time?'

'Oh, just you wait. In the next thirty minutes, I guarantee you it'll fill up,' Alanna said.

'Aaron told us about this place,' Peter said. 'I think it was one of the first restaurants in London that we tried. He specifically told us to make a reservation before six-thirty.'

'I'm sure between you two and Aaron, you know all the best restaurants in the city by now,' Henley said.

'We'd like to think we've tried all the awful ones, too, and weeded them out before letting our friends eat at them.' Alanna unfolded her napkin and set it in her lap. 'Let's get a bread basket.'

Peter motioned over our heads to summon our waiter.

'How may I help you?'

'Could we get a bread basket, please?'

Our waiter clasped his hands. 'Certainly. Could I take everyone's drink orders as well?'

Before I could even glance at the menu in front of Alanna and Peter, Alanna ordered for all of us.

'Let's start with four Pimm's, please.'

I didn't know what exactly that was, but I guessed I could try it.

'Would you like water as well?'

'No, thank you.' When our waiter turned to go, she said, 'Water is for the weak.'

'I believe Alanna's trying to get you tipsy,' Peter said to me. 'I think she wants to see it in person after hearing about it from Henley.'

'Tipsy? I'm trying to get her drunk,' Alanna said. 'This is our last meal together – it should be fun and memorable!'

I smiled nervously. I thought she was only joking but it was hard to tell.

'I do hope you both enjoyed your time in London, though,' Alanna said.

'We did,' I said. 'Lots to see . . . It's hard to pinpoint why, exactly, but it's a type of city you don't find in the States.'

'I get that,' Peter said. 'Having a long history, maybe?'

'No, I think it's something more,' Alanna said.

Our bread basket arrived with a dish of olive oil, and I took a moment to unfold my napkin.

'What do you think it is?' I asked her.

'A certain type of aura – if you will – that the people carry around with them. Different people have different ways of walking. Different motivations. Different ways of living.' Alanna took a piece of bread and skipped the olive oil altogether. 'Look at Aaron, for instance. He's satisfied with the hostel and himself. He takes sure steps. He isn't waiting to make something of himself.' She took a bite. 'I like to think it's different here. Special.'

'We all see things the way we want to perceive them,' Peter said.

I wasn't expecting anything that wise from someone who was currently swirling his piece of bread around the dish to make sure it soaked up the maximum amount of olive oil possible.

'We'll sure miss this city when we leave,' he said.

'Have you decided on a date?' I asked.

'We don't do that,' Alanna said. 'We typically move on when it feels like we've learned enough from one place. That's a distinct type of feeling – you just *know*.'

'We're almost done with our time here, just like you guys are,' Peter said. 'Then Alanna will probably be taking new photos of food in a different city and I'll trail along, just like always.'

'We're thinking of Prague next. I've always wanted to go . . . Or maybe somewhere in Switzerland.'

The waiter brought us our drinks.

Henley took the first sip. 'That sounds like an adventure.'

'I don't suppose you'd like to join us?' Alanna said. 'We'd love the company if you have the time.'

I shook my head. That was the one thing we didn't have. 'We've got to get going, unfortunately.'

'Back home to everyday life?'

Sure, if you can call running from a killer 'everyday life'.

The dinner went smoothly. The portions were big, so Alanna and Peter shared a quinoa bowl while Henley and I shared a steak. The food was good and my second Pimm's was giving me a flush. It tasted exactly how I imagined summer would. It was fruity, refreshing . . . and had that extra something that alcohol seems to give drinks. I decided I liked it almost as much as I liked apple martinis.

'Whenever you're ready,' the waiter said, placing the bill in the middle of the table.

Both Henley and Alanna dived for it. Henley's hand got there first, but Alanna batted it away.

'B-but you've paid for so many meals,' Henley said.

'I've paid for one,' Alanna corrected. 'And you can let me have this one with a clear conscience because I'm paying with my parents' money, not mine.'

Henley reluctantly gave up trying to claw the bill back to our side of the table.

'Fine . . . and thank you.'

The waiter came over and swiped Alanna's credit card through the machine. After a few beeps, two copies of the receipt came out, one of which Alanna signed and returned to the waiter.

'There is something you could do in return.' Alanna's lips curled into a smile. 'You could give us your home address so we know where to mail the invitation.'

'The wedding invitation?' I asked.

'Of course, silly. What else would I be inviting you to?' Alanna took the customer copy of the receipt, flipped it over and handed it to us with the pen.

I hesitated for a moment before writing down Miss Hatfield's address. I didn't want to imagine Alanna's face when we failed to respond to the wedding invitation. I hoped she would forget about us and not be too disappointed. I handed Alanna the receipt.

She pocketed it happily when she stood up. 'Shall we go?'

Our walk back was full of a comfortable silence. It wasn't too cold outside, just a chilly breeze to persuade us to walk faster. Henley held my hand, and it swung with his while we walked together. I noticed Peter matched Alanna's shorter strides just as Henley did mine so our steps were in sync.

We paused in the lobby of the hostel, wondering if we were going to part ways there, but we remembered our rooms were in the same section of the hostel and walked down the hall together until we got to our room.

'Well . . . This is us,' Henley said.

We stopped, but neither Henley nor I moved to get our key. Alanna and Peter didn't continue down the hall, either.

'If we don't happen to see you in the next couple of days, we really enjoyed meeting you and spending time with you,' I said.

Alanna took my hand. 'This isn't goodbye. We'll definitely meet up again . . . Just on a different continent.'

I tried to look like I believed her. 'Of course we will.'

'And you'll be there for the wedding,' she said, as if she could make it come true by sheer determination.

'You'll look beautiful on your big day,' I said as Henley unlocked the door and went in.

'They're such a nice couple. I can't wait to see them again,' I heard Alanna say, before closing the door behind me.

Chapter 15

It was Thursday at last.

I shot up too quickly and held my head, waiting for the rush to pass.

Aaron had agreed to knock on our door at four, just to make sure we were up in time for our flight. He hadn't knocked yet . . . Or at least I didn't think he had.

I gently shook Henley awake. 'It's time to get up. Aaron hasn't knocked yet, has he?'

'Not that I'm aware of.' Henley stretched both arms above his head as a knock sounded on our door.

'That'll be it,' I said. Louder, so Aaron could hear, I said, 'Thanks!'

Henley sat up. 'So we're really doing this?'

'Yes, today's airport day.'

I headed to the bathroom to start my morning routine, beginning with washing my face. Henley got dressed in the meantime.

'So, your first airport and your first flight,' I said as we switched locations.

'There's a first time for everything.' Henley's voice echoed in the bathroom. 'Any tips?'

'Not really . . . Just make sure not to get in anyone's way.'

'Sounds like a tip for life in general.'

We had time for a quick bite, so went to the Costa down the street and bought two sandwiches.

I handed Henley one as he came out of the bathroom.

'Nothing like a home-cooked meal,' he joked, taking it.

'If you don't want it, I'll eat both.'

He wolfed down his sandwich, finishing it just as I took my first bite.

'Hungry?'

'With this food? Always.'

'This makes aeroplane food look good,' I said.

'Aeroplanes serve food?'

'Or at least they claim to . . .' I said.

Henley didn't understand my joke and that made me giggle.

After finishing my sandwich and running my fingers over the corners of my mouth to make sure I hadn't smeared mayo all over my face, I grabbed the backpack. We'd put everything into it the night before and even wrapped the clock in clothing to ensure it didn't get bumped around.

Henley already had the door open.

Down in the lobby, Aaron smiled as we walked in and pulled out two brown paper bags from behind the desk. 'I took the liberty of fixing you a small lunch. Sandwiches. No meat, since I didn't know if you were vegetarians. Hope that's all right. No one's gluten free, are they?'

'That's wonderful! Thank you.' I couldn't complain about having sandwiches twice in one day. Food was food. I took the bags and tucked them into the backpack, on top of our other stuff so the sandwiches wouldn't be crushed.

'I believe everything's settled?' Henley checked.

'It is. Would you like me to find you a cab?'

'That would be great.'

Aaron headed outside and we sat down on the two chairs on either side of the door to wait.

'It's strange that I'm nervous, isn't it?' Henley said. 'Who gets nervous about something that apparently everyone does nowadays?'

'It's a new experience for you, though. It's normal to get a little jittery right before.'

'The airport I'm fine with,' he said. 'It's the hurtling through the air thousands of feet above the ground that I'm not too keen on.'

That made sense. I remembered trying not to think about that on my first flight.

A few minutes later, Aaron popped his head round the door. 'The cab's here.'

We grabbed the backpack and followed him out.

'Thank you, Aaron!' I said as I slid in after Henley.

'Have a safe flight!'

I sat across from Henley – I liked that you could do that in these taxis – and placed the backpack between our feet. Black cabs were so roomy compared with New York's yellow cabs.

'Heathrow, please,' I said.

As we pulled away from the kerb, I waved at Aaron. He was standing on the front step of the hostel building and waved back until he was out of sight.

Henley and I spent the taxi ride to the airport staring out of the window. The London Eye, Big Ben, Buckingham Palace – we saw all the touristy sights one last time. I should've been used to it by then, but it was still so strange to watch regular people going about their lives without a single visible worry, while I was hiding a secret from the world and trying to stay alive. It made everything else feel so trivial.

We drove away from all the people and got on a road that looked like a freeway. I watched the cars go by. Soon after that I started seeing signs for the airport.

'What terminal are we heading to?' our cab driver asked.

'Terminal three.'

'And what airline?'

I checked the tickets we had printed out at the library. 'Virgin Atlantic.'

Twenty minutes later, I felt the car slowing down.

We pulled up next to a sign that said 'Terminal 3' in bright yellow.

'Here we are,' the cab driver said.

'Thank you,' I said, handing the taxi driver a Visa gift card.

Henley and I watched him fumble with it before he swiped it slowly through his credit card machine. We held our breath.

Beep.

It didn't sound like a negative beep, if there was such a thing, and the driver didn't look peeved – in fact, his expression really hadn't changed for the entire journey. The cards had worked before, but every time I was still surprised when the transaction went through.

The driver handed us back the card. 'Thank you very much.'

Henley and I climbed out of the cab onto the bustling pavement in front of the airport terminal.

'My goodness, it looks as if everyone's here,' Henley said.

'Wait till you see inside,' I said, dragging him through the doors.

Henley wanted to stop and watch the automatic doors, but I didn't let him. We had things to do.

'My God . . .' Henley openly gawked at the number of people inside, all walking fast, rolling their suitcases behind them. 'So many people . . .'

I steered Henley into the correct check-in line. He played with the retractable rope set up next to us to help corral the crowd.

'Next, please!'

There were seven people working the nine or so ticketing desks. They were calling people from the line rather efficiently and we found ourselves moving forwards a few steps every couple of minutes.

'So . . . what are we in line for, again?' Henley stopped playing with the retractable rope and faced me.

'This is the ticketing section,' I whispered, having no other name to call it. 'It's where we check in. We'll ask if the flight's on time, since that's what most people do . . .'

Henley took this information seriously. I could tell he was trying to remember every twenty-first-century fact I told him.

'Next in line!' A woman wearing a red blazer was waving at us to approach . . . or maybe it was to hurry up.

'That's us,' I said and pulled Henley up to the desk.

'How can I help you today?' When she smiled, I noticed a smear of her pink lipstick on her top front tooth. Oddly, that reminded me of the first woman who had ever checked me in at an airport. I'd bought a last-minute ticket to Madrid from her that connected in Heathrow. That was the beginning of me being stuck in England.

'We'd like to check in, please,' I said.

Henley dug through the backpack for the print-outs of our tickets.

'Do you need these?' he said.

'I do.' I took the papers and handed them to the woman.

'Oh, good. You've already printed out your tickets. How smart of you – it's always faster that way. Any bags to check?' That must have been a routine question as she could see we only had the backpack with us.

'No.'

'Just carrying on that backpack, then?'

'Yes.'

She gave us a paper tag on an elastic band with instructions to write our address on it before tying it to the backpack.

'Is the flight still on time?' I had heard people asking this frequently.

'As of right now, nothing's changed. Gate twenty-three and the flight is still at eight-fifteen.' The woman smiled again and I saw a little more lipstick smeared on her teeth.

'Perfect,' I said.

'Is there anything else I can help you with today?'

I wondered if I should mention the lipstick on her teeth? *Better not. It's not my place.*

'No, that's it, thanks.'

'Security is over to your left.' The woman pointed. 'Have a pleasant flight.'

Henley and I walked in the direction she had indicated and joined the mob of people already waiting in line for security.

'Do exactly as the airport security officers tell you and you'll be fine,' I whispered.

'Who are they?'

'Those people in uniform,' I said.

A baby wailed as his mother tried to juggle him and the laptop she was putting into a tray.

'Why does this take so long?' Henley asked.

I pointed to a plastic sign with pictures of everything prohibited on flights. 'People have to take out their electronics, throw away their water and take off their shoes.'

'All for security's sake?'

'To make sure none of us are carrying explosives.' I made sure to whisper, so security wouldn't overhear me mentioning the word explosives. Thankfully we weren't so up near the front of the line that security would see us suspiciously whispering. 'And keep your voice down so they don't think we're terrorists.'

Henley solemnly nodded, but his attention was already elsewhere. He was watching the man in front of us intently. 'Shoes,' he whispered to himself as the man removed his. 'Into the bins.' The man placed his leather loafers into one of the grey trays he had already pulled out and put on the conveyor belt. 'Machine.'

A security guard signalled the man forward. He walked into the full-body scanner and raised his arms while the scanner spun around him.

When our turn came, Henley was already removing his shoes before I had to remind him. Off to a good start, then. I put the backpack on the conveyer belt. For the first time, I was glad of its obnoxious neon-green colour; there was no way anyone in their right mind would mistake it for theirs. I slipped off my shoes and placed them in another bin.

Henley had already put the boarding passes and the passports in a bin. He sent it through the scanner.

The security guard on the other side of the scanner motioned for one of us to enter.

'Do you want me to go first?' I asked Henley quickly.

He nodded.

I walked in and made a show of purposefully placing my feet on the coloured footprints stencilled onto the floor of the machine. I hoped Henley caught that. I raised both arms and froze while the scanner whirled around me.

'You're good,' the officer called.

He waved me on.

I stood by the conveyor belt intending to collect our stuff, but I was distracted by watching Henley walk into the machine. He put his feet on the coloured footprints. Good. He raised his arms and didn't move. Very good. He even stayed in that position for a second longer than he needed to after the scanner stopped.

'You're good to go, sir,' the officer called.

Henley walked past him and collected the boarding passes and passports. Then he joined me by the conveyor belt and collected his shoes.

'Why don't we sit on that bench over there while we put these on?' I pointed to a seating area in a corner near some elevators. Henley nodded and padded after me in socked feet.

'How did I do?' he asked before sitting down.

I joined him on the bench to slip on my shoes. 'Wonderfully. It couldn't have gone better.'

'Really? Maybe this flying business isn't too bad after all.' Shoes on feet, Henley stood up. 'I'm ready for the next step.'

I couldn't help but smile at his eagerness as I checked our boarding passes. 'We're gate twenty-three. I'm pretty sure that's not too far from here, and we still have a good hour.' I started walking.

On our way to the gate, we stopped by a currency exchange booth and managed to change from pounds to dollars without issue. There was a chance we might need the cash as soon as we arrived in New York.

Henley looked at the seats by the gates as we passed them. 'So do we sit by our gate and just wait now?'

'That's usually what happens.' Here I was, telling Henley what was 'usual' at airports even though I had only flown once before. That's usually what happened in the movies, though.

Henley spotted our destination first. 'Gate twenty-three. That's us, right?'

There was already a long line of people in front of the closed door that led to the plane. No one was moving, so I saw no sense in standing with them. They were probably all First Class and Business Class, anyway. Although the sitting area was getting crowded, we found two seats together towards the back, next to a nursing mother.

'I hope you don't mind,' she said as we sat down.

'Oh, no problem,' I said.

'I figured nursing Alex would be preferable to him having a screaming fit in the middle of the terminal.'

Henley crossed his legs and started to jiggle his foot. At first I thought he had some issue with the nursing mother, but then I saw that his eyes were unfocused and aimed lazily at the floor twenty feet in front of him. He was simply bored.

'You want to do something to pass the time?' I guessed.

'Yes – that would be nice.'

'Why don't you walk around the terminal and do a bit of window-shopping, then?'

Henley looked as if I had announced that animals could talk. 'They have shops in *airports*?' He was standing already.

'Yes, they do. You can even flip through the magazines in that small kiosk over there.' I pointed to the compact set-up across the walkway. 'But stay close to the gate – we don't have *that* much time left till we board. And be sure to use the restroom before we do.' I suddenly felt as if I was talking to a child or someone fifty years my senior.

He smirked at my babying him, but seemed too excited by the thought of airport shops to care. 'Yes, ma'am,' he said. And he was off.

The woman next to me had probably listened to the entire conversation, though she politely pretended she hadn't heard a thing. She must have thought we were a strange couple indeed.

I watched Henley walk over to the magazine stand, where he stared long and hard at the rows of bestselling books on the shelves. Knowing him, I knew he'd love the colourful covers almost as much as the words the books contained.

After a while, he moved on to the magazines in a spinning carousel and picked one up. From where I was sitting, I couldn't tell what he was looking at, but I hoped it was a motoring magazine. Henley would love to see how the cars of this time compared to the automobiles of his era. Or maybe it was a magazine like *National Geographic* where he would see full-page-spread photos of national parks and landscapes he was familiar with. Whatever the magazine was, Henley took his time flipping through it before finding an article he liked, and then spent several minutes studying one page. Maybe it was a humorous article, because his lips twitched as if he was trying to keep from laughing.

Watching Henley was the most wonderful thing, especially when he thought no one was noticing him. He was genuine. Maybe a bit naïve compared to the people of this time . . . but so was I.

He put the magazine down and spent some time turning the carousel. He was probably marvelling at how smoothly it moved. He even leaned down to look at the gears and wheels on the bottom. After briefly scanning the other magazines, he moved to the next kiosk. It looked like an airport gift shop selling teddy bears, no doubt wearing some sort of London-themed shirt; boxes of chocolates, probably with Big Ben on the lid; and of course the most obligatory tourist gift of them all – T-shirts emblazoned with the word 'London' in every type of script imaginable. I wondered what Henley thought of them, as he stood and gazed at the rack of T-shirts for far longer than I would have expected.

Eventually he moved on and out of sight, presumably to check out the stores further along the hallway. I sat for a while and studied the other people near me at the gate. They all looked busy, glued to the tiny screens of their phones and tablets. It wasn't that interesting to watch. I figured I would use the restroom while I waited and asked the woman next to me if she would mind saving our seats since I'd be taking the backpack with me. When I returned, she was still rocking her baby in her arms and murmuring to him.

'Thanks. Hope it wasn't too much trouble.'

'Not at all.'

I noticed our flight had started boarding. But it was still rows one through twenty. I looked at our tickets. We were row twenty-four. I noticed Henley walking towards the gate, presumably having heard the boarding announcement.

'We're going on soon?' he asked. 'Should we get in line?'

'Since it's almost our turn, why not?'

We stood to one side so people who were boarding first could still get past us.

'We are now boarding rows twenty-one through forty,' a voice on the intercom said.

'That's us.' I pushed Henley forward.

There was a clamour as most of the people waiting at the gate stood up and moved into line. A few inserted themselves ahead of us so we had to wait a little longer. They seemed to be hoping for room for their bags. Thankfully, that wasn't going to be a problem for us.

Henley was chewing on his lip as we approached the gate. 'This is where they check our passports again?'

I nodded and pointed out the airline staff scanning the passengers' boarding passes and checking passports.

Henley let out a long breath. He wasn't the only one who was nervous. There was a tightness in my stomach I couldn't easily breathe through.

Finally, our turn came and I went first. I handed the woman my passport and boarding pass. I watched her compare my face to my photo. She slapped the boarding pass onto the scanner. The light went off. It beeped. I was all good. She handed everything back to me.

I waited to the side for Henley. He was trying to look casual but I could tell he was holding his breath as the woman looked at his passport.

'Have a safe flight,' she said, returning his passport and boarding pass.

'Th-thank you.'

Henley's eyes were wide as he joined me. I started walking down the covered ramp before he could say anything incriminating in earshot of the attendant who had just boarded us. I was glad I'd taken that precaution when he spoke.

'I can't believe that worked.'

'Flight attendants, please prepare for take-off.'

I had spent the last five minutes watching Henley peer at the video demonstrating the plane's safety features that played on the little screen in front of him. Henley must have been the only passenger aboard who had pulled out the safety card in front of him and diligently followed along, just as the flight attendants in the video had requested.

As the engine whirred to life, I looked down to see Henley's hand gripping the armrest between us. He had an aisle seat and was gripping the armrest on that side as well. When we started moving, Henley unglued his eyes from the headrest in front of him to glance momentarily out of the window. Then the plane stopped and Henley tapped my hand.

'Is that supposed to happen?'

'We're just getting into position,' I said. 'We'll start moving a lot faster down the runway soon.'

Just as I said that, we heard the squeal of machinery shifting into place and the engine noise grew louder.

'This is it?' Henley looked at me.

I nodded and placed my hand on top of his as the plane started heading down the runway.

I hated planes. I hated taking off and landing most of all. But because I had a white-knuckled Henley next to me, I put on a smile as if I were an aeroplane pro and knew exactly what was happening. Thankfully, Henley calmed down once the plane reached cruising altitude and levelled out.

'You don't even realise you're flying once you're up here,' he said, craning his neck to see out of the window on the other side of me.

There was a woman on my right who had fallen asleep as soon as the plane started to move. She had a pink sleeping mask pulled over her eyes and I was glad she couldn't see Henley staring in her direction. I handed Henley his sandwich from the backpack so he could eat it whenever he got hungry. He put the paper bag in the pouch attached to the back of the seat in front of him and promptly fell asleep.

I took out the in-flight magazines from the seat pocket in front of me. The first one I looked at was a lifestyle magazine, detailing fitness tips, healthy eating habits and street style as seen on the current celebrities. It didn't hold my attention for long and I soon moved on to the other magazine. This one was a catalogue of the strangest things, all of which one could buy while aboard a plane. I could have a heated dog waterbed delivered to my house. I could get a wine cork carved into the shape of a friend's head. I could even buy an apron that lit up in the dark. *Whose job is it to sit around and think of these things? Who cooks in the dark?* I must have spent hours poring through the contents of that magazine. I read every description and studied every picture. It was all very curious.

I fell asleep with the magazine still in my lap. When I woke, I didn't know how long I'd been out for. I noticed that Henley had eaten his sandwich but was asleep again now, this time with his mouth slightly open. We hadn't exactly been on vacation, after all. I didn't blame Henley for being tired. I ate my sandwich and asked for a cup of water from the cart that came round. I got another for Henley and then fell back asleep.

The second time I woke, Henley's cup was empty. I peeked over to my left; sure enough, he was asleep again. It was as if we were sleeping in shifts.

Not having anything else to do, I opened the backpack, which I had stored underneath the seat in front of me. I pulled out the box with the phone in it. The man at the store had already set it up for us, but maybe I could learn how to use it? Perhaps it had some special features I didn't know about yet that might be useful when we landed.

'What do you think you're doing?'

It was the woman next to me. She'd obviously just woken up because her sleeping mask was pushed up onto her forehead and her curls were sticking out from the elastic band behind her head like little horns. She was looking straight at me with an angry expression on her sleep-creased face.

'Um . . . excuse me?'

'What. Are you. Doing. With that phone?'

'Uh, I just wanted to learn how to use it,' I said. I wished I could run, but we were stuck in our seats.

'You weren't thinking of calling anyone, were you?'

'Uh—'

'Do you want to kill us all?' She grimaced. 'You *do* realise that you can't call anyone from here because you'll cause the plane to go down?'

'Um . . . yes?' I had no idea what she was going on about and just wanted her to stop talking.

'You'd better not . . .' With that, the woman pulled her eye mask down as if she couldn't bear to look at me for another second and turned her back to me.

How could something as small as this simple phone affect something as big as the plane we were on? I didn't understand, but I put the phone away just in case.

I spent the rest of the seven-and-a-half-hour flight sleeping and reflipping through the magazines in turn.

When we landed, it was still light outside and that confused me for a moment.

'Ladies and gentlemen, the local time here in New York is 11:50 am. In just a few moments, the fasten-seatbelt sign will turn off and we will start disembarking. Until then, please remain seated with your seatbelt fastened. I hope you have a great day, whether New York is just a stop or your final destination. On behalf of the entire crew, thank you for choosing Virgin Atlantic. We look forward to seeing you again on your next trip.'

Henley had woken during our descent and laid his hand on mine.

I turned to him. 'Congratulations. You just survived your first flight.'

When the seatbelt sign was turned off, everyone immediately stood, even the passengers with the window seats who couldn't possibly get off the plane right away or even reach their luggage. I made sure the backpack was in my hands as we lined up in the aisle.

'Careful, Henley.' I pulled him out of the way of a man trying to lower his suitcase from the overhead bin.

'Let me help you with that,' Henley said.

It made me smile; that was so like him to offer a stranger assistance simply because he saw he was needed.

The line started to move but I was impatient. It wasn't moving quickly enough.

It took us ten minutes to get to the front of the plane. 'Thank you for flying with us!' a flight attendant said.

'You're welcome!' Henley responded.

I pulled him along towards immigration. Luckily the line wasn't too long, and the man behind the counter didn't ask us too many questions besides the address we were staying at in the US and the location and length of time we had stayed in the UK.

With immigration behind us, next I pulled Henley towards baggage claim. Although we didn't have bags to pick up, the exit was in that direction. Everyone was heading that way and I wanted to beat the rush to get a taxi.

The blazing New York summer heat hit us as soon as we walked out through the doors.

'Now this is something I didn't miss,' Henley said.

'From your time, or from the last time I was here?'

'The last time you were here, I had no body and didn't have to feel all this.' Henley waved his arm around in the air.

The air was heavy with humidity. I had forgotten what summer in New York felt like.

Just then, I saw a yellow cab heading towards us. I stepped to the kerb and put my hand up. I thought the driver saw me but he drove past. No matter, another taxi was coming. When he was close, I put my hand up again. This time I waved it around a bit to ensure I got the driver's attention. But he passed me, too.

What's wrong with these drivers?

I turned to ask Henley for help but he was nowhere to be found.

'Rebecca!'

I looked towards the voice. There was Henley, standing in a roped-off section of the sidewalk.

'The cabs are here – are you coming?'

By the time I jogged over, Henley was already near the front of the taxi line.

'Excuse me,' I said, passing a handful of people behind Henley. 'I'm not cutting in – I'm just joining my . . . boyfriend.'

'Took you long enough.' Henley smirked. 'Admit it – there are some things I'm still better at, even in times you're more familiar with.'

Two taxis pulled up to the kerb. The family of four in front of us took the first and we took the second. I gave him Miss Hatfield's address.

'Yes, yes,' he said.

I thought he'd heard and understood me, but I couldn't be certain.

As we left the airport, our driver asked, 'So is it your first time here?'

'No,' I said. 'It's been a while, though.'

'You've both been to New York before?'

'I was here a *long* time ago,' Henley said.

I couldn't tell if he looked sad because he was facing away from me, staring out of the window on his side.

'I bet a lot has changed,' the driver said. 'The city keeps changing. That's what makes New York the greatest city in the world.'

'"The more things change, the more they stay the same" – or at least, that's what they say, right?' Henley said, still looking out through the window.

It hadn't even occurred to me that this quick trip into Manhattan might be difficult for him, being his first time back since he'd lived here more than a century ago.

'I'm a New Yorker born and bred,' the driver said, taking one hand off the wheel to gesture wildly with it. 'My parents, too. And their parents. My grandpop used to sit me on his lap and tell me about the time when carriages filled the city. Can you imagine? Carriages. Horse-drawn carriages.'

Henley was looking up at the skyscrapers, ducking his head so he could see the tops of the buildings. 'No, I can't even begin to imagine . . .'

When we got to Miss Hatfield's brownstone, I waited for the driver to pull away before taking Henley's hand and dragging him past the front entrance.

'Why aren't we going in?'

'We will,' I said, 'but we have to get the spare key first – my copy didn't survive travelling to Tudor England.'

Miss Hatfield's brownstone wasn't on the corner of the street, but the house next to it was. Around the block to the side of the neighbour's house were four miniature trees in green pots.

'Let me see if I remember correctly . . .'

I walked up to the second pot and dug my fingers into the dry soil behind the plant. I didn't feel anything. I panicked for a moment, wondering if I'd chosen the wrong pot. I was just about to give up and try the other pots before suggesting breaking into the house somehow when my fingers felt cold metal.

'Here we go.' I retrieved the small key and brushed it free of dirt. 'Just like Miss Hatfield to hide keys in potted plants that aren't even hers.'

Henley tried to keep his face emotionless at the mention of his mother but there was tension behind his guarded expression. I wanted to say something comforting. Anything to make him feel better. But I didn't know what to say. What could you say to someone who never really knew their mother, but disliked her in every way because he hated what she stood for? I couldn't find the words and remained silent.

Back at the front of the house, the key turned with a familiar *click* and I pushed the door open. It was dark inside as we stepped over the large pile of mail that had collected on the floor. It was also a little dusty, but it had always been that way. Miss Hatfield kept dust covers over the furniture which wasn't used every day.

As I walked down the hallway, I almost forgot that Henley was following a few paces behind me. 'So what do you think?' I asked, as he hadn't said anything since entering.

'I'm not sure what to think.'

At least he was honest.

'I hadn't really thought about where my mother lived, but I guess I imagined it a bit differently,' he admitted.

'But it's not as if you haven't seen the place before. Granted, you weren't in a body, but—'

'It's different,' he said, and left it at that.

We entered the kitchen. It had always been my favourite room, despite all the horrible things that had happened there. Miss Hatfield slipped the water from the Fountain of Youth into my lemonade there. The fifth Miss Hatfield had supposedly killed herself there in front of my Miss Hatfield. But it was still the most homely part of this house – the most *normal*. Many things change when one becomes immortal, but the need to eat remains. It's universal and it's *normal*. Miss Hatfield had even occasionally baked here.

I flipped the light switch so we could see better but the lights didn't go on. I tried again before realising the electricity bills hadn't been paid in God knew how long. *At least we'll be out of here soon.* 'I just need to find the credit card Miss Hatfield had kept.'

'Are you sure there's even a credit card here?' Henley said. He was surveying the room, but of course he wouldn't know where to look.

I ran to Miss Hatfield's desk. It was a mess of spilled papers all coated with a thick layer of dust. I rummaged through it as best as I could. Not finding anything that resembled a credit card, I started looking through her drawers.

There. At the back. I grabbed the credit card. *Rebecca Hatfield*, it read. That was the upside of having the same name.

'Henley! I found it.'

Chapter 16

I woke up when Henley wrapped his arms around me and hugged me close from his side of the bed. It was dark in my bedroom because we had lowered all the thick blinds before going to bed, but I was sure it was already morning.

Henley's touch still made my breath catch. I hoped he didn't notice – he would only make some joke about it. Although I knew Henley well in so many ways – his thoughts, his words, his entire mind, really – his touch was still foreign. In the dark, if I tried really hard, I could almost make myself believe this was the same Henley I had known all those years ago in 1904, with his blue eyes and dark hair that flopped into them sometimes. In the dark, it was real. I could make it real with my imagination.

'Henley . . .'

'I'm sorry. Did I wake you?' he asked.

I assured him he hadn't.

'Was it that nightmare again?' He was referring to the dream I'd had once before of Miss Hatfield dying.

I nodded, but I didn't know if he could see it.

I turned to face him in the dark and ran my fingers through his hair.

'I wish I could stop them,' he said.

'I know.' I placed my hands on top of his, feeling how much larger they were than mine.

He gave my hands a squeeze. 'On the bright side, at least it's morning already. You're supposed to be up anyway. It's time for us to get going soon enough.' He let go of my hand and rolled away from me.

I sat up in the dark. 'Can you even see where you're going? You don't know the house well.'

'I think I'll manage. Don't worry about me.'

But I did worry about him. Henley had changed, whether he knew it or not, since the days when he had been ignorant of immortality in his own time at the turn of the twentieth century. New York had also changed in his absence and he was bound to notice when he saw more of the city.

'Let me open the blinds,' he said, moving towards the window. A flurry of dust arose as he did so. As I suspected, it was already bright outside and sunlight streamed in, momentarily blinding us. 'The first sunlight of the day is always dazzling, isn't it?' I said.

'Always . . . I'm just going to grab a glass of water,' Henley said.

I listened as his footsteps pattered away before I remembered there'd be no running water in the house. Henley would notice quick enough.

'Rebecca!' Henley's voice sounded urgent, but not like it was calling me to come to him. It sounded like a warning.

I shot up out of bed just as Henley burst through the bedroom door.

'He's found us.'

'The killer?' I asked, scanning his face.

Worry lines were carved into his face and his eyes were dark.

'Juana. Whoever it is. They've found us.'

It felt like I was punched in the stomach. I walked past him and headed to the kitchen. I didn't know what I would find.

In the middle of the room, a dead bird lay in a pool of its own blood. It was a large bird, almost the size of a small child, but its feathers were so matted that I couldn't tell what breed it was until I got closer.

'A peacock.'

'Its head has been severed, just like the snake's,' Henley said.

'What do you think it means?' I asked.

'The peacock's often used as a symbol for eternal life,' Henley said.

'Eternal life cut short,' I said, remembering what he'd said about the snake in the hostel room.

'I'll take care of this.' Henley gently ushered me out of the kitchen and I stumbled back to the bedroom, where I sat on the edge of the bed until he joined me.

'We have things to do today,' he said.

I assumed he meant buying plane tickets to Florida and reserving the hotel.

'There are things *I* would like to do. *Need* to do.' Henley's lips were in a grim line.

'What things?'

'I'd like to go to the cemetery. I'd like to see my home – my *former* home.'

'Do you really need to?'

I didn't know what seeing those places would do to him. This was different from meeting descendants with whom you shared a last name but didn't actually know. Henley would see that it wasn't *his* home any more. He would feel as if he didn't have a place to call home. As if the world had forgotten him. I didn't want to see him get hurt.

'Yes.'

I stood up slowly. 'Well, then . . .'

I found a clean pair of jeans and a comfortable sweat-shirt in my closet, untouched for ages. I put them on, sorry

I didn't have any clean men's clothing for Henley to change into.

Henley dealt with the peacock somehow. He didn't tell me what he did with the carcass, nor did I want to know.

I had a bit of time while Henley dressed to throw out the spoiled food in the fridge, which had all but rotted to a paste, covering the shelves, during the three years since I'd last been in the house. Luckily, the rotten food had dried out, minimising the smell. I also made sure the pantry had enough non-perishable food to sustain us for a day or two.

Henley met me downstairs with the backpack slung over one shoulder. We didn't talk about the peacock. He didn't ask me if I was ready to go, just looked at me expectantly. I didn't say anything, either. We simply left the house and started walking.

I knew the way from Miss Hatfield's house to the cemetery by heart. It was a half-hour walk, but it passed quickly. I struggled to keep up with Henley's pace. I knew we were getting closer when we passed St Patrick's Cathedral and the mob of tourists always milling around outside it. I didn't know what Henley was hoping to get out of this visit, but I would do my best to support him.

'Where is it?' Henley asked as we stepped through the gate.

Wordlessly, I led him down the lone path. I didn't have to count the rows of headstones to know where to turn. My legs remembered. Soon we were standing silently in front of an all-too-familiar grave. Henley drew a shaky breath, but he wasn't looking at the grave before me. He was staring silently at the one next to it.

Eliza P. Beauford, Loving Wife & Daughter.

I remembered the last time I'd visited this cemetery. Gazing at Henley's gravestone, I had realised I knew next to nothing about this man I had fallen in love with. All I had was his name etched into the tombstone – *Henley A. Beauford* – and I didn't even know what the 'A' stood for then. But now I knew. *Ainsley.* A little old-fashioned – to be expected – but a good middle name nonetheless.

'I had to pay my respects,' Henley said suddenly. 'You understand.'

'Of course,' I said, carefully positioning myself in front of his grave to block it from his sight.

'W-what are you . . .' Henley tailed off at the sight of his own grave.

I didn't want him to look at it. I had no idea what it would do to him or if he was even ready to see it. If anyone could ever be ready to see their own grave.

Finally, I couldn't stand the silence any more. 'Say something.'

'What is there to say?' He nudged me aside to get a better look at the tombstone.

A few more minutes passed in silence.

'So that's what they chose to put on my tombstone?' he said. '*Innovative Businessman & Loving Husband?*'

That might have been a funny moment had we not been standing in front of a grave and talking about Henley dying.

'I wonder who chose the words,' Henley said. 'Eliza wasn't there any more, and it's not as if we had any children to take on the burden of making the arrangements . . . It was probably a business acquaintance, maybe helped by some of the household staff. That's probably why "Innovative Businessman" came before "Loving Husband."'

He stood there a moment longer in silence and I put my arm around him, not knowing what else to do.

'Are you ready to go now?' I said quietly.

Henley nodded slowly. 'I'd like to see my – *the* house.'

'If you want.'

We walked from the cemetery to the Beaufords' city residence. I led the way for the first few minutes, but once we entered the historic district of Lenox Hill with all the old buildings, Henley knew exactly where we were and took the lead.

I hadn't been back to Henley's city home in modern times, and it didn't hold many memories for me as we had spent most of our time at the country house. But the city residence was still linked to him and that whole other life I had left behind. Being reminded of all that would have been too painful even for me when I thought I had lost Henley for good.

I didn't even know if the building was still standing. Maybe it had been knocked down decades ago and replaced with some shiny new skyscraper or apartment complex? I wanted to prepare Henley for the worst but didn't know how or what to tell him.

When we reached the street it was on, Henley started running. That made me run, too, but Henley shot ahead of me. I saw him stop on the sidewalk ahead. He had probably found the location. But was the building still there?

When I caught up, I saw what had made him stop.

Yes, the building was there. But more than that, the building – Henley's house – looked *exactly* as it had in 1904. The brick façade was free of telephone wires and satellite dishes. The front steps had the same weathered look to them as when Henley's father was still trudging up them.

The door was slightly ajar. I knew I shouldn't raise the possibility but I couldn't help myself.

'Do you want to see inside?' I asked, and climbed the first two steps leading up to the front door.

At first, Henley didn't budge from his spot on the side-walk, but he soon followed me. He was the one to push open the door.

What we saw inside was not what I expected. It wasn't supposed to be like this.

Henley's eyes had shown no emotion when he first laid eyes on Eliza's grave, or on his own, for that matter. They hadn't even changed when he saw the outside of his former house. But now they misted over.

We stood in the doorway, hand in hand, looking upon rows and rows of white plastic desks with people seated at each one in matching plastic chairs. The house had been completely gutted and turned into one big room with a high ceiling. Linoleum covered the floor and the walls were painted white. None of the grandeur of the previous age remained.

Henley broke free of my grip, went back outside and started walking down the street the way we had come.

'Excuse me,' I said to the closest man. 'Could you tell me what this is?'

'This office? It's Katara Designs.' Seeing the blank look on my face, he elaborated, 'We design stationery and fabric prints?'

'Um . . . Well, thank you.'

I headed outside and caught up with Henley.

'We should get going to a library or someplace we can find a usable computer,' he said, without looking at me.

'Don't you need a moment? We could take the rest of the afternoon—'

'I'm fine.'

I didn't argue with him.

Finding a computer we could use was much easier in New York than it had been in London. Miss Hatfield had insisted I get a laptop to 'assimilate into the technological era', so we headed back to the house to grab it. Then we found the nearest Starbucks, since that was the first place I could think of with free Internet access. We sat down at an out-of-the-way table and I handed Henley a Visa gift card. Maybe we could use all of them before we started using the credit card. We still had quite a few left. 'Could you go and buy a drink while I set up the computer? We should make a purchase if we're going to stay here and use their Internet.'

'What kind of drink do you want?' Henley was studying the menu on the wall. 'It looks like they have a lot of options.'

'Anything is fine. We can share it.'

I opened my laptop and plugged the charger into the wall. It took a few minutes for the laptop to boot up since it had been dead for the last few years. Once I'd logged on to the Internet, I launched the browser and researched plane tickets to Florida first.

I figured out that we could fly from JFK to Key West International Airport through Tampa, and then it would be another flight from Tampa to Miami, before taking a taxi all the way to the Keys. And although they were expensive because I was looking at flights that left tomorrow, it was still only a little over four hundred dollars per person – which was nothing compared to the international flight we'd just taken.

Henley came back with an iced coffee and a pad of paper and pen just as I was selecting the plane tickets.

'I figured you might need something to write down the information,' he said, passing them to me.

I thanked him.

'So when do we leave?'

'We can leave tomorrow,' I told him.

I gestured for the backpack, and when he handed it over I took out the credit card.

He sat down. 'What time?'

'Um . . . 11.20 in the morning is when the flight leaves, and we'd land at 5.34pm, according to this.' I jotted the information down on the pad of paper that Henley had thoughtfully asked for.

A few clicks and I'd booked the flights. I knew the credit card company would suspend the card soon, as it hadn't been used for three years. It was now a race to book the hotel room before the card got suspended.

Miss Hatfield had never bought a printer so I couldn't print out the tickets ahead of time like I had before, but that was a minor issue as they could provide us with boarding passes when we checked in. Another minor niggle was that I couldn't get seats together since the booking was so last minute.

'Are you okay with that?' I asked Henley.

'I'm fine. I survived my first flight, and if this one's anything like that, I'll be sleeping through most of it, anyway.'

I giggled. 'Now we need to book the hotel quickly . . .' I pulled up the website of the resort we had already settled on and took the phone out of the backpack to call the contact number at the bottom of the page.

'Why don't I do that?' Henley pushed the iced coffee towards me. 'Then you can drink this before all the ice melts and this becomes water.'

'You can, as long as you do it quickly. The card's going to be suspended soon.'

I passed him the phone along with the pen and pad of paper, and took a long sip of the sweet drink. Whatever Henley had chosen tasted more like sugar than coffee.

'How many nights am I asking for?'

'Um . . . two weeks,' I said. 'Actually, why don't we make it longer? Four weeks just in case. The card will eventually

get cancelled anyway, so we won't actually end up paying.'
I didn't even know if my body could handle staying in one
time for four more weeks, but I didn't tell Henley that.

Henley was already dialling the number on the screen.
'Hello? Yes, I'd like to make a reservation.'

Something told me that we wouldn't have trouble finding
a last-minute room at the Creekside Pointe Resort. The
Florida Keys didn't look like a destination you'd take the
time and expense to travel to only to stay at the cheapest
place. Also, Islamorada wasn't exactly the hottest spot on
the Keys.

'Yes, four weeks, please,' Henley said. 'Two adults. Arriving
tomorrow night. Yes, that would be fine. Under the name
Beauford. B-E-A-U-F-O-R-D. Yes, that's "B" as in "baby".'
He wrote down the booking information.

While Henley was on the phone, I used the laptop to
order a few gallons of water to be delivered to the house.
We needed something to drink and clean up with, not to
mention flush the toilet. I remembered to add a few candles,
too – the lack of electricity was a bit of a hindrance. I
drank half the coffee waiting for Henley to finish the call.

'Yes, thank you. Thank you very much.' He hung up
and tossed the phone into the backpack. 'Portable phones
are so useful.'

'So is same-day shipping.' I grinned, sliding him the
remainder of the coffee.

He took a sip. 'My God, that's sweet.'

But that didn't stop him from drinking it, I noticed.

'I know you probably don't want to talk about it,' I started,
'but are you all right? With everything that happened earlier
at your house, I mean.'

There was a pause as Henley gathered his thoughts.
Eventually, he said, 'I suppose I'm not. I-it took me off guard

. . . It was still a house but not a home . . .' Henley fiddled with the straw in the drink. 'I can't *expect* myself to be all right yet. I just need time. I'll be all right soon.'

That was an answer I could live with.

Henley finished the coffee and we packed up the laptop and charger before heading back to Miss Hatfield's.

'Who are all these people?' Henley pointed to the black and white photographs that dotted one of the walls in the hall.

I shrugged. 'I imagine some of these women must be the previous Miss Hatfields – or that's what I've told myself, anyway. And I guess the other people could be former family and friends.'

As Henley looked around the kitchen, I glanced at the wall with the mark where the clock had once hung. It had probably been there for years and the sunlight from the kitchen windows had faded the wallpaper around the clock, leaving a darker ring in its former position.

Henley walked back down the hallway, examining everything from the uneven hardwood floors to the dust covers hanging over the banister. Finally, he came to the parlour and sat down on the pea-green couch.

'Shouldn't we be preparing for Florida somehow?' he said.

'We bought the tickets and made the hotel reservation – what more is there to do other than wait?'

'Then we should prepare for our life afterwards.'

Henley sounded very sure that there would be an 'afterwards'. My brain couldn't process the thought of a time after this trip to Florida and after the killer was gone. In my head, there was no afterwards.

'We'll get through this, you know,' Henley said, intuiting what I was thinking.

I couldn't tell him that I thought he was wrong. 'What do you propose we do?'

'Well, once we're both immortal, we'll need to keep travelling in time, right? To retain our sanity and survive?' He spoke about it so lightly. 'And you said Miss – my mother – kept many things around the house that would come in handy, so surely she has period clothing you might be able to use?'

'She does.' I remembered the first outfit she dressed me in to pass for Mr Beauford's niece in 1904. 'But even if I take a dress, if I go too far back in time, the dress would disappear because it hadn't been made yet.'

'So just pick a really old dress, the oldest you can find.' Henley spread his arms along the back of the couch. 'Chances are it won't disappear on you if it's old enough. Then you'll have something to wear right away instead of having to "borrow" clothing when you arrive.'

Henley had a point. It *would* be nice to not have to arrive naked in each time period I travelled to because the clothing I wore didn't exist yet.

I started up the stairs. 'Are you coming?' I asked.

'To watch you play dressing-up? I think I'm fine where I am, thank you.' Henley talked over his shoulder at me from his spot on the couch in the parlour. 'Just pick an old dress and put it in the backpack. Make sure it's something that'll fit in wherever – or whenever – you travel.'

'So nothing too poofy?' I said, hoping to make him laugh.

He tried for a smile, but it was half-hearted at best. 'Nothing too poofy . . . and don't worry about me – I just want to take some time to myself.'

I knew it was hard for him to be here, but I was hoping he was starting to allow himself to feel something for his mother.

I went upstairs to the room where Miss Hatfield kept the chests filled with period clothing. She only collected women's clothing so I wouldn't find anything for Henley, but after opening all the chests, I did unearth a dress that looked old enough to be from Tudor times, although much less flamboyant than the dresses I had worn in 1527. It was rather plain, made of a linen-like material, with no jewels encrusted on it. Though the dress had probably once been a white-ish colour, the fabric had yellowed with age. Though I couldn't tell for certain, it looked like the oldest dress here. It would have to do.

The dress had been packed with a matching slip and undergarments that looked like petticoats and several garter-like pieces. I knew all that wouldn't fit into the backpack since we had other things to carry, so I only took the dress and the slip.

It was strange to be in Miss Hatfield's home without her, but good to have Henley there to share the lonely house. In a way, it felt like we were going back to our roots before one last great adventure.

Chapter 17

The next morning, we rose early to catch a taxi to the airport. Henley was already getting used to checking in and going through airport security.

'Where'd you go?' I was already standing in line at the gate with the backpack on the floor between my feet when Henley joined me. He had headed off more than half an hour ago to wander through the shops in the terminal.

He held up a brown paper bag. 'I bought sandwiches.' He looked pleased with himself as he took out his sandwich and handed me the bag. 'Best take yours since we're not sitting next to each other,' he said as boarding began for our flight.

'Remember not to hog the armrests,' I said as a flight attendant scanned our boarding passes. We both had middle seats on this plane.

'I'll see you when we land in Tampa,' Henley said as we boarded.

It didn't take long to get from New York to Tampa. I was impressed by the amount of beachwear that was already being worn on the plane. Half the people had sunglasses perched atop their heads. There were even women who spent the entire flight holding straw sunhats in their laps.

We had a short layover in Tampa – a little over an hour. Luckily, we didn't have to rush to another terminal as our second flight was only one gate over.

'This is such a small plane,' Henley said as we boarded our second flight of the day.

He was right. It was one of those planes with a propeller at the front. I thought Henley might be nervous in a smaller aircraft but he didn't appear to mind. His comment was only the result of his curiosity.

'At least we got seats together,' I said. I passed over the part about them being at the back next to the bathroom.

The next flight was much the same. This was the last leg of the journey. Neither Henley nor I could sleep on the short flight. I suspected he had slept almost the entire way on the previous flight from New York. My anticipation and anxiety kept me awake.

We were going to be in Islamorada in just a few hours. What then? Once we found the Fountain of Youth, Henley would only need to take one sip. With Henley immortal, we could proactively confront the killer, rather than wait for him and potentially be taken off guard. It would only be then that our worries would be over. It would be me and Henley together for the rest of time.

We caught a taxi when we landed. The 45-minute ride to the Creekside Pointe Resort in Islamorada was uneventful. The bellboy greeted us as we arrived, but he backed away when he saw we had no luggage with us save for the overstuffed backpack I was carrying. Henley was wearing his new shorts and looked suitably ready to spend time at the beach.

'Are you checking in?' a man asked as we approached the front desk. He didn't look surprised by our lack of luggage. Perhaps he thought the bellboy had already taken it.

'We are,' Henley said. 'The name is Beauford.'

'For four weeks?'

'Yes.'

I took out the credit card and handed it to the man. I finally relaxed when the transaction went without a hitch and he returned the card along with a couple of forms.

'Please sign in the indicated spots. Your card will not be charged until you check out.'

Henley signed for both of us.

The man handed us two copies of the room key. 'Two-twelve,' he said.

'Second floor?' I guessed.

'Yes. You'll find the elevator and the stairs on your left. And if you need anything else, my name is Albert – please call me Al – just ask and I'll be happy to assist you.'

We took the stairs up to the second floor and walked down the hallway to our room. Each room had a doormat outside and a potted miniature palm tree.

'So many palm trees . . .' Henley muttered as he unlocked the door.

Our room was only slightly bigger than the hostel room in London, but the sheets were fresh and the bathroom looked clean. That was all we really needed. I was glad to put the heavy backpack down on the bed for a moment.

'The window's so small,' Henley said.

I stood next to him to peer out of it. 'At least it over-looks the pool.'

'And that's a good thing? We're in earshot of screaming children.'

I ignored the part about screaming children. 'I think I'll go downstairs and ask Al what he knows about the lakes on Islamorada,' I said.

'Business already?' Henley said, but he knew we weren't here to enjoy ourselves. 'I'll go with you.' He walked to the door, leaving the backpack in the middle of the bed.

'I think we should keep that with us,' I said, collecting it. 'There are too many important things in it.'

Al was still in the lobby.

'Al,' I said, settling my elbows on the cold wooden surface of the front desk. 'We're looking to . . . hike a bit. What do you know about lakes in the area?'

'We're hoping to do a bit of swimming, too,' Henley added.

'We have the most beautiful beaches—'

'We prefer lakes,' I said.

Henley jumped in again: 'She's not one for saltwater – sensitive skin.'

'I see. Well, we have a freshwater pool on property. As for lakes, you'll find them further south in the Keys but not on Islamorada.'

'Not on Islamorada?' *He couldn't possibly be right.*

'It's a small island – they dried up a long time ago. If you're looking for a lake here,' Al said with a chuckle, 'you're a few hundred years too late.'

All dried up? A few hundred years ago? Not a single lake?

I blinked, trying to clear my mind enough to think clearly. 'Well . . . Could we have a map of Islamorada, then?'

'Sure thing.' Al handed me a folded map with the resort's name scrawled on the top. 'Here you go. Keep it. You'll definitely need it during your stay here. This map even has the good hiking trails marked in red.'

We thanked him and moved away from the desk towards an armchair set up in the corner of the lobby right next to a lamp.

'Why don't you sit down?' I said, handing Henley the backpack so I could open up the map fully.

'I'd rather you take the seat,' he said.

That was his old-fashioned nature talking. I doubted he would ever leave that behind. I was too tired to insist on him taking it, so I sat and spread the map out on my lap. My heart thudded in my ears. We were in Florida. We were so close to the Fountain of Youth. We were so close to turning Henley immortal.

Ads for beachside boutiques and historical sites to visit framed the map. Creekside Pointe Resort was clearly marked with a red star labelled 'You are here'. I scanned the map for any bodies of water.

Al was right. There wasn't a single lake. It was a tiny island and the only blue was the ocean around it. No lakes at all.

I closed my eyes and forced myself to inhale through my nose and exhale through my mouth. I had to get my heart to slow down.

'What if there's a lake in the middle of the forest that most people don't know about?' Even as I spoke, I knew it was a long shot.

'So you're suggesting we tromp through the forest looking for a body of water that might not be there? Where would we even start?'

Henley was right. Tears prickled in my eyes. 'So that's it, then.'

Henley looked down at me, slightly confused. 'What?'

'That's the end of it – we've come all the way here for nothing,' I said. 'There is no lake. There is no Fountain of Youth. It doesn't exist any more.'

'Yes, it does,' Henley said, starting to smile. 'The man at the front desk was right – we're just a few hundred years too late. We could fix that so that we're in the right time period.'

'You mean time travel?' I squinted at him through the tears that had welled up in my eyes.

'Precisely.' He looked so sure of himself.

275

I let out another deep breath. 'But you wouldn't be able to come – you're not fully immortal yet.'

'You'll only be gone for a short while,' Henley said. 'You've managed without me before. You can do this.'

The way he said it made it sound so reasonable. As if there was no way his plan wouldn't work.

'Okay . . .' I couldn't believe I was agreeing. 'Where do we start?'

The nearest historic location listed on the map with an exact date was called Sandy Cove. Having an exact date gave me a precise time to time travel to.

We walked there as daylight started to fade. It was quite close – just around the corner from the resort. When we got there, Sandy Cove turned out to be nothing more than a large cliff jutting out over the beach. Despite the advertising, the supposed tourist stop was completely devoid of tourists.

'Look at this.' Henley beckoned me over to a wooden sign staked in the sandy dirt.

On 25th July 1532, the third Spanish expedition to Florida set up camp here.

'Perfect.'

'Are you positive you want to do this?' Henley asked.

'Of course I am. I'm doing this for my sake as much as yours,' I said.

I opened the backpack and took out the old linen dress Henley had smartly told me to bring. I took off my jeans and T-shirt, and pulled on the dress. I looked silly now, but my dress would be time appropriate soon enough.

I gave him my room key. 'Hide this under the potted plant next to our door.' I figured that was slightly less obvious than hiding it under the doormat.

Henley handed me the clock but didn't let go of it immediately. 'Don't stay too long.'

'I'll be as quick as I can.'

'When you've settled in and have your cover story established, come back and let me know.'

'Of course I will.'

'And please be careful. Remember, someone's after you. There won't be many people around back then, so it won't take the killer long to find you.'

I gave him a kiss as my answer.

Henley finally let go of the clock. I held it with both hands and crossed the road we had walked along from the resort. On the other side of the road was the edge of a thick tropical forest. I stood by the treeline, where I could still see Henley. Against the backdrop of big sky, he looked small and alone. I probably looked the same to him standing next to the massive trees.

Henley held up a hand. He might have meant it as a wave goodbye, but it looked as if he was trying to touch me from far away.

I mirrored his gesture then turned the hands on the clock.

Chapter 18

Henley dissolved before my eyes. Saplings sprouted on either side of me and rushed to overtake the space where the road would eventually be and I was pushed aside by a tree growing where I was standing. I closed my eyes, feeling slightly nauseous as the ground rippled and my surroundings changed. When I opened them, the world was stable again. But everything was different. For starters, I was now in the middle of a dense forest.

My dress hung limply on my body. I looked down at my bare feet. I had forgotten about shoes. I was still holding the clock and realised I hadn't thought about what to do with it while I was here. I couldn't afford to lose it again; nor did I want it taken from me. It would probably be best to leave it hidden where no one was likely to come looking. I ripped an inch of cloth from the hem of my dress and tied the makeshift ribbon to the closest branch I could find, then buried the clock under a layer of dirt and fallen leaves at the foot of the tree.

I hoped to God it would still be there when I returned.

I could hear voices ahead of me, though I couldn't quite tell what they were saying. I took a few steps towards them and the sharp leaves and dirt on the ground pricked my tender feet. The trees grew so thickly that I couldn't see anything else ahead of me.

'Hello?' I called, then realised it would look strange if I came out of the middle of the forest alone and looking so clean. I scraped up a handful of dirt and rubbed it on my face and arms, then caked some mud into my hair. I even dirtied up my dress a bit.

I started to count my steps as I blindly thrashed my way through the trees. I took note of a tree that looked like it was bowing down and tried to memorise its location. The twigs and branches scratched my arms and legs and I tried to ignore the pain in the soles of my feet. I needed to keep an accurate count of how many steps I was taking away from the clock so I would have some hope of finding it again.

The voices had stopped now and all I could hear was the occasional squawk of birds.

I called out again as I stumbled through the leaves and branches and broke into a clearing. It looked like a camp. *The* camp. Tents made of leather and white cloth circled an open fire in the middle of the clearing, around which some people were gathered. Faces turned towards me in astonishment at the sound of my voice.

'Um . . . hello,' I said. 'I-I'm sorry. I was . . . lost.'

I counted five men near the fire. Some held knives in their laps. Most had swords by their sides. They were all looking at me. I took a step towards them. In an instant they were on their feet with their knives and swords in hand. I froze.

'Who are you?' one of them said in heavily accented English. His moustache tapered down into a pointy-looking beard.

I was so petrified, I couldn't form words.

As the men murmured among themselves, the altered tone of their voices brought several new faces out of the tents along with a shaggy yellow dog wearing a makeshift rope collar. The dog seemed to be a medium-sized breed, but looked lighter and skinnier than it should be.

'English.' One of the men spat on the ground.

Since America didn't exist yet, it made sense that they assumed I was English. They were also making it very clear exactly what they thought of the English.

A raven-haired woman from one of the tents raised her voice as she strode towards the fire. At first I thought she was shouting at me, but then I realised she was aiming her ire at the men. I was also suddenly very aware that I had no idea what she was saying. Everyone was speaking Spanish.

The woman walked between the men until she was face to face with me.

'English?' she asked. She also had a thick accent. 'No Spanish?'

I shook my head.

'Did you come from England? Who are you?'

That was a good question. It was time to try spinning a story that hopefully wouldn't cause the men to hate me any more than they did already.

'Yes – I came from England—' I started.

'An English ship?'

'Um, yes.'

'And what was your position there?'

'My position?' It took me a minute to work out what she meant. 'I-I snuck on board to escape my family.' It was the first thing I could think of since I didn't know the positions on a ship. 'It's just that I didn't have much money and—'

She interrupted me. 'What was an English ship doing in this part of the New World?' The woman frowned at me.

'Colonising.' I realised my mistake as soon as the word was out of my mouth.

'So the English think they can set up colonies in lands already claimed by Spain?'

A grumble of dissent arose from some of the men – clearly there were several English speakers among them.

I knew I had to turn this story around, and fast.

'That was their plan but . . . but the land was too harsh for them. Disease struck . . . Native tribes attacked . . . They wanted to return to England, but many of them became delirious from illness and died. So I fled.'

The woman crossed her arms, an expression of blatant incredulity on her face. 'You fled . . . Alone?'

'Um . . . No?' I said. 'Others ran with me, but they died. Some of those we left behind might have survived, but I don't know what has become of them.'

There was silence as I finished my story and the woman didn't appear to feel the need to fill it. She just stood there, staring at me, her arms still crossed. She gave no indication that she believed my story, but I was pretty sure she would have said something if she *didn't* believe it.

Finally, when she spoke, it was to the men around us and it was in Spanish, so I couldn't understand a thing. I kept listening for words that sounded like their English counterparts – I'd heard that Spanish was supposed to be full of those, but if that was true, I couldn't distinguish any of them through the woman's heavy accent. The men nodded slowly as she barked at them. I didn't know if they were agreeing to kill me or allow me to stay.

'Come with me,' the woman said.

'Me?'

'I *am* speaking your language, am I not?'

The woman took long strides like the men, her skirts swaying around her ankles as she led me to one of the tents. The men disbanded from the centre of the clearing and went back to whatever they had been doing before I appeared.

Inside the tent, aside from a hammock hung between two of the tent's wooden poles and some wooden chests pushed into the corners, there was no other furniture. The chests had papers spread over them; they looked like hand-drawn maps with 'x's marked on them, but I wasn't close enough to see what they were identifying. The woman followed my gaze and quickly put the maps away inside one of the chests. Then she turned and indicated for me to sit on the hammock.

I hesitated, not having the first idea how to do that without ending up in a heap on the floor. Seeing my unease, she dragged one of the chests into the centre of the tent.

'Sit.'

I obeyed.

She nodded her approval and said, 'Wait here,' before disappearing from the tent.

When she returned a few minutes later, she was carrying a basin of water and a smaller rag, plus a pair of leather shoes. She placed everything on the dirt floor, then knelt in front of me, dipped the rag into the water and started washing my feet. At first I pulled away in surprise but she grabbed my ankle to hold me still.

'This will hurt a little, but the pain will be nothing compared to what you might feel later if these wounds aren't cleaned,' she said.

As she gently wiped my cuts and scratches, I got a good look at her. She was strong and sturdily built, her plump hands deft and sure. Her hair was coiled out of the way at the nape of her neck. At first I thought it was pure black, but it had a reddish tint where the lamplight hit it. Her sharp nose was offset by her ruddy cheeks and her olive skin glowed as if she had diligently scrubbed herself clean. Though her linen dress was brown and caked with dirt around the hem, I couldn't see any dirt under her fingernails.

'W-why are you doing this? Helping me, I mean.'

It probably wasn't the best question to ask. These people hadn't killed me on sight, for which I was thankful, but reminding her that I was an outsider might not be such a good idea.

'Some of the men believe you're an English spy,' she said, not answering my question directly. 'I told them that the English are at least smart enough not to send a bumbling young girl to spy on us.'

I gritted my teeth as she dabbed at a particularly deep wound on the sole of one foot.

'So you believe me?'

'I'll help you stay here if that's what you want.' She licked her thin lips in concentration.

Her answer was puzzling.

'You speak English very well,' I said, trying a different tactic to try to find out more about her.

'I also speak French and Italian.' She stood to attend to the cuts on my arms.

'How did you learn all those languages?'

'My parents valued education,' she said. 'They believed it would find me a better match.'

It took me a moment to understand she meant marriage. 'And are you married?'

'You ask too many questions for someone who is not on the side with the power.' But she was smiling as she turned away. 'I'm unmarried. What husband would permit his wife to go on voyages to the New World alone?'

'Voyages? As in multiple?'

She tilted her head at me, apparently amused by all my questions. 'Just two, this being the second. Turn your head to the left.'

I did as I was told and the woman applied the damp rag to my face. My right cheek stung under her touch.

She saw me wince. 'It doesn't look as deep as it feels. Merely a scratch.'

I hadn't even noticed a tree branch catching me hard enough across the face to draw blood.

'And what are these voyages for? Colonisation?'

'They are for Spain. We found these lands on the first voyage. This second is to . . . chart the lands. Of course, there were a number of voyages between in which I had no part. Some of those involved colonisation for their Royal Majesties.'

'Their Royal Majesties?'

'Why their Royal Majesties King Ferdinand and Queen Isabella, of course.'

'And—'

The woman suddenly doubled over, clutching her side. I sprang up off the chest and was about to call for help when she said, 'Don't call anyone. Don't say anything. It'll pass.'

I stood over her, helpless. I placed a hand on her shoulder when she groaned in pain. I felt like doing anything more would be overstepping our relationship.

Minutes went by and the woman finally drew herself up to a standing position.

'Are you all right? Are you sure you don't need to see a doctor or something?'

'It just happens. No more questions,' she said. 'The time for interrogation is over.' She pointed at the shoes she had brought, indicating that I should put them on.

Save for a few beads of sweat on her forehead, there was no indication that she had been in agony only a few minutes before. I knew she wouldn't answer any questions about her pain, so I asked something else.

'Just one more question,' I said. 'I'm Rebecca. What might I call you?'

'Juana.' She smiled and her features softened moment-arily before she grabbed the basin and the rag and left the tent.

Juana. It was a name I knew so well from the stories Miss Hatfield had told me about the origins of the Fountain of Youth. There were two Juanas in the stories.

One of them – Juana Jimenez – went in search of the Fountain of Youth because she mistakenly believed it would make her younger. She got Ponce de León to trust her just so he might one day take her to the Fountain of Youth. When the day came, she spent hours floating in the lake, but of course nothing happened because she didn't drink the water. When Ponce de León found her body, it had a sickly pallor and there were claw marks on her face, either from her own fingernails or the result of some sort of struggle. Her cheeks were bloodied and her expression was one of utter horror. Some speculated that she had gone mad and taken her own life, while others swore that there was something sinister in the forest itself, but no one really knew how she died

Before Juana Jimenez was Juana Ruíz, the first European woman to set foot in the New World. She was also said to have been with Ponce de León the day he discovered the Fountain of Youth. This was the Juana who wrote that letter. And also the Juana who could be the killer. Without knowing its properties, she drank the water alongside Ponce de León. Eight years later, when Ponce de León was putting together another expedition to Florida, he was complimented on how he looked like he hadn't aged a day since his first voyage. Meanwhile, Juana Ruíz had disappeared. I didn't know why she disappeared from the records because Miss Hatfield hadn't thought it important to tell me the rest of her story. Perhaps she had gone into hiding somewhere.

I wondered if this woman who had tended to my wounds was one of those Juanas. A long shot, for sure, but it was possible. The answer to that question lay outside the tent.

'Ah, here she is,' Juana said, seeing me emerge.

She was sitting on a log outside by the firepit, above which some kind of animal was roasting. Only a few of the men were around, and none of them within earshot.

I sat down next to her. 'Where is everyone? All the men, I mean?'

'Working. Some still hunting. Some writing their letters back home. Some are taking their turn in confessional.'

'Confessional? Out here?' I said, before I remembered that Spain was very religious in this current time period.

'A priest from the colony encampment travelled a great distance to visit us. He only arrived two days ago, and today is the first day we've had proper Mass in a long time,' she said. 'Nature and a new world are not places where one should forsake God.'

'Yes, of course,' I mumbled.

Perhaps Juana knew more than she was letting on . . .

'Is Ponce de León at this camp?'

She looked sharply at me. 'What do you know of Ponce de León?'

'Not much.' That was true. I only knew what Miss Hatfield had told me and the generally known fact that he had discovered Florida.

286

'Clearly,' she said, turning the animal on the wooden spit. 'He's dead.'

'Pardon?'

'Dead. For a while now, too.' She squinted at me. 'Why do you want to know?'

'I-I just thought that . . . he would be the one leading all this.'

She nodded. That was a passable answer, thankfully. 'He was killed by a tribe of natives.'

Yes, Miss Hatfield said that, too. I just didn't know when that had happened in relation to now. 'Recently?'

'Depends on your definition of "recent". He died more than a decade ago.'

I had no response to that.

'I expected news of his death would have reached England by now.'

'Well . . . surely you must understand . . . We're concerned with our own explorers,' I said. 'You mentioned that the prior expedition was to chart this new land. Is that what you're here to do this time?'

'Of course,' she said, but she failed to meet my eyes. 'I'm here because I know these lands. That's my reason for being here.'

It would have sounded more convincing if she hadn't repeated herself.

'You said this is your second journey to the New World. Was anyone else here now on the first expedition with you?'

'No,' she said quickly. 'It was a long time ago.'

I was almost certain this was Juana Ruíz. Which meant a lot of things – primarily, it confirmed that Juana was immortal.

'Juana . . . What is your surname?'

She stared me down. 'I will not have this interrogation from you. If you cannot be sated by what you have already learned, I suggest you leave. If you would like to stay, you will not ask any more questions.' Her voice was icy.

'I-I'm sorry,' I said. I couldn't have her throwing me out. 'I don't know what came over me.'

Juana looked at me a moment longer to make sure my apology was genuine. 'I was a little too strong as well,' she said.

I didn't know why her last name would be such a touchy issue. Perhaps it would reveal more about her, like the fact that she wasn't a regular mortal. Or that she was the killer.

'You must eat,' Juana said, taking a knife out of a pocket sewn into her dress. I had absolutely no idea she was armed. 'I imagine you're hungry.' She began to cut off one of the roasting animal's meaty legs. It looked like a large rodent of some kind, but I couldn't be certain.

Then I noticed that Juana's hand was shaking. At first it was a little tremor, mostly affecting her fingers, but it quickly grew into a full-body shake.

'No . . .' she whispered.

She was shaking her head now, and kept shaking it and shaking it as if she couldn't stop. Then she started talking in Spanish. Not murmuring but talking loudly, as if there was someone in this tent who I couldn't see who could hear her and understand.

'Juana?' I reached out to touch her but she recoiled.

'No!' She screamed the word at me but I knew she wasn't seeing *me*.

I sat still. I waited to see if the men would come running after hearing her scream. A minute passed and no one came. Why didn't anyone come? Was this a frequent happening? Were they used to hearing her scream at night? Another minute passed and Juana quietened.

'Are you all right?' I said, after the shaking had stopped.

'I-I said the interrogation was over,' she snapped. She recovered the knife she had dropped during her convulsions and finished cutting off the animal's leg. 'Eat.'

There was still a foot attached to the end of the leg. It had nails that now looked crispy.

'Um . . . I'd like to . . . uh . . . I drank too much water . . .'

'There's a chamber pot in the tent. Alternatively, you could use the woods.'

That was what I needed.

I excused myself and started into the woods. I found the tree that looked like it was bowing down and began counting the steps between it and the clock.

37. 38. 39.

I had to talk to Henley – first to tell him that I was all right since he would be worried, but also to tell him about Juana and the strange shaking fit.

52. 53. 54.

I had counted 54 steps on my way to the campsite, so I looked around and saw the tree with the strip of fabric tied to one of its branches. I pushed the loose dirt aside and started digging with my hands. My fingers felt something smooth and cold.

I pulled the clock out and turned its hands forwards.

'Henley?' I looked around at the open road in front of me and the cliff.

He wasn't there.

Of course he wasn't there. He had no way to know when I would come back – I didn't even know how long I had been gone.

I started walking down the road towards the hotel, glad it was only a few minutes away. The leather shoes were now so old in 2016, it was a miracle the shoes even had their shape after so many centuries. I had just travelled more than four hundred years into the future in a few seconds – that never ceased to amaze me.

'Henley?' I knocked on the door to our room before retrieving the key stashed underneath the potted plant.

Henley wasn't inside. Maybe he was by the pool. I needed to find him soon, but the sight of the comfortable bed was too tempting. A short lie-down, just a few minutes off my feet, would do me good. I kicked off my shoes and stretched out on the bed. It felt amazing.

Unexpectedly, I heard fumbling at the door. I propped my head up with my arm in time to see Henley walk in.

Calling the look on his face 'surprise' would have been an understatement.

'What are you doing here?' was his first question when he was able to speak.

'You told me to come back to let you know I was doing fine and had come up with a plausible backstory?'

'But . . . it's only been ten minutes at the most since you left.'

That made me sit up. 'Ten minutes? No way. I was gone much longer than that.'

'I only *just* said goodbye to you – I walked back to the hotel and . . . here I am. And here *you* are. And what happened to your feet and your face?'

I sank back down onto the bed. 'The clock measures years, months and days, but not hours and minutes.'

'You almost gave me a heart attack,' Henley said, approaching the bed. 'Move over. And tell me what happened to that cheek.' He gently touched the side of my face.

'A scratch. Tree branches,' I said, moving his hand away. I didn't want him to worry. 'But I'm in. There's a camp of people there, exactly as we thought.' Then I told him the backstory I had invented.

'A little shaky,' he said.

'Like you could've done much better.' I teased him, but Henley ignored it, remaining serious.

'But they bought it?'

'Well, one of them did – this woman – and that's what matters,' I said.

'Who's this woman?'

And I told him all about Juana, which didn't take long since I knew very little. I also told him about the shaking incident and the other pain incident in the tent.

'Don't you think it odd that she snapped at me when I asked for her last name?' I said. 'She could be Juana Ruíz.'

Henley shook his head. 'You might be reading entirely too much into this. It could be a touchy subject for other reasons. Or maybe she snapped at you because you were aggravating her with all of your questions.'

'But we need to consider that possibility.'

Henley rolled over on the bed to face me. 'So what if she is the first Juana? That would only confirm she's immortal.'

'If she's immortal, she could have a way to travel in time—'

Henley filled in the rest of my thought. 'And that means she could be the killer.'

I swallowed hard. It was all conjecture, but it was a strong possibility. There was definitely something strange about Juana, and right then, she was the prime suspect. The only suspect, really. Who else could travel in time but another immortal?

I told Henley about the maps I glimpsed when I first walked into her tent.

'Probably maps of the island,' he guessed. 'You did say that they were charting it.'

'But then why would she hide them from me as soon as I noticed them? It doesn't make sense.'

'Maybe she's just wary of a stranger,' Henley pointed out. 'She could just be careful in case you report back to one of Spain's enemies.'

'Maybe . . . I just need to see what's marked on those maps – that could also be another clue to who she is.'

I forced myself up from the bed, wincing when my feet hit the floor. I put my shoes back on then grabbed the room key and the clock.

'Do be careful,' Henley said.

'Aren't I always?'

I replaced the key under the miniature potted palm tree on my way out. I walked the road to Sandy Cove with sure steps. Then turned the clock back.

'Where did you go?' Juana asked when I stepped out of the forest. I was surprised that she sounded more worried than suspicious.

I'd buried the clock in the same spot as before.

It was dark already. A lone man sitting on a log was tending to the fire, which was half the size it had been. Clearly I had been gone longer than the hour I had spent with Henley.

When I didn't respond quick enough for her liking, Juana continued. 'Taking a walk to clear your head after a long day is all well and good, but it's dangerous out there.' She held a lamp up to her face and examined me.

She had actually sounded concerned about me. I wanted to congratulate her on her acting skills. But I still didn't trust her.

'Everyone has already eaten. That's what you get when you leave for hours without saying anything.' She sighed and lowered her voice. 'I did save you a piece, though. Come.'

As we walked towards her tent, she said a few quick words in Spanish to the man near the fire.

'Alberto's keeping watch tonight,' she explained.

Inside the tent, a second hammock was hanging on the other side of the one I had seen earlier.

'You take that one.' Juana pointed to the new hammock. There even was a blanket on it.

Juana took off her dress, leaving only the slip underneath and her petticoats, and got into her hammock. She looked to me to do the same, so I took off my dress and put it on top of one of the chests as she had done. I noticed she was looking pale and damp wisps of her hair were stuck to her face.

I heard her mumble, 'It's happening more often now.'

'Are you feeling all right at the moment?'

'The food is over there,' Juana said, gesturing to one of the chests in the shadows. She tried to mask her weakness by speaking loudly, but her voice sounded strained. The pain was back.

'It's happening again, isn't it?'

Juana turned over in the hammock and faced away from me. That was all the answer I needed.

Her pain appeared to come suddenly and leave suddenly. Juana bore it well; she was clearly practised. The fact that it was happening 'more often now' made it sound a lot like the pain I experienced when I had lingered in one time period for too long. That was the curse of immortality – time rejected your body, your very presence, since you weren't supposed to be there.

I watched Juana. She was on her back again and I watched her chest expand and contract with even breaths.

She had fallen asleep. I couldn't help but sympathise with her pain, but if she truly was immortal then perhaps she was . . .

I shook myself out of it. I couldn't think that. Not when she had moments when she had been so gentle with me.

I glanced over at the food she had left out for me. A leg from whatever animal they'd had for dinner was sitting in a cracked wooden bowl on another chest. I hadn't eaten in hours, but the foot still made me feel nauseous. I also knew I had to eat it. I couldn't risk offending Juana again.

I retrieved the meat and sat on my hammock, staring at the leg in my hand and longing for the invention of vegetarianism.

The tent flap on my left moved. At first I thought I had bumped into it from my spot on the hammock, or maybe it was the wind, but the flap kept moving like something was on the other side. I almost called for Juana. Instead, I took a breath, counted to three and yanked the tent flap up from my spot on the hammock.

A furry face peered at me. It was the yellow dog with the rope collar I had seen earlier. I covered my mouth so Juana wouldn't hear my giggle, although she had looked so tired when she lay down that she must have been fast asleep by that point.

'What are you doing, buddy?' I whispered. 'What? You want this leg? Be my guest.' I wiggled it just above the dog's head to see if he would rise up on his hind legs so I could reach his head to pet him. He wasn't a big dog, maybe closer to fifteen pounds than twenty pounds. He looked a little on the skinny side, but luckily he didn't look too underfed.

The dog's eyes trailed the piece of meat but he didn't budge.

'Well, fine. Have it your way.'

He was probably tired after a long day, just like the rest of us. I held the leg directly in front of the dog and he started pulling the meat off the bone. I couldn't watch. The gnawing sounds were awful enough. When the dog stopped eating, I looked down to see a clean bone, albeit with some toothmarks here and there. The dog's tail was wagging.

'Good job. Good job, buddy.'

I carefully slid out of my hammock to return the bone to the wooden bowl on the chest. I turned around, hoping to scratch the dog behind his ears, but he was gone. At least one of us had enjoyed his meal tonight. I crawled back into the hammock.

The dog had saved me from having to eat the animal leg, so I was beyond thankful even though I was still hungry. My gratitude – not the killer, not immortality, not time travel – was the last thing I thought of as I drifted off to sleep.

My eyes shot open at the feeling of hands around my neck. They were gripping so hard. Strangling me. And I was staring into Juana's eyes.

'Juana—' I managed to choke out.

So this was how I would die. Strangled by the killer.

My arms flailed uselessly. Deprived of air, my mind was going foggy. Something wasn't quite right about this scene but I couldn't figure out what. I was too terrified to think coherently.

Think, Rebecca.

But all I could think was, *Why? Why is she doing this?*

I stared up at her, as if I might read the answer on her face. Even in the dark of the night, I could see that her eyes looked glazed. Her body was shaking . . . and it wasn't from the effort of strangling me.

'Juana . . .' I gurgled.

I thought I saw a flicker of recognition in her eyes.

'Juana!' I said, as loud as I could. I mustered the last bit of energy I had left and kicked blindly at her stomach.

All of a sudden, the hands relaxed. They were still around my neck, but all the strength had gone out of them and they were slack, resting against my collarbone.

'I-I'm so sorry,' Juana muttered. She took her hands off me and turned away before I could see her expression.

Then she climbed back into her hammock without another word.

I was wheezing, still trying to catch my breath.

She could have killed me. And she didn't.

I was terrified, but I didn't even know what for any more. *Was she even the killer, if she didn't kill me when she had the chance?* I didn't know what to think.

These thoughts kept flooding my mind, as I fought sleep for as long as I could. Eventually, my exhausted body won out and my mind quietened itself.

Chapter 19

I woke up to the sound of Juana rummaging around the tent. That was the problem with sharing a small space with someone, be it Juana or Henley – they always managed to wake you up even if they were trying to be quiet.

'Good. You're awake at last,' Juana said as I rolled over in the hammock to look at her. There was no sign on her face of what had happened last night.

Maybe she didn't remember . . . Or maybe she was pretending not to.

'You overslept. Everyone's done with breakfast. I left some for you but it's getting cold.'

I stared blankly at her, the sleep still in my eyes. Best not to mention it.

When I didn't move, she tutted at me like an errant child. 'Get up. Get dressed. That's what I mean,' she said.

I slid from the hammock and went over to the chest where I had put my dress. I noticed that the bone was gone but the wooden dish was still there.

'Damn it, dog,' I muttered. I had wanted Juana to see the cleaned-off bone to show I appreciated her taking care of me. Now it looked like I had taken the whole leg, bone and all, and disposed of it somewhere. She was going to hate me.

I pulled the dress over my head and glanced at Juana. She had frozen in place and was staring at me, her jaw slack.

I suddenly realised it was probably down to my swearing. 'Damn' was too strong from a woman. Much too strong. What did women say in this time? God's teeth? I needed to transition back to an acceptable level of swearing for the sixteenth century.

'The dog took the scraps?' Juana said, once she had recovered from her shock.

'There wasn't much left,' I said. I didn't mention the fact that there wasn't much left because the dog had eaten all the meat the night before. 'Only the bone, really.'

'We can't leave scraps around camp like that. Might attract wild animals,' Juana said. 'But the dog is old – she is much too feeble to have dragged a thick, heavy thigh bone like that very far.'

'I thought the dog was male,' I said.

Juana started looking behind some of the chests. 'Do you know your dogs well?'

'Not really. I never had one. I wanted one when I was younger, though.'

'Our family had a dog named Alegria. It means happiness. When she birthed puppies one day, my sisters and I couldn't bear to give them away, so we grew up always having a pack of dogs at our feet.' Juana lifted the tent flap at the front and laughed when she found the guilty-looking dog with the bone between her paws.

I petted the dog and she rolled over, exposing her stomach to be rubbed. She looked so content in the lazy way she turned her head to look at me and flattened out her tongue to pant in my direction. Simple, pure happiness.

'There you are,' Juana said. 'We've been looking everywhere for you.' She took the bone in one hand and grabbed the dog by the scruff of her neck. 'We need to get you back to José.'

'Who's José?' I followed Juana and the dog out of the tent.
'Her owner.'

'Oh.' I felt a slight twinge of sadness, and then surprise at what I felt for the dog. I didn't know why I had got so attached. For some reason, I had thought it was the camp's dog and belonged to everyone. Foolish of me. Besides, she had an owner. I shouldn't have cared that much.

'José!' Juana barrelled into one of the tents with the dog.

I hesitated and stood by the opening. I shouldn't enter. It wasn't my place to get involved in this.

A man had hopped out of his hammock and stood raking his hair back and staring disdainfully at both the dog and Juana. The dog looked guilty, as if she knew this was all about her. Juana said a few things in Spanish and led the dog over to him, but he didn't look that pleased to have her back. He stroked his beard and muttered something, then took a few steps towards the dog. I thought he was going to pet her, but instead he kicked the dog and sent her flying a few steps.

My heart in my throat, I automatically lurched forward but quickly stopped myself. What was I supposed to do? I couldn't help the dog. I *shouldn't*, at least. I had to remain as inconspicuous as possible.

But the man had seen my sudden move. He pointed at me and said a few words to Juana, then looked towards the dog again. Juana said something back and tried to get me to leave with her.

'No,' I said, holding my ground. 'What did he say?'

'He doesn't like you.'

'That much I can gather. But why kick the dog? I thought she was his.'

'She was supposed to be a hunting dog. One that would also catch the rats on board the ship. But look at her –

299

she's past her prime. She was the runt of the litter too; I suppose that didn't help.'

The dog was now lying at the back of the tent, her head on the ground and her tail tucked between her legs. She tilted her head as if she wanted to raise it but found it too heavy.

'José says it's only a matter of time before she dies. Until then, she's just another thing to feed.'

I looked hard at José. 'So he's waiting for her to die.'

Juana shook her head. 'He'll probably put her down. Conditions are harsh out here, no place for a useless old dog. Her portion of food could go to the men.'

'It's not fair.'

'No – but what ever is?'

'I want her,' I said, without thinking. In that moment, I couldn't stand by and let it happen just to remain inconspicuous.

Juana put a hand on my arm. 'The dog's not yours to want.'

'Tell him,' I said. 'Tell him I want her. I'll take her off his hands.'

Juana hesitated before translating my words but did so with a heavy sigh. José looked at me with new interest and simply gave me a nod that needed no translating.

He moved towards the dog but I was faster. I walked to the back of the tent and scooped up the dog in my arms. She was heavier than I anticipated and my shoulders protested under the strain of picking her up, but I didn't care. I thought Juana might have said something to José as I left with the dog, but she quickly followed me back to our tent.

'You have no idea what you're going to do with that dog, do you?' Juana said as I put her down in the middle of our tent.

'I don't,' I admitted.

Juana didn't chastise me, though. 'You think you're like her, don't you?'

'Perhaps,' I said, rubbing the dog's stomach. 'It's just not fair that she shouldn't be given a chance like the rest of us.'

'You don't want to be thrown away when you're no longer useful.'

It wasn't much of a question so I made no reply.

'Stay here.' Juana excused herself and walked out.

'It's just you and me again, buddy,' I said.

The dog appeared to understand, gazing up at me as I petted her belly.

'Yeah, I don't know what we're going to do with you either.'

The dog cocked her head.

'You don't have to be a hunting dog or a rat catcher to be useful, though. I'll take you the way you are, if you'll take me the way I am.' I scratched her chin.

She seemed to like that. Her tail feebly flopped from side to side.

'Neither of us is the way we would like to be. We've changed. I know that.'

Juana returned with two wooden bowls containing some kind of stew-like substance. She handed one to me and put the other in front of the dog. I was hungry and didn't want to ask what the ingredients were before I ate it . . . and probably not even after I ate it. There was no spoon, so I tipped the bowl to my lips and drank from it. Despite my best efforts, I couldn't suppress a grimace at the awful taste and texture.

'It's cold, isn't it?' Juana said. 'And runny. We have to add wine to stretch out the daily provisions.' I knew the explanation was her way of apologising for the food.

'Do you know the dog's name?' I asked.

Juana shook her head.

'Oh. Maybe we could ask José later.'

'I mean she doesn't have a name,' Juana said. 'We only have one dog. She answers to a whistle. There was no need to name her.'

I looked at the dog gobbling up the contents of her bowl. It wasn't right not to have a name of your own.

'We have to name her.'

'Pick something suitable. Something that fits her,' Juana suggested. 'That way, the name will really be *her*.'

I knew exactly what she meant. The dog was curled up by the now-empty bowl. She shouldn't have had wine, but I supposed there was no clean water. Still, her tail wagged feebly from side to side, showing her appreciation.

'I want something fiery,' I finally said.

'For her? "Fiery" isn't what I think of when I look at her.'

The dog was curled up in the middle of the floor now, wheezing a little in her sleep.

'I know, but she could be.'

'You shouldn't name living things with your expectations of them,' Juana said.

'I want to name her something hopeful.'

'What about "Alma"?' she suggested as she leaned down to stroke the napping dog.

'What does that mean?'

'Soul.'

I looked down on the dog's sleeping form. She had as much soul as we did.

'It's perfect.'

'Rebecca. I have to ask you something. Yesterday . . .'

Juana looked and sounded so serious that I thought she must have followed me into the woods and seen me disappear in front of her.

'Yesterday, you said you had drunk too much water.' She watched me carefully as she spoke. 'I meant to ask if you had found a fresh water source . . . Perhaps a lake?'

I knew exactly what she was talking about – the excuse I'd made up yesterday about needing to empty my bladder in the middle of the woods so I could return to Henley. Perhaps Juana really was just asking about plain old drinking water . . . But she might also have been feeling out what I knew about the Fountain of Youth.

'Um . . . No, it was a river,' I tried.

'And you're certain you didn't see a lake when you were journeying here?' Juana's face felt too close to mine. 'Perhaps the river flowed into the lake?'

'Uh, no. No lake.'

She sighed, but was it one of disappointment or relief? Juana definitely knew *something*. But what?

She walked a few paces away from me. 'I'm . . . I'm going to the confessional,' she said. 'The men went this morning and should be done by now. The priest is in the furthest tent across from the firepit. He's an educated man and speaks English – I suggest you make the time to go today, too.'

I told her I would before she left for the priest's tent.

I waited a full five minutes before peeking outside to check that she was nowhere in sight. With Juana at confession, this was my opportunity to check the maps that she had hidden from me.

As I crossed the tent to the chests, Alma whined. I guessed she was waking up from her nap.

'I know this isn't exactly the best, most honourable thing to do, but I *need* to know. She's hiding something.'

I opened the chest where I had seen Juana put away the maps and pulled out the rough pieces of paper, careful to maintain their order so she wouldn't know I had been there. As I'd thought, they were hand-drawn maps of Islamorada. Closer up, I could see the detail in certain areas of the coast and the part of the island I assumed we were on now. There were also writing materials and ink. Juana must have drawn the maps, charting out the areas the expedition had journeyed through.

But what was she trying to find? Each of the maps had one 'x', all in the same location close to the camp. What *was* that?

It crossed my mind again that she might actually be seeking supplies of fresh water, but if that was the case, there appeared to be rivers and small pools that would be more convenient to get to from where we were.

So maybe it was the lake – the Fountain of Youth. Juana had sounded too interested in the possibility that I had found a lake. If she was after one specific lake – the Fountain – then she must have known what its powers were. She was either trying to turn herself immortal, or was already immortal and seeking the Fountain for a different reason.

The maps were snatched out of my hands.

'I know exactly what you are.'

My head snapped up. It was Juana. Her face was red and her body shook as she stashed the maps back inside the open chest.

'You're not supposed to be here. Not like this. In this tent or in this world,' she said.

I opened my mouth but knew an apology wouldn't suffice. I also knew I didn't want to apologise to a killer.

As Juana moved towards me, I ran from the tent. When I burst out into the middle of the camp, heads turned, so I slowed my pace to a walk. All I wanted to do was talk to Henley, but I couldn't go into the woods to travel forward in time with all those eyes on me. Instead, I walked towards the priest's tent. That would have to be my refuge for now.

As Juana had said, it was set apart from the others beyond the firepit and consequently easy to spot. Inside, the tent was split into two 'rooms' by a simple opaque sheet that ran lengthwise across the space. I entered the left-hand side, where I presumed the raised tent flap indicated that it was empty. I pulled down the flap behind me and sat alone on the dirt floor, then closed my eyes and took a breath.

Those things Juana had said to me – she obviously knew that I was immortal. Maybe she had sensed something off about me all along. She also knew that I had worked out that she was looking for the Fountain of Youth. Of course she knew. It would make sense that she would know a lot about me and my doings if she wanted me dead. I just didn't know why she wanted to kill me.

Did she want the Fountain of Youth all to herself? And what did she mean when she said, 'You're not supposed to be here. Not like this. In this tent or in this world.' Did she mean that I wasn't supposed to exist, since I was an immortal? Was that the reason she wanted to murder me? But she was an immortal herself . . .

My thoughts felt unbearably heavy. I held my head in my heads.

'I just can't do this,' I whispered.

'Repent, my child, and the Lord will forgive.'

I looked at the dividing cloth. I could barely see the outline of the priest sitting on the other side.

'Forgive me, Father, I feel lost,' I began.

'Tell me how you have lost your way, my child.'

I remembered the last time I had been in a confessional. Although it wasn't in a tent and it had been in Henry VIII's court, it was very much like this. The priest had the same warm, soothing tone, and sounded like someone I thought I could talk to. I felt like I could do no wrong in a confessional.

'A woman called Juana has taken me in and helped me, and for that I'm grateful. But I fear that her reasons for doing so are not right.'

'And in what way are they not right?'

'I fear that she's exactly like me. Someone from whom God has turned away.'

'The Shepherd will always lead his flock.'

I placed my palms on the cool earth. 'Not if one of them is damaged irrevocably.'

'You believe you are damaged irrevocably?'

'I suffer an . . . abnormality that I can't fix or change, an unnaturalness that wasn't supposed to happen . . .'

After a pause, he said, 'And you think this woman has this same . . . disease?'

'I know it,' I said.

'Our Lord loves and forgives if you attempt to set things right.'

'I know,' I said, but I didn't mean it. This priest didn't understand. Immortality wasn't something I could ever 'set right'. And yet here I was, trying to get water from the Fountain of Youth to subject Henley to the same fate Miss Hatfield had inflicted on me. It was all a twisted mess, but there was no getting out of it.

'You're right,' I told the priest. 'I need to set it right.'

I left the confessional before he could say anything in reply.

When I came out of the tent, lunch was being served. Juana's eyes met mine as soon as I glanced in her direction.

She looked like she wanted to talk to me, but I figured if I didn't let myself be alone with her, she couldn't say anything about immortality or try to harm or kill me.

'Soup,' a man grunted to me in his heavy accent, handing me a bowl of stew much like breakfast.

'Thank you.'

The men were taking their places around the fire. I waited till Juana got her soup and sat down before choosing a spot on the other side of the circle. From there I could watch her and make sure she didn't come anywhere near me.

I looked at the men to keep my mind off Juana. They came in all shapes and sizes – some were broad and square, while others were tall and lean, but there wasn't an ounce of extra fat on any of them. I supposed expeditions like this would do that to you. The men glanced in my direction, too – a new face inevitably piqued their curiosity. Most of their expressions were surprisingly kind; suspicious, of course, but still gentle at the core. One man had the bushiest eyebrows I had ever seen. Another I recognised from yesterday, his pointy beard dipping into his soup as he drank it. José was also there. He glowered at me when our eyes met, but perhaps that was normal for him – he hadn't exactly been friendly in the first place.

The priest left his tent to join us for lunch and looked surprised when he saw me amidst the men. His neatly trimmed goatee sparked a memory. Maybe it reminded me of the way my – Cynthia's – father had worn his facial hair. Even with the beard, the priest looked young and surprisingly handsome. He was probably twenty-five at most – too young to be wearing all that solemn black – but his age matched that of most of the men there. There

307

were few grey hairs among them. It made sense that they would send the younger, stronger men on hard voyages like this one.

As the men were finishing their soup, some of them pulled metal flasks from their pockets. One was passed around and they took swigs of whatever was in it. I let the flask pass me by the first time, but the second time around, I decided to try it. I took a cautious sip and the liquid burned my throat. I coughed and tried to swallow simultaneously to get the taste out of my mouth and the men guffawed as I spluttered. More flasks came out, some of which weren't passed around. I guessed that these men were hoarding personal rations, not knowing when they would be able to get more . . . Or maybe these were the men who were sick of the expedition and just wanted to get drunk. Eventually they started to clear away their plates and return to their tents for what I assumed was siesta time.

I saw a flask that had been left behind and quickly picked it up, checking that no one was about to claim it. I'd had enough of whatever that drink was, but I could use the flask to collect water from the lake . . . once I found it. Finding the lake was another issue entirely.

All too soon, the area around the fire was almost empty, and only Juana, the priest and a couple of others remained. Juana still looked like she wanted to talk to me so I had to move quickly. I headed into the woods. The men would probably think I was seeking privacy to empty my bladder but Juana probably knew I was trying to get away from her. I had to tell Henley I was sure I had found the killer – I mean, she did try to strangle me in my sleep.

I found the tree that bent at the waist and mentally counted fifty-four steps from that until I made it to the tree I had marked. A voice startled me just as I started to dig for the clock.

'Rebecca?'

Juana had followed me into the woods and her voice didn't sound that far off. I dug frantically.

'Rebecca! I know you're here.'

My fingers hit metal and I scooped up the clock. I was turning the hands when the trees parted and Juana appeared. I looked up to see the scenery already dissolving around me. Juana's face had drained of blood and her hand was frozen in mid-air, as if she was about to say something.

It was too late.

She had seen me time travel.

'Henley!' I burst into our room brandishing the clock in one hand and the metal flask in the other.

I must have looked a sight but Henley wasn't there to see it. Damn it. Where was he? I wasn't sure, but it was probably the following day in this timeline as well. Henley must have slept one night since he had last seen me.

I ran back through the lobby, earning me a confused look from Al at the front desk, but there was no one else around. I could see the pool through the lobby's rear windows. Maybe Henley was there. I ran outside, oblivious to what the other guests must be thinking about me in my yellowed, dirt-stained antique dress.

'Henley!'

He was sitting at the edge of the pool with his feet in the water, wearing the swimming trunks we had bought him. It must have been the most modern outfit I had ever seen him wear and I would have commented on it if I hadn't been frantic to talk to him about more pressing issues.

'Juana's immortal,' I blurted out.

'What?' Henley managed to say once he'd got over the shock of my sudden appearance. 'And lower your voice – there are other people listening.'

I crouched down next to him. 'Juana's looking for the lake – actually, I think she knows its exact location.' I told Henley about the maps I'd seen and Juana's reaction to me finding them. I described the pain Juana felt in her stomach and how she had let slip that it was worsening. I also repeated what she'd said to me: 'I know exactly what you are.'

'There are too many matching pieces for all this to be coincidence,' I said.

Henley looked away from me to think for a moment. 'You're right. Too many points align. So you think she's the killer?' His eyes met mine.

'She tried to kill me.'

Henley froze. 'What? You couldn't have started with that? She didn't hurt you, did she? What the hell happened?'

I described how she'd tried to strangle me last night. 'That should be enough to prove it . . . But there was something off about her behaviour, as if she didn't know what she was doing. The whole thing felt like a manic episode of some sort. But there's no other suspect – who else could it be? No one else is immortal. Or at least not that I knew. Maybe there was someone else that I hadn't thought of who was actually an immortal . . . There's José, who doesn't seem to like dogs – or me either, for that matter – but I doubt he has any reason to want me dead. The rest of the men barely acknowledge my existence, let alone talk to me. There's the priest—'

Looking at Henley's face, I suddenly understood why the priest had seemed so familiar. That face. That voice.

'My God . . .'

'Rebecca?'

'It's the priest,' I said. 'It's the priest. He was at your father's funeral. He was at your house. He was at Henry VIII's court.'

'Father Gabriel?'

'He's the killer.'

We stared at each other open-mouthed, stunned into silence.

All those attempts on my life. He killed Miss Hatfield – he must have been in her house. He was there when I first met Henley. I saw him. He was at Richard's deathbed. My God.

My mind was whirling uncontrollably but I struggled to vocalise my thoughts. 'H-he was there. In each time period.'

'Every time someone tried to kill you,' Henley said.

I cursed myself for not seeing it sooner. I thought back to my conversation with him in the confessional. The fact that he didn't have an accent like the rest of the men and Juana should have made me suspicious. He'd done so much damage over the years.

'He murdered Miss Hatfield.'

In the silence between us we listened to the splashing of children playing in the pool.

'Do you think he killed my father?' Henley asked quietly.

The priest – Father Gabriel, if that was even his name – had been visiting Mr Beauford for months as his health deteriorated. Mr Beauford had developed a fascination with immortality towards the end of his life and begun collecting artefacts that might have any connection with it. Was that reason enough to kill him? I tried to take a breath, but it felt like my lungs were being crushed.

'He tried to smother you in Tudor England – and he tried to kill you in Heathrow Airport.'

'He ransacked Miss Hatfield's house before killing her. *He* sent me the text to meet at the location where she was killed. He must have been trying to kill us both at the same time.'

Henley's body shook as he sucked in a shaky breath.

'He was also in London before we came here,' I said. 'He was in our room – he wrapped the plastic beads around your hands.'

'Prayer beads,' Henley said softly. His face was devoid of colour and I knew mine was, too.

'And the dead snake. And the peacock, too. He was everywhere. He's been tracking our every move.'

Henley bit his lip. 'He must have his own way of travelling in time – his own clock or something.'

'That means we can't run from him for long.' I forced myself to breathe. 'I need to go after him and deal with him somehow on my own terms.'

'Rebecca. He wants to *kill* you – you'd only make it easy for him.' Henley was insistent.

'What other choice do I have?' I snapped.

Henley tried a gentler voice. 'Turn me immortal first so I can help you, at least,' he said.

I knew he felt helpless, but would turning Henley immortal really be the answer? I didn't know, but immortality would keep him safer, at least. Immortality meant Henley would be able to travel in time, far away from the killer's grasp, as long as he had access to the clock. I was willing to do anything to keep him safe.

I nodded and held up the flask, which was still in my lap along with the clock. 'I'll go back to fetch the water. I know exactly where the lake is now that I've seen Juana's map.'

Henley's forehead was creased with worry lines. I knew he didn't want me to return with the killer there but we were out of options.

'Now that we've identified who the killer is I can stay out of his way,' I promised.

'Be careful. Please.'

Chapter 20

I ran out of the woods and headed for Juana's tent. I kept
to the perimeter of the camp – it was dark, so I avoided
the central area where the man who was supposed to be
on watch was fast asleep by the fire.

Juana woke up as soon as I entered the tent. 'I was worried
that you—'

'I know everything,' I said.

I heard fumbling and Juana lit a lamp by her hammock.
'What—'

I walked up to her hammock to better see her face in
the flickering light. 'I know that you're Juana Ruíz. I know
that you've found the Fountain of Youth. I know that you're
immortal.'

Juana's face grew so pale, I worried she wasn't breathing.

'And I'm just like you,' I said. 'I know you suspected it.'

'The sudden appearance,' she whispered, sitting up.
'The disappearances – sometimes for hours. The curiosity
about my maps—'

'So you've been reading me as well as I've been reading
you?'

Juana rubbed her temples. She looked like she was still
trying to process everything.

'You can ask me as many questions as you like later,' I
said. 'Right now, grab the maps and let's get out of here.'

'Where to?'

'To the lake—'

'Why are you trying to find the lake if you're already immortal?'

Her tone wasn't accusatory – in fact, she sounded genuinely curious. But I knew I couldn't tell her I was planning to use water from the Fountain of Youth to turn another person immortal – I was pretty sure she wouldn't approve of that.

'I want to make certain no one ever finds it again,' I said. I surprisingly didn't have to think hard to make up an answer. The words seemed to come out on their own. 'I don't know what I'll have to do to accomplish that, but first I need to find it.'

Juana clasped her hands solemnly and nodded. She looked as if she believed my answer.

'Now hurry,' I said. 'We must be back before daybreak or people will notice that you're missing.'

'No, no. It's much too far from here. Maybe two hours away, even if you walk very quickly. Give it a few days – we're moving camp much closer—'

'I don't have a few days.' I thought it best to be blunt with her. 'And neither do you. Do you know why you're experiencing those pains?'

Juana looked confused. 'My disease? You know something about it?'

'It's not a disease, and yes, I know a lot about it. You don't have a few days.' I pulled her out of the hammock. 'I'll tell you what I know on the way.'

I opened the chest, grabbed all the maps I could see and handed them to Juana.

'The night watch looks like he's asleep. Which way do we go?'

Juana pointed the way I had come. 'But let's go around the camp so as to not wake him or the others.'

I started when I felt something cold move against my bare calf. But it was just Alma, half under my skirt.

'I know you don't want to be left behind but you can't come with us,' I whispered, but she followed us out of the tent. I took Alma by her rope collar and walked her back inside. 'You need to stay here.' She started whining.

Juana poked her head back into the tent. 'She might wake someone if she barks.'

'I know – I'm trying to quieten her down,' I said.

'Just bring her along. It'll be quicker.'

I looked down at Alma. 'All right, you win. You can come.'

I swear she stuck her tongue out at me.

We trod lightly, trying not to step on any twigs or dry leaves near the tents, with Alma trotting quietly behind us. Soon we were in the forest from which I had emerged just a few minutes before.

There was a crackle of twigs next to us and Juana jumped.

'That was probably just Alma,' I said, trying to calm her down. To say that Juana was having a complicated day would be the understatement of the century – any century. 'I'm sorry I couldn't talk to you sooner about any of this.'

'How long have you known about my . . . illness?' she asked, staring straight ahead as we walked briskly through the woods.

If the moon hadn't been full, we wouldn't have had enough light shining down through the tree canopy to see a thing.

'I suspected almost immediately.'

'Just like I suspected you,' she said. 'But how did you know my name?'

I smiled to myself, wondering if she'd believe me when I told her. 'I'm from another time. The future.'

Juana briefly closed her eyes. Upon opening them, she shook her head but didn't say anything, just kept walking.

'Have you ever sat for a painting?' I asked, changing my tactic.

'Yes . . .' Juana glanced at me, trying to judge where I was going with the question.

'There's one of you in a dark red dress, and you're sitting in a dark blue armchair.'

'My mother's favourite chair,' she said. 'I had that painted a year before my mother's death. It hung in the parlour. How do you know about it?'

Every detail of that painting was etched in my memory. 'Because I've seen it. I knew the man who will own the painting in the future.'

I thought of Miss Hatfield, who had instructed me to steal the painting from Mr Beauford as my first task. I didn't know then why that painting was of such great importance to her and had thought that stealing it was a random first test of some sort. But I soon found out that Henley's father was obsessed with immortality, and later learned of Miss Hatfield's personal connection with the Beaufords.

'What? A hundred years from now?' She sounded like she was joking.

'More like three hundred.'

A silence followed during which all we could hear was our own footsteps.

'You're serious, aren't you?' Juana said.

'Yes, I am.'

'How did you get here?'

'Now that's tied to your so-called "disease".' I knew I had to explain, but how? 'When you were turned immortal by drinking from the Fountain of Youth, it was as if your body was taken out of the loop of time,' I started, trying to explain it the way Miss Hatfield had explained it to me. 'Because of that, you don't belong in any time. You *can't* belong. Every time period you live in will slowly reject your body as something unnatural it cannot keep. That's why you feel the pain and the sickness.' I thought of her shaking episode and the pain spasms she felt. I also remembered her trying to strangle me. It wasn't her. It was the madness Miss Hatfield had described. So this was what it looked like.

'And you feel this, too?'

I nodded. 'Every time I stay in one time period for too long. Which brings me to the clock.'

'A clock?'

'A time-travelling device. It helps me move to different times when I start feeling ill.'

As we picked our way through the trees, Juana indicated we should turn left. I followed her, swiping at low-hanging branches that sought to claw my face.

'And where did you find such a thing?' she asked.

'It was given to me by my . . . mentor.'

She grew quiet. Then: 'So there are others like us? People who are not meant to be?'

'Yes . . . Well, there were. There were seven of us, including me, but only two were alive at any given point.'

'I don't understand,' Juana said. 'If they were immortal like us, didn't that mean they couldn't die?'

'They can't die of sickness or old age,' I corrected. 'Physical harm – accidental or deliberate – can still affect them.'

'They were killed?' she guessed.

'Hunted down,' I said.

'And someone's after you, too?'

I told her everything I knew about the priest and what I suspected he'd done.

Juana's eyes grew so large, I could see the parts of the moon that shone through the trees reflected in the whites. 'But—'

'It's him. I'm sure of it.'

I spent the next two hours answering Juana's questions about both my Miss Hatfield and the former holders of the name. I was amazed that Alma kept up with us so well despite her age. Perhaps she enjoyed our company or the break from the routines of camp. Juana asked a few questions about Mr Beauford and why he had bought her portrait, but nothing about the future.

'Don't you want to know what it will be like?' I asked. I'd have been curious in her position. 'I could tell you about Florida in the future. New inventions. How the fashions change.'

Juana smiled but declined. 'I don't want to know.'

'But why not?'

'Because I'm not supposed to,' she said simply. 'There are certain things I'm not supposed to know until they happen to me.'

'But you're also not *supposed* to be immortal and never die,' I pointed out.

'Yes,' Juana said. 'That's unnatural, too.'

Unnatural. That word again.

'You think you're some atrocity, don't you? A scar on the Earth.' I knew the feeling because I felt it often. 'You can't live thinking that way.'

'I don't intend to.'

Juana sounded so matter-of-fact that I did a double take.

'I don't intend to live this way,' she repeated. 'That's why I'm seeking out the lake again. I don't need to become immortal – I received that curse the first time. I'm going back to reverse it.'

I had never thought of going to the Fountain of Youth to reverse immortality.

'And you think it'll work?'

'It's the only chance I have. I couldn't spend my life – my existence – alone in Spain, wondering.' Juana smiled bravely into the dark. 'I'm looking forward to curing the discomfort and pain that come with immortality, too.'

That confirmed my instinct not to tell Juana why I was going to the lake. As I suspected, she would hate the idea of me inflicting this upon Henley.

Luckily, she didn't ask again.

The earth beneath our feet started to give a little where we walked. I paused to touch the ground and felt wet dirt.

'We must be close to the lake now.'

Alma pushed against my hand and I gave her a pat.

'The forest hasn't changed since I was here last,' Juana said.

'When you were here with Ponce de León?'

'When I made the mistake of drinking from the lake on my first expedition,' she said.

I knew she wouldn't have picked immortality if she'd had the choice – Juana and I were alike in that – but it was still strange to hear it being referred to as a *mistake*. It was a horrible fate. Maybe it was something forced upon you. But a 'mistake'? That word was too simple. That word almost make it sound benign.

'There,' Juana said. 'I can see it.'

She ran ahead, pushing aside the branches of the trees in front of us. The ground sloped down towards the lake and Juana skidded as she ran. I ran after her, and Alma limped after me.

'This is it. I remember it.' Juana was knee-deep in the lake by the time I got to the bank.

She flopped chest first into the water, immersing herself. When she resurfaced, her dark hair streamed down her face. She pushed her hair back and started gulping down handfuls of the water.

Poor thing.

Juana desperately wanted the lake to undo what it had done to her. She wanted to believe that the Fountain of Youth could work both ways even though she had no reason to imagine that it would. I think she knew that, too.

I waded in after her and took her in my arms. She was sopping wet and clung to me like her clothes clung to her skin.

'Do you see anything? Is there anything different about me?'

She was hysterical, and I didn't know if it was her emotions or the curse of immortality speaking. Her cheeks were wet and I felt moisture on my own as I held her. Tears or water from the lake? I didn't know. But I thought Juana understood the truth at last as she couldn't stop crying. Her body wouldn't stop trembling even though I tried to hold her still.

'Shh . . . We'll think of something,' I said. 'You could come with me and Henley, start a new life like Miss Hatfield and I did.' That was the best I could offer her.

Juana gradually calmed herself and walked back to the shore of the lake. But when she got there, she sat down with her feet still in the water. She couldn't bring herself to withdraw her legs, as if she still couldn't fully give up on her hope of the lake restoring her mortality.

Satisfied that Juana was as all right as she could be under the circumstances, I got back to my own task. I unscrewed the cap from the flask and half-filled it with water from the lake. Henley would only need a sip and too much would only weigh me down.

I heard splashing close by and looked in the direction of the sound but couldn't see anything. Then a dart of movement caught my eye from across the lake. Alma was on the other side, bounding through the water and drinking every few steps.

'No . . .' But even as I was saying it, I knew it was too late. The dog probably hadn't tasted fresh water in days and she was lapping it up gleefully. I glanced at Juana to see if she had noticed but she was still sitting at the lake's edge, arms crossed over her knees and head bowed. I decided to leave her alone and handle Alma on my own. As I circled the lake, I wondered if the Fountain of Youth worked the same on dogs as it did on humans. There was no reason to believe it wouldn't.

'Oh, Alma, what did you do?' I said as I guided her out of the water.

Alma looked positively bubbly as she scampered in circles around me with her tongue hanging out. Well, the Fountain of Youth certainly looked like it had already cured the effects of old age. I wondered what Henley would say when I returned with an immortal dog.

I heard more splashing and it wasn't Alma because she was on dry land right in front of me, so I looked towards the other side of the lake for Juana.

She was upright now, with her feet still in the shallows of the lake. She was standing at a strange angle . . . and then I knew why.

There was an arm around her neck, holding her up in the bend of the elbow, and a second pair of legs in the water behind hers. My eyes met the eyes of the priest.

'Father Gabriel,' I whispered.

And he slit her throat.

I watched her eyes go wide – maybe from the pain, maybe in shock at the amount of blood pouring from her neck. He stood there for a few moments, holding her up, watching the blood spew forth. Then he tucked the bloody knife into his belt, opened a small glass jar he'd produced from inside his robes and poured something that looked like white powder into the lake. When he let Juana go, her body toppled forwards and pitched head first into the lake. As soon as her body touched the water, she disintegrated.

I heard a scream. Mine.

I started to run, willing my wobbly legs to move faster. I didn't dare waste time looking back but I knew he was close behind me.

He had worked out that I knew he was the killer and followed us here, presumably to murder one or both of us a safe distance from the camp. But what had he poured into the lake from that glass jar? Poison – some kind of cyanide strong enough to contaminate the entire lake? Or maybe something to neutralise the source of immortality?

He had killed Juana because he knew she was immortal. And how had he known? Because of me. I was the reason she was dead.

I crashed through the trees, waving my arms to shove the branches out of my way. I thought I was heading the way we'd come. I needed to put distance and time between me and the killer and get back to the clock. That was the only way I was going to survive.

After what felt like a good twenty minutes of running, I risked a look back but saw no sign of him. He was still probably after me, but I had lost him momentarily. Trusting my gut, I rerouted and headed in the direction I thought the camp was. Once I found the clock, I could put a lot more time between me and the killer.

Juana had died the same way Miss Hatfield had. Neither of them deserved to die. How could I have been so stupid? Juana might have lived if I'd figured out the killer's identity just a few hours sooner. Her blood was on my hands.

I ran through the woods for what felt like an eternity. My legs and arms were slick with blood from scraping bark and my muscles should have been in agony from the running, but I couldn't feel anything. Numbness brought on by adrenalin or shock? No clue.

When I reached the edge of the camp, I found the bent tree, counted fifty-four steps to the hiding place and dug up the clock as quickly as I could.

I turned the clock's hands and held my breath.

As my surroundings started to fade, I heard a bark and something hurtled towards me.

'Alma, no!'

But it was much too late to stop her.

Chapter 21

I was running down the road before the scenery around me had settled into 2016.

It wouldn't take the killer long to work out that I had gone back to this time period. I had to find Henley and warn him. I had the clock tucked under one arm and the flask under the other. It was a miracle I hadn't lost either or both during my flight from the murderer.

I stumbled at the sound of barking and looked behind me along the road. Alma was bounding after me. A part of her must have been touching me when I used the clock. Apparently I had a dog now.

I ran into the hotel lobby.

'I'm sorry, miss. No dogs—'

I couldn't be bothered with that just then. All my attention was on the lobby's rear window in the hope of finding out whether Henley was at the pool or in the room. Yes – there he was.

'Henley!' I burst outside with a yapping Alma following close behind.

Children froze in the pool before some of them started to cry, while the women tanning in their bikinis lowered their sunglasses. I wondered if they were staring at the dog running past the 'No pets' sign or my bloodied body. Maybe it was the strange outfit I was still just about wearing.

Henley was also gaping at us. The only difference was that he got over his surprise much more quickly than everyone else. He was used to it.

'What happened to you?' he asked as he stood and came to meet me. He tried to hold my arms but I couldn't stand still enough to let him. 'You need to breathe and tell me what happened,' he said.

'The killer. Juana's dead. He's—'

Behind me, Alma started yapping so loudly I could barely hear myself.

I turned around. And screamed.

He was there.

Of course he'd worked out that I'd go straight to Henley.

The next thing I knew, I felt his hands on me, then all of a sudden I was underwater.

I blinked. Everything was tinted blue. Everything was quiet and still beneath the surface. I couldn't hear Alma barking. I couldn't hear the children crying. I couldn't hear myself screaming.

I pushed myself upwards and gasped for breath as I broke the surface.

At the side of the pool, I saw Henley and the priest with their arms locked around each other in a struggle. Neither of them appeared to be winning. I swam towards them and clambered out unhindered. The killer's attention was entirely on Henley.

I grabbed the priest by his shoulders and tried to prise him off Henley, but the killer got an arm loose and swung at Henley. He stumbled and crashed onto the poolside deck.

The priest turned to me immediately and I did the only thing I could think of. I grabbed the clock and turned the hands.

*

The world started to slip away as soon as the clock's hands were turned, pulling me beyond the grasp of the priest. After that, it was only a question of perfectly positioning the clock's hands in the exact orientation.

When I staggered back into the camp, I hit a log and toppled a pile of wooden bowls. At the sound of them hitting the dirt, the men began to appear at the front of their tents.

A shooting pain went through my back. I looked at my shoulder and I caught a glimpse of sticky-looking blood before the priest came at me again. He had found me much more quickly than last time – he must have grabbed hold of my arm when I time travelled.

He had a knife in his right hand and it took all my strength to hold him in a deadlock. Something dangling from a cord around his neck was swinging against my stomach. The knife was slick with blood. Was it mine? Or Juana's? Or Henley's?

I tried to shove him off again but he was too strong for me and angled his knife closer to my neck.

The men were running towards us from their tents, hopefully to help me . . . but maybe they'd help the priest instead.

Seeing the men approaching, the priest reached down for something.

All of a sudden, the men melted away, and the forest, and the dirt beneath my feet. We were travelling in time again.

We were back by the pool, where we had been standing just a few minutes before. We were only a couple of feet from the water and I tried to plant my feet so I couldn't be pushed in again. My shoulder was radiating pain now but my eyes were glued on the knife.

The men with their poolside drinks and the women with their oversized sunglasses must have been in shock after seeing us appear out of thin air, but I didn't have time to look at them.

'Henley!'

I gathered all my remaining strength and twisted my entire body to one side, momentarily unbalancing the priest. I took the brief chance to escape from his grasp and run.

I only managed a few steps before something caught hold of my ankles and I felt my body lurching towards the ground. My chest hit the cement. I tasted blood in my mouth. But for one small instant I felt fierce relief – I hadn't dropped the clock.

Hoping he wouldn't notice, I angled my arm to reach the clock's hands.

I drew a breath and kicked him. Hard. He did what I wanted and let go.

I turned the hands.

I felt dirt underneath my hands. Was it 1532 again?

No matter. The priest hadn't arrived . . . yet.

I forced myself upright and spat out the blood that had pooled in my mouth. I stood tall, waiting for him to appear, while I gasped for breath.

When he did arrive, he took me by surprise and tackled me from behind. As I hit the ground for the second time that day, I managed to twist just enough so that he took the brunt of the fall. I rolled over to gain some leverage and struck his head with my open hand. Meanwhile, the priest got in a few blows of his own, mostly to my stomach, but also a kick which buckled my knee.

He twisted, rolling away just enough that we weren't touching.

I took the chance to turn the clock's hands again.

I landed in a bush. Actually, technically, it was one of the potted miniature palm trees by the pool. Thankfully it was out of the way enough that none of the other guests noticed my arrival this time, although they were disturbed by the events of the previous few minutes. Behind me was the main building of the resort. I pressed my back against a wall and lay in wait for the killer. Any minute now, he would appear. And I would be ready for him this time.

I listened hard but couldn't hear anything through the commotion of the crowd. And the opportunity to catch my breath didn't bring me relief. It only gave me time to be concerned that I had missed something.

Peeking out between the leaves of the plant, I scanned the people by the pool. Unsurprisingly they were in a panic, having just seen two blood-soaked strangers materialise out of nothing and fight each other. Many of them had already left the pool, and those who remained were frantically calling the police and the manager.

I spotted the metal flask by the pool deck. It was half under one of the deckchairs, which was occupied by a woman who, judging by the bottle still in her hand, probably had been spreading tanning oil on her back only a few minutes ago, but now was screaming an incomprehensible series of yelps instead.

Something cold and wet touched the side of my leg. I looked down, expecting to swat away an insect, but it was only Alma.

'You stuck it out through this entire fight?' I scratched her under her chin and she panted, rolling her tongue out. My fingers must have found her favourite spot. 'Where's Henley?' I asked her. I scanned the pool area but couldn't see him. Perhaps he was back in the room.

I was about to make my way there with Alma when I saw a little boy heading towards us. He took in the blood dripping from my shoulder and the scrapes running the length of my legs before his eyes locked with mine. I held my breath. I knew I looked like something out of a child's worst nightmare and was waiting for him to scream. But instead, he just continued walking towards me.

'You have lots of ouchies,' he said, his tone serious.

'Yes, I do,' I replied, not knowing what else to say.

'Whenever I show Mama my ouchies, she tells me to scratch my forehead because it'll make me forget about them.'

He was so solemn that I felt the only appropriate response was to nod gravely back.

'That's good advice from your mama,' I said. 'Very wise.'

'Can I pet your doggie?'

I had an idea.

'If you help me, you most certainly can.' I pointed out the metal flask underneath the deckchair. 'Would you mind getting that for me? I lost it earlier and I'd really like it back.'

By then, police were swarming the area, pushing people aside and talking to a few witnesses, but the boy easily slipped into the mob unnoticed. I watched him toddle to the deckchair, pick up the flask and return, without attracting any attention at all.

'Thank you,' I said, taking it from him. I shook it to make sure the water was still inside.

'Now can I pet your doggie?'

I told him that he could, and he plopped down in front of Alma to stroke her entire body. Alma didn't appear to mind. In fact, she licked his face while he giggled and ran his fingers through her yellow fur.

I was still nervous about the priest, not to mention being caught by the police, and sent the boy on his way as soon as I could. The last thing I wanted was a child around when the killer came.

I took the back way to the room with Alma, avoiding the pool and the lobby. The fewer people who saw a dog and a bloody woman in the resort, the better.

I found the key under the pot as usual and pushed open the door.

'Henley?' Then I sighed; he wasn't here, either.

Alma stared up at me, as if curious about why I was talking to an empty room.

The first odd thing I noticed was that the neon-green backpack was in plain sight. We always took care to hide it under the bed when it wasn't with us. I approached the bed and saw the backpack's contents strewn across the duvet.

There was a note on the pillow. Frowning, I picked it up, then recognised Henley's handwriting. Miss Hatfield's address was at the top, and in smaller script at the bottom was today's date and the time '12.06'.

I had an idea what that might mean, but I didn't want to believe it.

I checked the stuff that was spread out on the bed. Henley's passport was missing, along with some cash.

Henley wouldn't leave without me, not willingly. The priest must have taken him. And the address on the note . . . They'd gone to Miss Hatfield's house.

I held my head. I couldn't breathe. The priest had seen Henley's – or rather Richard's – body in more than one time period and must have thought he was immortal. If that was true, Henley was in more trouble than I had imagined. He wasn't just leverage now – he was also a target. At that thought, my body started to ache all over as if it had just realised the extent of the damage caused by the fight it had gone through.

There was no time for thinking. Henley was alone with the priest. I had to get to him.

I picked up the phone and dialled.

'Hello? This is Al at the front desk.'

'Yes, um, hello, Al. This is Rebecca in Room 212. I'd like to check out as soon as possible, please – could you get all the paperwork ready for me?'

'Of course. Unfortunately you will be expected to pay the full amount for the four-week stay you booked even though—'

'Yes, that's fine. How long will it take?'

'I could have the paperwork ready in twenty minutes if you would—'

'Perfect. Thank you.' Just as I was about to hang up, I thought of something. 'You don't happen to have a gift shop here, do you?' I asked.

'Of course. It's next to the elevators on your right as you exit. It has the most wonderful selection of souvenirs, chocolates—'

'Yes, that'll be fine. Thank you,' I said, hanging up.

The priest must have sneaked Henley out of the hotel in the middle of the commotion. There was no way I could catch up with them, not even by turning back time to keep the priest from taking Henley, since like me the priest was immortal and there was only one version of him in all of time. If I were to travel back in time, I simply wouldn't find him.

I looked down at Alma, who was still staring at me. 'We need to get ready to leave.'

Walking into the bathroom, I was met with my gory reflection. One of the sleeves of my dress had been cut clean off and blood was dripping down my back from my sliced shoulder. My right knee was swollen and starting to turn purple. In other words, I was a mess. My saving grace was my face. I'd been smacked around but didn't look bloody and the bruises hadn't bloomed yet. I could hide everything else underneath clean clothing and look relatively normal. That was a good start.

Groaning, I started taking off my clothes to inspect the full extent of the damage. My entire chest was purple – probably from the fall onto concrete – but none of my ribs felt broken, thank goodness. I took a flannel and cleaned my cuts. The one on my shoulder was by far the deepest. Applying water to it burned and I had to grit my teeth to keep from shouting, but I needed to clean the wound thoroughly to keep it from getting infected, and to mop up as much blood as I could to prevent it from seeping through a clean shirt.

When I was done with all the cuts and had scrubbed most of the dirt off my legs, I tore off a sleeve from one of Henley's shirts and tied that around my hurt shoulder. Hopefully it would prevent further bleeding. I wore another of Henley's shirts on top to hide the make-shift bandage, one with long sleeves to hide the cuts on my arms. Jeans covered my scratched legs and swollen knee.

I checked myself in the mirror again. Not bad. I looked more like a person and less like something from a horror movie.

I shoved everything we owned into the backpack, taking special care with the clock and the flask. I'd have to remember to ask for a plastic bag in airport security because of the liquid. The flask looked like it would just about fit in one.

Alma was sitting patiently by the door. I couldn't leave her here. I had no idea if I'd be allowed to take her on the plane, but I had to try.

I slung the backpack over my better shoulder and headed to the lobby with Alma. The gift shop wasn't big but it would have to do. I scanned the glass-walled room filled with tropical-themed T-shirts, mugs, candles, glasses . . . thankfully, I quickly found what I had been hoping for. I chose a thin scarf with a fish print and the biggest sunglasses I could find. I set them on the counter along with a bag and pulled out the credit card. I doubted the bag was actually meant to be a pet carrier, but it was rectangular with a zip opening on the top and two mesh sides. It was perfect for getting Alma on the plane. Alma felt heavy for her size, but she couldn't have been too much more than fifteen pounds.

Once everything was paid for and the tags had been cut off by the helpful shop assistant, I draped the scarf over my head and tied it under my chin. I put the oversized sunglasses on and picked up Alma's bag. Not the best disguise, perhaps, but hopefully it would make me look different enough from the woman involved in the fight by the pool that no one would recognise me.

Al was ready with the paperwork for me to check out.

'Should I use the credit card on file?' he asked.

'Yes please.'

Al glowered at Alma by my feet but didn't bother to remind me that dogs weren't allowed at the resort, probably because we were checking out already. A couple of uniformed police officers walked in as I was signing the last of the papers Al had put in front of me.

'Why are the police here?' I asked.

'There was a bit of a bizarre scuffle outside,' Al responded.

I wondered how many emergency calls were made by the poolside patrons watching two people disappear and appear while trying to kill each other.

'Could you call me a taxi?' I asked.

'There should be a couple outside that just dropped off guests,' he said as he escorted me to the door.

Sure enough, a taxi was waiting for me. I coaxed Alma into her new carrier and we got in.

'Miami airport, please. As quickly as possible.'

Buying a last-minute ticket at the check-in counter was surprisingly easy since I was travelling alone. I only needed to tell the woman that a family emergency had come up and she sympathised to the point of giving me a discount on the fee for Alma, though money was now no issue since the credit card was a magical way to pay for everything and the money from the auction house wasn't going to run out any time soon. Naturally, I also knew that buying a last-minute ticket would probably result in additional security procedures.

As expected, a last-minute flight meant I was asked a few more questions, but the questions were centred around where I was planning to stay and what my residential address was, so they were easy enough to answer. I was escorted through the side and Alma was checked by her own officer. I remembered to ask for a plastic bag for the flask, so the backpack passed security without any trouble. A TSA officer was curious about the bulge at my left shoulder. I told her it was a bandaged injury and she was fine after she waved her metal detector wand over it.

Alma and I made it onto the plane in spite of all the potential complications. Then it was just sitting and waiting.

In a way, that was really the hardest part. There was even more waiting considering how many planes I had to take in order to make it back to New York.

I had time on my hands. Too much time.

In the middle of the struggle with the priest, I hadn't been able to think. When I realised that Henley had been abducted, my brain had frozen. Now I suddenly had three whole hours ahead of me with nothing to do *but* think.

Why had the priest taken Henley? To make sure I came to him? Probably. I couldn't leave Henley with the priest. And why was the priest doing all this in the first place? He was obviously immortal himself. I had more in common with him than anyone else in this world including Henley, yet he had some twisted vendetta against me. I just didn't get it. I had too many questions and no hope of answering them on my own.

I tilted my head back and stretched my stiff neck, staring at the plastic interior of the plane. My entire body was sore, especially my chest. It was probably black with bruises by now. I could only hope that the bruising on my face was minimal enough to avoid attracting attention.

When the last plane touched down in New York, I rushed off with the backpack and Alma in her carrier. I caught a taxi and gave the driver Miss Hatfield's address. As we made our way through the city, I fidgeted with my shirt, the backpack, anything I could lay my hands on. And still the unanswerable questions plagued me. What was going to happen when I arrived at the house? How was I going to get Henley out and avoid being killed by the priest? I hadn't come up with any kind of plan during the flight. What was I going to do?

I balled my hands into fists. *Okay*, I thought, *I have to take this one step at a time.*

The first thing I had to do was make sure Henley was all right. That was the most important thing. But . . . what if Henley was already dead?

I swallowed a burning in my throat. I couldn't think like that. I *shouldn't* think like that.

The taxi pulled up in front of Miss Hatfield's brownstone and I paid with the magic credit card. I gathered up my stuff and got out of the cab. I let Alma out of her carrier and walked up the stairs to the door.

It was ajar.

I willed my legs not to shake and walked in. I made sure Alma had followed me before closing the door behind us.

I took another step.

'Henley?'

I waited. No answer.

I walked slowly through the parlour, then the hallway, then the kitchen. In the kitchen, I opened the knife drawer and let my hands run over the knife handles. I hoped I wouldn't need it, but I took one before I continued checking all the rooms on the ground floor.

Empty.

I took the stairs to the upper floor and looked through each of the bedrooms. I checked behind each door.

Empty.

But now I knew exactly where they were.

They were in the room where it had all begun; the room I woke up in after Miss Hatfield slipped the water from the Fountain of Youth into my lemonade and turned me immortal. The attic bedroom.

I walked to the end of the hall and set the backpack down, still clutching the knife. Oddly, my steps were sure and steady now. There was no rush. He would wait for me.

The ceiling trapdoor to the attic was open and the steps that led up to it already pulled down. He was definitely waiting for me.

I walked up the stairs, each step deliberate. My body no longer hurt. I'd moved beyond physical pain now. This would be the end.

Chapter 22

'Rebecca.' Henley was the first to speak.

He was tied to a wooden chair. The cord the priest had bound him with was so tight it was cutting into Henley's flesh.

The priest stood behind him with a knife to Henley's throat, and I clutched harder at my own knife. It was the first chance I'd had to really look at him since working out that he was the killer. The only thing between us was a four-poster bed with a gilded headboard and a bare mattress.

The priest looked like a pillar of darkness in his black robes. He was tall enough that he could have touched the exposed rafters slanting above his head. Against the black fabric, his skin was pale and translucent. He looked as if he'd never set foot in the sun. But he was handsome. He had bright green eyes and they never left mine.

He looked *good*. Kind. Like a priest should.

'Put the knife down,' he said.

'Why are you doing this?' I asked, talking a step forward.

'Stay where you are.' It was the smooth voice I had heard in confessional. 'Put the knife down.'

I was hyperaware of how close the priest's knife was held to Henley's throat, and slowly put down my own by my feet.

'Good,' the priest said. 'Now kick it towards me.'

I did as he said.

'Don't you see? Don't you see what you've done?' The hand holding the knife began to tremble. 'This was supposed to be you.' The priest ran the blade down the front of Henley's throat. 'This would have been a fitting ending for you. We couldn't even call it death since you're not really alive, are you? You're merely *existing*.' He spat out the last word. 'You don't deserve death. You simply need an end.'

'And you're here to end me?' I said. 'Then why are you standing there with a knife against Henley's throat and not mine?'

He squinted his green eyes at me. 'Sometimes the innocent must be sacrificed to fulfil God's work.'

The innocent? So he knew that Henley wasn't immortal yet. 'You murdered Miss Hatfield to do "God's work"?'

'Miss Hatfield? Is that what you called her? Such respect for the person who damned you.' He smirked.

I had never seen anyone look so sinister, least of all a priest. 'What kind of God do you worship?' I asked.

The priest had an answer ready for me. 'One who created everything and everyone. Save for you and me.'

'You're just like me,' I said. 'Why would you want to end me?'

His answer surprised me. 'You're right – we're the same. You're *unnatural*. Something that was never supposed to be.'

Unnatural. There was that word again.

'The Lord never meant for you to exist.' The priest walked around Henley, trailing the knife's point across his neck. 'You cannot continue on to the afterlife without dying. You're stopping that from happening. Disrupting the way things are supposed to be.'

340

'This doesn't make sense,' I said. 'You had a chance to kill me in that hostel room in London. And then another chance when you left that dead snake. We were asleep. We couldn't have stopped you.'

He smiled. 'Very clever, Miss Rebecca. I did have the perfect opportunity to end you there. But I had to make sure no more immortals – deviants of nature – were created.'

'And so you followed me to the lake,' I finished off his speech.

'Precisely. You're much sharper than you look,' he said. 'I knew of the lake. I knew it was in Florida, but not it's exact location . . . Not until you kindly led me directly to it. With that knowledge, I was able to ensure more aberrants weren't created. You even led me directly to another who had already been turned.'

'Juana.'

'Indeed, and I must thank you for that. She might have slipped away from me, but the Lord wished her caught and finished, so I did my duty.' The priest moved to Henley's side, so I could see all of him apart from his legs, which were still hidden from view by the bed between us.

A glint of silver caught my eye.

There was a pocket watch hanging from the priest's neck. I recognised it even from where I stood across the room. I could describe the flowers and vines engraved on the cover without needing to see it up close because it had been made for me.

'Ah, so you've noticed my little time-travelling trinket?' The priest held it up with his free hand and watched as it swung on the chain and caught the light. 'I have you to thank for this as well, don't I? The court clockmaker created this for you and you were foolish enough to leave it behind. For me.'

I had left it on Richard's bedside table because I hadn't thought it was important. I commissioned the clockmaker to reproduce the golden clock – *my* clock – not some silver pocket watch he thought was more suitable for me. I never imagined it would be able to time travel.

'So many surprises.' The priest tilted his head and watched me.

I was still worried he would kill Henley. I needed to keep him talking until I could come up with a plan.

'So how did you become immortal?' I asked. 'I doubt you'd have done it voluntarily.'

The priest remained silent and I thought he would refuse to answer, preferring to move ahead with his killings.

'It *wasn't* voluntary,' he said at last. 'One of your Miss Hatfields was to blame.'

'One of the former Miss Hatfields turned you immortal?'

'No, not me – she turned my sister immortal,' he said. 'My sister was sick. Dying. She was going to meet her Maker. She was pious. She knew the Lord. But in a moment of weakness, she became scared and begged Miss Hatfield to help her—'

'And so she turned your sister immortal.' I was trying to figure out why I hadn't been told about her along with all the other Miss Hatfields.

'Did she become the next Miss Hatfield?'

'No.' The priest's face flushed. 'I ended her before that became her fate.'

My stomach turned. 'You killed your own sister?'

'I sent her to the Lord, where she belonged . . . But not before she turned me into this . . . this perverse insult to the Lord!'

I watched the knife at Henley's throat carefully. As the priest talked and became more agitated, the blade moved more erratically against Henley's throat. Right now it was so close that he could barely swallow.

'She thought it was a gift. A way to remain with me for ever. Even at the cost of paradise and salvation.'

'And so she sneaked water from the Fountain of Youth into something you consumed,' I said.

'Yes . . . She believed it would be some sort of twisted heaven on Earth.'

'And that sent you on a mission to hunt down all immortals?' I said.

'You're all the same.' The priest dragged the tip of the knife down to Henley's collarbone. 'All of you think you're more intelligent than you are. All seven of you sought to understand me. All of you tried to talk your way out. But at the last, it always ends the same way.' His green eyes glowed. 'I provide you with a last kindness – a choice in death. Death by arsenic. Or by the blade.' He swept his knife up Henley's throat in one swift motion.

My heart leapt at that sudden movement, but he only pressed down hard enough to mark Henley's throat with a thin red scratch. I had to remain calm.

'Arsenic?' I asked.

With his free hand, the priest drew a black pouch from inside his robes.

'I always give each Miss Hatfield the choice of a more honest death. Don't you think that taking the pills would be more honest than running, and thereby forcing me to kill them with a knife instead? The last Miss Hatfield chose to run instead. She chose a coward's death.' The priest tossed the pouch onto the bed. 'Go on – take it.'

I leaned over to the centre of the bed to retrieve the pouch. Soft black velvet. I recognised it from the lake. When I opened it, I saw two white tablets inside.

343

I finally had a plan . . . although I didn't know for certain if it would work or leave me dead.

'Wondrous pills. Maybe a little uncomfortable . . .' the priest said. 'Or a swifter death by blade. Have you made your decision?'

'Yes, I have.' I couldn't meet Henley's eyes.

'And what have you decided?'

'Arsenic.'

I took out one of the pills and tossed the pouch back onto the centre of the bed.

'Then let me die, too,' Henley said.

Both the priest and I looked at him.

No, Henley. You weren't supposed to say that.

'How gallant of you,' the priest said. 'Saves me from fretting about how to dispose of you afterwards.' He cut the cords securing Henley to the chair.

'Give me a pill,' Henley said.

I closed my eyes. This couldn't be happening. It was the wrong time to be stupidly gallant. Henley was actually going to kill himself.

The priest handed Henley the pouch and he shook out the remaining pill.

I tried to make eye contact with him. I tried to convey that I had a plan and that he wasn't supposed to kill himself, but there was no change in his eyes as he watched me.

Damn it, Henley.

'Well, on with it,' the priest said.

My eyes were locked with Henley's as we both put the pills to our lips.

I stuck mine in my mouth first. I tucked it under my tongue and prayed it wouldn't dissolve too quickly.

Henley took his tablet. And swallowed. *Oh, God.*

I felt the warmth drain from my face. I didn't know if it was the arsenic, or the panic I felt watching Henley swallow the tablet. I felt nauseous and lurched forward, retching, but there was nothing in my stomach to come up. Was that the arsenic or the dread? I saw Henley go white, but I couldn't keep my eyes on him. I felt faint and crumpled to the floor. I managed to make a pillow with my hands to cushion the fall but one side of my head still hit the ground. I didn't even feel the pain.

As soon as the bed blocked me from the priest's sight, I spat out the pill and quickly shoved it under the bed.

'Rebecca!'

Through the haze and my slit eyes, I watched Henley rush to my side. He made to bend over me but collapsed instead.

I dug my finger into Henley's mouth, looking to pull the pill out. We only had a few seconds until the priest came over to check that we were dying. Henley pushed my hand away and pointed under the bed.

In the middle of the floor beneath the bed were two white pills.

I was so relieved. I closed my eyes but still felt like vomiting. Maybe it was the arsenic, or maybe because I hit my head. I felt my consciousness slipping. Losing my grip on everything. Scared. And after the fear – nothing.

When I came to, the priest was standing over us. He reached down and felt the side of Henley's neck and I realised he was checking for a pulse.

Fear shot through me. If it was too strong, the priest would just run him through with the knife. If Henley's pulse was too weak or non-existent . . . he might already be dead. Maybe we'd both had the pills in our mouths for too long to survive.

The priest wouldn't desecrate a corpse without good reason – which was why I had come up with this arsenic plan in the first place – but nothing would stop him from stabbing us if he thought we weren't dead.

After what felt like an eternity, the priest stood. He looked satisfied. He started to mutter.

'. . . Hallowed be thy name. Thy kingdom come, thy will be done, on Earth as it is in heaven . . .'

I recognised the Lord's Prayer.

'. . . Forgive us our trespasses as we forgive those who trespass against us. And lead us not into temptation, but deliver us from evil.'

I couldn't see the priest's face as he prayed over us, but I suspected it would be showing a strange compassion.

His voice was strong until the end. 'For thine is the kingdom, the power and the glory, for ever and ever. Amen.'

I waited for him to check my pulse but he must have done it already while I was unconscious. Instead he walked over to the other side of the room again, muttering all the while.

'Arsenic draws out death, but death it does bring. It's only a matter of time before they're returned to the earth.'

I opened my eyes fully and looked at Henley. His glazed eyes stared back at me. *Maybe he was actually—*

He blinked.

Thank God.

Henley opened his mouth to say something but I gave a minute shake of my head, signalling him not to make a sound. I indicated where the priest had gone with a flick of my eyes in the direction of the slight shuffling noises coming from the other side of the room.

I couldn't imagine what the priest might be doing. It sounded like he had moved the chair Henley had been tied to.

I glanced at Henley. He had risen silently into a crouch, just barely peeking over the side of the bed. I knew it wasn't a good idea but I joined him anyway, trying to see what the priest was up to. That was the only way we could stay one step ahead of him.

The priest had moved the chair in front of the room's one window, which was small and circular, barely big enough to see out of. But the priest was facing away from the window so that the light shone down on him from behind. He was staring at the knife in his hands. When he turned the blade, it caught the light from the window and threw sharp streaks across the room. He appeared to be playing with the knife, waiting for something to happen.

The priest sighed as if he had to do something tedious and stood up. And then he plunged the blade into himself.

My hand shot out involuntarily and Henley caught it.

The priest remained standing for a moment, looking down at the knife embedded in his chest. Then he staggered and sat back down on the chair. There was so much blood. His robes couldn't soak all of it up and it dripped down the chair. His eyes were wide, as if in amazement at all the blood. As if he couldn't quite believe that he had done this to himself. But his lips were fixed in a smile.

Then I understood. His was the final death.

The priest hadn't argued when I'd told him we were the same. We were both immortals – and in his eyes, we were both aberrations in God's plan. He had killed all the Miss Hatfields before me. He thought he had killed me, too. His last duty had been to kill himself, to purge the world of the unnatural.

Henley started to stand.

I placed a hand on his shoulder. 'No.'

The right thing to do was to let him have his peace. He was already dying. There was no sense or compassion in showing him that his death had borne no meaning.

Chapter 23

The priest gulped his last breath and let it out in a final sigh. His body slumped forward, his duty finished. He disintegrated and I watched his ashes softly cover the chair he had been sitting in.

Henley stood, unable to tear his eyes away from the priest's remains as he helped me up.

'A-are you all right?' he asked.

He knew I wasn't all right. He knew neither of us was all right and wouldn't be for a while. But as the realisation of what had happened sank in, all we could do was fall back on our usual habits.

That was why I told him, 'I'm okay.'

'Good. Good. I-I'm fine, too. Very fine.'

He had forgotten to let go of my hand and I felt his tremors through his fingers.

We stood still for a moment before I pulled him towards the trapdoor in the floor. We couldn't stay in that room.

As we walked down the stairs I saw Alma lying at the foot of them, waiting for us. She had probably heard our voices in the attic and wanted to come up, but the first step was too high for her short legs.

'You've been waiting for us all this time, haven't you? You knew we'd come back for you.' When I crouched down to pet her, I realised the floor was wet. I put my hand on her head and she raised her eyes to look at me. Her eyes were tired. The light in them was dimming and there was grey in her fur again.

'I-I don't understand.'

Henley put his hand on mine.

Alma wheezed as she drew herself up onto her paws and slowly dragged herself away.

'No. No, she was immortal – she can't have aged. And not so suddenly. She looks like she did before she drank from the lake. It's as if she was never immortal . . .'

I saw the backpack by the foot of the stairs. I had left it open when I put it down and the small vial that Richard had given to me was out and crushed on the floor. The wetness on the floor was from that. Alma must have worried it out of the backpack and broken it. But why was she old again? It wasn't possible. Richard had said the liquid in the vial was useless. It didn't do anything when consumed. It couldn't be poison.

'Richard was searching for immortality,' Henley said. 'Is it possible . . .'

That he found mortality instead?

'He found a cure for immortality,' Henley said.

The water was fast seeping through the cracks between the floorboards.

'We need to make a decision right now,' I said.

Henley understood exactly what I meant.

I took out the flask containing the water from the Fountain of Youth and looked at Henley.

'Whichever decision we make, we won't be able to undo it,' he said.

Endless time with the man I loved or one meaningful life with him instead. Living *in* the world or being above it all.

I was human. I wanted to feel and experience everything human. I didn't want a cheapened experience.

We both understood how important this decision was, and yet we were calm as we dipped our fingers in the spilled water. We brought it to our lips. We were sure.

Epilogue

Henley and I kept the brownstone and lived in it for the rest of our days. Very little of our past lives remained, save for the sun-faded mark where the clock once hung in the kitchen. It didn't seem right to have the clock out on display, so, many years ago, I had asked Henley to put the clock up in the attic. As the decades went by, we started forgetting details of the existences we had once led.

But occasionally, on rare days, one of our older neighbours – the woman walking her chihuahua or the anthropology professor two doors down – would mention to me that a beautiful woman used to live in our house. They told me that she had lived alone and kept mostly to herself. She had seemed nice enough, but always very distant.

'You look so much like her,' they said.

'Such a shame she was so alone,' I replied.

And they told me I was fortunate that I couldn't imagine such a lonely life.

Our conversation usually ended with that. They would help me up the steps of my house, kiss me on the cheek and then return to their homes. I would wave and they would wave.

I would come home to Henley, who would be waiting by the fire in the parlour.

'Rebecca?'

My footsteps made the wood floors creak in familiar ways. 'Yes?'

A gust of wind came in through the door with me and knocked down one of the cards that lined the mantel.

'I was thinking minestrone soup for dinner tonight,' he said. 'Will that be all right?'

He knew I would eat anything for dinner, but he still asked every day.

'That sounds wonderful.' I walked to the mantel and picked up the card from the floor. It had fallen open, and the messy handwritten words seemed to spill out onto the floor.

Thank you so much for the mixer. It will make a great addition to our new kitchen. (I can't believe we've finally found a place to settle down!) I will have to make you brownies as soon as we unpack and officially move in after the honeymoon. I'm so glad both of you were able to make it to the wedding!

I didn't know why I was reading the card when I already had it memorised. It was the first thank-you card I had ever received, after all.

Closing the card, I set it back in its place on the mantel.

Alanna & Peter Santelli was embossed on the front in silver script.

'Now come and sit by me so I can take in what a beautiful sight you are.'

Henley always wheeled his chair into the parlour, next to the armchair that was my usual seat. Since he invariably complained of the cold, I put a blanket around his legs and pulled thick socks on his feet before sitting down next to him. He hadn't worn shoes in years.

Whenever I sat next to him by the fire, he always told me that my eyes hadn't changed. I still missed Henley's blue eyes, but I could feel them on me through Richard's hazel.

As the years went by, the world gradually grew darker for me. We didn't leave the house much any more and Margot came to carry groceries and help us with the food.

'Granny?'

'I'm in here, Margot. The parlour,' I said.

She sounded so mature, coming home from college. She almost sounded like her mother.

'I bet your mother's pleased to have you back for the summer,' I said.

'You know Mom – she likes to keep me close. She calls every other day when I'm in California.'

I had called every other day for the first year when her mother started college, too.

'I brought some apples and strawberries from the farmers' market,' she said.

'Strawberry season already?'

I extended my hand and Margot's was there to meet mine. I felt a few strawberries drop into my cupped hand. Their seeds gently scratched my palm.

'They're plump and a beautiful red, Gran.'

'Is that so?'

She took them from me. 'Let me wash them first.'

Margot's footsteps were soft as she exited the room.

'She looks more like you every day,' Henley said.

As the world grew dark, I saw Henley more clearly. He was young again and his blue eyes shone. He had this certain way he pushed his dark hair back when it flopped into his eyes. And also the way he would roll his eyes at me one moment, but then affectionately reach for my hand the next.

I felt Henley's hand cradle my own. He did the same thing every day, but somehow it felt warmer today – more comforting. His thumb stroked the back of my hand once before the world fell away. It wasn't the visual world that fell away – no, that had gone long before – but rather my tangible senses and the connecting emotions. They dissipated into nothing. The last thing to go was the feeling of Henley's hand on my own.

Is this death? If so, death felt like travelling in time. I felt the world slip away and welcomed the stillness. It shrouded me in silence and held me.

Acknowledgements

I would like to thank my agent, Maggie Hanbury, and the wonderful Rachel Winterbottom and Marcus Gipps. You are every author's dream team.

Thank you to the ever-patient Lisa Rogers and the Gollancz family for all their hard work on this book. There's only so much an author can do alone.

Rhean, I don't know where I would be without your guidance. You have taught me so much over the years.

Katie, your life advice is the reason I've survived these last nineteen years. Isaac, thank you for caffeinating me through my edits and keeping me company even when I'm frowning at my computer screen. Mark, I still believe socks with sandals are an abomination. Christian, there is no one with whom I would rather girl-talk.

To my parents – so many thank yous have already been said, but I know it'll never come close to being enough. In my opinion, so far, so good on the parenting. But then again, I might be a bit biased.

ANNA CALTABIANO was born in British colonial Hong Kong and educated in Mandarin Chinese schools before moving to Palo Alto, California; the mecca of futurism. She lives down the street from Facebook in the town where its founders reside, along with the pioneers of Google and Apple.

• • •

Find out more by following
@caltabiano_anna on Twitter.

ABOUT GOLLANCZ

Gollancz is the oldest SF publishing imprint in the world. Since being founded in 1927 Gollancz has continued to publish a focused selection of bestselling and award-winning authors. The front-list includes **Ben Aaronovitch**, **Joe Abercrombie**, **Charlaine Harris**, **Joanne Harris**, **Joe Hill**, **Alastair Reynolds**, **Patrick Rothfuss**, **Nalini Singh** and **Brandon Sanderson**.

As one of the largest Science Fiction and Fantasy imprints in the UK it is no surprise we have one of the most extensive backlists in the world. Find high quality SF on Gateway written by such authors as **Philip K. Dick**, **Ursula Le Guin**, **Connie Willis**, **Sir Arthur C. Clarke**, **Pat Cadigan**, **Michael Moorcock** and **George R.R. Martin**.

We also have a strand of publishing in translation, which includes French, Polish and Russian authors. Gollancz is home to more award-winning authors than any other imprint, with names including **Aliette de Bodard**, **M. John Harrison**, **Paul McAuley**, **Sarah Pinborough**, **Pierre Pevel**, **Justina Robson** and many more.

The SF Gateway
More than 3,000 classic, rare and previously out-of-print SF novels at your fingertips.
www.sfgateway.com

The Gollancz Blog
Bringing you news from our worlds to yours. Stories, interviews, articles and exclusive extracts just for you!
www.gollancz.co.uk

GOLLANCZ
LONDON